Iris Gower was born in lives. The mother she has written over She received an Honorary Fellowship from the University of Wales in 1999 and has been awarded an MA in Creative Writing from the University of Cardiff.

Act of Love is the first novel in her *Palace Theatre* series. Her new novel, *Bargain Bride*, the second book in the series, is now available in hardback from Bantam Press.

ACT OF LOVE

Iris Gower

CORGI BOOKS

TRANSWORLD PUBLISHERS
61–63 Uxbridge Road, London W5 5SA
a division of The Random House Group Ltd
www.booksattransworld.co.uk

ACT OF LOVE
A CORGI BOOK: 9780552154352

First published in Great Britain
in 2006 by Bantam Press
a division of Transworld Publishers
Corgi edition published 2007

Addresses for Random House Group Ltd companies outside the
UK can be found at: www.randomhouse.co.uk
The Random House Group Ltd Reg. No. 954009

Penguin Random House is committed to a sustainable future for
our business, our readers and our planet. This book is made from
Forest Stewardship Council® certified paper.

MIX
Paper from
responsible sources
FSC® C018179

Typeset in 11/13pt Plantin by
Kestrel Data, Exeter, Devon.

Printed and bound in Great Britain by Clays Ltd, St Ives plc

10 9

ACT OF LOVE

CHAPTER ONE

The early-morning street was deserted. Old news-papers huddled in the gutter as if fearful of the wind that chilled the autumn air. Helena Burton stood looking up at the imposing building before her. The red bricks of the Palace theatre looked sad and dull, with no lights to brighten the open doorway and no throngs of happy people, rich theatregoers in furs and diamonds, to adorn the pristine new foyer.

Helena paused, clutching her coat around her. Was she expected to use the back door? She was a cleaner, the lowliest of the low, and she hesitated to step on to the soft carpet in the foyer, bathed now in gloom, looking almost black in the dim early light. This was her first day at work and she had a feeling that her life was about to change for ever.

'Good morning. Can I help you?' The voice was cultured, like an actor's, and as Helena looked up at the tall man who swept towards her she felt her heart flutter. He was very handsome, with fair hair falling across his brow in soft waves, and Ella immediately assumed he must be the owner of the theatre.

'I'm the new cleaning girl, Sir – Helena Burton, but everyone calls me Ella.' She humbly lowered her gaze, half afraid to keep staring into the man's deep-blue eyes. He was what her father would call a namby-pamby toff, but to Ella he seemed the epitome of style and grace. She looked down at her shabby shoes and felt suddenly ashamed of her appearance. She wished now she'd put on her best boots, the shiny new boots that she cherished and polished until she could see her face in the soft leather.

'And I'm Anthony Weatherby Nichols,' he said. 'You'd better come this way.' He smiled down at her so charmingly that for a moment she felt as though she was beautiful and talented, like the performers who graced the stage at the Palace, but then he spoke again, reminding her of her place. 'As this is your first day you can come through the foyer and I'll call one of the others to show you around, but remember, in future you should use the side door.' He paused, then added, 'It was my assistant, Tim, who hired you, I understand? He should have advised you about that. He should have explained to you about our new recruitment policy as well. When the owner decided to refurbish the theatre he thought it best

8

to let most of the staff go – a clean sweep, so to speak. You'll soon be meeting the others – the ones who were kept on.'

Ella nodded, but he was already striding away from her. Galvanized into action, she scurried after him.

The carpet was deep and soft and a gracious staircase took pride of place in the foyer, the rich wood polished and gleaming. A noticeboard stood at the foot of the stairs and Ella read the boldly printed words with a sudden feeling of excitement.

2 December 1901 – GRAND RE-OPENING
AFTER EXTENSIVE REFURBISHMENT
Introducing Burlesque Actress, Dancer and Siffleuse
MIRIA VAUGHAN and Renowned Vocalist
MINNIE PALMERSTON.

She had no idea what a siffleuse was and she was too timid to ask. The names of artistes appearing that week was long, but Ella had no time to read it all as she followed the tall figure in front of her. Still, she could appreciate that this was a world of affluence and privilege, very different from the one she knew. Even the air smelled rich with the aroma of tobacco smoke and perfume.

Mr Weatherby Nichols was far ahead of her now and was opening a door that led on to

9

another, less glamorous part of the theatre. Doors led off corridors to the right and left – the dressing rooms, she guessed, of the famous performers. And then suddenly she was in the auditorium, a vast cavern of a place, filled with row upon row of seats that faced the stage. Ella glanced up at the gilt railings of the upper floors, overawed by the sheer size of the theatre.

Behind the stage was a kitchen. 'Here we are, then,' said Mr Weatherby Nichols. 'Perhaps you'd like a cup of tea before you start work. Kathleen!' A young girl appeared, wiping her hands on the sacking apron tied around her slim waist.

'See to . . . What did you say your name was?'

'Helena Burton, Sir. Ella, if you please.'

'Well, Ella,' he smiled, 'our little Irish colleen here will show you where to start. The rest of the staff will already be at work, though as I expected our Kathleen has been boiling the kettle for a brew.'

'By the blessed Virgin I have not!' Kathleen protested. 'I'm getting more water for me bucket, that's all. There's a lot of back-breaking work to do now the place is opened again. No work been done for months, if you ask me.'

Ella wondered if her dismay was showing on her face. The prospect of cleaning all those long corridors was not a pleasant one.

'Look,' Mr Weatherby Nichols said kindly, 'fit

in here as best you can, work hard and you'll be all right. I've got to go.'

As he disappeared, Ella felt suddenly lost, cast adrift in a strange world where she was nothing more than the tiniest cog in the wheel that ran the theatre.

''Bout time you got here.' Kathleen looked her up and down. 'Sure you're a bit on the small side, so you are so.' She rubbed her hands on her sacking apron and then smiled, tugging a loose curl of red-gold hair back under what appeared to be a man's cap. 'I hope you're a hard worker. We need somebody with a good dollop of elbow grease.'

Ella had difficulty understanding what Kathleen was saying; she had a lovely Irish accent but she spoke quickly, as though she had no time to mince her words. Ella smiled and held out her hand. 'I might be small but I can work hard,' she said.

'You'll need to work hard round here.' Kathleen smiled to soften her words. 'Most of the cleaners were paid off when the Palace closed down for a few months. In any case, to be sure they couldn't hang around waiting for the theatre to open again – some of them had little kiddies to feed.'

'But there are other staff, aren't there?' Ella was alarmed at the thought of cleaning the huge building with only Kathleen to help her.

11

Kathleen laughed. 'Not many! There's my Irish pal Tim, who probably took you on. He styles 'imself as the under-manger, though he don't do much managing. And then there's old Doris. The chief scrubber, I call her, just for a joke, you know. She's off work today – bad cold. Used to be a fine singer, so she says, and I've got no reason to call her a liar. Mind, she's old now and half blind. She don't even see the fag ends the toffs throw away.' She paused and looked sharply at Ella. 'Good bit of tobacco in them fag ends – not to be wasted. But that's my business, right? Any fag ends you pick up belong to me. Understand that and we'll get on just fine, so we will.'

Ella had no interest in fag ends and wondered why Kathleen collected them.

'And the man who let me in,' Ella changed the subject. 'What does he do?'

'He's the manager of the place.'

'Is he a good manager?' Ella asked hopefully. 'He seems to have a very nice way with him.'

'Don't be fooled by his chat. Anthony likes to think he's the boss, but he don't own the Palace. Mind you, he's the one who forks out the wages so you'll have to be nice to him.' She giggled. 'Not *too* nice, mind. Come on then, take your coat off. If I was you I'd tuck your skirts up into your bloomers. We got a lot of cleaning to do.'

Ella had hoped for the cup of tea Anthony had mentioned before they started work – it was cold outdoors and even colder here in the bowels of the theatre. But Kathleen had already lifted her bucket into the sink and turned on the tap, and as the water drummed into it she tucked up her skirt, revealing her shapely legs with no sense of shame.

'I can't work like that,' Ella said quickly. 'I'll be all right as I am.'

Kathleen shrugged. 'Suit yourself. But you'll soon have a wet and dirty skirt dragging round your ankles.'

'You don't like working here, do you?' Ella said gently.

Kathleen glanced at her, surprised. 'So you're not as dull as you look, then,' she said.

'Why do you stay here, then? There must be other jobs in Swansea.'

Kathleen heaved the heavy bucket to the floor, slopping water in small pools round her feet. 'What, for instance?'

'You could go into one of the big houses as a maid, perhaps.'

'And I'd still be scrubbing floors, wouldn't I? *And* I'd have some fancy woman lording it over me. No, I'll stay where I am, thank you.' She stood for a moment, her hands on her hips. 'Anyway, there's the night time. Magic, it is.' Kathleen had a faraway look in her eyes and her features seemed softer. 'You should see the place with all the lights on and the posh audience coming in, the men all dressed up and the women in lovely frocks and fur coats. It's a real sight.'

'But you don't have to stay here all day and all evening too, do you?' Ella saw the hours stretch before her like a long dark tunnel. The prospect of the night-time glamour did nothing to comfort her. She wanted to get home, pick up her books and do a bit of studying in the peace and quiet of her bedroom. Helena Burton didn't intend to be a cleaner all her life.

'We often do, yes. Who do you think sweeps up after the rich folks?' Kathleen sighed. 'Tim is supposed to help us but he's too busy patting the behinds of the rich ladies as they leave.'

Ella was shocked. 'Don't the ladies slap his face for taking such a liberty?'

Kathleen shook her head. 'You got a lot to learn about the theatre, girl. Brings out the best and the worst in folk, so it does. All the soft lights and the music and the excitement of the show make the women ripe for a bit of jiggery-pokery on the side, if you get my meaning. Come on then, let's make a start or we'll never get finished.'

Ella shivered as she slipped off her coat. The big empty theatre was a cold place – but she'd have to get used to it. The Palace was her life, at least for now.

*   *   *

14

'Not bad looking, that new girl. Even though she's only been here a few days so far, I've found her to be a good worker. She seems cut out for better work than scrubbing floors, though. I've heard she's from a respectable family.'

Anthony sat in his office, his feet resting on the polished surface of his desk.

Tim looked up from the table where he was bent over the receipts for the previous night's takings and frowned. 'Aye, she looked as if she'd work hard. That's why I gave her the job. Find her beddable, do you?'

'Not at all.' Anthony felt oddly affronted by Tim's remark. 'She's what I'd call a good woman, and God save me from good women – it's the bad ones I like.' Somehow he took no pleasure in his flippant remark.

'I don't know,' Tim said. 'The good ones present more of a challenge, don't you think?'

'Maybe,' Anthony mused on the question. The new girl was sweet looking, though he sensed an iron determination lurking behind her meek manner. 'Anyway,' he changed the subject, 'the takings for last night, are they as good as we expected?'

Tim looked at the sheaf of notes in his hands. 'Full house. The acrobats seem to pull in the crowds,' he laughed. 'The good rich folk are hoping one of the performers will fall to their death.'

Anthony slid his feet down from the desk. 'Well, I'd better do some work, I suppose, since old Simons is hardly ever here. What sort of director is he?'

Tim nodded gloomily, but Anthony could see that his attention was on other matters, and he suspected that he knew exactly what those other matters were. 'Are you going to marry young Kathleen, then?'

Tim looked at him in alarm. 'Whatever gave you that idea? I'd like Kathleen and me to have some fun, that's all.'

'In other words, you haven't taken her to bed yet?'

Tim looked uncomfortable. 'She talks like a peasant but she's got strange ideas about . . . well, that sort of thing.'

Anthony shuffled the pile of papers in front of him. He had Alice Leamar coming to the theatre soon and the event would have to be properly advertised; she was well known and would not appreciate a half-empty theatre.

'I'll get along and open the box office,' Tim said, taking the hint and grinning as he got up.

'You should smile more often, Tim. You almost looked handsome there for a minute or two.'

'I'll never have the sort of charm you're famous for.' Tim stood at the door for a moment. 'Don't be modest now, it doesn't suit you. You know as

16

well as I do that not even the made-up actors who grace the boards with their artificial presence can hold a candle to you.'

'Get away with you,' Anthony said. As he leaned back in his chair his thoughts strayed to the new girl, Helena Burton. She was pretty in an elfin sort of way, thick curly hair framing her small features, but she had a surprisingly large and generous mouth, a mouth it would be a pleasure to kiss.

He sighed. There was one drawback: he'd learned that the girl had a stern father, a tin-plate worker who guarded his only child as though she was the Virgin Mary. There would be no pleasant dalliance with Helena Burton. He pushed the thought away. He'd better get on with his work, which right now meant arranging the production of the posters that would advertise the appearance of the wonderful Alice Leamar.

He smiled to himself, glancing around his office with a look of satisfaction. He was pleased with his job at the Palace: he had made it his own and ran the place like a well-oiled machine. The absent owner, Simons, was only a trifling concern; he, Anthony, ruled the roost – he did all the work, he hired and he fired, he chose the artistes who performed at the theatre. It was his domain.

With a smile of contentment, he picked up his pen and settled down to work. Everything else was pushed from his mind – everything except for the pretty young creature who'd gazed at him with such awe. He didn't usually spend time mooning over some girl or other. And yet there was something about Ella that had got into his blood and he was finding it hard to shake the image of her lovely face from his mind.

Ella's back ached, her knees ached and so did her arms; and, as Kathleen had predicted, her wet skirts clung to her with tenacious coldness, hanging heavily around her legs. After a few days of putting up with the discomfort, she wondered if she should take Kathleen's advice and tuck her skirts into her bloomers.

Kathleen appeared at the end of what always seemed an endless corridor. 'Come on, slow-coach,' she said amiably. 'I've made us a brew. I think it's time we took a break, don't you?'

Gratefully, Ella got stiffly to her feet, almost tipping over her bucket of cooling water as she did so. She looked down at it in distaste: a film of scum rested on the top and the soap had turned into a shapeless slimy blob.

In the small kitchen, Kathleen had already put the kettle on the battered stove. As she waited for it to boil, she peeled down her thick stockings and placed them over the rail that ran round the stove. The warmth of the stove was the only source of comfort in the bare kitchen, whose stone floor seemed to hold the chill. A small window let in the thin grey light; a high wall outside blocked all sunlight. The only furniture was one battered chair that had seen better days.

'Give me your things,' Kathleen said.

Ella looked down ruefully at her stockings. They were wrinkled round her ankles like elephant skin.

'Go on, take them off,' Kathleen insisted. 'There's no one here but me to see your legs, is there?'

Ella lifted her wet skirts and peeled off her stockings. Defiantly she tucked her sodden skirt into her bloomers, thinking with a smile how her father would have a fit if he could see her.

'Is it always this cold in here?' she asked, shivering as the stream of cold air from the corridor touched her skin, bringing out goose bumps all over her legs.

'Make the best of it while we're in here by the stove,' Kathleen said easily. She wrapped her arms around her thin body and looked rapturously around the room. 'You haven't worked late yet, but just you wait until tonight,' she said. 'Then you'll see our Palace at its best, full of people, warmth and excitement. Full of magic, so it is.'

Ella stared at her in surprise. 'You love the theatre, don't you?' she said. 'When you're not cleaning it, I mean.'

Kathleen dropped her hands to her sides and a

steely expression seemed to come over her. 'Sure make no mistake about it, I won't be a cleaning girl for ever,' she said with some force. 'I'll be an actress, a singer, an *artiste*. I'll walk the boards and be better than all of them, you'll see.'

Ella smiled, suddenly feeling close to Kathleen. 'And I'll still be scrubbing the floors, no doubt.'

Both girls looked round as they heard shuffling steps approaching the door.

'That'll be old Doris wanting her tea.' Kathleen fished in the cupboard for another cup. 'You'll be doing this tomorrow, mind,' she said.

Ella didn't mind at all – it would be good to stand near the warm stove, good to spoon the tea into the old steel pot. It would be a welcome break from kneeling in the draughty corridors.

An old woman came into the room. She looked tired and her skin was lined, but she carried herself well and her eyes were as sharp as a bird's as she looked curiously at Ella.

'Not given up the job yet, then?' Her tone was sharp.

Kathleen laughed. 'Take no notice of Doris,' she said. 'She's one of a kind, there's no one like her. And she can work, mind. She cleans the fixtures and fittings, as the boss calls them. Good worker, aren't you, Doris?' She spoke loudly but the old woman ignored her.

'You're going to make a name for yourself, my girl,' she said, looking at Ella carefully. 'You got a

20

brain in your head and you'll learn to use it. You'll learn the hard way, mind, but learn you will.'

Kathleen sighed. 'Doris is in one of her sooth-saying moods. It would pay you to listen to her, she has the sight right enough.' Kathleen looked pleased with herself. 'Doris told me I'll be a famous performer one day and she's right, I'm determined on it.'

'Come on then, where's that tea?' Doris's tone became brisk and the thoughtful look left her face.

'Sit down for a minute, Doris,' Kathleen said. 'I'll pour the tea as soon as it's steeped.'

Doris sank into the worn leather chair. 'I'm getting too old for this sort of work,' she said.

'Why not give it up, then?' Ella asked gently, thinking how Selma, her mother, would die rather than do menial work. But then her mother had a good man to look after her, a man who brought his money home at the end of the week instead of squandering it as many of their neighbours did.

'I got to eat, girl,' Doris said sharply. 'It's slave away here or end up in the workhouse.' She smiled. 'It's not so bad here, mind, 'specially on the nights when we get to watch the show.'

Ella took the cup that Kathleen held out to her. The tea was pleasingly hot and the sugar rested sweetly on her tongue. Guardedly, she studied

21

Doris. She looked very ordinary now, resting as she was in the chair, her cup in her hand. She could have been anyone's grandmother: her green eyes shone out from her wrinkled face, but her hair, tied tightly in a bun at the back of her head, was surprisingly dark with hardly a hint of grey.

'Know me next time, will you, girl?' Doris said.

Ella blushed, realizing she'd been staring. 'Sorry.' She bent her head over her cup and felt the steam warm her face. She wanted to prolong this moment of relaxation because all too soon she would be out there again in the hub of the theatre, scrubbing and cleaning.

'Come on, then,' Kathleen said. 'Drink up. The work won't get done if we stand around all day doin' nothing.'

Reluctantly Ella drained her cup. She looked at Kathleen with her wet skirts tucked into the legs of her bloomers and all at once she began to laugh. Kathleen looked at her in surprise.

'Don't we look a sight?' Ella said. 'Well, I may have a brain in my head, as Doris tells me, but at this rate I'll have sores on my knees to go with it.'

Kathleen returned her smile. 'That's the spirit, laugh away your troubles and you'll always have friends.'

But once she was in the corridor again with a fresh bucket of water, Ella felt far from laughter. She took up her scrubbing-brush and knelt once again on the cold floor. If she was going to make a name for herself one day then it couldn't come too soon. In the meantime she must make the best of things. Sighing, she began to scrub the grey unyielding floor.

CHAPTER TWO

The darkness of the night had closed in and Ella welcomed it, looking forward to going home to fall into bed and sleep.

Kathleen came into the kitchen, where Ella was sitting in Doris's sagging old chair, and put her hands on her hips. 'Come on, slowcoach,' she said. 'You've had a few days to get used to the work, and haven't me and Doris been good and let you go home early?'

Ella looked up pleadingly at Kathleen. 'Can't I go home now?'

'No, you can't! I'm taking you to look at the theatre, so I am. You'll see it in all its glory, with the new electric footlights all agleam and ready to welcome the artistes.'

Ella sighed. 'I just want to sleep, I'm so tired.'

Kathleen shook her red-gold curls. 'This is the best part of the day, you daft girl! Come on, dash some water on your face to wake you up a bit and we'll creep on to the stage and peep through the curtains at the crowd – that's a sight you don't want to miss.'

Ella felt she would miss anything if only she could go to sleep. Reluctantly she got up from the chair. 'All right, let's go and look at the audience and then perhaps I can get some rest.'

'You won't be getting any rest for a while yet. It's about time you did your share and stayed on till the last performance to help clean the clutter the rich folks leave.' Kathleen sounded exasperated. 'Jesus, Mary and Joseph! Wake up, won't you? Even old Doris has got more go in her than you have. It's early yet and all you want is to miss the best part of the day and go home to bed.' Kathleen shook her head. 'I don't know, just look at you! Pretty face, lovely thick hair – with those looks you could be a performer yourself if you wanted to be.'

Ella forced herself to smile. 'Well, I don't want to be a performer. Oh, go on, then, I'll come with you. I suppose I've got no choice.'

Kathleen knew her way around the theatre perfectly and Ella stifled a yawn as she followed her through the warren of corridors. And then they were mounting the steps to the stage. It was shaped like a triangle of cheese, with the widest part facing the audience. Heavy plush curtains hung down from the flies; surreptitiously Kathleen drew one of them back a fraction so that she could peer into the auditorium. Her nose disappeared and all Ella could see was the curve of Kathleen's cheek. She had a sudden urge to laugh, and put her hand across her mouth to stifle a giggle. Her tiredness vanished and she felt a thrill of excitement as she listened to the soft murmur of voices from beyond the curtains.

Kathleen beckoned to her urgently and a moment later Ella had taken her place. She grasped the thick curtain and peered through it at the throng, rich people with diamonds gleaming in the hard electric light. Peering down beyond the footlights, she could dimly make out the figures of the bandsmen, but the lights were too fierce for her to make out any faces.

Kathleen took her arm and drew her to the side of the stage. 'Stay here,' she whispered. 'We'll watch a bit of the show.' She crouched down on her knees, gesturing for Ella to do the same. Ella preferred to sit on the floor with her legs crossed; her knees had taken enough punishment over the past week.

As the members of the band began to tune their instruments ready for the performance, Ella felt another thrill of excitement. It was as if she was in a new world, a world quite different from the one in which she lived with her strict father and her timid mother. This was freedom, she thought; it was a heady sensation.

The band struck up the strains of the National Anthem and Ella heard the rustle of people rising

26

to their feet; although she could not see them now, she imagined the scene: the ladies refraining from waving their fans; the gentlemen with their shoulders held back stiffly with patriotism. Unaccountably, tears came to her eyes. Ella wiped them away, ashamed of her foolishness.

'I'm waiting for Minnie Palmerston to come on,' Kathleen hissed. 'Such a voice – you've never heard the like before.'

As soon as the last chord was struck, the curtains began to open with a sweeping sound. Alarmed, Ella shrank into the shadows, but Kathleen was unperturbed. She knelt, her hands clasped in wonder and her face aglow, and as each act appeared on the stage she told Ella who the artistes were.

'See him?' She pointed to the man striding confidently on to the stage. 'That's J. T. Daniels. Isn't he handsome?'

He didn't seem handsome at all to Ella. He was very short and his hair looked as if he'd put boot black on it. He leaned towards the audience as if confiding a great secret to them. His face was covered in greasepaint and after a few minutes the heat of the footlights made his skin slick and shiny. But she had to admit he was clever. The audience responded to his jokes, stamping their feet on the floor and clapping loudly.

Minnie Palmerston was the last act. She came

quietly out of the shadows, passing Ella and Kathleen without looking at them. She seemed unusually shy for a performer, but as soon as she launched into her first number she was transformed. Her face glowed, her hands stretched to the people in the auditorium and her voice rose triumphantly, reaching easily to the poorer folk seated high up in the gods.

When the curtains finally closed, Kathleen turned to Ella. 'See? What did I tell you? Wasn't the show worth seeing? And we didn't even have to pay a penny piece for the privilege.'

Ella's head was still full of the magic of the performance; the stirring music still rang in her head. She left the wings in a dream, finding it difficult to focus on the reality of the work that waited for her.

'Shall we go home now?' she asked as she followed Kathleen back to the kitchen. Doris was there already, seated in the chair, a cup of tea in her hand. She nodded to the large steel pot. 'Help yourself. It's hot and fresh, make the most of it.'

'Aye,' Kathleen said. 'Sure a cup of tea will go down well. It will fortify us for the job of picking up the rubbish the rich folks have left behind.'

'Can we go home after that?' Ella repeated. Now that the excitement of the performance was over, she was once again longing to fall into her own comfortable bed and sleep.

'You're as innocent as a newborn babe!' Kathleen's voice was filled with scorn for Ella's ignorance. 'There's a second house, mind. Only when we've cleaned up after that will we be able to think of going home.'

All Ella's tiredness had returned. She leaned against the sink, taking the cup Kathleen held out to her with gratitude. 'Perhaps this will wake me up a bit,' she said. 'Do you ever get used to the long hours?'

'Ask Doris. She's worked in theatres longer than I have.' Kathleen perched on the arm of Doris's chair. 'Haven't you, you old crone?'

'That sharp tongue will get you into trouble one of these days,' Doris said mildly.

Kathleen smiled. 'I won't get into trouble. I'm going to be a great performer like Minnie Palmerston. I'll have the audience in the palm of my hand.'

Doris's face seemed to grow pale and her eyes took on a dreamy look. She was silent for a long moment and then she spoke.

'You will too, girl. One day your dream will come true.' She hesitated. 'But it comes with a price, mind. There'll be trouble out there, and heartache. But you will be famous one day, and when fame comes don't forget your old friends, will you?'

Kathleen nodded earnestly. 'I'll remember you, both of you, don't you worry.'

'What about me?' Ella asked a little fearfully.

Doris looked at her. 'Oh, you'll make a name for yourself too, girl, but not treading the boards. Oh no, you'll live like a respectable lady.' She shook her head. 'Someone get me another cup of tea. All this soothsaying has made me right parched.'

Ella pondered on Doris's words. How could she make a name for herself when she came from a poor family? It didn't make sense. She shrugged the thought away. Probably Doris was just humouring them, teasing them with a bit of silly nonsense to pass the time.

The second house was just as stirring as the first and Ella felt herself drawn into the magic of it afresh. She laughed with the comedians, was thrilled by the singing and felt almost sad as the haunting strains of the final National Anthem faded away.

'Come on then, let's get to work,' Kathleen said. 'We'll clean the foyer first and then Doris and I will do the theatre. While we're doing that, you can sweep the stage.' She smiled at Ella. 'Sure I'm being kind to you, but I know you'll pull your weight once you're used to the work.'

Later, when Ella was alone on the stage, she stared out into the body of the theatre. It was eerie now, only dimly lit, and the silence seemed overpowering. She stood for a moment with her broom in her hand and mused on her future. One day she would make a name for herself, so Doris said, but it wouldn't be as a performer. Ella knew that without anyone telling her; she was not cut out to be an artiste, travelling from town to town, never settling. What Ella wanted was a respectable job, a position where she could use her brains, and then a good marriage, a few children and a nice little cottage to call her own. It wasn't very ambitious of her, she recognized that, but then she was different from Kathleen, who lived and breathed the theatre.

When she was finished with the stage Ella went into the auditorium. Looking round, she was amazed at the rubbish strewn across the floor. Cigarette butts had been ground into the carpet and paper wrappers had been tossed aside along with used theatre tickets. On an impulse, Ella picked up one clean-looking ticket and put it in her pocket.

At last the work was finished. It was almost midnight when Ella finally left the building. As she stepped out on to the pavement, she felt the weight of a hand on her shoulder.

'Well? Are you getting used to working in the theatre?'

Ella was startled but she recognized the voice at once and answered politely, strangely moved by the warmth of his hand as it rested on her shoulder. 'Oh, yes, Mr Weatherby Nichols.'

He stood looking down at her, still touching her, and as he bent his head towards her she thought for a moment that he was going to kiss her. She felt a thrill run through her to the pit of her stomach, and she was strangely disappointed as well as relieved when he drew away.

'Don't be late in the morning,' he said briskly. 'I don't like having to give lectures for unpunctuality.'

Ella watched him as he strode away along the street. One minute his tall figure was washed in the pool of light from a street lamp, and then he was hidden in darkness. When at last he was out of sight, Ella felt strangely lonely. She turned towards home, pondering on her new job in the theatre. Her first week had been strange – exhausting, but exciting too – and unaccountably she looked forward to the following morning, when she would inhabit the strange world of the theatre once more.

'I'm not at all sure it's right for her.' Ella's mother twisted her apron between her fingers. 'The hours are so long, Arthur.'

'I'm all right, Mother,' Ella protested. 'I'm getting used to it now and my knees don't ache as much as they did the first day.'

'The girl has to work,' Arthur Burton said, 'and if she was in service we'd see even less of her.'

'I realize that, Arthur, and of course you're right, but if Ella was in service she'd be looked after, she'd be safe.'

'I'm safe now, Mother,' Ella said quickly. 'And wherever I worked, the hours would be long. In any case,' she glanced at her father, 'the wages are good in the theatre.' She knew that would sway her father more than any of her protestations that she liked the job.

He nodded and took his pipe out of his pocket, pressing the tobacco into the bowl with practised fingers. As he set the pipe into his mouth, Ella studied him as objectively as she could. He was not a bad father. He was distant, it was true, and he never showed her any affection, but he was fair and honest and he never kept back his pay packet as many of his fellow workers did. Her father was highly regarded by the neighbours. He didn't drink strong beer, his house was always clean and well run and the Holy Bible always had a place on the table after supper. Ella realized that she could almost be called privileged. She'd heard tales from Kathleen about her father walking out on them, running off with some fancy piece. Kathleen's mother had to take in other folks' washing so she could put food on the table.

Her own mother's voice broke into her reverie. 'Don't stand there daydreaming, girl.' Her soft tone belied her words. 'You got some sewing to do, or were you hoping I'd do it for you?'

'No, of course not, Mother.' Ella slipped her arm around her mother's thin waist. She was always on the go, half fearful of the strict rebuke she would get from her husband if she let her standards of housekeeping drop even a little.

Ella sat near the lamp and took up the skirt she was mending. She'd caught it on the arm of one of the seats last night when she'd been cleaning the auditorium.

She liked her job – she hugged the thought to herself. Her father would take a dim view of anyone who admitted to liking work; his idea of a job was to toil away and hold out his hand for his money at the end of the week.

Her stitches were neat and even, and she soon had her skirt mended. Anyone with half an eye could see the patch, but then her thick calico apron would cover that nicely. Again she thought of Kathleen, who wore a sack around her waist as a makeshift apron. But Kathleen always looked neat and clean and her shoes, though worn, shone with polishing.

Ella was glad to go to bed; she knelt down on the rag mat in her bedroom and pressed her hands together to say her prayers. She did it every night, just out of habit. Her work at the Palace had shown her another side of life: there people smoked, drank strong drink in the interval, and some of the men peppered their talk with oaths when they thought there were no ladies around.

And then there were the men of low morals who brought with them women who were not their wives. Kathleen always went to great pains to point out the philanderers to Ella.

And yet Ella had come to love it all: the smell of greasepaint, the sounds of the band tuning up their instruments. And most of all she loved the occasions when Anthony Weatherby Nichols paid her a compliment.

She climbed into bed with a feeling of anticipation; now she was free to think about Anthony, free to relive the feel of his warm hand on her shoulder, the softness of his breath on her face as he leaned towards her. Whenever he spoke to her, he always leaned close as if he was about to kiss her and she relished those magical moments.

Ella snuggled down under the blankets. The night outside was cold and crisp and the stars were bright in the sky. And here she was in the warmth and safety of her room, thinking how exciting her life had become.

She wondered often about Doris's fortune-telling. Could there be a new life out there for her, perhaps as the wife of the theatre manager? Warmth surged through her body and she felt her cheeks grow hot. She would give Anthony as many children as he wanted, she would always obey him, as her mother obeyed her father. But her marriage would be different because she and

Anthony would be so in love with each other. She turned her face into the pillow and tugged the blankets over her shoulder. She was being silly; why would Anthony want to marry a cleaner, the daughter of a tin-plate worker? But then stranger things than that had happened.

At last she slept, and when she woke the sun was poking inquisitive fingers in through the thin curtains. Ella slipped out of bed with a sense of excitement. Another day had begun, a day she would spend in the magical realms of the theatre.

CHAPTER THREE

Ella hurried through the narrow streets towards the Palace theatre, her heart in her mouth. She didn't want to be late and spoil her record for punctuality. She imagined Anthony's displeasure and her heart beat faster. He was so wonderful, so awe-inspiring, and soon she would see him again. Sunday had been her day off and her father had been satisfied that his daughter was observing God's day of rest. She had gone with him to church as usual, but at bedtime her thoughts had been less than holy as she dreamed of being back at the Palace.

Once she was inside the theatre doors, the reality of the day swept up on her: more scrubbing, more picking up trash left by the audience, more hard, grinding work. Kathleen was in the kitchen, a cup of tea in her hand, and Doris was seated in the chair she had claimed as her own. It almost seemed as if they'd been there all night, just waiting for the morning to come.

'About time you put in an appearance.' Kathleen spoke in a theatrical voice, with no trace of her Irish lilt, as if she was the performer she longed to be. 'I was beginning to think you weren't coming and I'd have to do all the work on my own. Tim was supposed to get us more cleaners, but the boy never does a job properly.' Then she smiled one of her warm smiles and her face was transformed. She really was a beautiful girl, Ella thought.

'I wouldn't let you down,' Ella said, and Doris poked her in the ribs.

'She loves it here already,' Doris said shrewdly. 'It gets into your blood, girl, don't it?'

Ella smiled and pushed the kettle back on to the hob. 'I could murder a cup of tea,' she said, avoiding Doris's comment. But the old woman was right – the theatre had got into her blood. As Kathleen had predicted, she loved the evenings, the scent from the ladies, the flash of jewellery in the bright electric lights. The lighting itself was a miracle: no hiss from gas mantles, just a clear bright light that illuminated the stage and the performers on it so that even the people in the back seats of the theatre could see them clearly.

'Look,' Doris drew a faded cushion from the back of the chair, 'take this with you when you scrubs the stairs, it'll save your knees a bit.'

Ella took the cushion. 'The stairs?' she asked.

Doris grinned. 'Aye, girl, the stairs. How do

you think the folk get up to the gods? They can't fly like the birds, can they?'

Kathleen smiled and added, her Irish accent in place once more, 'We kept the stairs as a treat for you today, so we did.'

'A treat, she says.' Doris chuckled. 'Fair breaks your back and ruins your hands, does doin' the stairs, but you got to do it sometime, girl. Might as well be first as last.'

Ella wondered again what had brought Doris to the theatre, what she had been like when she was younger.

Doris seemed to guess what she was thinking. 'I used to be a performer,' she said. 'I was the best singing-and-dancing act the Palace ever saw, but that was when I was young and fit. Now I just do the fixtures and fittings, and sometimes when Tim is busy I take care of the box office.'

'Don't you listen to Doris's nonsense. She opens up the place and then spends her time taking tea to that Tim who thinks he's God's gift to the theatre,' Kathleen said drily.

'I do more than that,' Doris said indignantly. 'I count the tickets at the end of each performance.'

'And Tim counts all the takings.' Kathleen poured another cup of tea.

Doris got swiftly to her feet. She was surprisingly spry for her years. 'Don't drink it all or there'll be none left for Tim at all,' she said, seeming to remember her duties. She poured the tea from the steel pot into a large cup and added several spoonfuls of sugar. Without another word she left the kitchen and disappeared into the maze of corridors.

Kathleen shook her head. 'They keep Doris on out of pity, really,' she said. 'It's not a proper job, but she can't let go of the past. She'd die without the theatre, would our Doris.'

'Well, that's kind of Anthony . . . Mr Weatherby Nichols, I mean.'

Kathleen looked arch. 'Don't go letting that man turn your head,' she warned. 'And it's not up to Anthony who he keeps working here. Doris is here by the kindness of the owner, Mr Simons.'

'What's he like?'

'He's a bit stuck up but he's nice enough. We don't get to see Mr Simons very often, mind, but he's the man with the money all right. It's him we answer to, when push comes to shove. Go on now, start your work, girlie, or you'll never be done. And take Doris's cushion with you – you'll need it.'

Ella soon found out that cleaning the stairs leading to the gods was as bad as Doris had told her. While the stairs leading to the circle were covered with rich red carpet, those to the upper floor were bare and cold and grimed with the constant movement of many feet.

By the time she reached the door that was signposted 'Upper Circle', her back ached and her arms felt as though she would never be able to use them again. She stood up and threw her scrubbing-brush into the rapidly cooling bucket of water, rubbing her back with her hands. After a moment, she pushed open the double doors and stood looking down at the stage far below.

A rehearsal was in progress and a large woman was singing in a clear ringing voice, her arms outstretched towards the empty theatre as if embracing an audience. This must be the famous singer Anthony was so excited about. Ella didn't remember her name but it was clear that she was a special artiste. Her voice filled the auditorium with little effort, soaring like a bird up into the vaulted ceiling.

Intrigued, Ella made her way to the front of the balcony and sat on one of the steps. She had tucked her skirts into her bloomers, following Kathleen's lead, and her knees gleamed palely in the lights shining down from above. She was so engrossed in the performance taking place below that she failed to hear the doors opening and the soft footsteps coming towards her.

'Enjoying the performance, are you?' a voice whispered in her ear. She turned, startled, to see Anthony standing next to her. She was suddenly conscious of her bare legs and made an effort to pull down her skirts.

Anthony sat beside her and pressed his hand

over hers. 'Don't worry, working at the theatre I often see more than a pair of bare knees.' He smiled and sat beside her, his hand still resting on hers. She wanted to move away, to put a little distance between her and the large impressive man sitting so close to her, but she felt he would see it as a snub if she did.

'I'm sorry, Sir. I didn't mean to stay here long. It was just that I couldn't resist listening to that wonderful voice.'

'That's Alice Leamar,' he said. 'A very fine singer indeed. You have very good taste, Helena.' He was still holding her hand and she felt the warmth of his shoulder next to hers. She knew she should be modest and move away, it wouldn't do to give him the wrong impression, and yet she felt so alive, so happy that he was taking an interest in her, and the truth was she didn't want to break the spell that seemed to hold them in a moment of intimacy.

It was he who moved first. 'Well, my dear little Helena, much as I enjoy sitting here with you I'd best go downstairs and tell Miss Leamar that her wonderful voice reaches even the furthest corners of the upper circle.' He rose at once and, without looking at her again, headed for the door and disappeared as silently as he'd come.

Ella hugged her knees in a burst of happiness. Anthony had been kindness itself. He hadn't told her off for wasting time, he'd sat with her, touched her hand and shared the joy of the singing with her. Anthony liked her, and the thought gave her a feeling of joy.

Back in the kitchen, Ella sluiced the dirty water out of her bucket and sat for a moment in what she thought of as 'Doris's chair'. Her aches and pains seemed to have vanished and she leaned back and smiled, thinking of Anthony. He liked her, she told herself over and over again, and somehow that made the hard work of cleaning the Palace seem worthwhile.

'What are you grinning at?' Kathleen came into the room, her shapely legs protruding from under her skirts. She stripped off her stockings and hung them over the rail to dry. Ella wondered why she didn't take her stockings off before she started work, then they wouldn't get wet. She didn't dare suggest it to Kathleen, who seemed to know everything there was to know about the theatre, but she decided she would try it herself the following morning.

'Come on, girl, wake up. I asked what are you grinning at?' Kathleen repeated. 'As far as I can see there's nothing to smile about. You've taken so long to do the stairs I thought you'd given up and gone home.'

'I just had a little rest in the gods, that's all,' Ella said defensively. 'I'm sorry if I'm a bit slow, but I'm still getting used to it. Soon I'll be a real help to you.' She was suddenly worried that

43

Kathleen might report back to Anthony, telling him that the new girl was no good at her job.

'Aye, I suppose you're right, you're better than nothing, but you'll have to shape up as a cleaner, mind, or I might have to talk to Anthony.' She seemed to know about Ella's fear of being reported. 'You'll do the corridors for me this afternoon, won't you?'

Ella was well aware that she was being taken advantage of, but she nodded her head in agreement.

Kathleen smiled, well satisfied. 'I'm going to sit in the wings,' she said, 'and listen to Madame Leamar. Such a voice, have you ever heard the like?'

Ella would have liked to have sat in the wings herself, enjoying the privilege of hearing a private performance by the famous Alice Leamar, but she was too wise to say so.

When at last it was time for the evening performance, Ella felt sick with weariness. She had done the work of two cleaners that day, and she made up her mind she would not be so foolish again. If she gave in to Kathleen every time she asked a favour, she would soon look as old and worn as poor old Doris. But it would take a great deal of courage to stand up for herself against Kathleen. The Irish girl had such a feisty personality.

A juggler was the first act on stage that evening and Ella sat in the back row of the stalls and watched him without much interest. He was clever, there was no doubt about that, but in the few weeks she'd been at the theatre she'd seen a lot of clever performers. They were there to 'warm up' the audience, as Kathleen put it. She cruelly called them 'has beens', artistes who had passed their best days on the London stage and now were looking for work wherever they could find it. Only the people who headed the bill, like Alice Leamar, were known countrywide. Although it was often difficult to get such stars to perform in the provinces, Anthony had the charm to coax anyone, however high-flying, to come to the Palace and give of their best to the audiences of Swansea. Ella felt warm again as she thought of his hand on hers.

She must have fallen asleep, because the next thing she was aware of was that Kathleen was beside her, digging her elbow into her ribs.

'Come on,' Kathleen said. 'The first house is over. We have to clear the litter up now, or have you forgotten?'

Ella sat up in confusion. 'I couldn't have slept during Alice Leamar's act, could I?'

'Looks like you did. Talk about stupid. Folks pay a fortune to come and listen to such a singer and there's you missing it all, *and* you took up a seat that could have been bought and paid for. I don't know what Anthony will make of this, I'm sure.'

Ella pressed her lips together to stop the hot, angry words from spilling out. She'd done Kathleen's work cleaning the corridors as well as her own work on the endless stairs. She shook away the cobwebs of sleep and got to her feet, thankful that at least she'd pulled her skirts down over her legs. She wondered who had been seated next to her and what they must have thought about sitting next to a girl with a rough calico apron over her clothes. She was lucky that no one had protested about her presence in the theatre.

'I couldn't help it,' she said, following Kathleen along the row of seats. 'Those stairs really kill me.'

'That's just bad luck then, isn't it? I had to do it before the Palace closed for sprucing up, and I'm as sure as hens lay little eggs that I'm not doing the stairs now I'm senior cleaner round here.'

'That's all right,' Ella retorted, 'but I'll make sure I only do my own work from now on.'

To her surprise, Kathleen burst out laughing. 'Glad to see you got guts, Ella. At first I took you for a snob, but you're not so bad after all.'

At last Ella was free to go home. She left the theatre and walked quickly along the quiet streets, anxious to get into her bed, to think of

Anthony and of the way he'd touched her hand. He was a big man in every way, a kind, honourable man, and she was falling in love with him.

Her mother was waiting for her and smiled as she saw Ella. 'Come and sit down, love, you look so tired.' She put a pan of milk on the hob. 'This will do you good. It will help you get a good night's sleep.'

'Where's Father?' Ella asked, gratefully sinking into a chair and stretching her feet out to the blaze of the fire. The night air was cold and the wetness of her stockings made her feel even more chilled.

'He's gone up to bed.'

'He didn't go to that meeting in the Adelphi, then?'

'Not tonight.'

Ella sighed in relief. On the nights when her father mingled with the hotheads in the public bar, complaining about nothing and everything, he was apt to be pompous and demanding when he came home. She loved him dearly, but he sometimes made life hard for his wife and daughter.

She took the cup her mother handed her and drank gratefully.

'You know that your father is a good man underneath all his bluster. He reads his Bible every day and he brings home his pay to me, which is a lot more than most of the men round here do.'

'I know,' Ella said. 'It's just that he could be a bit kinder, that's all.' As she drank her milk she brooded on how her father expected clean clothes and good food to appear whenever he lifted his little finger, not realizing that his wife was getting worn out.

'I'm going up.' She put down her cup, wanting to be alone in her room, to curl up in her bed and think of Anthony. She kissed her mother's cheek. 'Don't be long now, you need your rest too.'

On the landing she stood for a moment outside her parents' room. She could hear her father snoring and smiled to herself. Her own husband would be so different: kind, considerate, making her blood tingle with desire. Now that was something her father would never understand.

Anthony closed the door of the theatre and locked it securely. 'That's it for tonight then, Tim,' he said to the young man at his side.

'Thank the Lord for that,' Tim replied. 'I thought the public meant to stay all night!'

'Well, they enjoyed Alice Leamar and they wanted encore after encore,' Anthony said with satisfaction. 'I knew we had a good thing going when she agreed to come to the Palace.'

The two men stood in the street and Timothy looked up at Anthony with a sly smile. 'Getting anywhere with the new girl? She's a bit of all right, isn't she?'

48

'I wish you wouldn't talk like that, Tim. Helena Burton is a respectable young lady. I wouldn't dream of taking advantage of her.' Although, he thought silently, he felt a tug of attraction whenever he was near her.

'It's Kathleen *I'd* like to take to bed.' Tim made a vulgar gesture. 'She's got a fine pair of pins on her and I'd like to see the rest of her.'

'Kathleen is too wise to take any notice of you,' Anthony said easily.

'I suppose you're right. Well, see you tomorrow.'

Tim loped away into the darkness and Anthony looked after him for a long moment, knowing that Tim was all talk. He'd never get anywhere with Kathleen. She was wiser and tougher than most girls her age.

And then there was Ella Burton – a lovely, innocent girl. Somehow, deep down in his soul, Anthony was glad she was untouched.

'Stupid fool! She means nothing to you!' he said out loud, and began to make his way home through the dark streets.

CHAPTER FOUR

Anthony sat in his room and looked around him. It was a pleasant room, with a high ceiling and new electric lighting, but the place resonated emptiness. It was dark, it was past midnight and once again he was alone. He needed the company of a good woman, and yet the thought of settling down was anathema to him.

Ella was pretty and modest and he felt himself drawn to her. But she wasn't for him, he told himself quickly; she was a lowly cleaner, not the stuff that wives were made of. When he did marry, it would be a good match to a lady who would bring him a fat inheritance. He needed to get on, to achieve his aim in life – one day to own a theatre of his own.

His thoughts turned to that night's performance. Alice Leamar had been on fine form, her pure and strong voice ringing in the far reaches of the upper circle. The show had been a sell-out, but then Anthony was used to achieving a full house. He chose the artistes himself, mixing the acts with just the right amount of comedy and pathos – the audience loved a touch of pathos – and the success of the theatre was all down to him. And yet he didn't even own a share in the place.

He turned to the table beside him and picked up his glass, his thoughts returning again to little Ella. He didn't seem to be able to get her out of his mind.

Ella was used to the building now. Below the theatre was a large number of rooms – eerie rooms, for the most part, filled with dummies wearing costumes of all kinds, which appeared lifelike in the gloom. Ella hated cleaning the still, dusty rooms. She preferred the upper floors where there was light and warmth and where the kitchen was always open for making tea.

She knew her way round the place now, knew the stairs and corridors intimately because she cleaned them every day. Like Kathleen, she now tucked her skirts into her bloomers without hesitation, laughing as she imagined her father's look of disapproval if he could see her with her legs bare – he would order her to leave the theatre at once. But that must never happen. She was in love with the Palace, and she was in love with Anthony Weatherby Nichols, too.

In the kitchen Kathleen was waiting for her

with a look of impatience on her face. 'You're to take tea to the office,' she announced, her tone sulky. 'I don't know why Anthony chose you above me, but there it is.'

'The boss has come for a visit,' Doris said. 'Mr Simons himself. You're honoured, girl. Anthony must think a lot of you to have you wait on him and the boss.'

Kathleen cast Doris a venomous look. 'What do you know about it, you old crone?'

'Temper, temper,' Doris said. 'No need to get nasty.' She looked at Ella. 'You'll find the good china in that cupboard in the corner. And while you're at it, take your skirt from out of your bloomers or you're going to look a proper fool.'

'Best china?' Ella repeated, ignoring Doris's sarcasm.

'Aye, you don't think the owner is going to drink out of the chipped cups that we use, do you?'

Ella opened the cupboard and found not only an entire service of white and gold china with a teapot, sugar basin and jug to match, but a cake stand and a fruit bowl. Well, there were no cakes and no fruit, so Mr Simons would have to be happy with just tea.

The tray was heavy by the time Ella had it set up ready to take to the office.

'May the luck of the little people go with you.'

Kathleen had recovered her good humour. 'Don't drop anything on the way.'

Ella didn't bother to reply. She was too busy balancing the tray on her arm while trying to push open the kitchen door with her foot.

Anthony opened the office door to her knock and gestured her inside.

She placed the tray on the table and glanced surreptitiously at the big man sitting comfortably in Anthony's leather chair. Mr Simons was a good-looking man of about fifty, with touches of grey at his temples but a good head of hair for all that. She'd heard Anthony refer to the owner as 'Old Man Simons', but he wasn't all that old, not really old.

He met her eyes and smiled. 'Helena Burton, isn't it?' he asked.

Ella nodded her head, not sure if she should curtsey to him or not. It was said that the men in the tin-plate works still touched their caps to the bosses, but Ella was never sure if that was right. It was hard to imagine her father touching his hat to anyone.

'Do you like the work?' Mr Simons enquired.

Ella nodded again. 'It's quite hard, Sir, especially doing the stairs, but I'm happy enough here.' She smiled. 'I particularly like watching the shows, Mr Simons. The theatre is the most magical place to be at night time.'

'Oh, an educated girl, I see,' Mr Simons

remarked. 'How do you get on with the rest of the staff?'

'Very well, Sir,' she said. 'The other women are most helpful and Mr Weatherby Nichols is a kind man to work for.'

'A glowing reference, Anthony, should you ever need one.' Mr Simons took the cup Ella held out to him and Ella sensed an undercurrent. She glanced anxiously at Anthony. He wasn't going to leave, was he?

When she finished serving the tea she quietly left the room and headed back to the kitchen.

'What's the matter with you?' Kathleen shot her a questioning look. 'Dropped the tray, did you?'

Ella shook her head. 'No, of course not!'

'What, then? You're looking really flushed. Did Mr Simons tell you off about something?'

'No, he didn't!' Ella took the cup of tea Kathleen held out to her. 'There's nothing wrong. I wish you'd leave me alone.'

'Oh pardon me, Miss Grumpy Bloomers!' Kathleen glared at Ella. 'Sure an' wasn't I just taking an interest. I don't know why you're being so touchy.'

Ella sighed. 'I think things are going to change in the theatre,' she said. 'It looks like Anthony . . . I'm worried that Mr Weatherby Nichols might be going to leave. You don't think there's a problem with the theatre, do you?'

Kathleen's eyes widened. 'How do I know? We'd be the last to hear if there was.'

'You don't think he'll get rid of us, do you?' Ella couldn't keep the anxiety out of her voice.

'Why would he do that?' Kathleen said. 'We're the best cleaners he could get, we come in to work on time and we do our job well. What more could any boss ask?'

Doris came back into the room, a duster in her hand. She always carried a clean duster when she was out in the foyer so that she could look busy if Anthony came along.

'What's going on?' she asked, her voice sharp. She edged her way past Ella and took possession of the old leather chair.

Ella bit her lip. She said at last, 'I could tell by the way Mr Simons was talking to Anthony that there was something going on. I was just worried in case one of us was getting the sack or something.'

Doris sighed. 'Well, I hope I'm not going to get the sack. I've been a good and trusted employee, I have, and I'm not too old to do my share.'

Kathleen's eyebrows shot up. 'You can fool yourself, but you don't fool us,' she said. 'Still, I hope Anthony keeps you on. The place wouldn't be the same without you.'

'Thank you,' Doris said. 'How about getting me a cup of tea? My old legs are aching a bit today. Must be the weather.'

Kathleen shook her head. 'I don't know why I put up with you. You were just saying you're not too old to work and here you are asking to be waited on.' In spite of her sharp tone, Kathleen poured the tea and handed it to Doris. 'Here, you old crone, make the most of it, but remember I'm not your servant.'

Ella tucked her skirts back up into her bloomers and picked up her bucket. 'Well, I don't know about you two but I'm going back to work.'

'You go ahead,' Kathleen said. 'You got the stairs again today, I'll carry on down here.'

Ella left the room and struggled along the corridor with the bucket full of water. Whatever happened, there was nothing she could do about it. All she could hope was that things stayed the same at the theatre. It was like another world to her, and all she wanted at the moment was to be part of it.

'Well, my girl, you've kept your word to me and your mother these past few weeks and brought your money home to us as you said you would.'

'I'm glad to help out, Father,' Ella said. 'I know how hard you work and I'm only too happy to ease the burden.'

'Well, I've decided you can keep half your wages this month and buy yourself some new clothes.'

Ella looked at him in surprise. 'Thank you,

Father. I do need a few new things. My old clothes are looking a bit shabby.'

'Well, there's nothing wrong with a bit of mending, mind. I didn't have a pair of new boots until I started to work in the tin-plate. My folks couldn't afford to splash out and neither can I, so don't expect such generosity every month.'

'No, I won't, Father.' She removed the last of the supper dishes and took them out to her mother. 'You've had a word with Father, then?' She put her hand on her mother's shoulder.

'Aye, I thought I might get some money out of him for you.' She smiled. 'I told him he must keep his daughter looking well shod or folk wouldn't think good of him.'

Ella could see that her father would be influenced by such things. 'Here, let me wipe the dishes for you, Ma.'

'Go and sit down, it's your day off and they don't come round very often, so make the most of it.'

Ella took the cloth from her mother and began to wipe the dishes. She was sorry it was her day off – she missed the theatre. The people there had become like another family, a family who didn't have strict rules of behaviour.

'How are things at the theatre these days?' her mother asked.

'Well, much the same as ever,' Ella said. 'Mr

Weatherby Nichols has taken on another woman to be dresser to the stars.'

'Dresser?' her mother said sharply. 'Why would anyone need help to get into their clothes?'

'Well, sometimes the artistes need to change quickly,' Ella said. 'Then the wardrobe mistress must have everything ready for them to go on for another appearance.'

'Ah well, it's another world to me,' Mrs Burton said. 'I don't understand it. I was never one for the theatre and I'm surprised your father let you work there. Mind,' she said drily, 'I think the wages you're getting helped make up his mind.'

'I'm glad something did,' Ella said. 'I love the job, even though it's hard work. I'd hate to be below stairs scrubbing and cleaning for some posh family – your life isn't your own then, from what I've heard, you're at folk's beck and call even through the night.'

'Aye, that was another thing. Your father likes the idea of you sleeping in your own bed. He's heard enough tales of maids getting into trouble in these big houses.'

'Well, I wouldn't let anything like that happen to me,' Ella said stoutly. 'I've got too much respect for myself. Anyway, the only men working in the theatre are Anthony and Tim, and I don't think either of them would set their sights as low as a mere cleaner.'

'You're as good as anyone,' her mother said

gently, 'and you can hold your head up in any company.' She looked at her daughter. 'You look ready for bed, but you'd best say goodnight to your father before you go up.'

Ella nodded and walked back into the parlour, where her father was sitting reading his Bible. 'I'm going to bed, Father,' she said, 'so I'll say goodnight and God bless, if that's all right.'

'Come and sit down,' her father said. She noticed he had a glass of beer standing beside him. He rarely drank and when he did the beer made him loquacious. Her father read to her for over an hour and Ella had great difficulty in keeping her eyes open. At last he closed the heavy cover of the Bible and laid his hand on it. 'It's time I went to my bed,' he said. 'Tell your mother not to wake me when she comes up.'

Ella breathed a sigh of relief, and headed for bed herself.

CHAPTER FIVE

Ella's father was out at one of his meetings, so it was peaceful and quiet in the little parlour. Ella and her mother were both engrossed in their sewing. The sheets they were mending were old and faded, but they would do another few months and Ella knew that was important to her mother. Selma Burton hated wasting anything, and bedlinen was so expensive to buy.

'We're having a visitor for tea tomorrow,' Selma announced suddenly. Her tone was almost hearty and Ella looked at her in surprise.

'Who?'

'Some friend your father's made at work. It seems they get on really well together.' She rolled her eyes heavenward. 'They both like their Bibles. But I must be charitable, the poor man has lost his wife and has five children to care for. Anyway, he's coming here for his tea. His name is Richard Mortimer, but for some reason he's called Jolly. A funny name for a man, but that's what your father calls him, so it must be right.'

'Oh well, if he's like his name Sunday tea might be more entertaining than usual,' Ella said flippantly.

'We are not here to be entertaining,' Selma remonstrated. 'We're going to make this man welcome, whether he lives up to his name or not.' She gazed speculatively at her daughter. 'Your father seems keen to have this man meet you.'

'I don't know why,' Ella said. 'If he's old like Father I can't see that we'll have much in common.' She hesitated. 'He's not bringing his five children, is he?' The prospect of a gaggle of little ones running around her mother's neatly kept house was not a pleasing one.

'No, thank the Good Lord,' Selma said quickly. 'It seems his sister-in-law is looking after them for an hour or two. What the man really needs is a good wife, I suppose.' She glanced at Ella again. 'But who would want to take on such a responsibility? With five children to raise it would be a daunting task for any woman.'

'Well, I wouldn't, for one.' Ella concentrated on her sewing, trying to shake off the uneasy feeling that her father had something more in mind than inviting a friend to tea.

'As well as working together, it seems they like to meet at the public bar sometimes and your father tells me that this Jolly is quite well off, with a big house in the Uplands.'

'Teatime is going to be more of an ordeal than a pleasure, by the sound of it,' Ella said ruefully. With a sigh of relief, she put her sewing away. 'Thank goodness that's done. I never did like sewing. I'm not good at it like you, Ma.'

'Well, you have to practise, my girl,' Selma said reprovingly, 'same as you should learn cooking. One day you might have a household of your own to look after and then you'll need to turn your hand to anything.'

The front door slammed and Ella and her mother sat up straighter in their seats. Arthur Burton came into the parlour and looked at them both with approval. 'I see you are busying yourselves, keeping the household well maintained for me.' He rested his hand on his wife's shoulder. 'Seeing my friend Jolly struggling along without a wife has made me realize that I'm a very lucky man.'

Ella looked at her father in surprise. It was not like him to hand out compliments to anyone. He was obviously in a good mood.

'Put away your sewing and come to bed, Selma. You've done enough work for today and I don't want you looking pale and peaky when my friend comes for tea tomorrow.'

'Yes, Arthur.' Obediently Selma put down her sewing, snapping the cotton between her teeth and folding the sheet carefully. She didn't look at her daughter but Ella knew that tonight her mother would be suffering the attentions of her husband, and come morning she would be out of sorts, with shadows under her eyes.

This was not what marriage was all about, surely? A couple should love one another, delight in being close to each other. They should feel the same thrill of happiness that she felt when Anthony was close to her. Her mother must have loved her father at some time in the early days of their courtship, but perhaps that feeling faded away with time.

Later that night Ella dreamed about Anthony. He was holding her in his arms, kissing her gently, touching her intimately. She woke up abruptly, staring round her darkened room in a daze. She recalled her dreams and was ashamed. It was not proper that a young girl should imagine such physical delights. She turned over and settled down, and when she slept again, it was a dreamless sleep.

On Sunday morning, Ella and her mother prepared the house for their visitor. It seemed that Jolly was not a tin-plate worker himself, but held the heady position of manager in the company.

Arthur Burton watched as Ella blacked the bars of the fire. She was rubbing with all her strength,

63

knowing he would be quick to criticize if the job wasn't done to his satisfaction.

'Jolly Mortimer has a fine house,' he said. 'He's a good Christian man as well as being fair-minded and a fine man to work for. I want you and your mother to treat him like the gentleman he is.'

'Oh, we will, Father,' Ella said quickly. 'Of course we will. Any friend of yours will be well looked after, don't you worry.'

Her father got up from the table and closed the thick Bible in front of him. 'I expect you to come to church this morning, mind.' Her father's stern tone reminded Ella that his wishes would be obeyed to the letter.

'I'll attend church, of course, Father.' Ella owed a great deal to the church. It was there she had been taught to be a better scholar than was usual for the daughter of a tin-plate worker. The vicar's wife said Ella had a good mind and readily absorbed her lessons, which pleased Arthur Burton, at the same time making him stricter about what he called her 'studies'.

Since she'd been working at the theatre, Ella had had little time for poring over books, but she knew she was already better read than most and was clever at numbers, too. All of that was wasted at the theatre, but one day Ella hoped to be better placed to use her education. She had no ambitions to work as a performer at the Palace, like Kathleen did, but she might one day aspire to Tim's job. Cashing up, handling the books and generally keeping check of the theatre's finances – now that job would really appeal to her. Until she met the right man, of course.

By the afternoon, with the roast dinner eaten and the dishes cleared away, the little house gleamed with cleanliness. Whoever this Jolly man was, Ella thought, he would find no fault with her father's domestic arrangements. As the clock hands moved towards four o'clock, Arthur set the Bible in pride of place on the polished table in the parlour. By the time the knock came on the door announcing the arrival of Jolly Mortimer, Ella was a bundle of nerves.

'Go and let our guest in, then.' Her father made an impatient gesture with his hand. 'And straighten your skirts. You don't want to look like a hoyden, do you?'

The man Ella found standing at the door was large and round, and had several double chins that wobbled above his starched white collar as he inclined his head in greeting. A cheerful smile spread across his face, revealing strong white teeth. Jolly might be good-looking if he lost a bit of the weight he was carrying around.

'Miss Burton, is it?' he said, removing his hat. 'I've been looking forward to meeting you. Might I step inside?'

Ella moved back from the door. 'Of course, Mr

Mortimer. Father is expecting you and we've all been looking forward to your visit very much.'

'That's very kind of you, my dear.' As he attempted to move past Ella, she quickly stepped aside.

'My father is in the parlour, I'll show you the way.' She led the visitor along the hall to the parlour. Her father was reading his Bible, but he looked up with a pleased smile when Ella opened the door.

'Come in, Mr Mortimer,' he said, almost bowing to his visitor. 'Shall we read a little of the Good Book before we partake of tea?'

Jolly handed Ella his hat. 'A capital idea,' he said. 'May I?' He seated himself in the large armchair near the fire and Ella hid a smile. It was a good thing he hadn't decided to use one of the wooden chairs around the table – it was doubtful whether they would have held his weight.

'Fetch your mother, Ella,' her father said, and as she left the room, she heard her father extol her virtues to his visitor. She paused in surprise.

'My daughter is a fine, well-behaved girl,' he said. 'She's a good scholar and she's also a good little housewife. Helps her mother with all the work, as well as bringing money in from her position at the theatre.'

'She's very beautiful, too,' Jolly Mortimer said. 'You have a family to be proud of, Arthur. Everyone knows that. But then again, do you think it's suitable for a girl to be working at the theatre? You know the Palace customers are drinkers and smokers, and there's a great deal of coarse language that goes on in such an establishment.'

Ella held her breath. How dare Jolly Mortimer try to influence her father against the Palace?

Her father coughed a little before replying. 'My Ella works at the cleaning, she doesn't come into contact with the folk who attend the shows or with the people who perform on the stage. The money is good, better than the girl would get in service, that's something I have to consider.'

Ella heard Jolly sigh. 'Well, you know your own business best. Now, what are we going to read – one of the gospels or some of the psalms? You know I always like the psalms.'

'The psalms it is, then.'

Ella hurried to fetch her mother. 'Come on, Mother, they are waiting for us.'

Selma looked flustered. 'I've got cakes in the oven. How am I supposed to get tea for us all if I'm listening to Bible readings?'

'It will be all right, Ma. I'll excuse myself in a few minutes and come back into the kitchen and see to the cakes.'

'Well, make sure you use the best tray-cloth, mind, the one with the rose decoration. We don't want Mr Mortimer thinking we're too poor to provide a decently prepared tea.'

It soon became stuffy in the parlour and Ella,

listening to her father's sonorous voice intoning his favourite psalms, felt she could have easily dropped off to sleep. She hoped her closed eyes made her seem pious rather than bored and tired. When her father paused before starting a fresh psalm, Ella took the opportunity to speak.

'May I be excused to attend to the tea?' she asked meekly.

Her father frowned, but even he saw the necessity of presenting well-baked cakes for their visitor. 'Very well, go about your duties. We need Marthas as well as Marys in this life of ours.'

Ella left the parlour smiling to herself, knowing her father was trying to impress their visitor with his knowledge of the Bible. In truth she didn't see herself as much of a Martha. She wasn't content to serve and do the practical chores; she was more interested in improving her mind. She had taken the job as a cleaner only because it would bring in money to help with the housekeeping. The fact that she loved being at the Palace was her good luck.

The cakes were a pleasing golden colour when she took them from the oven, shielding her face from the heat as she did so. Carefully, she slid the cakes on to the cooling tray. Her mouth watered at the aroma. Her mother was a good cook and a good housewife. Sometimes Ella thought her father didn't deserve such a good woman.

She found the best tray-cloth and put out the

china. She would need to make several trips to the parlour to serve the food and the pot of tea. Fortunately, her father had finished his Bible reading and he looked up with a rare smile as she came into the room.

'Well timed, indeed.' He sounded almost genial, and even though Ella knew it was an act for their visitor's benefit, she felt her shoulders relax. 'What have we got for tea, then?' Arthur peered at the tray.

'We've got beef sandwiches, Father, and Mother's special butterfly cakes.' She put down the tray and stood waiting for her father to speak again.

'Good. Now sit down and talk to Mr Mortimer. Your mother can see to the rest of the things.' He leaned back in his chair as Ella handed out the plates. Mr Mortimer was still seated in the big chair and Ella smiled at him.

'Can I tempt you with some of these, Mr Mortimer?'

'You certainly can.' He helped himself to a handful of beef sandwiches and looked Ella over carefully. 'You have a comely daughter, Arthur. She'll make someone a good wife.'

'Oh, she really will, I know that,' Arthur replied. 'Her mother has taught her all the household skills she needs to run a good home.' He sighed. 'So far there is no one on the horizon, though. Ella hasn't much time for the young men she

69

meets at church. Keeps them all at arm's length, she does.'

'Modesty is a laudable trait in a young lady. You've brought Ella up well, Arthur.'

Ella was glad when her mother appeared with a second tray. She didn't much like the way Mr Mortimer was appraising her as if he was about to make an offer for her. She took a seat as far away from him as she could. She was uncomfortably aware that her father was looking speculatively at her and then at Mr Mortimer.

She kept quiet, listening as the two men talked together. She was tired; she would have liked a nap on her bed. It was a luxury to spend time in her bedroom, reading, resting, just enjoying her own company. But their visitor had put paid to all that, and Ella was forced to sit in the parlour until her father pushed aside his cup and signalled for her and her mother to leave the room.

In the kitchen Selma sank into a chair. 'Thank goodness that's over. I've never felt so uncomfortable in all my life.'

'Me too, Mother. I didn't like the way Mr Mortimer kept staring at me as if I was a piece of merchandise in a shop.'

'Well, your father likes him, so we'll have to put up with him.'

'He's not going to make a habit of coming to tea on a Sunday, is he, Ma?' Ella dreaded having to suffer the stifling presence of her father's friend every week.

'Mother,' Selma said, automatically correcting her. 'I keep telling you, don't let your father hear you calling me "Ma", you know he doesn't like it.'

Her father had ideas above his station and sometimes Ella almost felt sorry for him. He was a tin-plate worker, a man who worked with his hands. Why on earth was he cultivating a friendship with one of the managers?

At last, the visit was over and Ella heaved a sigh of relief. Her father returned to the kitchen looking pleased with himself. 'You've both done well,' he said, seating himself at the table. 'More tea, Selma.'

His wife got up at once to serve him, and then looked to her husband to see what he wanted next. Arthur was in a good mood and said cheerfully, 'Sit down, both of you.'

Ella felt a sudden chill come over her. She had a feeling of foreboding, expecting her father to say something she didn't want to hear.

'Well, Ella, you've made quite an impression on Mr Mortimer. He's very taken with you.'

'I'm glad, for your sake, Father. Though I'm not sure why your friend is taken with me. We hardly exchanged a word.'

Arthur's expression changed. His brows creased and he glared at Ella. 'That was your fault. I gave you every chance to talk to Mr Mortimer, but you didn't do what I expected of you.'

'You said yourself she made a good impression,' Selma broke in, her words rushing out nervously. 'And Mr Mortimer might be the sort of gentleman who would rather talk himself than listen to a mere girl.'

'Aye, you could be right, woman.' He seemed mollified. 'Well, next time he visits it will be to see you, Ella.'

'Me? Why?' She felt the hairs on the back of her neck stand up. She'd been dreading this moment since teatime, somehow knowing deep down that Mr Mortimer's visit didn't bode well for her. 'Are you going to ask me to be governess to Mr Mortimer's five children, Father?' Well, if he did she would refuse – she loved her work at the theatre and she had no experience of dealing with children.

But her father had much worse than that in mind for her. 'You should be honoured, Ella. Mr Mortimer is coming to visit to pay court to you. He wants you not as a governess, but as a wife.' His look became steely. 'And mark my words, on this I will be obeyed.'

Ella was speechless. She sat back in her chair and tried to stem the rebellious words that rose to her lips. Getting angry with her father would gain her nothing. She looked to her mother for help, but Selma was staring down at her hands clasped firmly in her lap.

'May I be excused, Father? I'm rather over-come by what you've just said. May I go to my room to think things over?'

'You may think all you like, my dear girl. Such an honour is bound to make a young lady nervous.'

As Ella rose and made for the door, her father's voice followed her. 'I am determined on this, Ella,' he insisted. 'You may think all you like, but put your mind to it – you are going to marry Mr Mortimer.'

She took the stairs two at a time. 'I won't marry Mr Mortimer! Not until hell freezes over,' she said, and closed her bedroom door against the world.

CHAPTER SIX

As soon as she was back at work the next morning, Ella decided to put all thoughts of Jolly Mortimer's visit out of her head. It didn't help that Kathleen was in a foul mood. She'd been visited at her lodgings by one of the artistes and it seemed it had not been a success.

'I took him to my room and deliberately left the door open,' she said, hands on hips, eyes gleaming. 'I warned him that the landlady – in other words old Doris here, I'm lodging with her now – wouldn't put up with any nonsense and still he tried to get me into bed. Jesus, Mary and Joseph, what's wrong with men these days?'

'Not so much of the "old", if you don't mind. And he took liberties because you're one of the cleaners at the theatre, love,' Doris said, unable to hide her mirth. 'That Danny Malone thought his luck was in.'

'Well, he thought wrong!' Kathleen's voice

cracked a little and Ella realized she was deeply upset by the incident.

'Perhaps you should have arranged to meet Danny in a tea shop or the park or something,' Ella said mildly. 'I suppose taking a man to your bedroom could seem like an invitation.'

'But I left the door open!' Kathleen's voice became almost a wail. 'I thought he was a nice man! Well, I soon learned different, didn't I?'

'Don't look in the theatre for a sweetheart,' Doris said. 'You know the performers are here today and gone tomorrow. They're just after a bit of loving, only human they are, see? Now simmer down and drink your tea. We'll have to get to work soon or we'll never get the place cleaned up ready for tonight.'

Kathleen threw her a scandalized look. 'You're a fine one to talk about cleaning up. It's me and Ella who do all the work while you flick a duster around and pretend to be busy. Still,' she said grudgingly, 'I suppose you're right. I won't see hide nor hair of Danny for the rest of the week.'

But Kathleen was wrong. Danny arrived for the first house carrying a huge bunch of flowers. He came into the kitchen with a sheepish look on his face. 'I'm sorry, Kathleen. I was a fool to be so disrespectful to you, but you're such a beautiful girl, I couldn't help myself.'

Kathleen sniffed. 'Never mind the excuses. I'm still angry with you, but I'll keep the flowers

75

anyway. They'll brighten up my bedroom, if nothing else.'

When he'd gone, Ella smiled at Kathleen. 'I thought that was sweet of Danny. I don't think he meant to offend you. He'll probably be on his best behaviour from now on.'

'You're such a dimwit, Ella. Men are all out for one thing and it's about time you were wise to their little ways.'

'They can't all be like that,' Ella protested.

'Well, they are, so take a lesson from me and don't go out with any of the performers. Doris is right. They're here at the theatre for a short time, so they are, and then they're off again. Anyway, why did you come in this morning looking so glum? You been in a tizz all day. Got out of bed the wrong way, did you?'

Ella shook her head. 'You're a fine one to talk about looking glum. You've been in a bad mood since you came in.' She lightened her words with a smile.

'Get on with it,' Kathleen said. 'There's something on your mind or I'm not an Irish Catholic'

Ella shook her head. 'It's nothing really.'

'Go on,' Doris put in. 'You can tell us anything and it won't go no further.'

Ella could see she wouldn't get any peace until she told them what had happened on her day off. 'It's just that my father invited this man to tea at our house yesterday. He's a widower more than

76

twice my age, with five children and five chins to go with them.'

'So?'

'So my father actually thought I'd make a good wife for this man.'

Kathleen was all ears. 'Marriage? Well, that's not to be turned down in a hurry. There are plenty of men out for a good time but very few who'll make an honest woman of you.'

'When I marry it will be because I love the man,' Ella said quickly. 'Anyway I'm still young. I want to see a bit of life before I settle down.'

'At least think about it. You might not get the offer of marriage again.'

'Well, in that case I'll be an old maid,' Ella said bluntly. 'I thought you would be on my side. I won't and I can't marry a man I don't even know.'

'Ah well, you must do what you think best, I suppose.' Kathleen smiled. 'And I'd baulk at the thought of taking on five little monsters.'

'I'm glad to hear it,' Ella said. 'For a minute there I thought you'd side with my father and tell me to marry this Jolly Mortimer.'

'Who? The manager of the tin-plate works, you mean? But he's the richest man you're likely to meet.'

'I don't care how rich he is. He's plump, to say the least, and so old.'

'Well, that's your business, I suppose. Come

on, let's forget our problems and get to work. Keeping busy usually clears the mind, so it does.' She rested her hand on Ella's shoulder. 'Look, no one can make you marry Jolly Mortimer, so don't look so worried. I'll tell you what, I'll do the stairs today and you can sweep up down here.'

It was a generous offer and Ella accepted quickly. 'Thanks, Kathleen, that's really good of you.'

'Right then, let's make a start, shall we?' Kathleen left the room with Doris trailing behind her and silence descended on the kitchen. Ella stood for a moment, thinking of her father's orders. Well, whatever it took, she would refuse to marry Jolly Mortimer, even if it meant being turned out of the house. She squared her shoulders. She would find lodgings, just as Kathleen had. She wouldn't let her father have his way on something as important as this.

That evening, Ella took her place with Kathleen and Doris at the edge of the stage, eager to watch the night's performance. She thought Danny was very good. He raised a lot of laughs and he kept glancing towards the wings, hoping, Ella thought, to see Kathleen. But Kathleen wouldn't look at him. She was probably still sulking. At any rate, as soon as Danny finished his act Kathleen hurried away, determined not to let him forget his mistake.

Later, Danny appeared as the band was tuning up for the second house. Ella was listening to the scratchy sounds of the instruments as she made her way to the auditorium, looking in despair at the mess the audience had left behind. It would take her a good half-hour to pick up the discarded tickets and crumpled programmes. She was startled when Danny caught her arm.

'Where's Kathleen?' he said abruptly. 'She's not ill, is she?'

Ella shook her head. 'No, I expect she's already started on the gods. She's doing up there to-night.'

But Kathleen was not upstairs; she was in the foyer, and Ella had the distinct feeling she had manoeuvred this so that she would bump into Danny. He was top of the bill, after all, and a very handsome man into the bargain. It seemed Kathleen had decided she'd punished Danny enough.

Ella noticed that Kathleen actually blushed when she came face to face with Danny and quickly averted her gaze. Undeterred, Danny went up to her and apologized yet again for his rudeness of the previous night. 'Come out with me tomorrow morning,' he coaxed. 'We'll sit in the park and feed the ducks. No harm in that, is there?'

'I don't know if I can get time off.' Kathleen's face was turned away from Danny but Ella could

79

see a smile playing at the corners of her mouth. Finally, after Danny had pleaded with her for several minutes, she agreed she would see him on her day off.

'When's that?' Danny asked. 'I'm travelling to Devon next week.'

'I'm off on Sunday, will that do you?' Kathleen asked. 'If not, then that's just your bad luck, so it is.'

Ella felt she was intruding into something that was not her business. 'I'll start to clean up, then,' she said. But Kathleen ignored her. She was busy staring at Danny; she was smiling and her eyes sparkled at the attention she was getting.

Ella returned to the theatre, almost bumping into a tall figure in the dim light. 'Oh, Mr Weatherby Nichols! You gave me a fright,' she said breathlessly.

'Sorry about that. On your own?' Anthony asked. 'Where's Kathleen?'

'She's doing upstairs,' Ella said quickly. 'We take it in turns, you see.'

Anthony reached across her to lean his hand on the pillar behind her. She felt trapped in his embrace, recognizing that it was a feeling she very much liked.

'I suppose that's fair enough.' He was looking down into her eyes and Ella felt her colour rise. 'I've got a proposition for you.' He was smiling, his teeth gleaming in the dim light. 'I need your help very badly, you see. I don't know why I didn't make you an offer sooner.'

Ella stared up at him doubtfully. What on earth did he have in mind? Perhaps with Kathleen's experience fresh in her mind she was reading Anthony's words wrongly.

'What do you want?' She had a chill edge to her voice that Anthony didn't fail to notice.

'Nothing bad, I assure you.'

He was so close she could feel his breath on her cheek. He always leaned into her when he talked. It meant nothing, she assured herself.

'The dresser I engaged has left. It seems her mother is sick and she has to go home to nurse her.'

'I see.' Ella didn't see at all but she didn't want to appear dim. 'What do you want me to do, then?'

'I want you to be wardrobe mistress. I think that's a position more suited to a lady of your intelligence.'

Ella felt her mouth go dry. Anthony was praising her, offering her a job she would love. She couldn't believe her ears.

'Well, what do you think?'

'I think that's wonderful! But what will Kathleen say? She can't clean the theatre on her own.'

'We'll leave things as they are for the next few days. That will give me time to employ another full-time cleaner. Don't you worry your head about that, that's my job.' He paused and touched her cheek gently with the tip of his finger. 'Will you take the job then, or should I offer it to someone else?' He was teasing and Ella knew it.

She smiled. 'Of course I'll take the job.'

He straightened and moved away from her. She longed to pull him into her arms. She liked it when he smiled at her and teased her. It seemed to make them closer, more than just employer and employee.

She watched as Anthony walked away, her heart beating fast with joy. She, Ella Burton, was going to be a dresser, assistant to the many stars who came to perform at the Palace.

Kathleen was too enthralled with the attention Danny was paying her to take too much notice of Ella's new job.

'I think Danny's learned his lesson,' she said, her lips curving into a smile. 'I might forgive him if he plays his cards right.'

'Well, what do you think about my new job?' Ella asked impatiently.

'I suppose it will come to the same thing in the end. You'll help the lady performers dress and clean up their rooms for them. Looks like you'll be put upon even more than you are now,' Kathleen replied grudgingly.

Nothing anyone could say would dampen

Ella's happiness. She'd been promoted! She imagined she'd receive extra wages and she'd meet the famous artistes face to face. It was like a dream come true.

She debated with herself all week: should she tell her parents about her new job or not? Perhaps her father wouldn't like the thought of her mixing so closely with the performers, and even the prospect of more money might not be enough to convince him she was making a good move.

She was still pondering on Friday evening as she made her way back home; she was earlier than usual and as she let herself into the house her heart sank at the sight of Jolly Mortimer's large coat hanging in the hall. So Father was pushing on with his idea of marrying her off? Well, he could forget it, nothing would make her marry a man she didn't love.

She smiled politely as she went past the parlour, hoping to hide in the kitchen, but her father spotted her and called for her to come and chat to their guest.

'Been hard at work all day?' Jolly smiled at her. 'I hear you're a cleaner at the Palace theatre.'

'I am that,' Ella said quickly. 'I work hard but it's a job I very much enjoy. I have good friends working with me. The other cleaners, I mean,' she added hastily, glancing at her father to see if he was displeased. If he thought she was 'hob-nobbing', as he called it, with the performers he'd have her out of the theatre with a snap of the fingers.

'Ah, but I'm sure you'd like a home of your own and a family to look after. That's what all women want, when it boils down to it.'

'I don't know if I'll ever marry,' Ella said hastily. 'I haven't met anyone I'd like to share my life with.'

'That comes, my dear. You have to get to know a man before you can talk about sharing your life.' He glanced at her father with a knowing look. 'And you've got all the time in the world, I'm a patient man.'

Ella didn't know what to say, so she closed her lips and waited for her father to release her. But instead of telling her to go to see her mother in the kitchen, he gestured for her to take a seat.

'I'm so tired, Father,' she said hesitantly. 'I think I'd like to go straight to bed.'

'Nonsense!' her father said genially. 'Spare your father a little bit of your time, girl. It's not much to ask of a daughter, is it?'

Reluctantly, Ella sat down on one of her mother's best chairs and stared tiredly down at her hands. Suddenly, so that she was taken by surprise, Jolly leaned forward and covered her fingers with his plump hands. 'Looks like you're working too hard,' he said. 'A woman's place is in her own home. Why, my dear departed wife had an easy life, what with a couple of maids to help her with the housework.'

'I should think bringing five children into the world and caring for them was work enough.' Ella realized she was speaking forcefully and she tried to lighten the moment. 'Your wife must have been a wonderful, remarkable woman.'

'Of course she was. But now I've mourned her passing for long enough. I must try to get on with my life, don't you agree?'

Ella edged her hands away from his grasp. 'You must do as you think fit, Mr Mortimer.'

'It's best I find a new wife,' he said. 'Best for me and for my poor motherless children.'

Arthur coughed and Ella looked at him pleadingly, trying to communicate her distress to him. 'I'm not thinking of marrying for some time yet, isn't that right, Father?'

He stared at her with a stern expression on his face. 'You marry when you can, Ella. When a man asks you to be his wife it's a very great honour and it must be considered as such.'

Ella rose to her feet. 'If you will both excuse me, I'm sure you have a great deal you want to talk about and I'm bound to be in the way.'

'Sit down, Ella.' Her father's voice was quiet, but she knew by the expression on his face it would not be wise to disobey him.

'Now listen to me – ' he began, but Ella broke in before he could say any more.

'I've had promotion at the Palace,' she said. 'It will mean more wages, Father.'

He paused and looked at her for a long moment. 'What job will you be doing, then?'

'I'll be looking after the business side of things,' she lied. 'You've said yourself I'm good at words and figures, didn't you, Father?'

'I suppose I did. But for all that, I must think this over very carefully. Do you really want to go on working in the theatre all your life?'

'It won't be all my life, Father. It's just until something better comes along.'

'There we are, you see?' Arthur said in satisfaction. 'Until something better comes along. Well, "something better" might come along sooner than you think.'

'I don't understand.' Ella understood only too well, but she could hardly blurt out her dismay at the prospect of marriage to Jolly Mortimer.

Her father smiled indulgently. 'Well then, you're nothing but an ignorant girl. Now go and join your mother in the kitchen and leave us men to talk about the important things in life.'

Ella left the parlour with a sense of relief, but that quickly faded when she heard Mr Mortimer's next words.

'I think she will suit me very well, Arthur. Your daughter is comely and hard-working, and that is all a good man can ask of a wife.'

Ella held her breath for a long moment, then

went towards the kitchen clenching her hands into fists. Mr Mortimer was a decent enough man, he had a kindly expression on his face when he looked at her, but she would never marry him, never.

CHAPTER SEVEN

Christmas had come and gone, but the start of the New Year was a dreary affair in the Burton household. Selma had cooked a fine roast dinner of shoulder of lamb with plenty of mint sauce, followed by a toffee pudding, but Ella couldn't enjoy the meal, dreading as she was Mr Mortimer's teatime visit. Her father still seemed intent on marrying her off to him and Ella was still determined to refuse the proposal, even if it meant alienating her father.

Now, as she carried the pristine tablecloth into the parlour she glanced out of the window and saw grey sleety rain falling like tears against the gleaming glass panes. She sighed. Mr Mortimer would doubtless arrive in a good humour; she had come to learn that he was a good-natured man, likeable and kind, but when she married it would be to someone she loved. Someone like Anthony Weatherby Nichols.

She shook the cloth and set it billowing like a

white cloud before coming to rest on the polished surface of the table. Nothing but the best was good enough for Father's guest. The house, already spotless, had been scrubbed to within an inch of its life and any surface that needed dusting had been given her mother's full attention. As usual, no word of praise passed Arthur Burton's lips.

'I'm not looking forward to this tea at all,' Ella said, turning as her mother entered the room. 'You know I don't have feelings for Jolly Mortimer, and the thought of meeting all those girls fills me with dread.'

'Don't say anything to your father, there's a love.' Selma's voice was low and she glanced anxiously over her shoulder as if expecting to see her husband standing over her listening to her every word. 'Just be polite, that will satisfy your father. He knows you've been well brought up and are not given to fussing over a man you've only recently met.'

'But he expects me to marry the man,' Ella said, copying her mother's hushed tones. 'I'll never agree to that, Ma.'

Selma held up her hand. 'All right, just go along with things for now and keep your father happy. I think Mr Mortimer realizes he must give you time to get to know him. He can't expect you to fall into his arms like some loose woman.'

Ella opened her mouth to reply, but heard her

father's footsteps coming towards the parlour. He stood in the doorway and looked round, satisfying himself that the room was warm and welcoming, with a good fire burning in the grate. He looked heavy-eyed, but then he had eaten more than his fill of roast lamb and Ella knew his inclination, after a big meal, was to fall asleep. But he would stay awake if it killed him. He was looking forward to Jolly Mortimer's visit and would do anything to please his friend – even hand over his daughter to him, sincerely believing it to be for her own good.

At last there was nothing left to do in the parlour and Ella followed her mother back into the kitchen, sighing with relief as she sank into a chair. 'I could murder a cup of tea,' she said.

Selma frowned at her. 'Do you have to bring such common language into our home, Helena? It's bad enough that you mix with those people from the theatre, without picking up their crude manners.'

'Mother, we're just an ordinary family. The folk from the theatre are probably better off than we'll ever be.'

'And how do they earn their living, Miss?' Selma sniffed. 'Cavorting about half dressed on the stage in front of all those people. I'm sorry in my heart that your father let you work at the Palace in the first place.'

Ella grimaced. If her father realized that she

came into daily contact with the artistes he would have her out of the Palace in the blink of an eye. Fortunately, he believed she simply kept in the background, doing the clerical work and minding her own business. Which, Ella realized with surprise, is largely what she did.

Her elevation to the job of dresser to the stars had added to her workload rather than diminishing it. She worked with the artistes, helped them into their stage clothes and also cleaned their rooms. The performers might as well be a crowd of children the way they left litter and discarded costumes for her to pick up.

But on the days when there was a matinée in the afternoon and a show in the evening, when all outside was dark and cold and the interior of the theatre was brightly lit, filled with music and laughter, those were the moments she lived for.

'Here, have a cup of tea and don't speak a word about the Palace in front of Mr Mortimer, will you?' Selma's voice shattered her thoughts. 'Please, Helena, be good just for me,' her mother pleaded. Suddenly Ella felt a deep pity for her. Selma Burton had given up her freedom for the respectability of marriage and all it had brought her was hard work and little joy. Well, Ella would not give up her own freedom so lightly.

When Mr Mortimer arrived, Ella was waiting, wearing her best dress as her father had instructed. She opened the door and stepped aside

91

as Mr Mortimer ushered his five children into the tiny hallway. As they filed past Ella into the parlour she viewed them with misgivings. They were all girls, the youngest being about six and the eldest about fourteen years of age, Ella guessed. They were all well dressed, but Ella could see small signs of the lack of a mother's hand. Their boots needed polishing and one of the girls had a button missing from her good woollen coat.

Mr Mortimer reeled off the names of his daughters, smiling all the time, proud of his brood. 'Leticia here is the eldest, then comes Charlotte and the twins, Vicky and Lizzie, and last but never least, our dear little Mary.'

Ella smiled shyly and the girls stared back at her with solemn faces as if they knew she was an intruder in their lives. She offered to take their coats and hats and obediently the girls took off their outdoor clothes.

Selma had made a plateful of small beef sandwiches garnished with pickles, and as soon as everyone was seated, she nodded to Ella to hand them around. The girls ate daintily; it seemed that someone had taught them good table manners.

Ella smiled again encouragingly, but none of the children returned her smile. They looked at her blankly with identical blue eyes and Ella felt they were putting up with the occasion just as she was, none of them enjoying it.

Selma had suggested putting silver sixpences into the cakes in lieu of presents, but Arthur had told her not to be so foolish. 'What if one of them choked on a sixpence? What would Mr Mortimer think of us then?'

Selma always did what she was told, and so making twists of paper into crackers with sixpences inside had been her second choice. A good one, it turned out, because the youngest girl actually smiled, rubbing the sixpence against her skirt to polish it. Ella guessed that their father, although he loved them dearly, rarely thought of little treats for them.

After tea, Selma, with a nod from her husband, swept the children away to the kitchen with the promise of dandelion and burdock cordial. Ella rose from her chair too, but her father waved his hand at her. 'Sit down and talk to Jolly,' Arthur said. 'I'll help your mother with the little ones.'

Ella knew her father would do no such thing; it was just an excuse to leave her and Mr Mortimer alone. Arthur left the parlour and the stern look on his face showed Ella that he expected her to be pleasant to his friend.

'Well, what do you think of my girls?' Mr Mortimer smiled at her and his chins spread out over his collar. 'Aren't they lovely?'

'They are a credit to you, Mr Mortimer.' Ella fidgeted uncomfortably in her chair.

'Please, Helena, call me Jolly, everyone else

does.' He leaned forward conspiratorially. 'Though my real name is Richard. You can use that if you like.'

'Thank you.' Ella, knowing he was making an effort to be kind to her, settled for not using his name at all. 'You have a wonderful family. The girls must be good company for you.'

'Do you like children, Helena?'

She looked across the room at him, careful to hide her sense of unease at being left alone with him. 'I must confess I've never been in contact with children. I am an only child myself, as you know.'

He brushed this aside. 'Well, it all comes naturally to women, my dear, and I'm sure one day you'll make a splendid mother.'

'Oh, I won't have children for a long time yet,' Ella said. 'I'm still only nineteen, you see, and I don't feel ready for the responsibilities of married life.' If she thought she'd deflect his attentions with her statement she was wrong.

'Oh, nonsense! You are cut out to be a wife and mother, anyone can see that just by looking at you. And you have a superb example in your dear mother. She is a jewel of a woman.'

'Subservient and obedient, you mean?' The words were out before she could stop them.

Mr Mortimer looked at her in surprise, as if she had suddenly reared up and kicked him. 'Your mother is a very sweet, amiable lady.' He sounded bewildered. 'I'm sure she goes about her business with pleasure. She certainly keeps a good home. Your father is a very lucky man.'

Ella wanted to ask him why he didn't find a woman just like her mother then, instead of wasting his time with a girl young enough to be his daughter. But she closed her lips and kept silent. It was pointless to upset the man, he was nice enough and she didn't want to hurt him. The best thing she could do was try to put Mr Mortimer off the idea of marriage in small, discreet ways.

'I'll never be the cook my mother is,' she said, 'and I don't think my talents at housekeeping are to be compared with hers, but then I'm still very young.' She emphasized the last part of the sentence, hoping this time he would take the hint that she was too young for him.

He smiled. 'You are very mature for your age, Helena. Old enough for marriage, my dear.'

Nothing she said seemed to put him off his clumsy attempts to woo her. After an hour of his company Ella was tired of making small talk, but she concealed her feelings well and it was with a smile that she welcomed the children back into the room, all dressed for outdoors. They stood obediently close to their father, waiting for him to take them home.

'Thank the Good Lord that's over!' Ella exclaimed as she stood with her mother at the window, watching the little group walk down the hill towards the centre of town.

'He's a very good catch, mind,' Selma said. 'Mr Mortimer has a fine big house and several maids to wait on him.'

'Why does he need a wife, then?' Ella asked quietly.

Her mother's glance slipped away. 'Men have needs, Helena.'

Ella understood men's 'needs' only too well: she had witnessed her mother's pale face and shadowed eyes the morning after her father had satisfied his, unaware that his wife was over-worked and tired.

She glanced at her father as he came into the room. He was smiling, and in an uncharacteristic gesture, he rested his hand on his daughter's shoulder. 'You've really got Jolly in a state, my dear,' he said. 'All he can talk about is you. The man is besotted.'

Selma gave her a warning glance and Ella held her tongue. There was a moment's pause while her father waited for Ella to speak and then Selma intervened. 'I think I'll make a fresh pot of tea. Would you like a cup, Arthur?'

'I'm ready for something stronger than a cup of tea, thank you. Open a bottle of the barley wine you made last year. This is a special occasion, after all.'

Ella felt the hairs on the back of her neck

rise. 'How's that, Father?' she asked, her voice cracking a little in apprehension.

'Why, Mr Mortimer has paid you the greatest compliment in the world, Helena. He's asked me if he can propose marriage to you, and of course I've said yes. It would be an honour to have him in the family.'

Ella felt as though the earth had tilted under her. A rush of angry words rose to her lips, but she felt her mother's hand on her arm and she remained silent. But she didn't want to marry Mr Mortimer – she would rather die first.

CHAPTER EIGHT

Ella slipped through the side door of the Palace with a feeling of anticipation tingling in her veins. The place felt like home to her now, and every day there was the chance of seeing Anthony, listening to his voice, feeling his hand touch her shoulder.

Once inside the now familiar warren of corridors, she pulled off her gloves and rubbed her chilled fingers together to bring life back into them. Outside it was snowing, light dry flakes that had touched her face like a kiss. She smiled to herself: how would she know? She had never been kissed.

Kathleen, as always, was there before her, but the big chair was empty and Ella glanced enquiringly at her friend. 'Where's Doris?'

'She's been taken poorly. The winter weather has got to her chest. Still,' she smiled brightly, 'when I left her she was swearing she'd be better in a day or two. She can't bear to be away from the Palace for longer than she has to.'

Kathleen waited a moment and then dug an elbow into Ella's arm. 'Well, are you looking forward to it?'

'Forward to what?' Ella knew full well what Kathleen was getting excited about. Anthony had arranged a competition – supposedly to find new talent, but he had explained to her that it was a ploy to save the Palace the expense of hiring new artistes in January, a time when business was usually slow.

'The singing contest, of course! You *are* going in for it, aren't you?'

Ella shook her head. 'Not me. It's you who wants to be famous and tread the boards.'

Kathleen sighed and pushed the kettle on to the hob. 'Oh, I can't wait! Just imagine it – me on the stage and everyone watching. By all the saints, it's enchanted they'll be.'

'What will you do if you don't win?' Ella asked anxiously. 'You won't be too disappointed, will you?'

'Oh, don't you worry, I'll win all right. You haven't seen the ragtags and bobtails that are competing against me, have you?'

'That's true. I've been busy tidying up the costumes.' She gave Kathleen a conspiratorial smile. 'I'm dresser to the stars, remember?'

Kathleen's face fell. 'Now you come to mention it, that's my problem – I haven't got a decent frock to wear.' She looked down at the sacking apron around her waist. 'I can't go on like this, can I?' She made a pot of tea in silence, as though waiting for Ella to say something. Then Ella understood.

'You want to borrow something from the wardrobe?'

Kathleen turned, beaming. 'That's a wonderful idea!' She hugged Ella. 'I promise I'll be good. I'll make the tea every morning as soon as you come in to work. You won't be sorry you've been kind to me, because one day I'll be as famous as Alice Leamar and then you can be my own personal dresser and travel all over the country with me.' She smiled happily. 'We'll probably have to spend a lot of time in London in the big theatres, so we will.'

'Anything would be better than marrying old Mr Mortimer,' Ella said, giggling at the thought of travelling all the way to London with Kathleen and watching her perform on the stage of one of the great theatres. But it was all dreams – it would never happen.

'Come and see what you'd like to wear, we might as well do it right away,' Ella said. She led the way along the corridor towards the room where the costumes were kept, and as she opened the door Ella smelled the now familiar odour of old clothes. The costumes were cleaned only once every few months, and between shows they just hung up on hooks like limp, headless bodies.

Along the shelves were ranged numerous wigs on faceless stands. Ella shivered: the room had no windows, it was underneath the theatre and always felt a bit creepy.

Kathleen glanced at her. 'If there's a ghost in the building, sure it would be haunting down here,' she said. She was already rifling through the clothes and Ella watched her with a feeling of indulgent amusement. Kathleen was like a child at a party – her face was alight and Ella felt a pang of affection for her. She hoped that Kathleen would realize her dreams and become a famous star, but being successful in the theatre with so much competition was a difficult nut to crack.

'Nothing I like there,' Kathleen said at last, her disappointment evident in her voice. 'The clothes are either too big or too small or too old-fashioned.'

'Look in those.' Ella pointed to the huge baskets ranged against the wall. 'The best stuff is kept neatly packed away, so as not to damage the good material.'

'Why didn't you say so right away?' Kathleen didn't wait for an answer, she hurried over to the first basket and flung back the lid. 'Ah, this is more like it.' She carefully lifted out a red velvet dress and stared at it with a look of longing on her face. 'Can I try it on?'

'Of course you can.' Ella helped Kathleen into

the gown and stepped back to admire her. 'It fits you perfectly,' she said. 'I think it was once worn by some famous singer or other.'

'You're useless, so you are. I'd have found out by now exactly who wore this gorgeous gown. Oh, it's lovely.' Kathleen lifted her arm and sniffed. 'It smells of sweat, though. Can I wash it, do you think?'

Ella shook her head. 'No, that would be too dangerous, it might fade. Look, I keep some rose scent here – I'll spray under the arms with it. That usually removes sweat stains.'

At last Kathleen was happy with the dress and handed it back to Ella with a reluctant look on her face. 'I don't suppose I can take it home with me, can I?'

Ella shook her head. 'I tell you what – I'll keep it separate from all the other clothes so it will be ready for you to slip into before you go on stage.' She paused. 'I suppose I could put it in Dressing Room One – we've got no stars on tonight. Except for you,' she added hastily.

Kathleen nodded. 'You're a real diamond, Ella, and I'm not a bit jealous of you having all these lovely clothes to play with.'

Ella hid a smile, knowing Kathleen would give her eye-teeth to work in the wardrobe room. She watched as Kathleen walked slowly to the door, saying, 'I'd better get on with my cleaning, I suppose.' She paused a moment, glancing back at the jewel-like costumes with such longing that Ella felt sorry for her.

'You'll win the competition, Kathleen. You've such a good voice – you're bound to be picked at the end of the night,' she said.

Kathleen smiled. 'You know something, Ella Burton? I thought you were a stuck-up so-and-so when you first came here, but you're not such a bad stick after all.' She vanished into the corridor and Ella smiled to herself. She supposed Kathleen's words were meant as a compliment.

Ella was busy in the kitchen, using steam from the kettle to brush up the collar of a gentleman's velvet jacket, when she became aware of a presence behind her. She glanced round quickly, remembering Kathleen's mention of ghosts, and sighed in relief as she saw Anthony smiling down at her.

'You look as if you're enjoying your work.' He came and stood next to her and peered over her shoulder. She felt his soft breath on her cheek and had the foolish impulse to turn into his arms and lift her lips to his.

'This has come up quite well, as you can see.' She held the jacket out to him and he took it gingerly.

'Here, have it back. It looks as if it's been worn by a ghost from the past.' He smiled. 'Come to

103

think of it, perhaps it was – the Lord only knows who wore this jacket last.'

'Anthony . . .' Ella looked at him, trying to breathe calmly. His closeness was disturbing but she forced an even note into her voice.

'Yes, Ella?' As he smiled, dimples appeared in his cheeks. He was so handsome, so lovable, that she could hardly remember what she was going to ask him.

'Oh, I just wondered if you'd like me to make you a cup of tea. As we're here in the kitchen anyway, it seems like a good opportunity.'

'Why not?' Anthony said amiably. 'Doris used to bring a cuppa to my office, regular as clock-work. I do hope she'll be well enough soon to come back to work – I miss the old girl.'

'I can bring you tea every morning – just until Doris returns, of course,' Ella said eagerly.

Anthony looked at her for a long moment. 'That would be very nice, Ella. I think it's time I got to know more about you. For instance, I don't even know if you've got a sweetheart.'

'Of course I haven't! My father's so strict he hardly lets me step outside the door except to come to work.'

Anthony placed the tips of his fingers together like a tent and looked at her for a long time. 'A girl like you will soon be snapped up, I suppose,' he said. 'And then I'd lose you; I wouldn't like that one bit.'

Ella felt her colour rise. It was the first time Anthony had said anything so personal to her. But did he mean he would miss her just as an employee?

'I love it here,' she said quickly. 'I think my father would like to see me married off, but I haven't found the right man . . . yet.'

Anthony drained his cup and put it on the table. 'Thanks for the tea, Ella. And I'm glad.' He touched her cheek gently before he moved to the door.

'Glad about what?'

'Glad you haven't got a sweetheart.'

As he left the kitchen, Ella put her hand over her heart; it felt as though it was beating loud enough for Anthony to hear. Did he mean he cared about her? She hardly dared hope so, and yet his words seemed sincere: he had said he was glad she didn't have a sweetheart. It was a good thing he didn't know about Mr Mortimer's foolish hopes that she would wed him.

The day seemed to drag by, but at last it was time for the first house. The competitors were lined up in the wings and as Ella made her way to dressing room number one, she sent up a prayer that Kathleen, even if she didn't win, would give a good account of herself.

'Thank God you've come!' Kathleen had the red velvet half on, half off, and was trying to pull the sleeves up over her arms. 'Help me, Ella, I'm stuck.'

Gently Ella eased the heavy material over Kathleen's shoulders. She did up the fastenings at the back and pulled the skirt straight and then she stood back to admire her friend. Kathleen did a twirl, happy and nervous at the same time.

'How do I look?'

'You look lovely. Here, let me comb your hair, it's so red and so curly it always looks beautiful.'

Ella combed Kathleen's curls into a glossy twist at the back of her head, which showed off her friend's graceful neck and the fine bones of her face. 'I've brought you these from Wardrobe.' She took out a pair of glittering earrings and clipped them into place.

Stunned, Kathleen stared at her reflection. 'Oh, Ella, I can't believe it! You've transformed me – I look almost pretty.' She turned her head from side to side, watching the gleam of the earrings. 'Are they real diamonds?'

'Of course not!' Ella smiled at her friend. 'They're probably made from paste, but they'll look good to the audience.'

'Well,' Kathleen heaved a sigh. 'If I sing half as good as I look, I'll be sure to win the competition.'

'Come on,' Ella said. 'We'd better go and wait in the wings. I think you're the fourth act to go on stage.' As the two girls left the dressing room and made their way along the corridor towards the stage, Ella noticed Kathleen was trembling.

Waiting in the wings was an older woman who looked familiar to Ella, though she couldn't think where she could have met her. The woman nodded to her. 'Don't you remember me, Miss Burton? I'm Aggie Bodycombe. I live a little way down the street from you. I'm looking for a job.'

Ella felt a trickle of apprehension run through her. A neighbour seeing her like this, walking towards the stage as bold as brass, would be sure to talk to her mother or – worse still – her father about her.

'Can you find me some work, then?' Mrs Bodycombe asked.

Ella shook her head. 'Oh no, I'm one of the cleaners, that's all.'

'Oh, that's not what I was led to believe.'

'What do you mean, Mrs Bodycombe?'

'I was told you help the so-called stars get their clothes on. You must have curried favour to get that job. By the way, does your father know about your new position?'

Ella swallowed hard. 'I haven't told him yet. I thought it would be a nice surprise when I brought home a little bit more money to help out at home.'

Anthony came into the wings and ushered the next act towards the stage. The girl was little more than a child and was clutching a teddy bear in her arms. Anthony was gentle with her and Ella's heart softened. He was such a good, kind man. He came and stood next to Ella, touching her shoulder in the familiar way he had, and she blushed as she saw the stare Mrs Bodycombe threw at them both.

'Good worker, is she?' Mrs Bodycombe directed her question at Anthony.

He looked a little surprised but replied courteously. 'Our Ella is a fine worker. I don't know what I'd do without her.'

'Well, you'll have to do without her soon, because from what her mam tells me she's going to be a married lady before too long.'

Ella froze as Anthony removed his hand abruptly from her shoulder. He moved slightly away from her and was silent, waiting for Ella to say something. She couldn't talk; her voice seemed to have deserted her. In any case, Anthony ignored her and turned to Kathleen. 'Look, my little nightingale, I think it's time for your turn. Go on, give them your best out there. I know you can do it.'

As Kathleen strode confidently on to the stage, Anthony cast a fleeting glance at Ella. 'So it looks like I'll be taking on new staff soon,' he said. 'And I had such high hopes of you being a real help to me.'

As he moved away, Ella hurried after him. 'Anthony, it's not what you think. I don't want to be married to this man. It's just an idea my father has got into his head.'

He didn't stop to listen and the words died on Ella's lips. In that moment she hated Jolly Mortimer, Mrs Bodycombe and her father, but most of all she hated herself for being so weak. She shouldn't have tried to please her father. She should have made it quite clear right away that she didn't want to be married, that she just wanted to be left alone to run her life and make her own choices. And yet the picture of her mother's pleading face came to mind and she felt trapped like a bird in a cage. It was not a feeling she liked.

CHAPTER NINE

Ella stood facing her father across the shiny table in the parlour and her nerve almost failed her. After a moment she squared her shoulders and declared, 'I can't marry Mr Mortimer, Father. I just don't love him.'

Her father flushed. 'You will do as I say, child. I know what's best for you.'

'I don't think you do, Father.'

'How dare you answer me back, girl? I told you I've given Jolly my permission to ask for your hand in marriage and that's an end to it.'

'No, it isn't, Father!' Ella's voice rose. 'I don't see why I should take on a man twice my age who simply wants a nursemaid for his five children.'

'Jolly can offer you so much – can't you see that? He's got a fine house, and as for the children, he's got nurses and such to see to their needs. Do you want to be an old maid?'

'Father, I'm only nineteen. Of course I don't want to be an old maid, but I want a loving marriage, not one that would bring me nothing but discontent and unhappiness.'

Arthur Burton came round the table and caught her arm. 'You *will* marry Jolly Mortimer, do you hear me? And I don't want any more nonsense about love. I ask you, who marries for love? It's a just a dream, girl. You marry a man who can look after you financially. I won't always be here to support you, mind.'

'I can support myself, Father. I'm earning a good wage, or have you forgotten that?'

He waved his hand in dismissal. 'And how far will that take you? Will it be enough to put a roof over your head or food on the table and clothes on your back? You have no idea how much it costs to live well, Helena.'

Selma appeared behind her husband, putting her finger to her lips, urging Ella to be silent. 'Come on now, Arthur,' she said. 'I've made a nice cup of tea. Let's all sit down and talk calmly, shall we?'

Arthur looked at his wife for a moment, his head jutting forward, his eyes blazing. 'Talk calmly?' he echoed. 'I should take my belt to the girl, that's what I should do. Talk about biting the hand that feeds you. She is ungrateful and foolish and I won't stand for it.'

He paused to get his breath. 'Jolly is calling on you this evening. He will be ready to ask you to marry him and you will say yes, do you understand?' His eyes narrowed. 'God help me for having an ungrateful girl instead of a fine son. Now I'll have no more on the subject, do you understand?'

Ella bowed her head. This was the first time her father had ever voiced his desire for a son. The white, gaunt face of her mother stilled her tongue. Her thoughts were racing. She'd go upstairs and pack a few of her clothes – there was nothing to do but leave home.

Ella could well imagine the way her father would treat Selma, blaming her for everything that was wrong with his life. He was a discontented man who wanted to live above his station and that's why he was so keen to marry her off to his boss.

Later, when it was dark, Ella slipped out of the back door and crept along in the shadow of the wall outside the garden, clutching her bag. Soon Jolly Mortimer would be arriving at the house expecting to find a bride-to-be, but he could go whistle because she wouldn't be there.

Only when she was on the street heading towards town did she stop to wonder where she would stay that night. It was cold and bleak, with the threat of snow in the air. Ella shivered. Almost without thinking, she began to make her way along the High Street towards the Palace. She could sleep in one of the dressing rooms, at least for tonight, and then tomorrow she could look for lodgings.

The lights in the theatre were ablaze – the second house was about to begin. No one questioned her as she walked in through the stage door. She was a familiar face and no one would remember it was her day off.

The dressing rooms were all in use. Though Kathleen had not won the talent competition, she'd put on a good show and was more anxious than ever to tread the boards like a real star. Tonight there was a full cast of performers getting ready to go on stage. Ella smelled the greasepaint, heard the soft murmur of voices. As always, the excitement of the theatre made her blood tingle. It was her world now, a world she loved, and she vowed she would remain part of it as long as she had breath in her body.

She took her bag to where the costumes were kept. All the clothes for the coming performance would have been removed by now, and as it was the last house, no one would bother her tonight. The artistes would simply undress and leave their costumes hanging over chairs or even on the floor of their dressing rooms, ready for Ella to find them in the morning, brush them down and put them away.

She sat on one of the baskets, looking round at the headless mannequins. Some of them were naked and looked like pallid corpses in the harsh electric light. But at least it was a warm shelter from the cold night air. Weary now, she pulled out some of the covering sheets from a stack in the corner and lay down. Her eyes were heavy and soon she slept.

Ella woke to feel a light touch on her face. She sat up quickly and blushed as she saw Anthony kneeling beside her.

'Thank God you're all right,' he said. 'For a moment I thought you were dead. What on earth are you doing here?'

Ella decided to tell him the truth. Perhaps Anthony would listen to her now, without the interfering Mrs Bodycombe putting her oar in.

'My father's friend was coming to ask me to marry him this evening. I don't love him and I don't want to be married. Not yet.' She sighed. 'I just felt I had to get away, and the only place I could feel safe was here in the theatre.'

'Well, you know your own mind best. But one thing is sure, you can't stay here.' Anthony caught her arm and drew her to her feet. 'You'd better come home to my place.' He saw her flustered look and smiled. 'I have a spare room. Don't worry, I'm not harbouring any evil intentions.' He took her arm and led her from the room. 'Mind, you'll have to face my battleaxe of a landlady. She'll make sure there's nothing untoward going on. She thinks of me as a child and often tells me to mind my manners.'

'But I can't stay with you,' Ella said, though she could think of nothing better than sharing a house with Anthony.

'Well, stay for tonight, at least. Tomorrow you can find a more suitable place to live. It might be that Doris will have a room free. Kathleen lodges with her so you'd be with friends.'

He drew her towards the doorway. 'Look, I have to stay on here until the end of the show. Do you want to go on without me or wait until the curtain falls on the last house?'

'I'll wait,' Ella said firmly. 'I don't want to face your landlady on my own after all you've said about her.' She didn't add that the walk home from the theatre with Anthony at her side would be wonderful. She would wait all night for him if she had to.

'All right, just wait in my office. Take a little of my port – it will warm you up. You look frozen.'

He took her hand and led her up the stairs and she felt suddenly light-hearted. Anthony was holding her hand, he would be taking her to his home – he must care about her, at least a little. The thought sent the blood coursing through her veins.

When he'd gone, she looked round the office. It was pleasantly warm; the coal fire burned brightly and Ella took Anthony's advice and helped herself to a glass of his port, which had a ruddy glow in the firelight. Soon she began to feel better. Leaving home was hard, especially leaving her mother, but it was for the best. She couldn't be forced to marry Jolly Mortimer if she kept out of sight. As for her father, he could make any excuse he liked to his friend, but in the end he'd have to accept the truth that his daughter had a mind of her own. She could only hope that Jolly would take the hint and give her up as a bad job. Surely he could tell by now that she didn't want to be married to him? She actually felt some pity for him: he was a nice man and didn't deserve to be led on by her father. Ella drank a little more of the port and closed her eyes, feeling wrapped in a cosy glow where everything, even finding love with Anthony, was possible.

'I'm sorry, Jolly.' Arthur Burton stepped back to allow his boss into the small hallway. 'Helena has been taken suddenly sick with a bad cough. I'm afraid her mother has put her to bed with a hot-water bottle and a hot toddy.' Arthur cursed Helena for running off into the night like the foolish child she was. But she would come home soon enough when her belly was aching for food.

'Is the girl often sick?' Jolly handed his hat to Selma without looking at her. 'I don't know if I could cope with a wife who is sickly. I had enough of that with my first one.'

'She's hardly seen a day's illness in her life,' Arthur said quickly. 'She's been working too hard, that's what the trouble is, not getting a proper night's sleep.'

'Well, Helena would be well cared for in my home,' Jolly said. 'You may be assured of that, and I believe she'll make a good obedient wife.'

'I'm sure she will,' Arthur agreed. 'Come and sit in the parlour. Perhaps we could play a hand or two of cards – what do you say?'

Jolly nodded. Relieved, Arthur led him into the parlour, where a good fire burned in the grate. 'I feel in the mood for a little light entertainment,' he said as he picked up the deck of cards.

'You're a good man, Arthur,' Jolly said. 'I'll see that you get a rise at work, perhaps even a promotion.' He smiled. 'I know that's what you'd really like.'

Arthur beamed. Promotion – the word was like a magic spell. He would be better than his fellow workers, he would wear clean shirts and the cuts on his hands from the tin would heal and he would have baby-pink fingers like Jolly.

As Arthur settled in his chair opposite Jolly, his smile hid his anxiety. He would send his wife to fetch Helena home: there was only one place she could have gone to and that was the Palace.

When Selma came into the parlour with a tray of cold meat, cheese and pickles, Arthur stood up, took the tray from her and placed it on the table. She looked surprised but said nothing. 'Excuse me a moment, Jolly,' he said and ushered his wife out of the room. 'Go and fetch her home, Selma. I'm worried about the girl.'

Selma looked at him with tears in her eyes. 'Arthur, if she doesn't want to come I can't make her. In any case, we don't know where she's gone.'

'She's gone to that blasted theatre!' he whispered, shocked at his own language. 'Fetch her home before she ruins her reputation.'

Selma drew herself up to her full height and stared at him with a look he'd never seen before. 'No, I will not!' she said, far too loudly for his comfort. 'I know she doesn't want to—'

He stopped her words by putting his hand over her mouth. 'Get back to the kitchen. We'll talk about this later.'

Selma looked as if she would defy him, but finally she pushed away his hand and went into the kitchen.

Arthur was relieved when at last Jolly decided to go home. As he put on his coat, Jolly glanced up the stairs. 'I hope that Ella is well by tomorrow. I want the wedding plans to get underway at once – the sooner we're married, the better.'

Arthur saw him to the door, then went back into the parlour and stared at the embers of the fire. He was worried now, really worried that he'd driven his daughter away, when all he'd wanted for her was a good marriage. Well, her fate was now in the hands of God. Arthur prayed that

God would be kind and save his daughter from a life of shame.

It was comfortable in Anthony's small spare bedroom. The fire was blazing and a glass of hot milk stood on a tray beside the bed. Anthony had even provided her with a nightgown to wear in bed. She imagined from the old-fashioned cut, the large floral pattern, faded now and almost colourless, that the nightgown had once belonged to his mother. She was touched by his kindness, and as she slid between the sheets she wished it was as his wife that she was being welcomed into his home. She picked up the glass of milk, curling her fingers around it for extra warmth. She felt so happy, Anthony had taken charge of her and shown her every kindness, and she was hopelessly in love with him.

There was a gentle tap on the door and Anthony stepped inside. 'I see you've made yourself at home.' He left the door open and came to stand beside the bed. He gently lifted a curl of her hair and let it slip through his fingers, smiling. 'I never noticed you had such silky hair.'

She ached with tenderness for him and on a whim took his hand and raised it to her lips. 'Thank you so much, Anthony. I'm so grateful to you.'

He patted her head as if she was a child and drew his hand away. 'Don't worry, Ella. No one can force you into a marriage you don't want.'

She longed for him to kiss her, and as if reading her thoughts, he bent his head and pressed his mouth briefly against hers.

Before she had time to think, he was walking away from her. At the door he paused. 'Look, have a few days off work. I've got three more people starting tomorrow, so you needn't worry.'

'No, I want to come to work,' she said. 'The theatre is in my blood.' She wanted to add that he was in her blood too. She loved him, she wanted him, and the touch of his lips against hers had sent thrills racing through her.

'All right, come into work if you like.' He smiled and her heart began to thump. Quickly she pulled the blankets up around her shoulders.

'Goodnight, Anthony.'

She heard his footsteps dying away along the landing and hugged herself, remembering the touch of his hand, the feel of his mouth on hers, the way he smiled and looked at her in such a caring way. 'Oh Anthony,' she sighed. 'I do love you.'

Selma lay still beside her husband. She knew he wasn't asleep, but she wanted him to think she was sleeping. He began to grumble to himself. 'Fine life, being ruled by two rebellious women. It would never have happened in my father's day.' He nudged Selma. 'Wake up, I want to talk.'

She lay still, hoping he'd give up, but he nudged her harder. 'Come on, Selma, wake up, please.'

Giving in, Selma sat up. 'Arthur, it's no good trying to force Helena into a marriage she doesn't want. Jolly might be a good man, but he's too old for her.' She lay down again and turned her back on her husband. 'Now let me go to sleep, Arthur.' As she closed her eyes she prayed that Helena was safe and warm; in the morning, she would go to the theatre and speak to her daughter, beg her to come home. She hoped that her husband had now seen the error of his ways and would stop pestering their daughter to make a thoroughly unsuitable marriage.

CHAPTER TEN

Ella was brushing a velvet cape the next morning when Kathleen came in and stood, hands on hips, staring at her.

'What's wrong?' Ella hung up the cape, careful not to crease it. 'Why are you staring at me like that?'

'You're a dark horse, to be sure, Ella Burton.' Kathleen's voice had an edge to it and Ella knew exactly what was coming next.

'You've heard I stayed at Anthony's house last night, then?' She took up the flat iron from the hob. 'You'll excuse me if I don't stop, won't you?' There was a hint of sarcasm in her voice, but Kathleen either didn't notice or didn't care.

'You could have told me!' she rushed on. 'I felt such a fool when he mentioned it.' Kathleen sat on one of the large square baskets. 'Did you warm his bed?'

'Of course not!' Ella was angry now. 'If you must know, I had a bit of trouble with my father

122

and Anthony was kind enough to take me in when I had nowhere to go.'

'That's funny, he's never offered to take anyone else home, not even for a cup of tea.' She paused. 'But then, look how quickly you got promoted to dresser. You must be sleeping with him.'

'I only wish I was.' The words were out before Ella had time to consider what she was saying, and Kathleen was quick to respond.

'I thought so! You've got a soft spot for our Anthony. I could tell by the way you're always mooning after him.'

'Maybe my liking for him showed,' Ella said. 'But as to sleeping with him, I wouldn't do it. My father hasn't drummed the words of the Bible into my head all this time for me to go and shame him by being a kept woman.'

'Well, come on, you might as well tell me the whole story.' Kathleen, reassured, was her old self again. She pulled her skirts loose from her bloomers and made herself comfortable.

Ella sighed and put away the iron. 'It's nothing, really. My father and I fell out with each other, that's all.'

'And he chucked you out?'

'No, not exactly. I suppose I ran away, if the truth be told.'

'So that's why your mother has come by the theatre, is it? Poor soul wanted to check that you were all right. What's she got to say about you staying with the boss?'

'She doesn't know,' Ella said quickly.

'Well, come on, sure I might as well have the full story.' Kathleen folded her arms and waited.

Ella sighed. 'Well, you know that my father wanted to marry me off to Jolly Mortimer, who's got five girls to bring up. I'd be a drudge before I could turn around.'

'But the man is rolling in money. I think you're a lucky girl, Ella Burton.'

'I don't feel lucky,' Ella said. 'He's so old, for one thing.'

Kathleen smiled. 'He isn't that old – he's about forty-five, I'd say.' She paused for a moment and waited for Ella to speak but Ella just sighed. 'So what are you going to do, then? Are you going to live at Anthony's place for ever or are you going to be sensible and get some lodgings?' She rushed on without waiting for an answer. 'Folks will talk, mind – look on you as a loose woman. Sure you should make your move as soon as you can.' She paused, then added, 'Doris has got rooms going spare.'

Ella felt a cold chill at the thought of leaving Anthony's spare room, but she knew she had no alternative. 'Where does Doris live?' she asked reluctantly.

'On the edge of town, just off Walter Road. I'll take you there myself. I know Doris will be glad of some extra money coming in.' Kathleen had warmed to Ella again now she knew the truth. She smiled. 'The old girl will be back at the theatre as soon as her chill is better. You can talk to her later about renting a room, but I'm sure she'll agree.'

'Perhaps you would ask her for me, Kathleen?'

'Better speak to her direct – you can go along when you knock off here.' Kathleen plucked some cotton from her skirt. 'Doris used to be a famous performer, you know, entertaining the rich folk in London.'

'What did she do? Was she a singer?'

'Sure, she was a fine singer. But when she was a young colleen she was the finest trapeze artiste you'd ever hope to see. But she had a fall and that finished her career for good, 'cause the funny thing was she never sang a note after that.'

There was silence for moment while Ella thought of poor Doris, earthbound but still loving the theatre.

'I'd better get up to the dressing rooms,' she said finally. 'I don't want to keep the stars waiting. They can be real prima donnas when things don't go according to plan.'

Kathleen sniffed. 'I wouldn't know, I'm only a humble cleaner, not a wardrobe mistress like you.' She raised her eyebrows. 'You'd better get out of Anthony's house before folk start saying you are *his* mistress.'

'All right, you don't have to keep on about it. You've said your piece.'

Later that day, Ella took a cup of tea to Anthony's office. As he took it from her their hands touched. She moved away from him as though her fingers were burned. She took a deep breath and said, 'Kathleen suggested I talk to Doris about renting a room in her house.'

Anthony glanced at her quickly but didn't speak.

'Look,' he said at last, 'you don't have to move out of my place. We'd be well chaperoned by my landlady, so no one would be able to talk about us, would they? And even if they did, it's no one else's business.' He paused. 'The truth is I'd like you to stay, Ella.'

He moved close to her and rested his hand on her shoulder. Ella breathed in his aroma: he smelled of the theatre, of plush curtains and rich cigars. She began to tremble. She wanted to be in his arms, to feel the thrill of his touch, his mouth teasing hers, but she drew away from him.

'I'm a respectable girl and I wouldn't like to hurt my family by causing nasty gossip.'

Anthony moved away from her. 'I respect you for that, Ella. I know you've been well brought up. Your father is a God-fearing man and your mother would break her heart if she thought you were living in sin with me.'

He gazed down at his desk and Ella drank him

in: the tilt of his head, the shape of his shoulders. She felt her body throb with strange new feelings. Was it love, this breathless longing to submit to the passion that raced through her?

'I must get back to work,' she said quickly. 'Thank you, Anthony, for . . . well, everything.'

Back in the kitchen, she pressed her palms against her hot cheeks. She had wanted to stay close to Anthony, to satisfy the urges he aroused in her. 'You foolish girl!' she said in a whisper. 'That's the way girls fall into trouble.' The sooner she found somewhere else to stay, the better. Kathleen was right: to stay with Anthony would be foolhardy; she needed to find some lodgings without delay.

Doris was only too glad to see Ella standing on her doorstep. 'Come in, girl. Hurry, before the chilly breeze gets into my lungs.' She shut the door and pushed Ella along the dimly lit passage-way. 'There's a good fire in here,' she said. 'I can't afford fires all over the house so I spend most of my time in the kitchen.'

It was a comfortable kitchen and Doris watched as Ella looked round approvingly. The grate was leaded, the brass fender gleamed in the flickering firelight and a good chenille cloth covered the kitchen table.

'Cosy, isn't it?' Doris pointed to a soft arm-chair. 'Sit yourself down. I'll make a cup of tea and then you can tell me why it is you want a room in my house.' She smiled drily. 'Not that I don't know already.'

'How do you know?' Ella asked.

Doris chuckled at her surprise. She tapped her head. 'It's all up there,' she said. 'And in here.' She rested her hand on her heart. She pushed the kettle on to the stove and giggled like a girl. The truth was that Kathleen had already told her all about Ella's split with her family. 'Is it true your father wants to marry you off to Mr Mortimer, the boss of the tin-plate works?'

'Aye, it's the truth,' Ella said flatly. 'And when I marry I want it to be a love match. It's just a pity my father can't see that.'

'Well, I expect he wants what's good for you.' Doris made the tea and handed Ella a brimming cup. 'When you've drunk that, I'll tell your fortune in the leaves, if you like.'

Ella smiled. 'All right – and thank you for being so kind.'

Doris looked at her knowingly. 'I expect your father, being a Bible-bashing churchgoer, has drummed into you that reading the future is the Devil's work.'

She observed the look of embarrassment on Ella's face. For a time there was no sound in the kitchen except for the coals shifting in the grate. Doris sat still and waited for Ella to speak.

'So – about the room. Can I lodge with you,

Doris?' Ella avoided the issue of her father's religion.

Doris nodded. 'Aye, you can have a room in my house right away. I see you've drained your cup. Pass it over to me, there's a good girl.' Doris stared at the sodden tea leaves at the bottom of the cup.

'What is it, Doris? Have you seen something about me?' Ella asked anxiously.

Doris played for time, studying the mess of leaves, turning the cup around in her still slender fingers. 'I see that our Anthony will shortly be leaving Swansea, so don't pin your hopes on him.' She put down the cup abruptly. 'I can't tell you any more, my love.' Doris sat upright in her chair. 'Right, you can move in here tonight, if you like. I'll take a few shillings towards the food and fuel, but I'll expect you to help Kathleen clean the house for me. My old bones hurt like tooth-ache these days. It's all I can do to manage my bit of dusting at the Palace.'

Doris looked at Ella, a feeling of pity running through her. Life was going to kick the girl hard, and there was nothing any of them could do about it.

Anthony watched with dismay as Ella packed her few possessions into her bag. 'Do you really have to go?'

'You know I do, Anthony. People will talk, and

129

in any case my mother is worried. She left a letter at the theatre door this morning. She won't come inside the theatre, you know that. When I've settled in with Doris my mother can visit me whenever she likes.'

'Look,' he said. 'Can I at least call on you at Doris's? No one can talk about us then, can they?'

'Do you really want to call on me, Anthony? Isn't it true that you are going to leave Swansea soon?'

'Leave Swansea? Where on earth did you get that idea from? Of course I'm not leaving Swansea. I have plenty of work to do at the Palace.'

He took her hands in his, and when she smiled up at him her face was illuminated with happiness. 'Old Doris read my tea leaves. She saw something there about you leaving. She must have got it wrong.'

Anthony smiled. 'Look, old Doris has strange ways. It's best to humour her, just so long as you don't believe all she tells you.' He wanted her to stay with him, but realized it was impossible. 'Come on,' he said. 'I'll walk with you over to Doris's place. It's the least I can do.'

'You've done a lot for me, Anthony,' she said gently. 'I don't know how I would have managed if you hadn't taken me in.'

Anthony felt a pang of regret. He liked Ella's

company, but perhaps it was just as well she was leaving. He was a young man: he couldn't afford to be tied to anyone, not just now when his career was blossoming.

It was cold in the street, and Anthony took Ella's arm as they stepped out briskly towards Walter Road. It felt so right, he and Ella close together, but he told himself he needn't feel despondent. He'd still be seeing Ella every day at work, and he had ample time to think about things, to make up his mind whether to develop their friendship into something stronger. Anthony told himself that he had made the right choice in not declaring his feelings for Ella. After all, he needn't rush into anything. He was young and he had all the time in the world.

CHAPTER ELEVEN

There was an air of excitement in the theatre, because the popular Miss Nellie Belmore was making her first appearance in Swansea. Ella had never heard of her, but then she was no expert on the performers. When Doris told her the artiste had once been one of the best in the world, Ella pulled a face. 'Well, I'll have the privilege of dressing her ready for tonight's performance.'

'And you remember to give her the respect she deserves, my girl.' Doris was now fighting fit and was making her presence felt. 'Miss Belmore is a star and should be treated like one.'

Doris sighed. 'I was treated like a queen when I was at my peak, Ella. I could sing, I could dance, and I loved the trapeze. A one-woman show, that's what I was.'

Ella tried to be patient with Doris, who had held the position of assistant wardrobe mistress since returning to work, but she got tired of hearing about the past. She'd rather dream about the future, about she and Anthony being married and bringing up a brood of wonderful children.

Her reverie was shattered when Doris spoke to her in a loud voice. 'Are you listening, girl? You never know, you might learn something if you listen to old Doris's tales of the theatre.'

Doris had cajoled the scene-shifters to bring her armchair from the kitchen into the costumes room, and she sank into it now, fanning her face with her hand. 'You know, it was through Anthony's insistence that I was kept on at the theatre,' she said. Ella was surprised. 'Mr Simons wanted to get rid of me when I became ill, but Anthony stuck up for me, told him that my long years of experience in the theatre were an invaluable asset.'

Ella's heart warmed, as it always did when she thought of Anthony. Since she'd moved in with Doris he'd taken to calling around of an evening and spending a little time with them, drinking tea, playing cards or just sitting talking.

Doris picked up on her thoughts. 'He's a fine man, a good man, is our Anthony,' she said. 'But never forget he is a man, and men have only one thing on their minds and that's to get under a girl's skirts.'

'Anthony isn't like that,' Ella retorted, but Doris only frowned at her.

'All men are like that. It's their nature, they can't help it.' Seeing that she wasn't convincing

Ella, she changed the subject. 'What about these dresses: will Miss Nellie be wearing the red or the green?' Doris picked up two gowns of soft velvet and held them up to the light.

Ella looked at them doubtfully. 'Haven't we anything else in her size? Those dresses have seen better days.'

'Tush! Don't you know anything, girl?' Doris didn't wait for an answer. 'In the bright new lights these clothes will look like new.'

'Will they?'

'I tell you what, you go to the back of the theatre when first house opens and you'll see how good the costumes look.'

Ella nodded. 'I'll do that. But don't you think that Miss Belmore should be bringing her own costumes, seeing she's so important that even Mr Simons is coming to tonight's performance?'

'People like Miss Nellie Belmore are never in one place for very long, so they don't carry too much baggage. In any case, thank your lucky stars she's wearing our costumes. We'd be stuck with a heap of ironing if she brought her own.'

The door was pushed open and Kathleen came into the room with a tray balancing on her arm. 'I'm taking my break in here with you two lucky souls.' She put the tray down on one of the baskets, slopping some tea into the saucers.

'We'd have come to the kitchen as usual if only

134

you'd said, and look, you haven't brought us any biscuits,' Doris grumbled.

'Don't carry on.' Kathleen sat on a pile of costumes and Ella winced; they would all have to be ironed again, but that wasn't Kathleen's concern.

'Those new cleaners Anthony got are bloody useless. I've spent hours showing that Aggie Bodycombe what has to be done and she still hasn't got the foggiest notion what cleaning a theatre means. All she wants to do is natter.'

Doris chuckled. 'It's the oldest trick in the book. Pretend ignorance and let some other fool keep on doing the donkey work.'

Kathleen took her cup of tea from the tray and held it between her fingers in an effort to warm them. Ella could see that Kathleen's hands were chapped from constantly being in water.

'I'm going to have a word with them,' Ella said. 'Right now.'

The corridors were freshly scrubbed and Ella felt sorry for Kathleen, who seemed to be doing the bulk of the work. The three new cleaners were sitting in the kitchen, drinking tea. Ella couldn't quarrel with that; they were taking their break, just as she was.

'I'd like to have a word, ladies,' she said. 'I expect you'll want the same wages as Kathleen when pay day comes, won't you?'

They looked at her as if she'd grown two

heads. 'Of course we will.' Aggie Bodycombe glared at her. 'It's only fair, mind.'

'And it's only fair that you do the same amount of work as Kathleen, don't you think?'

'We're still learning the ropes.' Aggie spoke for the three of them and the other women nodded their agreement.

'Didn't you come to us as experienced cleaners, then?' Ella's voice was deceptively quiet.

'Yes, we did. Well experienced, we are – we've worked in places far bigger than this poky theatre and . . .' Aggie Bodycombe's words trailed away as she realized the trap she was falling into. 'But every place needs learnin' about.'

'Well, I'll expect you to learn about the Palace by the morning,' Ella said without raising her voice.

'And who do you think you are to order us about, Madam?' Aggie folded her arms across her thin chest. 'I thought you was the wardrobe mistress, not head cleaner.'

'You're quite right,' Ella said. 'But I do see a great deal of Mr Weatherby Nichols and I'm also on good terms with Mr Simons, the owner. A word in the right ear . . . you know what I mean?'

'You'll tell on us if we don't do the work to your satisfaction, is that it?' Aggie Bodycombe's colour was high. 'I've a good mind to walk out right here and now.'

'Please yourself.' Ella allowed herself a smile.

136

'That would be fine by me. I could have three really good cleaners lined up before morning, as you well know.'

The silence in the kitchen was profound and the three women looked uneasily at each other. At last, Aggie Bodycombe backed down. 'I think we've got a good idea of the work now. You'll see a difference in the morning.'

'I'm sure I shall,' Ella said. 'And I trust I'll see a difference after the Palace closes its doors tonight as well. You know there's the auditorium to be swept and polished, don't you?'

'Yes, Miss Burton, right.' Aggie Bodycombe's face was sour and Ella knew she'd made an enemy of the woman for all time. Still, she wasn't here to be taken advantage of, and neither was poor Kathleen.

'Well, now we understand each other we can get on and enjoy our break. Work starts again in five minutes, thank you, ladies.'

Ella returned to Wardrobe just as Kathleen was tucking her skirts into the elastic of her bloomers. 'No you don't,' she said. 'You'll do no more work tonight, Kathleen. You've done enough. Now, you just go and watch the show from the wings and enjoy yourself.'

Kathleen smiled broadly. 'You've licked those new cleaners into shape, then?'

'I'm pretty sure we'll have no more slacking. Indeed, I guarantee it.'

'Dash it all, I underestimated you, Ella Burton. Right, it's off to wait for curtain up, then.' As she passed Ella she rested her hand on her shoulder. 'I could get very fond of you, given half a chance.' Giggling, she planted a playful kiss on Ella's cheek and went out into the corridor, eager to see every act and every turn that graced the stage of the Palace that night.

Doris looked at Ella and nodded her head. 'I was right about you. You'll go far in this business, but just don't lose your head over our Anthony, my girl, or you'll rue the day.'

'I won't lose my head,' Ella said. 'I've been brought up to know the difference between right and wrong.'

'Knowing doesn't stop you wanting. Just take care of yourself and don't be blinded by the charms of a man – any man.' She paused. 'Now, which gown shall I take up to Miss Nellie's dressing room?'

That night, it was crisp and cold with a hint of snow in the air again and Anthony insisted on walking Doris, Kathleen and Ella home. To Ella's disappointment, he didn't stay and she watched him walk away with a lump in her throat. However many times Doris warned her about Anthony, it did no good. Ella knew it was too late for advice: she was in love with him and nothing would ever change that.

The next morning, Ella woke early to the sound of repeated banging on the front door. She met Doris on the landing; the old lady was white with fear, her eyes still half closed in sleep.

'I'll go,' Ella said. There was a sick feeling in the pit of her stomach. Something was badly wrong: no one came thundering on the doors of respectable people's homes so early in the morning unless there was a crisis.

The young boy who stood on the pavement looked up at her, his face pale and anxious. 'You got to come home, Miss,' he said. 'There's been an accident at the tin-plate works.' Before she could reply he spoke again quickly. 'I don't know what's happened, but your mammy wants you home.'

'You run back to my mother,' Ella said. 'Tell her I'm coming right away.'

Ella dressed quickly, her hands shaking. Doris fussed around her, her lined face full of sympathy. 'Things might not be so bad, girl,' she said, but her tone was unconvincing. They both knew it was bad news.

When Ella arrived at the small terrace of houses the street was full of women. Most of their menfolk were tin-plate workers; whatever had happened at the tin-plate works it was bad, very bad indeed.

Her mother was sitting in a chair, her hands folded tightly across her lap, her knuckles white.

'What is it, Mother?' Ella knelt beside the chair and took her mother's hand.

Selma took a deep breath. 'There's been an explosion. One of the boilers burst. A few of the men were scalded – we don't know how bad it is yet, but there's a lot of workers injured, we do know that.'

A shadow fell over the room as Jolly Mortimer's big frame filled the doorway.

'You should be ashamed to show your face here, Mr Mortimer!' Aggie Bodycombe had been up at the crack of dawn in anticipation of the hard work she would be doing at the theatre, and had seen Jolly Mortimer arrive. She put her hands on her hips and challenged him. 'Perhaps if things were better managed the accident might not have happened.' She hoped by taking sides she would ingratiate herself with Ella and perhaps get some of the lighter jobs at the Palace.

Jolly Mortimer shook his head to and fro as if in pain. 'I manage the place to the best of my ability. But for a trick of fate I would be right in there with my men.'

'Oh, and what trick of fate was that? A cup of tea or a drink of porter, was it?'

'I had to go out of the building – urgent business in the office. I regret what's happened more than any of you.'

'And I suppose the only compensation for the

140

ones who have lost their lives will be a coffin,' Aggie Bodycombe mumbled.

Selma lifted her hand. 'Please, don't go on like that. I can't bear arguing, not now while I'm waiting to see if my man is alive or dead.'

She didn't have to wait long; four men from the tin-plate works were carrying what was left of Arthur Burton home on an old wooden door. They brought him indoors, avoiding Selma's eyes.

Arthur Burton's face was unrecognizable. He had been scalded by the steaming water from the boiler; his skin was peeling and his eyes were invisible in the swollen folds of his face.

Selma let out a cry and fell into Ella's arms. 'He was a good man,' she sobbed. 'He read his Bible every day, he went to church on Sundays, regular as the clock. Why didn't God save him?'

Jolly Mortimer coughed. 'I know it's not much consolation at a time like this, Mrs Burton, but I will personally see to the expenses of the funeral, you need have no worries there.'

Ella nodded to him. 'We accept your offer, Mr Mortimer, with thanks.' She knew her mother had very little money of her own. Anything her father had been able to spare he had given to his church, buying his way into heaven. Well, she hoped it was money well spent, because her father had gone from this life now, leaving a widow behind him.

Ella patted her mother's shoulder. 'Don't worry, I'll come back home and live with you. We'll manage all right on my wages from the theatre.'

Selma looked up at her gratefully. 'I'm going to need you very badly now, Helena, but I don't want you to give up your life for me.'

'I won't be giving up my life. I'll still go to work every day, but I'll be coming home to you when the last house at the Palace is over.'

Jolly Mortimer leaned towards her. 'You and your mother need never go short of anything, I promise you. Arthur was a dear friend of mine and we were both churchwardens. I won't stand by and let his family suffer.'

'That's very kind.' Ella looked up at the people crowded into the room in silent respect for the dead. She wished they would all go away. She glanced briefly at the man on the stretcher: he was no longer her father, but a disfigured stranger. She couldn't bear the sight of his ravaged face any longer. 'Will some of you men kindly take my father into the parlour? I have arrangements to make.' She spoke more to herself than to anyone in the room.

Jolly put his hand on her arm. 'No need for that. I'll have the carpenter send a good coffin up to the house as soon as he can. Your father will be treated with the respect he deserves, don't you worry about that.'

Aggie Bodycombe gave a snort of derision. 'What did I tell you? A coffin for the dead and a few insincere words of sympathy, that's all you'll get from the management, Selma.'

Ella ignored her. 'Thank you, Mr Mortimer,' she said tiredly. 'Will you do it now? I can't bear to look at my father's body for a moment longer than I have to.'

He nodded and left the house. Ella warmed to him; Mr Mortimer had proved his friendship to her father and for that she would always be grateful to him.

When at last Ella was left alone with her mother, Selma began to cry in earnest. 'Oh, what am I going to do without Arthur to look after me?' She looked at her daughter, a pitiful expression on her pale face. 'I did love him, you do know that, don't you, Ella?'

'Of course I know that, Mother, and don't worry, we'll manage all right. I'll be able to look after the two of us while I'm working at the Palace.'

Selma caught her hand. 'Think about marrying Mr Mortimer, won't you? It would solve all our problems.'

Ella took a deep breath. 'Yes, I'll think about it. But for now we've got too much to do, arrangements to make.'

'Leave it all to Mr Mortimer, Helena. He'll see that your father has a good send-off.'

Ella nodded. A good send-off was important among the tin-plate workers. She rested her hand on her mother's shoulder. 'Don't worry, we'll make sure Father is sent to his rest with dignity.'

It was only later, when her father was laid out decently in his coffin and her mother had gone upstairs to 'rest her weary bones', as she put it, that Ella was able to let the tears of grief roll unchecked down her cheeks. She sat in a kitchen chair by the fire and whispered the name she called her father when she was little more than a baby. 'Oh, Dadda, why did you have to die? Is there no justice in this world?'

CHAPTER TWELVE

Five days after burying her father, Ella went back to work at the Palace, only to find the theatre in uproar. The front page of the *Daily Post* declared to the township of Swansea that Mr Simons, owner of the Palace, was going to be summonsed to court.

Kathleen drew Ella into the costumes room, her face white and her eyes filled with tears. 'Mr Simons is ruined. His reputation is in shreds, so it is.'

'Why?' Ella was bewildered. 'What on earth has happened?'

'He had a blazing row in the street with a man called Mr Jarvis and punched him on the nose. It seems Mr Simons owes him a lot of money – he's been gambling away the Palace's takings,' Kathleen said, her eyebrows raised. 'Can you believe it?' She handed the newspaper to Ella. 'If Mr Simons goes to jail we'll all be out of a job. The Palace will close down.'

Ella saw clearly now the reason for Kathleen's tears. 'Perhaps Mr Simons will be cleared in the court and will keep the Palace going.'

'Not a hope in hell.' Kathleen shook back her red curls. 'The new cleaners and the stagehands have already gone. Even Anthony is looking out for a new job.'

'Talking about the lies in the paper, I see,' said Doris, coming into the room and sitting in her armchair. She looked up at Ella, her face pale and lined. 'I've lived for the theatre all my life. I'm nothing without the smell of greasepaint and the applause of the audience.'

'Don't be so selfish, Doris!' said Kathleen. 'What about Ella? She's got to keep her mother as well as herself now. How's she going to do that without a job?'

Doris nodded. 'I know, I know.'

Kathleen didn't let up. 'At least you've got your house. You can let out more of the rooms or something, you'll easily make a living for yourself.'

'I bought that house when I was a successful performer,' Doris said slowly, 'and it will be hard to see strangers sharing my home. But you're right, Kathleen – I suppose I can make a living from the place and the sooner the better.'

Kathleen settled herself on a pile of old curtains. 'Will you try to find another job, Ella?'

'I'll have to,' Ella said, fear clutching her heart.

146

'I've saved some of my wages but a couple of pounds isn't going to last me long.'

'Well, it doesn't look too hopeful for me, either,' Kathleen said. 'I've made enquiries at the Grand and the Empire, but they've got enough staff already.'

'Well, we'll have to try something else, then,' Ella said.

'What else?' Kathleen's gloom was unshakeable.

'I can't take a job where I have to live in,' said Ella. 'I'll try one of the big shops – Ben Evan's, perhaps.'

Kathleen chewed her fingernail. 'Sure, don't we all love the theatre too much to work any-where else.'

'Well, we've got a few more days while the acts work the week out. They'll have to allow them that.' Ella forced a positive note into her voice. 'You'll see, tonight we'll open as usual. We can't let the illustrious Miss Belmore down, can we? Come on, girls. We'll put on a show tonight to a full house. The crowds will flock in because of the scandal, you'll see.'

'Aye.' Kathleen smiled briefly. 'Sure we might as well enjoy ourselves while we still can. You'll both have to pitch in and help with the cleaning for as long as we stay open, mind. I can't do the whole theatre on my own.'

'We know that, Kathleen,' Ella said. 'Of course we'll help.'

* * *

It was later than usual when Ella got home. Her mother was still up, sitting in the kitchen with her hands in her lap, her face a picture of despair.

Ella put her arms around Selma and hugged her, feeling her mother's misery and fighting back her own tears.

'I miss him so much,' Selma said.

'I know you do, Mother.'

'What am I going to do with my life now? I sit here every day and think of him. I miss him reading the Bible to me; I even miss polishing his boots and doing his washing.'

'I'll make us a cup of tea,' Ella said, 'and I'll put a tot of brandy in it. Father always recommended it for a good night's sleep.'

As she made the tea Ella told herself she would never be dependent on any man, not to the extent her mother had been. Now Arthur was gone, Selma had nothing to fill her days. Her whole life had revolved around her husband; she had no knowledge of anything in the outside world. She had lived for her family and her home, and now everything had been stripped away from her.

Ella bit her lip. She must find another job, and soon. The rent was paid up until the end of the month and she could probably keep the place going for another few weeks, but after that there was a frightening void.

* * *

Ella turned up for work early the next morning. It had been a struggle to get up: she'd become used to going in late – her duties as wardrobe mistress didn't demand her attention until later in the day. But now, somehow, the theatre must go on as normal until its fate was decided.

To her surprise, Anthony was already in his office. 'Good morning, Ella. I'm glad you're here – I want to talk to you,' he said. He coughed as though he didn't know where to begin.

A cold hand clutched at Ella's heart. 'What is it, Anthony?'

He sighed heavily and rubbed his eyes. 'I've got to go away. I've tried desperately to find work in Swansea, but the other theatres are well supplied with staff. There's a job going at a theatre in Yorkshire. It's a long way but I'll come back as often as I can.'

'I see.' She waited, hoping he would tell her his intentions. Was he speaking to her just as an employee of the theatre or was there something more personal in his words?

'When will you be leaving, Anthony?' Ella forced herself to speak calmly, though she waited with bated breath for his answer.

'I'll leave on Sunday. Mr Simons is going to make a statement to the public on Saturday night. I'll stay for that.'

She waited for him to go on. If only he would

ask her to wait for him, because wait she would if he gave her even the smallest encouragement. Instead he shuffled some papers on his desk and refused to meet her eyes.

'You go back to work now and tell Kathleen and Doris I'm very grateful for their loyalty.'

'Anthony . . .' she began, but then her courage deserted her. 'Take care.'

'And you, Ella. I know this is a bad time for you, having just lost your father. You could do with all the help you can get just now.'

As she left the office, Ella was uncertain: was Anthony bidding her a fond farewell? Was he saying they had no future together now he was leaving Swansea? She just didn't know.

Kathleen and Doris were waiting in Wardrobe for her to appear. 'Well?' Kathleen stood with her hands folded across her chest. 'I saw you talking to Anthony in his office. What's going to happen now?'

Ella shrugged hopelessly. 'Anthony is leaving Swansea, he's found a job in Yorkshire.'

'He'll be back,' Doris said slowly. 'I can tell that his heart is here in Swansea. Yes, he'll be back.'

'We'd better get to work,' Ella said, forcing a note of lightness into her voice. 'Those corridors and stairs aren't going to clean themselves.'

It was hard going back to her role as cleaner. Her hands, softened now by her work handling fabrics, stung as she plunged them into the hot water, and the soda seemed to burn her skin. With heavy heart, Ella tackled the worst job of all: the many stairs that wound up towards the gods.

'What are we going to do, Ella?' Selma looked up as her daughter came into the kitchen. The fire was almost out, but Ella would build it up again. She was a good girl and Selma didn't know what she would do without her.

'We'll manage, Ma.'

Selma could see that her daughter was tired. She tried to rise but her legs seemed weighted down with lead boots. 'Just let me sit a minute and then I'll put the kettle on.'

'I'll do that, don't you worry.'

As she watched her daughter work, Selma noticed the dark shadows under Ella's eyes. She was tired, that was obvious, but there was something else on her mind. Selma didn't want to probe, she had enough to deal with as it was. Perhaps she should find work herself. She didn't have many skills, but when it came to stitching and washing clothes she excelled. She could take in other people's linen, mend and wash it and return it as good as new. That's what she would do, but not just yet. She still felt the sting of loss too painfully, she'd give herself a little while to come to terms with her grief.

'Our problems would all be solved,' Selma

said, 'if only you could make a good marriage. If only you'd marry Jolly Mortimer all our troubles would be over. He's got a lovely house and plenty of money, he's a churchwarden and a good father. I don't know why you can't even consider him.'

'I don't love him, Mother.'

'Love! Look what love has done for me – left me a grieving widow with nothing to do with my time, no man to care for, no one to bring in the money we need to keep us.'

Ella turned her face away from her mother and busied herself attending to the fire.

'I suppose you think you're in love with that man from the theatre, that Anthony whatever his name is. Well, his kind look after themselves, so don't pin your hopes on him.'

'You needn't worry about Anthony. He's going to Yorkshire to work.'

'You see? He's footloose and fancy-free, and can pack up and leave you behind without a thought in his head for your feelings.'

'He has to earn a living, Mother.'

'Well, if he cared about you he could have offered you marriage.' She saw Ella's face grow pale and knew her words had hurt her daughter badly. 'I'm sorry, Helena, but it's best we face facts. We have to earn our bread, but even with both of us working we won't be bringing in the sort of money your father earned.'

'You can't work, Mother.'

'I can and I will, just as soon as I can build my strength up.'

'But what will you do?'

'I'll find something. I'm good with a needle and you know how fine my bedlinen looks when it's blowing on the line. Yes, I'll take in washing and mending, and I hope in the meantime you'll consider Mr Mortimer's proposal.'

Ella turned to her. 'Look, Mother, if I did marry him where would that leave you? Worse off than you are now, because you wouldn't have my money to depend on.'

'You'll be out of a job soon, remember?' Selma said. 'In any case, Jolly has offered me a place in his house if you marry him.'

Ella sank down into a chair, holding her coal-blackened hands away from her skirt. 'You have no right to be talking to Mr Mortimer like that, Mother,' she said in a hopeless tone.

For a moment Selma felt guilty, but she brushed the feeling aside. Ella would do well as Jolly's wife: she would have standing in the town and would be respected by everyone. No need to feel guilty for trying to do the best for your fatherless daughter, was there? Selma waited patiently for the fire to burst into life and watched as Ella made the tea. 'There's some cheese and pickles in the larder,' she said. At the thought of food her own stomach heaved; since

153

Arthur was gone, food seemed to be the last thing she wanted.

When Ella set a plate of neatly cut bread and a slice of cheese in front of her mother, Selma tried to eat but the food stuck in her throat.

'Why aren't you eating, Ma?'

'I'm not hungry just now. I'll have it later.'

Ella seemed to accept her words, but once her daughter had gone to bed Selma knew she would throw the food out for the scavenging animals that roamed the narrow streets outside. She would build up her appetite soon, but for now a fresh hot cup of tea was all that she wanted.

It was closing night at the Palace and Ella stood at the back of the auditorium with Kathleen and Doris, waiting with bated breath as Anthony stepped in front of the curtain and addressed the audience. His voice soared to the gods – he was a fine speech-maker, as good as any actor. 'As you all know by now,' he announced, 'the theatre is closing tonight. Mr Simons has had to leave Swansea unexpectedly, but he has asked me to pass on the following message to you, his loyal supporters.' Anthony unfolded a letter he was holding, and read out:

'I'm devastated to leave the Palace theatre and such a fine audience behind me, but it's in the best interests of the theatre that I hand over the reins to someone else. To all those who have worked for me, my heartfelt thanks. Though it might take several months for everything to be sorted out, I'm confident that the Palace will come into its own again one day in the not-too-distant future.'

When he had finished, the audience rose in unison and gave him a standing ovation. There were whistles and cheers and Ella had tears streaming down her face as she looked at Anthony, who stood on this stage for the last time.

'Come on,' Kathleen sniffled. 'Bugger the work for tonight. Whoever takes the Palace over can do the cleaning.'

'You go on home,' Ella said gently. 'You too, Doris. I want to lock up the costumes before I leave.'

As she walked along the corridors that led to the heart of the theatre, Ella began to cry in earnest. This part of her life was over and done with, and she wasn't just saying goodbye to the theatre, but to the man she loved.

CHAPTER THIRTEEN

The Palace had closed its doors, perhaps for ever, and Ella, out of sheer necessity, found a job of sorts serving on one of the butchery stalls in Swansea market. It was so different from anything she'd experienced before that at first she couldn't take it all in. She found it difficult boning the joints of beef and mutton and the cold, dead feel of the meat nauseated her. After a few days at the market, her hands were red and swollen and Ella thought for the umpteenth time how fortunate she had been to work at the Palace.

Ella had arranged to meet Kathleen at Doris's house that evening. Though she felt guilty leaving her mother alone, she found Selma's company depressing and was desperate for a change of scene. Her mother now read the Bible avidly. She had become remote and withdrawn, and Ella found it almost impossible to get any conversation out of her. She knew her mother was grieving, and Ella could understand that. She was grieving too – she was missing her father more than she would have thought possible. He had been strict, but she knew he had always had her best interests at heart.

'Come on, girlie, it's time to pack up and go home.' Billy the stall-holder was standing before her, his apron red with bloodstains.

Ella would be glad to leave the market. The air had turned chilly and her poor hands were burning with pain. 'All right, Billy. I'll see you in the morning.' She took off her own apron, rolled it up and pushed it into her bag.

'Early, mind. There's a lot of pickling of hogs' heads to do tomorrow,' Billy said.

Ella nodded. She didn't know anything about pickling hogs' heads but she could guess it would not be pleasant.

When she knocked on Doris's door, Kathleen answered with a glum expression on her face. 'I'm glad you've come. Me and Doris have been talking over old times and it's got me down, so it has.' She stood aside to allow Ella into the warm passageway. 'There's a pot of tea brewing. You look as if you need cheering up as much as I do.'

It was cosy in Doris's house and the front room was spotlessly clean, as usual. 'It's lovely here, I wish I was still living here. Life at home is . . . well, difficult.' Ella looked round enviously. 'Doris must be kept busy with all the cleaning.'

'I'm doing it all now, in exchange for board and lodging,' said Kathleen. 'I've no money to speak of.'

Ella looked at her in surprise. 'You haven't found a job, then?'

Kathleen shook her head, her curly red hair shining like molten copper.

'How is Doris managing to buy food for both of you, if neither of you is working?' asked Ella.

Kathleen tapped her nose. 'I've learned that our Doris has a bit of money put by, saved from when she was a big success in London. I think she only worked at all because she didn't want to lose touch with the theatre.' She shrugged her shoulders. 'In any case, Doris has taken in a few lodgers – remember we talked about it before we left the Palace? I do the cooking for them. It's better than being out on the streets.'

Doris was seated in a chair near the fire in the kitchen. She looked up as Ella entered the room and lifted her hand in greeting. 'About time you came to see me.' She waved towards the teapot. 'Go on, pour yourself a cup. It's freshly made.' She caught sight of Ella's reddened hands and clucked her tongue in sympathy. 'Working on the meat stall, I hear?'

'It's all I could get.' Ella helped herself to tea. 'I hate every minute of it – I wish we were all back at the Palace. I didn't realize how lucky I

158

was to have a job there. Even cleaning the stairs was better than handling salted meat.'

'And have you heard from Anthony?'

Ella's heart sank. 'I expect he's very busy getting used to the new place. He'll write to us soon, I'm sure.'

'Well, he was sweet on you, Ella,' Doris said. 'He didn't try to hide his feelings, either. I'm surprised you haven't had a letter by now.'

Ella was surprised too, but she didn't want Doris to know she was worried. 'I expect he'll write when he's got a minute to himself. Starting a new job in a different theatre must be hard. I expect it's taking up all his time getting to know the place.'

'That'll be it, then,' Doris said, but Ella didn't miss the hint of pity in her voice. She suddenly felt deflated. All the excuses she'd made about Anthony to herself seemed silly now. Of course he could have found time to write if he'd wanted to. She might just as well accept it: Anthony's interest in her had been a passing phase, it meant nothing and she'd been an idiot for reading anything into it.

'How's your sainted mother, Ella?' Kathleen was sitting cross-legged on the floor near the fire. The appetizing smell of toast drifted towards Ella, but suddenly she didn't feel hungry. There was a lump in her throat as she thought of her mother, endlessly reading the Bible, looking thinner and sadder each day. She swallowed hard and forced a smile. Her friends didn't want to know of her miseries; they had enough of their own.

'I think she's getting better,' she said cautiously. But her mother was anything but better; she was drifting more and more into a world of her own. She didn't eat all day and only picked at her food when Ella put it in front of her.

'You don't sound too sure.' Kathleen was looking at her closely. 'Give her time, I expect losing a husband takes the stuffing out of you.'

'You're right, I'm sure Mother will perk up soon. I've just got to be patient.'

Sitting with Doris and Kathleen in the warmth of the kitchen, Ella forgot her own problems and fell to thinking about the Palace again. 'Who do you think will take the theatre over?' she said suddenly.

'I've heard some gossip about that in town,' Kathleen replied. 'I think Lady Mansel is interested in buying the Palace, but I'm not sure, mind.'

'Well, Lady Mansel was at the grand reopening,' Doris said. 'Though I doubt she'd take all the responsibility on her own shoulders. She'd be bound to have a partner.'

'Well, I wish they'd hurry up and get on with it,' exclaimed Kathleen, spreading butter liberally on the hot toast. Ella watched as the butter melted enticingly and all at once she was hungry again. Kathleen pushed the plate towards her. 'Have some. You look as if you could do with a good feed – there's nothing left of you.'

'It's all the worry about my mother,' Ella said, though that was only part of the reason she wasn't eating well. Handling meat all day put her off her food, and then when she got home there was the daily disappointment of finding no word from Anthony. Her heart lifted a little – perhaps today when she got home there would be a letter standing on the mantelpiece, waiting for her. 'I wonder if we'll get our old jobs back,' she said. 'Whoever takes over the Palace, I hope they'll think of us when they're handing out the work.'

'I don't know whether I'd go back if they asked me,' Kathleen replied. 'I might go and live in London and try to find work as an entertainer.'

'Don't do that, Kathleen,' Doris said quickly. 'You need polishing in a provincial theatre before you go to the big city.'

'What do you think, Ella?' Kathleen put the last piece of toast on the plate and scrambled to her feet. Her normally pale face was flushed from the heat of the fire and her red hair glowed.

Ella looked at her, trying to see her dispassionately. 'You have the look of a star,' she said. 'But maybe Doris is right – you need to work here in Swansea before you go travelling.'

'I tell you what,' Doris chipped in. 'What if I give you singing lessons?'

Kathleen looked at Doris doubtfully.

'I did a bit of everything, me.' Doris's face was alight with her fondness for her memories. 'I told you all about that, didn't I, love? You see, Kathleen, when you work in a show you have to be an all-rounder. Some theatres don't want plain singers, they need something extra. But singing was my first love.'

'Surely you could have stayed on in the theatre as a singer, then, even if you couldn't do the trapeze acts any more.' Kathleen finished her piece of toast and dabbed the crumbs from her lips.

'I was sick for a long time, Kathleen, though I kept up my singing practice, thinking one day I'd take to the stage again.' She looked sad. 'But I never did.'

'I'll have singing lessons from you.' Kathleen smiled. 'Can't do any harm, and it might even do some good.'

'Tomorrow you might be a star,' Ella said with a hint of envy in her voice, 'and I'll still be pickling meat.'

Doris's face became dreamy and her eyes closed. 'I see great things for you, Helena Burton,' she said. 'I see a wedding ring on your finger. But take care, the marriage will not be the one of your dreams. You'll have a good, kind

162

man, but he's not the one for you. Still, one day you will make your mark, you'll make a name for yourself.' She opened her eyes and blinked. 'Pour me another cup of tea, Kathleen, I'm parched.'

'Does your second sight always prove to be true?' asked Ella, pushing away the crusts of her toast. She wanted to dash home and see if Anthony had written to her. If she ever had the luck to marry him she would make sure the marriage was a happy one.

'Oh, never mind all that.' Doris was her old down-to-earth self again. 'Don't keep all that lovely toast to yourself. Push the plate over to me, there's a good girl.'

'Tell us about your days in London, Doris,' Kathleen said enthusiastically. 'What was the biggest thrill of your life?'

'Oh, there were many thrills,' Doris said. 'I worked with the best in the business. Honour Strong was a fine performer – I shared the stage with her at the Pavilion more than once.'

Ella listened to Doris's happy chatter for a while, but a great weariness had come over her. She got to her feet at last. 'I'd better get home,' she said apologetically. 'I told my mother I wouldn't be late. But it's been lovely talking to you – can I come and visit again?'

'Of course you can. Need you ask?' Doris sounded exasperated. 'Come whenever you like, Ella, I'm always glad to see you.'

Kathleen saw her to the door. Ella wrapped her arms around her body as the chill wind caught her unawares. 'I'd better hurry,' she said, 'my mother doesn't like to be on her own at night.' She sighed. 'I don't suppose she'll even think of lighting the lamps.'

But as Ella reached the small terraced house, she saw the soft glow of the lamps shining through the windows. Hope filled her heart. Perhaps her mother was feeling better. If she was, life would be bearable again. She could go out without feeling she was deserting Selma. Even going to work caused problems: the long hours in the market meant that Selma was on her own for most of the day.

When she opened the door and stepped into the hallway, Ella heard voices. Her mother spoke softly and deferentially, and Ella had a moment of sheer joy, thinking that Anthony had travelled from Yorkshire to see her. She opened the door of the parlour eagerly, but her heart sank when she saw Jolly Mortimer sitting in the chair that had been her father's.

'Ah, here she is.' Jolly lumbered to his feet and grasped her hand. 'I'm so pleased to see you, Helena. I would have come before, but I felt I had to give you time to come to terms with your grief.'

Thank you, Mr Mortimer.' Ella moved away from him and sat close to her mother on the old worn sofa.

'I do wish you would not be so formal with me, Helena. After all, I consider myself part of the family.'

'Listen to what Jolly tells you, Helena,' her mother said quietly. 'He's been very good to us.'

'I'm very grateful to you,' Ella said, forcing some warmth into her voice. After all, Mr Mortimer had paid for the funeral and her mother was right, they owed him a debt of gratitude. 'Can I get you a cup of tea?'

'No, thank you, Helena, but a little drop of brandy would go down well. Keep the chill out, you know what I mean?'

Ella poured Jolly some brandy and wished with all her heart he would go away. She couldn't wait to ask her mother if there was a letter for her. She looked at the mantelpiece eagerly, but there was no sign of one.

The time passed slowly. Ella wanted nothing more than to crawl into bed, but Mr Mortimer seemed intent on staying. At last, it was Selma who made a move. 'If you'll excuse me, Jolly, I'm away to my bed. I'm very tired these days – I don't know what's the matter with me.' As she rose, Jolly put down his glass and pushed himself to his feet.

'I mustn't keep you, then.' He spoke as though he was reluctant to go, but Selma didn't seem to notice. Ella led the way to the front door and Jolly took her hand. 'I can see your mother still isn't herself,' he said. 'I do worry about you both. You know that.'

'There's no need,' Ella said quickly. 'I've got a job and we're managing very well. But thank you for your kindness.'

'The market isn't the place for a delicate lady like you, Helena. Your dear father made sure you had a good education. You are made for better things than handling meat all day long. You were happier working in the theatre, weren't you?'

'Yes. But once the theatre opens again I hope I'll go back to being wardrobe mistress.'

'Well, I may have some influence there.' He winked and stroked her hand. 'But it's all top secret at the moment, so I'll say no more.'

Ella was too tired to wonder about Jolly Mortimer's secrets. She was relieved when he set off along the road towards his home.

As soon as she'd dampened down the fire and turned off the lamps, Ella went to bed. There was still no news from Anthony. In spite of her disappointment, she fell asleep quickly, only to dream that Anthony was putting a slim gold band on to her finger.

Selma crept downstairs, holding her candle high as she made her way towards the small table in the parlour. She opened the brandy bottle and, without waiting to pour it into a glass, took a great gulp of the liquid. As it burned its way down her throat she felt comforted: the drink helped her to sleep, and for a time it took away some of her loneliness.

She sank into a chair, Arthur's chair, and pondered on her situation. It wasn't as though she and Arthur had had a perfect marriage, but it had been a steady marriage, and as the wife of a man who had brought home good money at the end of the week she had felt she had some self-respect. Now she was nothing; she was a ship without a sail.

She wished that Helena would see sense and marry Jolly Mortimer. He was such a fine catch. Admittedly, he was older than her, but that was all to the good. He had money, a fine house, and, most important of all, standing in the community.

What if she was to die, Selma thought, and follow her husband to the grave? It was something she often thought about these days. In some ways it would be a relief to be finished with the pain and struggle of her everyday life.

She took the letter from her pocket and stared at it. It was addressed to Helena and she knew exactly who it was from: that upstart from the theatre, the man who had dropped everything, including her daughter, and made his way to a better life in distant Yorkshire.

'We don't want anything to do with your sort, Anthony Weatherby Nichols,' she whispered, and, poking the embers, she thrust the letter into the heart of the fire. She saw it turn brown, curl up and fall to pieces, and sighed. How much longer before the man gave up pestering them and left them in peace?

Selma put the bottle to her mouth again and took another gulp. Weariness was creeping over her; tonight she would sleep with an easy mind.

CHAPTER FOURTEEN

Ella looked at the pair of hogs' heads with distaste; their vacant eyes seemed to stare at her. She was standing with Billy in a cold, stone-built outhouse behind the market stall and the smell of dead meat was nauseating.

'We're doing wet pickling today, Ella. Have you got that?' Billy had an irritating habit of treating Ella like a child or an idiot, or both.

'You need one gallon of water and just over a pound of salt.' He coughed into his hand and Ella shuddered. 'Then add some brown sugar, allspice, saltpetre, and just half an ounce of black pepper. Are you following this, Ella?'

She nodded. 'Then you boil it all up together, is that it?' Her attempts to cut short his long-winded directions failed dismally.

'Lift the pan of water on to the fire, then boil it all up for about fifteen to twenty minutes. You keep skimming the scum off the water and be careful not to scald yourself – I don't pay out no compensation.'

'Then you put in the hogs' heads, do you?'

'No, no, no, girl! Listen to me, will you?'

Ella sighed. She'd proved Billy's point – that she was a foolish girl – and she wished herself anywhere but here in this cold wet building with dead meat all around her.

'You have to strain the liquid into this pan, and when the water's cooled – and not before – you put in the meat and cover it. Now have you got that, Ella? Tell me if I should go over it again with you.'

'That's all right, Billy. I think I know what you mean now.'

'Right then. The water's nearly boiling, so keep an eye on it.'

Ella stared at the pot as a thick layer of scum rose to the surface. She stamped her feet on the cold floor in an effort to bring life to them. Surely she could find a job she was more suited to than working on a meat stall in the market – and for very little pay at that.

Straining the water proved tricky. She found a length of linen, thinned by many washes, and wrapped it round the pan on the floor. Lifting the pot from the fire was difficult; Ella remembered Billy's words about compensation and held the pot carefully by the handle, well away from her body. At first, all went well, but when she had almost finished straining the water the cloth sank into the pan and Ella knew she'd have to start all over again.

She sighed. If only she could go back to the days before her father died, before the Palace closed, before Anthony went away. But she couldn't turn back the clock, so she would just have to make the best of things.

'You getting on all right there, girl?' Billy's voice carried to the outhouse.

Ella stared down at the mess in the pan and took a deep breath. 'Nearly done!' she lied, and began the process of straining the water all over again, her eyes filling with tears at the miserable turn her life had taken. But soon it would be dark and the meat stall would close, and then she could go home to a warm fire and a cup of hot tea.

'For heaven's sake, Helena, go and wash the stink of meat from your hands, will you?' Selma looked at her daughter and saw by the downward tilt of her mouth that she was unhappy. What she needed was a good man to look after her; it wasn't right for her to be slaving in the market all day long when she could be married to a fine man like Jolly Mortimer. Selma smiled to herself. She'd gone to see Jolly, to invite him over for supper, and the eager way he'd accepted showed he still harboured hopes of marrying

171

Helena. Her plan would work, she would see to it.

'Have you eaten today, Mother?' Ella removed her apron with its revolting stains of blood and obediently washed her hands. Selma noticed that they were red and raw and her heart filled with pity for her only child. But the answer to all their problems lay with Jolly Mortimer: he was a good, sensible man, he had plenty of money and he could keep Helena in comfort. What more could a woman ask?

'I want you to look nice tonight,' Selma said pleadingly. 'Jolly is coming to visit. I wish you would be nice to him, for my sake. Could you do that, Helena?'

'I'm always polite, Mother.'

Selma rubbed her eyes; they were misted with tears, though she didn't know why she was crying. 'Just think about your future,' she said. 'I'm not a well woman, Helena, and I don't want to leave you all alone in the world.'

'You're not going to leave me all alone, Ma. You've got years ahead of you yet.'

'Maybe and maybe not,' Selma said. 'If only this dratted cough would go away I would feel better, but I'm so tired, Helena, and my mind is so confused; half the time I don't know where I am or what I'm supposed to be doing.'

'It's the shock of losing Father,' Ella said quickly. 'Come and sit down. I'll see to the meal and I'll be nice to Jolly, just to please you. You'll buck up soon, you'll see.'

'I'm not well, Helena,' Selma insisted. 'There's no use in pretending any different. Sometimes I fear that I'm not long for this world.' She took a deep breath. 'If you were married to Jolly he would see me all right, get me a good doctor, I just know he would. And let me tell you, you're wasting your time pining after that Anthony fellow. He's gone away for good and has forgotten about you already, can't you get that into your head?'

Selma thought about the last letter that had come from Anthony Weatherby Nichols and frowned at the recollection. He'd begged Helena to answer his letters – but she had made quite sure her daughter knew nothing of them.

'But Mother, I can't marry a man I don't love. Can't you understand that?'

Selma shook her head. She was feeling muddled again, what was Helena talking about now? She could see the girl's mouth moving but she couldn't understand the words. She felt shaky; she would have to sit down. She held her hands out to her daughter and allowed herself to be led to a chair.

'Mother, what is it? Are you really ill?'

Selma waved her away. All she wanted to do was to close her eyes and never open them again. She wanted to lie in the rich earth of the cemetery beside her Arthur. But she tried to pull herself

173

together: she must be strong, at least until she saw her daughter safely married.

By the time their guest arrived, Selma was feeling a little better. Ella made every effort to be nice to Jolly to please her mother. The meal was plain and simple: they couldn't afford steak or even a leg of lamb, so they were eating rabbit stew followed by crusty bread and cheese.

'You'd think Billy the butcher would give you a bit of meat to bring home.' Selma saw the confused look on Jolly's face and realized she must have interrupted a completely different conversation. 'I'm tired,' she said. 'I'll go to bed.' As she left the room, she paused for a moment on the stairs. There was something she had meant to do, but what was it? Well, it didn't matter. Jolly was here and he'd keep them safe.

'I'm so worried about my mother,' Ella confessed, looking anxiously at Jolly.

He took her hand at once. 'She is looking poorly, I'll grant you that. What she needs is to see a doctor and then have a nurse come in and look after her in the day while you're at work.'

Ella stared at him. 'Do you think she's that bad?'

He nodded. 'I do, Helena. She's weak in mind as well as body.'

Ella felt a chill run through her. 'Are you saying my mother is losing her senses?'

174

'I'm afraid so, my dear. Did you notice how she broke into our conversation with that bit of nonsense about the meat? She had no idea we were talking about my girls.'

'I can't give up my job,' Ella said. 'The money is poor enough but it does pay for the food on the table.' But not enough to cover the rent, she thought worriedly. The arrears were mounting up and she didn't know how she was going to explain to the landlord that she couldn't pay him.

'I know you are not in love with me, Helena, but don't you think you owe it to your mother to accept my proposal of marriage? I would be very happy to look after both of you. Surely you know that by now?'

'It's very kind of you, Jolly, but I don't really want to be married. I'm hoping the Palace will open again and I'll have a better job with more money. I've heard that another owner might be found before too long – then I can get my old job back.'

'Such a job still wouldn't provide you with enough to pay for doctors and nurses. You must realize that, Helena.' He paused. 'Just think about marrying me, my dear. It wouldn't be so bad, would it? I'd always be kind and considerate, I can promise you that.'

'But why do you want to marry me?' Ella heard the desperate note in her voice and bit her lip.

'For lots of reasons. You're a respectable girl – I

175

was very close to your father so I know you've been brought up to be a good Christian. I think you would be a good influence on my daughters: you're young and you'd understand their needs better than I can. Also, I've always wanted a son. You are young and healthy and you could give me a boy. But lastly and most importantly, I've fallen in love with you, Helena.' He looked at her earnestly. 'Just say you'll consider my proposal and I'll be happy.'

'I'll consider it.' Ella couldn't believe she was uttering words that would give Jolly hope of a future with her, but at the moment he was offering her a way out of her dilemma and she couldn't dismiss it out of hand.

'Is there anyone else, Helena?'

She thought of Anthony, of his long silence. He'd not even tried to get in touch with her since starting his new life in Yorkshire. 'There's no one else,' she said firmly.

'There we are, then. What's to stop us getting wed as soon as we can?' He looked at her pleadingly. 'Just name the day, Helena.'

'Please give me a bit of time,' Ella said. 'Marriage is a huge step and I'm not at all sure I'm ready for it.'

'I'll give you time, my dear, but don't take too long. Your mother is getting worse by the day – I can see the change in her and I'm sure you can.'

Ella nodded. 'You're right, I know you are. I'm just not sure . . .'

'There's nothing to fear, Helena. I'm a gentle man – I'd never hurt you.'

She warmed to him, despite herself. He was offering her a way out of the hardship her life had become. She looked down at her hands, red and sore from her hard work. 'Just give me a week,' she said. 'I promise I'll give you my decision then.'

Jolly smiled, lifted her hand and kissed it gently. 'You're a lovely girl, Helena, and I'll pray to God every night that your answer will be the one I'm hoping for.'

Ella was sitting in Doris's warm comfortable kitchen again, and so far the talk had all been about the theatre. Suddenly she announced, 'I've promised Jolly Mortimer that I'll think about marrying him.' She rubbed her face tiredly. It felt as if the salt from the butcher's had got into her eyes, they were stinging so badly. 'I don't know what to do. He's rich and kind, but . . . well, I don't want to marry him, if I'm truthful.'

'What do you want, then, Ella?' Kathleen asked. 'I wouldn't mind having a rich old man offer me marriage.'

'I suppose I expected to be married to a handsome young man. 'That's every girl's dream, isn't it?'

'And I know who put those dreams into your head,' Doris chimed in bluntly. 'That two-timing Anthony Weatherby Nichols, that's who.'

'What do you mean, "two-timing"?' Ella asked anxiously. 'What have you heard, Doris?'

'I've heard that our Anthony is walking out with the daughter of the theatre owner in Yorkshire. Pretty and well placed as she is, he'd be a fool not to offer her marriage, I suppose. Still, he might at least have written to you and told you his plans – you two were so close when he was here in Swansea.'

'Where did you hear that bit of gossip?' Kathleen asked. 'Perhaps it's not true.'

'Well, his aunt keeps the hotel on the seafront, you know – that big hotel with a fancy name.'

'And what would you know about a rich woman who owns a hotel?' Kathleen asked.

Ella held her breath, fearing Doris's reply.

'I do a reading of the tea leaves every month or so for her, Miss Clever Clogs.'

'So that's why you go out on the sly now and then – you tell people's fortunes. I should have guessed.'

'It's not fortune-telling, it's good honest reading of the leaves. I'm not a charlatan, I'll have you know.'

Ella leaned back in her chair. So Anthony had found himself a more suitable woman to court. No wonder he hadn't bothered to write to her.

'I'd better be getting back home,' she said. 'I don't like to leave my mother alone too long. It's bad enough when I go to work, but I feel even more guilty spending time with my friends when I should be with her.'

'You have to have a break, girl,' Doris replied. 'You're not looking too well yourself.'

'I'm just tired, that's all.' Ella pushed back her chair. 'Working in the market is much harder than being a wardrobe mistress, I can tell you.'

'You should take Jolly's offer of marriage seriously.' Doris had a faraway look on her face; she was clearly having one of her 'visions'. 'I see you with his ring on your finger. I see you in a fine house, being looked after like a queen. I see you having no choice in the matter; however much you protest, you will walk down the aisle with Jolly Mortimer.' She blinked rapidly and rubbed her eyes, as though waking from a deep sleep, and then asked Kathleen to pour another cup of tea. 'Come on, girl, I haven't got to wait all night for you to make a fresh pot, have I?' She turned again to Ella. 'And as for you, young lady, take the easy way out of your problems, that's my advice.'

'I'll think about it very seriously,' Ella said.

The walk home cleared her head. She still had a few days to think about Jolly's proposal; she would spend time looking for a better job with more money, then perhaps she could afford to have her mother properly cared for.

When Ella reached home she could see that the front door was open and light spilled out on to the pavement. She quickened her step. Something was wrong with her mother, she just knew it.

Jolly was standing in the hallway, talking to a man who held a bag in his hand. 'Ah, Helena,' he said. 'I've had the doctor to your mother. I fear her condition has deteriorated. It looks as if she will need a nurse to tend her sooner than we thought. Just look what she's done to the parlour.'

Ella stood in the doorway and stared in disbelief at the chaos her mother had wrought. Cushions were torn, the stuffing covering the floor like snow. Ornaments were smashed, and coal from the fire had burned holes in the rag mat which Ella had helped her mother make as a child.

'Where is she?'

Jolly touched her arm reassuringly. 'Don't worry, she's in bed. The doctor has given her a sedative – it will work soon and then she'll sleep.'

Ella hurried up the stairs and found her mother sitting up in bed. Her lips were moving continuously, though no words came out of her mouth.

'Mother, are you all right?'

She might not have spoken for all the notice her mother took of her. Selma was deathly pale, and her hands plucked feverishly at the bedclothes. Ella became aware that Jolly was standing next to her.

'Let me take you both home to my house,' he said slowly. 'I'll settle the rent on this one, so you'll have no worries there.'

'We owe a lot of rent,' Ella said bleakly. 'I'm afraid I've fallen behind with the payments. I can't ask you to clear my debts for me.'

'Don't worry about that now,' Jolly said. 'Look, Selma will sleep till morning and then I shall send someone round to pick her up.' He took her hand. 'Have you thought about my proposal, my dear?'

Ella felt so tired. She needed someone strong to help her right now, and the only person offering any sort of solution to her problems was Jolly Mortimer. He was a good man, no wonder her father had become such firm friends with him. She nodded her head wearily. 'I'll marry you, just as soon as you can arrange it.'

CHAPTER FIFTEEN

Ella had been trying all day to pluck up the courage to tell Billy she was leaving. But they were kept so busy that she wasn't able to broach the subject until he was about to close up the stall at the end of the day. 'I'm sorry, Billy, but I'll be leaving at the end of the week.'

'Don't you like the work then, girlie?' Billy stuck out his lower lip as though he was going to cry. 'I've treated you right, haven't I?'

'Of course you have, Billy, but – well, the truth is I'm getting married.'

Billy's face cleared. 'Married, is it? You do right, girlie. Marriage is a fine thing for the young. I'm glad for you. Look, I'll even give you a fine piece of topside and a leg of lamb as a wedding present.'

Ella couldn't believe that she was talking about marriage so easily. She'd spent sleepless nights going over it in her mind. Sometimes, lying awake in the dark, she felt she really couldn't go through with it and she'd have to tell Jolly it was all off. But in the cold light of day she thought about her mother's worsening condition.

'That's very kind of you.' She forced a smile. 'I'm very grateful, really I am.'

'I'll be sorry to lose you, mind. You was getting the hang of the job really well. When you were slicing bacon the other day you was almost as good as me.' He paused and then smiled warmly. 'Ah, go on, you might as well finish now. I'll clean the place up.'

Ella was relieved, as she hated washing the blood from the wooden block and the dangerously sharp knives. Cleaning the pans used for pickling was even worse: it was a back-breaking job and played the very devil with her hands. As she removed her apron, she examined her raw hands and sighed. They looked awful, and in only a few weeks she would be wearing Jolly's ring on her finger. At the thought, her heart dipped in fear. She took a deep breath. Before her wedding she must get some ointment to take away the redness.

She felt tears burn her eyes. But however miserable she felt, she had to admit that Jolly had been wonderful. He had arranged for a nurse to stay with Selma throughout the day, and had paid off their outstanding rent. And yet she saw that as another tie to bind her. But she had to be realistic: she had no choice but to marry Jolly. If she didn't, the rent arrears would pile up again and soon she and her mother would be out on the street.

Because she was leaving work early, Ella took the opportunity to visit Doris and Kathleen and tell them her news. Doris had already predicted that she would marry Jolly, so she shouldn't be surprised.

'Come in, my girl, it's good to see you,' said Doris, waving Ella into the kitchen.

'Sure and didn't you smell the tea.' Kathleen looked at her and then frowned. 'You're looking bad, girl. Not sickening for something, are you?'

'No, it's just my mother, all the worry about her, and the job, and . . . oh, I might as well say it first as last – I'm getting married in the spring to Jolly Mortimer.'

'You never are!' Kathleen said. 'Do you hear that, Doris? Ella's going to marry Mr Mortimer! About time she came to her senses and got over Anthony Weatherby Nichols.'

'I knew it,' Doris said. 'My second sight is not very often wrong. Jolly Mortimer is a good, kind man and you're lucky to have him. So that mother of yours is worse, is she?'

Ella sank into a chair. 'Most of the time she rambles on, talking nonsense, but now and again she has a sensible moment or two and then I can see the mother I used to know. When she's lucid, she tells me how lucky I am to be marrying a fine man like Jolly.'

'There you are, then,' Kathleen said. 'You've seen sense at last. It was obvious you couldn't go on as you were.'

Doris sat opposite Ella and stared at her with the faraway look Ella associated with Doris's visions. 'I see you back at the theatre, mind,' Doris said. 'I can see us all back there again before very long.'

'Well, that's daft!' Kathleen retorted. 'How can Ella be married and work at the theatre at the same time? It doesn't make sense.'

Doris tapped her nose. 'It will all happen and very quickly, you'll see.'

'Ah well, now it's my turn to tell you both some news.' Kathleen beamed. 'I've been offered a little part in the chorus at the Empire. What do you think of that?'

'There, you see, I'm right again, aren't I?' Doris was triumphant.

'Yes, but you're talking about working at the Palace, and I'm talking about singing in the chorus at the Empire. I don't want to go back to scrubbing floors again, not if I can help it.'

'You'll be with me and Ella at the Palace before too many weeks have passed,' Doris insisted.

'Never mind all that second-sight business, Doris. Let Ella tell us what she's going to wear for her wedding.'

Ella frowned. 'I don't know what to wear, I haven't thought about it.'

'There's a bride's gown hanging about doing nothing in the Palace costumes room,' said Doris. 'Remember it, Ella? It's white silk, with a veil to match. Just about fit you, it would.'

'I remember the dress – you're right, it would be perfect. It would save me money if I borrowed it, but how am I going to get hold of the dress?'

'I'll get it for you,' Kathleen said. 'I'll get in touch with Mr Simons myself. He'll be only too pleased to help out, you know what a sentimental old stick he is.'

Ella sighed. 'Well, that's enough about my wedding. I'd better get home now and see to my mother – she'll be fretting if she doesn't see me soon.'

'But if her mind is fuddled, how by the name of the Blessed Virgin can she miss you?' Kathleen was shaking her head. 'I don't understand.'

'Neither do I.' Ella smiled wryly. 'But it's true all the same. If I'm not in at my usual time, she's difficult to manage.'

'What do you mean, difficult?' Kathleen was curious.

'Pipe down, Kathleen, it's none of your business. Show a bit of tact, can't you?' Doris said.

'Sorry, I didn't mean to be inquisitive.'

'It's all right,' Ella said. 'It's no secret. Soon everyone will notice how muddled my mother is.'

186

'Why?' Kathleen asked.

'Well, the other day she wrecked our house. She cut open all the cushions, broke the dishes and made a real mess of the place. If it wasn't for Jolly I don't know how I would have coped.'

'There!' Doris sounded triumphant. 'Didn't I say Jolly would make a good husband for you? You want to thank your lucky stars you've found such a fine man.'

Ella sighed. 'I know. Look, I'd best be going, but it's lovely to see you again. Doris, I hope you're right and we'll all be working at the Palace again before too long.'

'Aye, I'm right. But before that happens you'll be Mrs Jolly Mortimer.'

Ella let herself out of the house and began walking briskly towards home. She tried to clear her mind, but Doris's words kept popping into her head. 'Mrs Jolly Mortimer.' It had a strangely unreal ring to it, and Ella shivered.

Selma was in good spirits. She was wearing a clean skirt and blouse and her hair was neatly combed; the work of the nurse, Ella guessed.

'That awful woman was here again, mind.'

Ella knew her mother was referring to the nurse.

'And Jolly's been,' Selma said. 'I'm marrying him soon, you know?'

Ella's heart sank. Her mother might look

187

normal, but her mind was far away with the fairies.

'What do you want for supper, Mother?' Ella took Selma's hand, which felt cold. She sighed as she noticed that the fire had gone out. She would have to re-light it before she could make them a meal.

'Has the nurse been looking after you, Mother? Did she make you anything to eat?'

'Nurse? What are you talking about, girl? The nurse only calls when someone is sick or has a new baby.' She smiled coyly. 'And I'm not even married yet, so I can't be with child, can I?'

Ella felt tears burn her eyes. How could such a cruel thing happen to her mother? Selma was living in a dream world and seemed perfectly happy, and yet she had lost a great deal of weight and her eyes did not seem to focus on anything at all.

Ella rolled up her sleeves. 'You sit down, Ma,' she said firmly. 'I'm just going to light the fire.'

As she knelt on the floor, Ella's finger caught in one of the burn holes in the mat. She sat back on her heels, feeling the tears roll down her face. Instead of dreading marriage to Jolly she should be thanking him with all her heart for solving her problems for her.

Jolly had taken to calling in to see her each evening and that night was no exception.

'How are you today, Helena?' he inquired, kissing her chastely on her cheek.

Ella resisted the childish urge to rub his kiss away. 'I'm all right, Jolly,' she said. 'Thank you for asking.'

He took both her hands in his and frowned at the redness of her fingers. 'I hope you've given Billy your notice,' he said. 'The work is ruining your poor hands.' He kissed her palms tenderly. 'You'll never have to work again, my dear, I promise you that.'

Ella felt weary. She allowed herself to lean against Jolly's plump shoulder and closed her eyes. It would be so good to have someone strong to manage her life, to take the weight of all her responsibilities from her shoulders. 'Thank you, Jolly, for being so kind. Are you hungry? Do you want some supper?'

'Bless you, my dear. I have one of the best cooks in the whole of Swansea. Don't worry about me, I've eaten my fill.' He followed her into the parlour. 'I've had such a feast for dinner tonight. Turbot cooked with almonds, followed by juicy lamb and mint sauce, and a delicious milk pudding to round it all off. You see, my dear girl, I'm going to make sure you eat well. I'll look after you and bring the colour to your cheeks again.'

Ella thought of her own frugal supper and wondered how she would manage to eat heartily as Jolly did.

'Where's your mother?' Jolly asked as he seated himself in the parlour.

'She's gone to bed,' Ella said with relief. 'The nurse called again this evening and helped me wash and undress her. I'm so grateful for all you've done for us.'

Jolly took her hands and drew her on to the sofa beside him. 'As we are alone, this seems just the opportunity I've been waiting for. I've been meaning to talk to you about our future for some time.'

Ella took a deep breath, smoothed her skirts across her lap and waited for him to begin.

'I don't wish to be indelicate, Helena,' he said, 'but I shall expect certain duties from you when we're married. Do you know what I mean?'

Ella bit her lip, afraid to speak. She looked away from him, feeling the heat rise to her face.

'Don't be embarrassed, dear girl. You will be my wife, it is right and proper that we share a bed.'

'I understand.' Ella's voice was muffled.

'Do you?' Jolly asked. 'Wifely duties don't mean just organizing the household and the staff. Admittedly I'm older than you by a good few years, but I will still want you to be my wife in deed as well as in name. As I told you, I want a son.'

Ella plucked up the courage to look at him. 'I

190

will be a good wife, Jolly – in and out of the bedroom. Don't worry, I won't fail you.'

He touched her cheek and sat back, relieved. 'Thank you, my dear. Now let me tell you of my other plans.' He smiled, his eyes sparkling with excitement. 'I've taken an important step today. You're going to be pleasantly surprised when I tell you what's happened.'

He paused to make sure he had her full attention. 'I've given up my job as manager of the tin-plate works. Since the accident and your father's death the place doesn't hold the same appeal for me. Can you understand that, Helena?'

'Of course.'

'And this is my big news – I've bought the Palace theatre, lock, stock and barrel. Do you approve?'

So this was what Doris's vision must have meant: they would all be involved with the Palace in one way or another, only Ella's role would be as wife of the owner.

'But Mr Simons, isn't he coming back?'

'He's been through enough, what with the court case and the consequent slur on his good name. No, he will not be seen at the Palace again, my dearest.'

Ella sank back against the horsehair cushions of the sofa and felt as though the world was crashing in on her. It was all too much to take in. What did Jolly know about running a theatre?

'I want all the old staff to be reinstated,' Jolly continued. 'Your friends Kathleen and Doris, and, if I can entice him back, Anthony Weatherby Nichols as well. Between you, you ran the Palace like clockwork, so we have every chance to make a go of it.'

Ella's heart began to pound. She would be seeing Anthony again, maybe even working with him, but there would be a gold ring on her finger that would put an insurmountable barrier between them for ever. Suddenly she began to cry. Jolly put his arms around her and she rested against him, too weary and dispirited to object.

CHAPTER SIXTEEN

Ella stared at her reflection in the mirror. The wedding dress borrowed from the Palace fitted her perfectly. It was white silk, the bodice encrusted with tiny pearls. The waist was nipped in, accentuating her slim figure, and the skirt hung loose to her ankles.

Kathleen had taken the only chair in Ella's bedroom. She gazed at Ella in admiration. 'Holy Mother of God, you look beautiful, so you do.' As bridesmaid, Kathleen was helping her friend to dress, and now stood back to admire her handiwork. 'You look like a fairy queen. Jolly Mortimer will be so proud of you.'

At the mention of the man she was going to marry, Ella trembled. 'Oh Kathleen, what am I letting myself in for?'

'Don't be silly, it's just wedding-day nerves. Everyone gets them.'

'But I don't want to be married.' Ella bit her lip as tears threatened to overflow.

'Look.' Kathleen touched her shoulder gently. 'Most women marry a man they don't love, for security if nothing else. No one wants to be an old maid, do they?'

'It's all very well to say that, but would you marry Jolly Mortimer?' Ella watched Kathleen's face closely.

'I don't know,' Kathleen said honestly. 'If I was in the position you're in, with a sick mother to care for and money troubles, I suppose I would marry him like a shot.' A smile spread across her face. 'I must admit I've got a soft spot for Jolly, especially since he's taken over the Palace. He's fair and kind and . . . Yes, I would marry him if he asked me.' She hugged Ella impulsively and then stood back, her hands held wide. 'I hope I haven't crushed your frock, Ella. You look so lovely, it would be a shame to spoil your dress and—'

A sudden noise from downstairs interrupted Kathleen's flow. 'What on earth is that?' she said.

'Oh dear.' Ella guessed at once what was wrong. 'It's Mother. The nurse is trying to get her ready for church, and by the sound of it she's protesting.'

'You stay there,' Kathleen ordered. 'I'll see to things.'

Ella sat gingerly on the bed, careful not to crease her dress. The sun was shining in through the window, an early pale spring sunshine that should have cheered her up, but the way she was feeling now, nothing would lighten her spirits.

Soon, Kathleen came back into the room. 'I don't think your ma is going to make it to the church,' she said. 'The nurse had to give her a soothing tablet and now she's nodding off to sleep.'

'Perhaps it's just as well,' Ella said. 'She might have made a scene in the church and that would have been awful.'

'Look,' Kathleen said. 'After today, all your troubles will be over. Jolly will see that your mother is looked after properly. All you have to do is be a good wife to him. That shouldn't be so hard – anyone can see he loves you with all his heart.'

Ella heard the sound of bells from the street outside and her heart began to pound: the carriage and pair Jolly had hired had come to take her to church.

As Kathleen looked through the window, her face lit up. 'You're going in style! Come and see the carriage, it's all decked with flowers, and the pair of white horses have been done up like a dog's dinner. You're a lucky girl, Ella Burton, and don't you ever forget it.'

'For one minute I thought it was a handsome prince on a white charger coming to rescue me,' Ella said drily.

Kathleen turned to look at her. 'I suppose you

thought that Anthony would come for you. But that's just a silly dream, Ella.'

'I know,' Ella said hopelessly.

Kathleen took her arm and propelled her towards the door. 'Come on, let's get this show on the road.'

Ella smiled for the first time that morning. 'The theatre is in your blood, Kathleen. You even talk like an entertainer.'

Downstairs, Selma was asleep in a chair. Her hat fell lopsidedly over her eyes and her pretty new dress was rumpled around her knees. The nurse nodded to Ella. 'Your mother is better off sleeping here,' she said. 'She got over-excited and I had to give her something to calm her down.'

'Thank you, Nurse Carmel,' Ella said warmly. If the truth be known, she was relieved her mother wasn't coming to the wedding. It would be hard enough to go through the ceremony without having to worry that her mother might cause a disturbance.

At that moment Doris stepped through the door. She took Ella's hands and held them wide. 'You look beautiful, Ella Burton,' she said. 'That gown fits you a treat. Mind, I had a figure like that when I was your age. Good luck to you, my lovely girl. You deserve the best that life can offer you.'

When they stepped outside, Ella paused for

a moment, taken aback by the large crowd of onlookers waiting in the street. But then, Jolly was an important man around these parts and it was natural folk would want to see his bride.

A footman in livery helped her into the carriage and Kathleen climbed in beside her. Doris found it difficult to negotiate the steps but at last she was seated opposite Ella, panting a little but with a smile on her face that would have lit up the whole of the Palace theatre.

'We're all going to get our old jobs back because of you,' she said breathlessly. 'It's a strange world, when a marriage can change everything.'

'Do you think my marriage is going to be a good one, Doris?' Ella asked in a small voice. 'I seem to remember you saying something about it bringing me tears.'

'I think once you've settled down to being a wife, you'll be content,' Doris said warily. 'But don't take too much notice of me. We all have times when we weep. That's life, my girl.'

The women fell silent; only the jingling of the horses' bells disturbed the quiet. Ella sat rigidly in her place, worried that her veil would fall off. If she was going to be married she wanted the wedding to go without a hitch.

The door of the church stood wide open, and another group of onlookers had gathered outside. As Ella was helped down the steps of the carriage, she heard murmurs of approval from the crowd.

Waiting for her at the door were Jolly's five daughters, looking lovely in primrose-coloured dresses and clutching small bouquets. None of them looked very happy, though. Ella made up her mind to do her best for the girls: they were probably dreading her presence in their household, this stranger whom their father was marrying.

It was cool and dim inside the church and Ella blinked, trying to accustom her eyes to the gloom. She could see Jolly's rotund figure standing before the altar and she lifted her head high, determined that no one would see her reluctance to walk down the aisle towards him.

The vicar smiled benevolently at her, pleased to be officiating at such a prestigious ceremony, and bowed his head to her as she took her place beside her husband-to-be. She had made her bed, as her father would have said, and now she must lie on it.

Anthony sat staring out of the train window without seeing the passing villages and rolling green Yorkshire farmland. He stared at his reflection, wondering why it had taken him so long to make the journey back to Swansea, to see Ella for himself and find out why she had never answered any of his letters. If Jolly Mortimer hadn't offered him a job back at the Palace, he wouldn't be going home now.

He had had a good career ahead of him at the large theatre in Yorkshire, but in spite of everything he felt incomplete. He realized now that he wanted Ella at his side; he needed to make her his wife, to see her bear his children. He felt sure she loved him too, but then why the long empty silence?

He must have dozed for a while, because the next thing he knew, the train was shuddering to a halt. He sat up and looked out of the window. It was time for him to change trains; in one swift movement he got to his feet and picked up his bag.

His connecting train was late and Anthony stared stolidly into the distance, waiting impatiently to see the plume of steam that would herald the train's arrival. What was Ella doing now? When the Palace closed down she would have found other work – probably as a domestic. His heart ached as he thought of her scrubbing floors and wearing herself out in such a tough job.

Although she'd come to the Palace as a cleaner, he'd soon realized that she was cut out for better things and had treated her accordingly. He admitted to himself that he'd been attracted to her from the first time he'd seen her. He'd played a waiting game, treading carefully, unsure if marriage would be a good move for him. But now all that was swept aside as he confessed to himself that he loved her.

At last the train arrived, puffing and gasping like an old goat. He climbed on board with a feeling of relief and settled in a corner, closing his eyes so that no one would interrupt his thoughts with conversation. The chugging of the train made him drowsy and soon he slept again, knowing that when he woke he would be in Swansea, close to his darling Ella.

At last, the celebrations were over and Jolly had taken his new bride home to the house he'd redecorated especially for her. He knew he had a jewel in Helena Burton; she wasn't one of the flighty girls he saw around the streets of Swansea, she was modest and sweet and she would do her best to make him happy.

The maid had shown her to the bedroom to help her change out of her wedding clothes into something more comfortable. When Jolly learned that Ella had borrowed her wedding dress from the theatre his heart had been touched, but he knew he must allow her this last act of independence. As his wife she would have more clothes than she knew what to do with.

His daughters stood around him like fallen flower petals, waiting for him to dismiss them.

'Go on, girls,' he said. 'Run and get changed

out of your pretty dresses and get ready to visit Auntie Mena. If I'm not mistaken she'll spoil you with sweeties until your teeth fall out!'

His eldest daughter looked at him with penetrating blue eyes. 'It's all right, Father, you needn't baby-talk us or bribe us with sweets. We all know you want us out of the way.'

'Letty!' Jolly rested his hand on her shoulder. 'You are all precious to me and I love you all. Don't you forget it.'

The twins, Vicky and Lizzie, gazed up at him, as alike as two peas in a pod, then ran obediently up the stairs, and after a moment's hesitation the others followed. He smiled to himself: he was blessed with five beautiful children, and now with a beautiful young wife as well. He would soon sire a son, he felt sure of it.

His heart quickened: tonight he would take Helena to his bed and teach her the delights of marriage. For a moment he was touched as if by a cold hand – what if Helena could never love him? He was older than she was and far too plump to be a hero in her eyes. Still, he loved her dearly and he would take care of her all his life. Tonight they would be undisturbed, as the girls would be staying with their aunt. Helena's mother was still in the little house in Tinman's Row with the nurse he'd provided for her. Jolly was determined his first night with his new wife would be free of problems. He decided that he would eat a frugal supper and drink only a little wine, so as to be alert for his new bride. He smiled to himself again. He had loved his first wife dearly and had mourned long for her, but now it was time he made a new life for himself, and Helena was just the person to help him do it.

Ella sat beside her husband and marvelled at the shining array of cutlery and the glasses that gleamed brightly on the long dining table. She smiled at him, feeling suddenly warm. She liked Jolly, he was a fine man. But there was no room in her heart for love; she loved another man and always would.

When the meal was finished Jolly led her to the comfortable parlour full of rich, plush furniture. Although it was spring, the evening air was still chilly and a good fire burned in the ornate grate, warming the room and casting a glow into the corners.

'Would you like a little medicinal brandy, Helena?' Jolly asked tentatively.

'I think a medicinal brandy sounds like a very good idea.' Ella looked down at her hands, afraid to meet his eyes, knowing she would see his love for her plainly writ across his face. She watched as he poured the golden drink into a glass and their hands touched as he handed it to her. She didn't draw away; she was Jolly's wife now and he was entitled to touch her hand if he so wished.

He took a seat beside her and she felt the warmth of his thigh against hers. She looked up then. 'Don't be nervous of me, I'm not going to bite,' she said, smiling. He didn't reply and Ella struggled to fill the silence. 'It's so quiet here. It's such a lovely house, you must be very proud of what you've achieved.'

'Without a woman in my life the achievements have been hollow,' he said. 'I've needed a wife so badly, Helena, but I wasn't content to marry just for the sake of companionship.' He took her hand and kissed it. 'I wanted more, my dear. I wanted a soulmate, and in you I feel I've found one.'

'I'll do my best to be a good wife, Jolly,' Ella said quietly. 'And a good mother to your girls.'

There was a gentle tap on the door and the young maid popped her head into the room. 'Mrs Prior asked me to tell you there's a fire in the bedroom and the bed is turned down ready, Sir.'

'Thank you, Jenny.'

The maid disappeared and Ella emptied her glass, then waited until Jolly had finished his drink. He took her hand in his again. 'You go on up first,' he said gently. 'Jenny will be there to help you undress.'

Ella climbed the stairs slowly, admiring the polished bannister, studying the patterns in the rich carpet – anything to take her mind off what was to come.

In spite of the fire, the bedroom felt cold and Ella shivered as the maid helped her to take off her clothes. It was strange being attended by a maid, but Ella knew the girl would be offended if she sent her away.

At last, she was in bed. She lay quite still beneath the sheets, waiting for her husband. Finally, just as she was about to fall asleep, she heard Jolly's tread on the stairs and immediately she was wide awake.

Jolly seemed to take a long time to prepare for bed. She heard him in the bathroom, listened to the rush of water drumming into the basin, and then at last he came to the bedroom. He slid into bed beside her and lay still for a moment without speaking.

Ella was tense, wondering how she should behave. Did it become a new bride to offer herself to her groom?

It was Jolly who made the first move. 'Helena, may I . . . ?' His voice trailed away and Ella turned her head to look at him.

'Of course you may, you are my husband.' She lifted up the hem of the cotton nightgown she had donned a short time ago and felt her cheeks burn red with embarrassment at her nakedness.

But Jolly was gentle; he kissed her and touched her and when at last he made love to her it was not the fearful experience she had dreaded. Jolly was patient with her and through the night he turned her from a maiden into a fully fledged wife.

CHAPTER SEVENTEEN

The Palace theatre was silent, the stage empty, the flats in the wings gathering dust. Ella stood in the auditorium that still smelled of smoke and scent and looked around her, thinking how lifeless it all seemed without people thronging the aisles, without music from the band and, most of all, without the magical presence of Anthony Weatherby Nichols. She knew Jolly had managed to persuade Anthony to come back but so far she hadn't met him face to face. She didn't even know if he was in Swansea yet.

The doors swung open and Ella turned to see Kathleen and Doris making their way down the aisle.

'There we are then.' Kathleen helped Doris into one of the seats and fanned her face. 'Jesus, Mary and Joseph!' she exclaimed breathlessly. 'Now we're here, perhaps you'll tell us what's going on?'

'Nothing, really,' Ella said. 'It will be a few

weeks before the theatre can open again, but in the meantime I don't want it feeling sad and neglected so I thought we'd give the place a good cleaning.' She laughed as she saw the pained look on Kathleen's face.

'Cleaning? Sure haven't we had enough of cleaning this place? In any case, you are a respectably married woman now and I'm going to be a singer, so we don't need to go cleaning for a living.'

'I'm only teasing,' Ella relented as Doris panted and flapped her hand in front of her face as if she was about to fall into a vapour, as the performers in melodramas often did. 'We're not going to clean – I've got a team of young women in for that. We are going to supervise, though, and I might just ask one of you to make us some tea.'

Kathleen beamed. 'For a minute I thought you were serious. But I'll gladly make the tea – I could do with a cup myself.'

'Wait a minute, Kathleen,' Doris said. 'This is important. Ella, when exactly is that husband of yours going to re-open the place?'

'As soon as he can. There's still a lot of business to be settled, papers to sign, and he needs to hire scene-shifters and lighting men, that sort of thing, but he'll get all that done as quickly as possible.'

'I can't wait to get back in here.' Doris had a

dreamy look on her face. 'I can't wait to see the performers do their stuff and to hear the applause of the crowd. How well I remember when the applause was for me.'

'You must have a good memory!' Kathleen joked.

Doris nudged her with her elbow. 'Go and make that tea before I give you a backhander.'

'All right then, Grumpy Guts. But don't be putting on me all the time. This is the last time I'll be making the tea – the new cleaners can do that in the future.'

When Kathleen left the room Ella took Doris's arm. 'We'll go and sit in the office,' she said. 'I might as well get used to it, I suppose. Once Jolly opens the place the office is where I'll be spending a lot of my time.' At least that's what she dreamed of: she wanted to be involved with the theatre. Sitting at home all day being a house-wife was not what she planned to do.

Doris mounted the stairs slowly, clinging on to the bannister and panting for breath. 'I don't think I'll be doing this very often,' she said.

'Sorry, I didn't think. Anyway, I want you downstairs working in the box office, checking the tickets and the money. That's going to be your job now.'

'Isn't Tim coming back?'

Ella shook her head. 'He's left Swansea. I don't know what he's doing now. But in any case, I want you to do the job. I know I can trust you to do it properly.'

The office was stuffy from being closed up and Ella pushed open a window. It looked out towards the sea, but the lane at the back of the building was strewn with rubbish. A thin cat slunk its way through the filth, scavenging for food. The theatre's air of neglect was so depressing and Ella felt impatient to see the Palace gleaming with lights and full of life again. Suddenly she was filled with pride for her husband. Jolly was a good man, and in some ways he'd taken the place of her father. She smiled to herself: Jolly was not as strict as Arthur Burton, but he had the same way of talking to her as though she was a beloved child.

'You're not looking half bad,' said Doris as she settled wearily into the big chair behind the desk. 'I really think that marriage suits you. Are you happy, Ella?'

Ella thought for a minute before answering. 'I'm content,' she said. 'My mother has settled well into the family. Jolly's girls have endless patience with her – they really are lovely children.' Her smile faded: all except Letty, who didn't approve of her father's new wife and made no attempt to hide her feelings.

'They won't be children for much longer,' Doris commented. 'That eldest girl, Leticia, she's going to be a beauty just like her mother before her.'

Ella was suddenly curious. 'What was Jolly's first wife like, Doris?'

'She was lovely. Tall, willowy, with lovely blond shining hair. Jolly thought the world of her. You should feel honoured that he married you – he was a widower for so long.'

'I'm very fond of Jolly,' Ella said honestly, 'but it's not the earth-shattering love I thought I'd feel for the man I would marry.'

'Love is often an illusion,' Doris said sagely. 'Just as the footlights make everything seem colourful and beautiful, so the dream of love takes on a magic all of its own. But believe me, Ella, you don't want to exchange the dream for the reality. You've got a fine man in Jolly, a good man who loves you, and that is worth the world.'

'I know,' Ella said softly, 'and I'm very grateful for what I've got.'

The door opened and a red-faced Kathleen pushed her way into the room, balancing a tray on her arm. 'God help me! I'm not climbing those stairs too often, it's killing on the poor legs.' She put down the tray and lifted her skirts to examine her ankles.

Doris burst out laughing. 'Climbing stairs is good for a young thing like you,' she said as she took her tea. 'It makes the body strong and supple. And you need to be strong and supple if you're to be an artiste, believe me.'

Kathleen looked hopefully in Ella's direction.

'Do you think Jolly will let me sing for the audience sometimes?' she asked. 'I don't expect to be featured on the bill, mind, but I would love to do a warm-up before the proper show starts.'

Ella patted her friend's arm. 'I'm sure Jolly will be only too happy to include you in the line-up of artistes.'

Kathleen smiled happily. 'To tell the truth, your husband will agree to anything you say. That man is so in love with you he lights up like a candle when you're in the room. An' isn't he losing some of that weight he put on after his first wife died? You must be keeping him happy in the bedroom.'

Ella felt her colour rise. She would never get used to Kathleen's outspoken ways.

Doris looked at her shrewdly. 'Don't be embarrassed, girl. You should know by now that nothing is private in the world of the theatre, where the chorus girls walk around in next to nothing and the men make coarse remarks about them. Don't be too much of a prude, Ella, the theatre is different from any other world. We're like family, don't you feel that? So don't turn into a toff now you're married to the boss.'

'No chance of that with you around,' Ella said with spirit. 'I've learned some very unladylike expressions since I first worked with you two and my poor father would turn in his grave if he knew half of what went on behind the scenes.'

The sound of the side door closing caught Ella's attention. 'It looks as though the new cleaners have turned up. Come on, girls, let's show them how we want things done around here.'

Kathleen rubbed her hands together. 'I'm really looking forward to this,' she said with a cheerful smile on her face. 'It will be a real treat to be supervising instead of getting down on my knees and scrubbing the place. I'll see the cleaners do a good job, don't you worry.' She left the room and clattered down the stone steps.

Ella took Doris's arm. 'Come on, we'd better see fair play is done, otherwise Kathleen will frighten the new girls to death.'

Together they slowly made their way down to the ground floor. 'I'm getting old,' Doris said breathlessly. 'I suppose it's time I was sent to the big stage in the sky.'

'Nonsense! You've got many years ahead of you yet.' But Ella realized with sadness that Doris's health was failing. Still, she could take care of her, see that her work was not too arduous. All at once she felt a surge of gratitude to her husband for changing the lives of her friends as well as her own.

Once she had instructed the cleaners as to their new duties she would go home and organize the menu for tonight's dinner. She would make sure that Jolly's favourite foods were served. Her husband deserved nothing but the best, and she would see that he got it.

Anthony stood outside the theatre and looked up at the faded billboards. The front doors were closed, so he made his way slowly round to the back of the building.

He had stepped off the train only yesterday. He'd arrived a day early – his meeting with Mr Mortimer was not scheduled until this afternoon. In the meantime, he had booked into the Mackworth Hotel on the High Street. But he had been unable to sleep last night. He wanted desperately to find out where Ella was living now. He'd been to her home in Tinman's Row only to find that Ella and her mother had moved out. The new tenant, an elderly gentleman, had spoken to him rudely.

'You was mixed up with that ruffian Simons and the court case, wasn't you? I've got nothing to say to the likes of you.'

Anthony sighed. He was guilty by association with Mr Simons, and there was nothing he could do about it. Now he stood outside the Palace, hoping for news of Ella.

As he entered the doorway, he breathed in the familiar smells of the Palace with a feeling of nostalgia. This was where he belonged, the place where his love for the theatre had been born. He stood for a moment in the dusty silence and breathed in the atmosphere. He loved the Palace and was delighted to be back. If only he could find Ella his happiness would be complete.

He heard the sounds of activity in the distance: the clanking of a bucket, the rushing of the tap in the kitchen, and all at once he was transported back to when he'd been manager here, working night and day to make the theatre a success; when, more importantly, he'd fallen in love with Ella Burton. Would she be coming back to work here? His heart leaped at the thought. Any minute now he might take a turning in the corridor and see her lovely face smiling at him.

Perhaps he'd been a fool not to declare his love for her while he was still in Swansea, but he hadn't realized the strength of his feelings until he left. Now, with the security of a job at the Palace again and some savings put by, he was ready to offer Ella marriage. Somehow, deep in his soul, he knew she returned his love. But why hadn't she replied to his letters? A small rebellious voice in his head taunted him.

He heard laughter in the kitchen and with a light heart he made his way there, almost breathless with happiness. Doris would be drinking tea as usual, Kathleen would be warbling some tune and Ella, his lovely Ella, would be waiting patiently for him to come back to her.

The girl in the kitchen turned to look at him questioningly. She was a stranger and he saw at once that she was new to the job. Her skirts hung wet around her ankles; she had not tucked them into her bloomers the way the experienced cleaners did.

'Good morning. I'm looking for Ella Burton – is she still working here?' Anthony stood in the doorway, waiting.

The girl frowned, lowering her bucket of slopping water on to the floor. 'Don't know any Ella Burton,' she said. 'I'm one of the new girls. There's three of us and none of us is called Burton.'

Anthony felt his heart sink. 'When did you start work here?'

'Only today, Mister.'

'So is the theatre to open soon?'

The girl shrugged. 'Bless you, Sir, I don't know. No one tells me anything like that. I'm just here to do a bit of scrubbing, that's all.' She chewed her fingernail for a second, frowning in concentration. 'Mr Mortimer is the new boss, mind, I do know that.'

'Yes, I know.' Anthony had difficulty keeping the impatience out of his voice; it was not the girl's fault she'd never heard of Ella.

She paused, then added, 'He was here earlier, but I think he's gone out.' She smiled at Anthony. 'He's a lovely man, is Mr Mortimer. I suppose his new wife has got something to do with him looking so content these days.'

'New wife? Does that mean he's moved house?'

'No, Sir, he's still living in the big house in the Uplands. Needs a big house, I suppose, with five daughters and a new wife to look after.'

'Thank you for your help. I'll go to his house.' He paused and grinned. 'I think you might find it helpful to tuck your skirts into your bloomers – saves them getting too wet.'

'Oh, aye, so that you can peek at my ankles, is it?' She paused. 'Still, sounds like a good idea. Thank you, Sir.'

Anthony smiled at her. 'It's the way the old cleaners used to work.' The way Ella used to work until he'd promoted her to wardrobe mistress.

He left the theatre and made his way to the Uplands. It was a fine day and the walk would be good for him. In any case, he needed time to think. As he walked, all his memories came flooding back: the warmth of the theatre when it was full, the way the cigarette smoke drifted like a haze across the footlights, the smell of the greasepaint. It was all so precious to him. And most precious of all were his thoughts about his darling Ella. Soon he would be seeing her again, and he couldn't wait. As soon as possible, he would ask her to be his bride.

CHAPTER EIGHTEEN

'Helena, I'm home!' Jolly walked through the hall and was greeted by his eldest daughter, Letty.

'She's supervising dinner.' Letty kissed her father. 'She's been at the theatre today. I told her you wouldn't like it, but she went anyway.'

Jolly pinched his daughter's cheek. 'It's all right, my darling, we've agreed that when the Palace re-opens Helena will be involved with the running of it.'

'But do you think it proper for your new wife to be consorting with cleaners and such? I know she's from a low-born family, but she should abide by our standards now, shouldn't she?'

'Helena's from a good Christian home,' Jolly said firmly. 'She was brought up properly, even though her father was a tin-plate man. It doesn't do to stand in judgement on folk, Leticia.'

'Well, her family couldn't have been all that good – just look at her mad mother. How we put up with her, I don't know.'

'I won't have you speaking like that, Letty, it's uncharitable. You've been brought up to have compassion for those less fortunate than yourself.'

'So, Father, your new wife is more important to you than your own daughters, is she? Are you going to take her part whenever there's a hint of friction?'

Jolly felt exasperated, but did his best to reassure his daughter. 'My dear Letty, I love all my daughters more than anything in the world, but you have to accept that I was lonely without a companion by my side.'

'But you had us!' Leticia sounded tearful and Jolly took her hand.

'I know, and you children have been wonderful, but . . .' He struggled to find the right words. 'I need a wife's company. Please try to understand that.'

'You mean to have more children, I suppose?' Now Leticia's voice was cold. 'Sons who will take the place of my sisters and me in your affections. That's what will happen, won't it?'

Jolly sighed. 'Helena and I don't intend to have children for a long time yet. I have to give my wife every opportunity to get used to her new lifestyle, and I look to you as the eldest of my children to behave like a fond daughter to her.'

'May I go now, Father?'

'Yes, Letty, you can go. I'm sure you have

plenty to do. I hope you are intending to work at your studies this afternoon?'

Before Leticia could answer, the door opened and Helena came in. Jolly could see by her expression that she guessed at once that something was going on between her husband and his eldest daughter.

'Am I interrupting anything, Jolly?' She spoke softly and her eyes met his anxiously.

'Not at all, Helena. Come and tell me what we're having for dinner tonight.'

'Cabbage soup and boiled liver, I suppose,' Leticia said spitefully. 'That's the sort of cooking you're used to, isn't it, Stepmother?'

Helena turned pale. 'I'm no cook, but when my mother was well she made us rabbit stew with dumplings. My father was very fond of cooked ham and vegetables – good plain food. As for tonight, I've arranged to have salmon for the first course, braised beef and kidney for the second and a good rich treacle pudding to finish with.'

'No soup?' Leticia asked. 'Mother always made sure we had at least four courses. But then I suppose you're not used to such luxuries.'

Jolly frowned at his daughter. 'You may leave us,' he said firmly, 'and for your information, the dinner menu was my idea.'

When his daughter had left, Jolly apologized to Helena. 'Please take no notice of Letty. She's very temperamental at the moment.'

Ella sat on the sofa and arranged her skirts around her ankles with minute attention, as if the folds of the material were of the utmost importance to her. 'She resents me,' she said. 'She thinks I'm taking the place of her mother. But I know I can never do that and I wouldn't want to try.'

Jolly sat beside her. 'Give her time, my dear. I'm sure she'll come round to my way of thinking.' He took her hand and kissed it. 'And I am thinking I'm the luckiest man in the world to have such a wife.'

He saw the tension in her face relax a little.

'The other girls are well behaved and listen to me with respect,' Ella said, 'but I have a feeling they all wish you'd never brought me here to share their home.'

'As I said, give it time. Soon the girls will grow to love you as I do.' He tilted her face up to his. 'And I love you more than words can say. That's the most important thing to remember. One day my girls will marry, have homes and children of their own, and then they'll realize what a good woman I've gained as a wife.'

'I hope so, Jolly, I really hope so.'

Selma sat in the strange living room and stared around her. Nurse Carmel, ever attentive, put a hand on her arm.

'Is there anything you need, Mrs Burton?'

220

Selma tried to think – what had she been about to say? For the moment the thought escaped her, so she substituted another that seemed to make sense.

'What are we having for supper?'

Nurse Carmel smiled. 'I'll go and find out from Cook.' She seemed anxious to be out of the room and Selma realized, albeit dimly, that the room she was in was as much of a prison to the nurse as it was to her. As Nurse Carmel went to the door she glanced back a little anxiously. 'You're sure you'll be all right?'

Selma nodded. It would be good to have a few moments alone. She waited until the nurse had left the room, then crossed to the window and looked out at the gardens below. They were wide and spacious and full of colour. Selma was confused. She thought she had a small garden, planted with vegetables – no point buying them half dead at the market, much better to grow your own.

After a minute or two, she wandered out of the room and peered around anxiously. She knew she shouldn't go out, but she was tired of sitting looking at the same four walls every day.

The landing was large and airy and Selma didn't recognize anything: not the rich carpet on the floor, nor the big picture window that let in so much light. It dazzled Selma. She blinked and tried to focus, but then a figure appeared before her, a ghost all in white with long, golden hair. Was she an angel? But no, her features were stern and there was no kindliness in her eyes.

Selma cowered against the wall. Perhaps the vision was Death coming to claim her. She fumbled her way along the corridor back to her room and closed the door quickly. Death couldn't get her now, she was safe here.

She sat in her chair with her hands folded in her lap, waiting patiently for Nurse Carmel to come back. No wonder she was told to stay in this room – she was safe here, angels and demons couldn't touch her. Suddenly tears rose to her eyes. She missed her Arthur, he had put a ring on her finger and now he was gone, she knew not where. They hadn't been married very long – he shouldn't desert her in this way.

The tears dried and a weariness crept up on her. She closed her eyes and found peace in a deep sleep.

'She's a mad woman.' Leticia confronted Nurse Carmel on the stairs. 'You shouldn't allow her to wander about the house the way she does.'

'She doesn't wander about the house – I see to it that she stays in her room.'

'Well, I just encountered her on the landing,' Leticia said coldly. 'My father would be very cross if he knew you left her alone like that. She's a danger to everyone.'

'I only left her for a few minutes,' Nurse Carmel replied. 'Mrs Burton wanted to know what was for dinner, so I went to find out. There's no need to feel afraid of her. She's harmless enough, just a bit senile, that's all.'

'Well, I'll let it pass this time,' Leticia said haughtily. 'That old woman should be in a mental institution if she's senile,' she added. 'I shall have a word with my father about it.'

Leticia smiled to herself. The nurse would be worried now, afraid she would lose her position in the household. And serve her right, her job was not an arduous one, she merely had to keep a batty old woman in check. She should be very grateful for her position, but then her father was always inclined to let people take advantage of him. Leticia swished her skirts past the nurse and hurried down the stairs. She burst into the drawing room and saw to her disgust that her father was holding Ella's hand.

'Father!' she gasped. 'I've just had the most horrid experience.'

To her satisfaction, he left Ella's side at once. 'What on earth has happened?'

'It's her mother.' She pointed at Ella. 'She almost attacked me there on the stairs. She stared at me so strangely I feared for my safety.'

She saw Ella's look of distress, but pressed on. 'Please, Father, can't Mrs Burton be taken to a hospital or something? I'm so afraid of her.' She was careful not to sound unkind. 'I know she's sick in the head, but she could do herself harm. You should have seen her, poised on the stairs as if she was going to fling herself down them. I tried to talk to her, but when she saw me she stared like a mad woman and returned to her room.'

'Come along now, Letty darling, things can't be as bad as you say. Where was Nurse Carmel when all this was going on?'

'Gone on an errand for Mrs Burton, so she said, but I think she just wanted to gossip in the kitchen as she usually does.'

'I've found Nurse Carmel very trustworthy,' Ella said at last.

Leticia concealed her impatience. 'Oh, I'm sure she "acts" trustworthy when other people are around, but the fact remains that she left your mother alone long enough for the poor lady to go wandering around the landing.'

'I'll have a word with her, don't you worry.' Her father patted her shoulder. 'I'm sorry Selma frightened you, but it won't happen again, I promise.'

Triumphant, Leticia smiled at her father. 'I know you'll keep us safe, Father. Well, I'd better go and see if my sisters are ready for dinner. I've got to act like a mother to them, since they haven't got anyone else.'

Jolly looked uncomfortable and Leticia thought

for a moment that he was about to admonish her, but he just cast a helpless look towards Ella and shrugged. 'Go along then, Letty, and try not to frighten your sisters, promise now? No ghoulish stories.'

'Of course not, Father.' She left the room with her head held high. She'd got her father's attention at last and also found a way to upset his new wife. She hadn't missed Helena's anguished expression as she'd talked about her mother.

She found her sisters in the sitting room and smiled as she closed the door behind her. Everything was falling into place: now she could tell her tales and turn the girls against Helena and her mad mother.

As Anthony reached the Uplands region of Swansea, the sky had darkened. Clouds had gathered and the wind had risen, rushing off the sea like a serpent roused from sleep. The house where Jolly Mortimer lived stood on its own, a lovely elegant building with spacious gardens surrounding its mellow walls.

Anthony had come to talk about his new job at the Palace. He had a lot of questions to ask Mr Mortimer – they needed to discuss his salary, working hours and what his new role would involve. And his hopes ran high that his new boss would know where Ella had gone. Mr Mortimer was a sensible, practical man, by all accounts, and he might have felt he owed those who had left the Palace at least the courtesy of a final payment for their services. For that he would need the addresses of the workers.

He rang the bell, and after a time the big front door swung open and a small girl stood there. Anthony guessed it was one of Jolly's daughters.

'Good afternoon, young lady,' he said. 'I wonder if your father is at home.'

The small girl looked at him gravely, but didn't reply. He imagined she was taken with his theatrical appearance; his wavy hair and richly coloured cravat appeared to intrigue her.

An older girl came across the hall whom Anthony recognized as Leticia, Jolly's eldest daughter.

'Mary!' She took her sister by the hand. 'How many times do I have to tell you? You do not answer the door to anyone! Leave that to the maid.'

Mary began to bawl and Anthony shifted from one foot to the other. 'I'm sorry to trouble you,' he said. 'It was your father I wanted to see.'

'You're Mr Weatherby Nichols, aren't you?' Leticia said. 'You used to manage the Palace until you were summoned to court.'

It was obvious that everyone round here thought him just as guilty as Mr Simons. 'That's not quite correct, young lady, but never mind. Is your father at home? I have an appointment with him.'

'He's just about to sit down for a cup of tea and some cake. Can you tell me what you want to see him for? A job, was it?'

Anthony was irritated by the girl's imperious attitude, but he realized he wasn't going to get very far if he didn't cooperate with her. 'The interview is about my post at the theatre,' he said evenly, 'but I'm also interested in finding Miss Ella Burton.' He smiled as charmingly as he could. 'I would like to see her again, but I don't know where to find her.'

'I can solve that problem for you. Step into the hall, Mr Weatherby Nichols.' She had an expression of delight on her face that puzzled him, but he went into the hall and removed his hat, handing it to the embarrassed maid who had just appeared.

Leticia departed, dragging her small sister with her, and Anthony waited uncomfortably. He felt as if he was intruding, but he stood his ground, expecting to see Jolly Mortimer appear in the hallway. Instead, a door opened and a young woman in a fine lavender sprigged dress came towards him. Her face was shaded by the dim light in the hall, but he would have recognized her anywhere.

As she came closer his heart missed a beat. 'Ella!' He met her halfway across the hall and took both her hands in his. 'Ella, I'm so glad I've found you!'

She looked away, as if it hurt her to meet his eyes. At her side stood Leticia, a triumphant smile on her face.

'Mr Weatherby Nichols,' Leticia said, 'may I introduce Helena Mortimer, my new stepmother.'

It was as if a great gulf had opened at his feet. He couldn't move. He just stared stupidly at Ella, at the gold band gleaming on her finger, the fine dress and the well-styled hair, and his heart began to thump. He had come to make her his own, but he was too late. She was married to another man.

CHAPTER NINETEEN

The months passed slowly for Ella. Though she had settled into her new role as Jolly's wife, she was still haunted by the look in Anthony's eyes when he realized she was married. She deeply regretted that she hadn't waited a while before agreeing to become Jolly's wife, and yet she knew that even if she had the time over again she would take the same course of action. She had needed help with her sick mother and Jolly had been there to give her all she needed. And give it with a warm heart, she must never forget that. And now there was going to be an additional responsibility.

She was arranging late-summer roses in a tall vase in the hall when Jolly came in, bringing a fragrant breeze from the garden with him. He crossed the hall and kissed her, his arm around her waist, and for a moment Ella rested her head against his shoulder. He was a safe refuge from the troubles of the world, and for that she would be eternally grateful to him.

'How is Selma today? Has she been behaving herself?' he inquired.

Ella turned in his arms and looked up at him. He was illuminated by a ray of sun slanting in from the open door, and she saw, quite suddenly, that Jolly was looking well. He had a happy smile on his face and such a contented look in his eyes that she felt a great responsibility settle on her shoulders. She was the reason for the change in him and she must never disappoint him.

'Mother's so quiet these days,' Ella said. 'She's almost always asleep. I worry about her, Jolly, I really do.'

He touched her cheek. 'I know, my dearest, but we are doing the very best we can. Nurse Carmel is with her all the time, and in spite of her state of mind she seems very well in herself.'

Ella smiled. 'Come on, let's go into the sitting room, where we can talk in comfort. I've something to tell you.'

His eyes lit up. 'Helena, do you mean . . . ?' His words trailed away as Ella put her hand over his mouth.

'Not here. Little ears might be listening.' She led him by the hand into the sitting room and closed the door behind her. Jolly took her in his arms and looked down into her face. 'Tell me, Helena, is it the news I've hoped and prayed for?'

She nodded. 'We are going to have a baby, Jolly. I'm two months gone.'

Jolly had tears in his eyes as he kissed her gently on both cheeks. 'I'm so happy, Helena, so very happy. I think I'm the luckiest man in all the world.'

The door opened and Leticia came into the room. Her quick glance took in everything: the tears of happiness in her father's eyes and the gentle way he was holding Helena.

Ella bit her lip. She knew there would be no hiding anything from Jolly's eldest daughter. 'You can be the first to know our news,' she said, trying to rescue something from the awkward moment. 'I'm having a baby. I hope you're happy for us.'

Ella saw a quick flash of anger in Leticia's eyes, which was rapidly concealed by a forced smile. 'Congratulations. I'm sure this is exactly what you wanted.'

'It's what we both wanted,' Jolly said quickly. 'Send in the girls, Letty, and I'll talk to them.'

Soon Charlotte, Vicky, Lizzie and Mary were lined up before Jolly, looking up at him expectantly. Letty stood aloof a little way off, a sullen expression on her face.

'Girls, you are going to have a brother.'

'Or maybe a sister,' Ella added quickly.

'Where are you going to get the baby from?' Mary asked, her eyes large with wonder.

Jolly smiled, suddenly embarrassed. 'Helena will explain it all to you,' he said, with an

231

apologetic look in Ella's direction. 'I'll leave you to it, my dearest.' He left the room and Ella was faced with the daunting task of telling his daughters how a baby was conceived.

'I don't know how to begin . . .'

'I'll do it,' Leticia said suddenly. She stood in front of her sisters and smiled a tight smile. 'Father sleeps with Helena, you know that, don't you?'

'Of course we know that,' Lizzie interjected. 'But I sleep with Vicky and we don't have a baby.'

'Well, when father sleeps with Helena he does things to her.' She stopped and looked spitefully at Ella. 'You'd better explain, after all.'

'Sit down, girls.' Ella felt angry with Letty. She was doing her best to make things awkward.

'You've seen how the rabbits mate with each other, haven't you? Well, it's the same sort of thing with a husband and wife, only nicer, of course.'

'Does Father stand behind you and push his thingy into you?' Lizzie asked.

Ella felt her colour rise. 'It's not exactly the same. Fathers and mothers face each other and they mate because they love each other. That's the way people make babies.'

She wished she'd never started this. It might have been a better idea to ask Nurse Carmel to talk to the girls.

'But you don't love Father,' Letty said. 'You married him so that he could take care of you and your mad mother.'

Ella wanted to lash out at Letty to slap the smirk from her face, but she bit her tongue and forced a smile. 'Of course I'm fond of your father. Love grows when you marry someone.'

'But I thought you loved Anthony Weatherby Nichols,' Letty persisted. 'I saw the way you looked at each other when he came to the house that time wanting to know where you were. He was so disappointed to find you married.'

Ella rose to her feet. 'I think it's time you returned to your studies, girls. Your tutor will be cross if I keep you away from your lessons for too long.'

The girls trooped obediently towards the door.

'Not you, Leticia. I want to have a word with you.'

Leticia pouted sulkily. 'I need to go to the bathroom.'

'This won't take long.' Ella stood with her back to the door. 'I'm surprised and cross at the way you spoke to me just then.'

Letty glanced at her from under her long dark eyelashes. The girl was already blossoming into womanhood. She had lustrous brown eyes and her blond hair curled enticingly around her face. She would break hearts one day.

'I don't understand.' Leticia was all wide-eyed innocence. 'What have I said to upset you?'

'You called my mother mad, for one thing.'

'Well, I apologize for that. It just slipped out. I didn't know how else to put it. She is mad, isn't she?'

'She is old and weary and her memory isn't what it used to be. My mother suffered very badly when my father was killed. We have to make allowances for her.'

'As I said, I apologize, but I felt I was telling the truth.'

'Letty, why can't you be kind and gentle like your sisters?'

'I'm the eldest and I don't like to see my father taken for a fool.' Suddenly all pretence of politeness was gone and Leticia was openly hostile. 'You were a poor woman, you had nothing and my father was a good catch. When he offered you a way out of your troubles you jumped at the idea.'

'That's not true!' Ella said quickly.

'But it is true. You didn't love my father and you don't love him now. Your word for what you feel is "fond". Well, you can be fond of a dog or cat, but you are supposed to be in love with your husband.'

She spoke the truth and Ella knew she had no defence. 'This is getting us nowhere, Leticia. Go back to your studies.'

'Oh, by the way,' Leticia said. 'I met Anthony in Victoria Park the other day. He was very attentive – I think he wants me to put in a good word to Father about him working so hard at the Palace. He's working such long hours – I expect he's angling for a rise in salary. Actually, I've asked Father to invite him over for dinner tonight. Didn't he mention it?' She smiled and her eyes glinted with spite. She stared at Ella's red cheeks for a long moment and then made her way gracefully to the door. There she stopped and turned the full glare of her dislike on her stepmother.

After a long pause, she gave one last parting shot. 'You can tell Anthony your good news, can't you? About the baby, I mean. I'm sure he'll be delighted for you.'

When Leticia had left the room, Ella sank into one of the chairs and put her hands over her face. Her feelings for Anthony rushed back to the surface like a high tide and she knew she still loved him with all her heart.

But she was a married woman, and was now carrying her husband's child. She must put all her silly thoughts about Anthony out of her mind. She was determined to make Jolly happy – it was no less than he deserved.

Perhaps things would be easier when she gave up her involvement with the theatre. The thought was depressing: she loved going to the Palace, loved meeting with Kathleen and Doris, and she always had the hope that she would catch sight of Anthony. But she would have to stay at home once her pregnancy was more advanced. At the thought of her baby, her heart lifted. Soon she would have a little spark of life to love and care for. She must look forward to motherhood and forget the Palace and the people who worked there – that part of her life would soon be over.

Anthony stood looking round the foyer, feeling very satisfied about the way the theatre looked now. The sad, faded hoardings had gone, re-placed by bright colourful new posters advertising the date of the grand opening.

At the front of the building the freshly painted doors were open and the steps were scrubbed and gleaming, ready to offer a welcome to the people who would soon fill the theatre again.

'What do you think, Mr Mortimer? Is everything to your satisfaction?'

'You've done well,' Jolly said. 'Glad you came back?'

Anthony rested his hand on Jolly's plump shoulder. 'Very glad. I would work here for nothing if I was a man of private means.'

'I know, and I do appreciate the effort you've made to get the Palace up and running again.' He clapped his hand to his forehead. 'Oh, I've just remembered! I've been asked by my eldest daughter to invite you to dinner tonight – if you can bear the company of my brood of children, that is.'

As Anthony hesitated, Jolly looked up at him and winked. 'I've got an ulterior motive for inviting you over. Perhaps when we've eaten and the ladies have taken their leave of us you could give me some pointers about how I should run the Palace. You know more about it than I ever will.'

'I would be delighted,' Anthony said reluctantly. It would be torture to sit close to Ella and know she belonged to another man.

'Good, good. We'll look forward to seeing you then – about seven thirty suit you?'

Anthony nodded. In spite of everything, his spirits rose at the thought of spending the evening in Ella's company. He knew she was out of his reach, but that didn't stop him longing to see her.

Anthony forced his mind back to business. 'It looks spick and span here now,' he said. 'No one would believe the place has been lying empty for months.'

'Come along,' Jolly said. 'Let's have a good look round. We'll need to stock the bar and to get in a good supply of cigars. I take it you can deal with all that?'

'Of course I can,' Anthony said quickly. 'I have a good working relationship with the suppliers.

They know me and I hope they still trust me, in spite of my long absence.'

'I'm sure they will. After all, there was no hint of you being involved in Mr Simon's difficulties.'

'Some find me guilty by association,' Anthony said as he followed Jolly upstairs. The familiar smell of the plush carpet imbued with years of tobacco smoke rose to greet him, and above it rose the fresh smell of cleaning fluid. Anthony took a deep, thankful breath. The theatre was almost ready to open and soon he could throw himself into the task of making it successful once again.

Ella presided over the dinner table with all the serenity she could muster, though it was strange sitting with Anthony on one side and her husband on the other. The girls had been allowed to dine with the adults, and Leticia dimpled and smiled at Anthony as though she'd known him for years. Ella felt a dart of triumph because Anthony seemed oblivious to Letty's attempts to draw attention to herself. He responded with the utmost courtesy when she spoke to him, but his eyes were constantly meeting Ella's. This did not go unnoticed by Jolly.

'You think, as I do, that I have the most beautiful wife in the world,' he said genially. 'And no one can blame you for that.'

'Oh, Father, don't be so silly,' Letty interjected.

'Mr Weatherby Nichols and my stepmother used to work together, so there's bound to be feelings between them.' Her mouth puckered and she turned to Anthony. 'In fact, I've heard that you went calling on our dear stepmother before you went away, didn't you?'

Jolly looked at Ella. 'Is that so, my dear?'

Ella smiled reassuringly at her husband. 'No, it was nothing like that,' she said. 'We were all friends – Kathleen, Doris, Anthony and I – and we wanted to keep in touch with each other, that's all.'

'But didn't you stay at his house? That sounds like more than friendship to me,' retorted Leticia.

'Letty!' Jolly said sharply. 'Don't talk about matters that don't concern you.' He was pale and his eyes were anguished as he looked at Ella.

'Yes, I stayed at Anthony's lodgings one night,' she said quietly. 'But nothing improper took place, I do assure you.'

Anthony fixed his gaze on Letty and his voice was tight with anger. 'I can confirm, Miss Mortimer, that my landlady was there to chaperone us at all times.'

Letty's cheeks turned pink. She was making no headway with Anthony and she was becoming angry. Ella wondered anxiously what she would say next.

'Perhaps the baby she's expecting isn't yours, Father. Have you thought of that?'

For a moment, Jolly was unable to speak. Then, tight-lipped, he said, 'Leave the room, Leticia – at once!'

There was an awkward silence as Letty delicately wiped her mouth with her napkin and then got slowly to her feet. Her spiteful gaze turned on Ella. 'You would have married Anthony if he'd asked you, do you deny that?'

Ella stared the girl down. 'My marriage to your father is an honourable one. If we are going to be blunt, I can assure you I was still a maid when I went to my marriage bed.'

Jolly reached out his hand and covered hers. 'Don't be bothered by all this nonsense, my dear. I know what sort of woman you are and my daughter's vile tongue will not change my love for you.'

Beaten, if only for the moment, Letty left the room and Ella sighed with relief. For a few moments there was silence in the dining room, and then Jolly rang the bell for the maid. 'Well, I can only apologize for my daughter's dreadful manners and offer you a drink of my best cognac, Anthony,' he said.

But the evening was ruined and Ella was not surprised when Anthony got to his feet. 'If you'll excuse me, I should be running along. Perhaps we can talk more tomorrow about the business.' He held out his hand and Jolly, to Ella's relief, shook it firmly.

'Tomorrow, then.'

When Anthony was gone, Ella looked at her husband. 'I'm sorry about all that, Jolly. I've never been anything but a good and faithful wife.'

'I know that,' Jolly said heavily. 'But you didn't deny that you would have married him if he'd asked you.'

'But I was young and innocent then. How did I know anything about love? Anthony is handsome and charming, and like all the other women I was taken with him. But it's you I married, Jolly, and I'm having your child and that makes me very happy. Please drop the subject. But from now on be aware that Letty resents me. I've tried to win her friendship but I've failed.'

'Do you love me, Helena?'

'Of course I love you.' And she did, in a way. She would give him all the love and attention that was his due. 'Let's go to bed.' She held out her hand to him, and after the slightest hesitation, Jolly took it. But a seed of doubt had been planted in his mind that night, and it might never go away.

CHAPTER TWENTY

Kathleen stood on the stage behind the heavy curtain, excited by the buzz of voices in the theatre. It was all so familiar to her: the smell of good cigars mingled with fine perfume had been part of her life for so long. But now it was different: she would be opening the show, 'warming the audience up', and for a moment her nerves got the better of her.

'All right, Kathleen?' Anthony stood beside her, looking down at her with an understanding smile. 'It's not so bad once you're out there in front of the audience. And isn't this what you always wanted?'

'To be sure it is. But what if I fail out there? What if I'm booed by the crowd? Perhaps I only imagine I've got talent.'

'That's a chance every artiste takes, Kathleen. Have faith in yourself, believe you can please the crowds, just like you did when you took part in the competition. Remember how the audience cheered until you came back on stage again?'

Kathleen felt the hard knot inside her begin to relax. 'Well, all I can do is give of my best.'

'That's the spirit.' Anthony patted her shoulder. 'Hold your head high and open your throat and let that mellow voice come out. You've got the talent, Kathleen. All you need is the confidence and that will come with experience.' He paused. 'Now go and get some rouge on those pale cheeks and you'll feel better.'

Kathleen drew a long breath. Anthony was right – there was nothing for her to do now but get on with the show.

And as Anthony predicted, once she was ready for the performance she felt more cheerful. She was hidden now, her identity submerged beneath the make-up and the costume. True, the dress – emerald green and fastened at the side with a white flower – was worn and shabby, but no one in the audience would see that. All they would see was a young Irish girl singing her heart out.

She stared at herself in the dressing-room mirror. She thought she looked so different, even her friends wouldn't recognize her. But she was wrong.

'You look lovely, Kathleen. A real star.'

Kathleen saw the smiling face of her friend reflected in the mirror. 'Ella! Sure 'tis lovely to see you! Are you staying for the performance?'

'You didn't think I'd miss your first night, did

you?' Ella took Kathleen's hands. 'I'm afraid to hug you. Dressed up in all your finery you look so . . . well, so professional. You're going to wow the audience tonight and I'll be in our favourite spot in the wings, watching you.'

Kathleen's insides turned over with fear. Her legs were suddenly weak and she gripped Ella's hands tightly. 'I don't think I can do it. I can't go on, Ella – I'll let all of you down, I know I will.'

'First-night nerves,' Ella said at once. 'Even the best performers get them. We've seen stars sick with stage fright, haven't we?'

A chord of the opening music filled the silence and suddenly Kathleen straightened her shoulders. She was a performer; she would do her very best to please the audience.

Ella came with her to the wings and Kathleen watched as the heavy curtains glided back, revealing the stage with its painted backdrop of a park, and artificial trees strategically placed around rustic benches. She walked out on to the stage and was blinded by the footlights. She blinked as she tried desperately to remember the song she was going to sing. Of course, it was 'Parks Were Made For Lovers' – she'd been rehearsing it all week.

Someone began to clap and Kathleen knew it was Ella, urging her on. She struck a pose, her hand on her hip and her leg revealed through the clipped-up skirt of her dress. She looked like a music-hall entertainer; now she must play the part as best she could.

The musicians struck up the opening chords and, after a moment's hesitation, Kathleen began to sing. Her voice surprised her – it was strong and tuneful and seemed to fill the theatre, soaring high into the gods. Soon Kathleen had the courage to move across the stage, staring up into the boxes, smiling, flirting with the audience, strutting as she'd seen the best performers do. And when the song came to its bawdy conclusion, Kathleen turned her back on the audience and flipped up her skirt to show her frilled knickers.

There was a moment's silence. And then the theatre became filled with the sound she'd always longed to hear: hands clapping, feet stamping as the audience called for another rendering of 'Parks Were Made For Lovers'.

At the end of the encore, Anthony had to come to her side and take her hand to get her off the stage. And then she stood in the wings, being hugged by Anthony, with the sound of the audience calling for more ringing in her ears.

'You did it, Kath!' Ella appeared from out of the gloom, her face shining. 'I've never heard you in better voice. You're a real performer now – no more scrubbing floors for you, my girl.'

In the dressing room, Doris was waiting with a bottle of wine. She was smiling broadly. 'I'm so proud of you, Kathleen,' she said. 'Come and sit down and be treated like a star, because that's what you'll be in no time at all.'

Kathleen felt dazed as she re-lived the appreciation of the audience, the way her head had buzzed as though she had somehow come out of her own skin and taken on that of someone else. Someone confident, strong, willing to take on the audience and win them over.

She sank into a chair and took the brimming glass from Doris, and as she drank she knew she'd changed for ever. Gone was the poor Irish girl living like a shadow in the theatre. She was now becoming part of it, a real, honest-to-God performer.

Doris held the bottle out to refill Kathleen's glass, but Kathleen shook her head. 'Doris, know what I'd really like?'

'No, but I'm sure you're just dying to tell me.'

'Can we go down to the kitchen and have a nice cup of tea? It's thirsty work being a star!'

It was early afternoon as Ella made her way through the theatre to the office upstairs. She hesitated outside the door: Anthony was working in there and Ella wasn't sure how she would react to him. Since that disastrous dinner he'd been polite but distant with her, and her heart ached to think of what might have been if things had been different.

She opened the door and stepped inside. 'Good afternoon, Anthony.' She smiled as she looked down at him. He was seated at the desk, his head in his hands, but he looked up quickly when he heard her voice.

'Ella, what can I do for you?' His voice was formal and Ella felt her heart sink.

She went closer to him and rested her hand on his shoulder. 'Anthony, can't we still be friends?'

'Of course we can be friends – we can never be anything else, can we?' he said bitterly.

Ella sat opposite him and stifled the desire to reach out and touch his hair. He was lost to her now, nothing more than a colleague, and his tone was warning her to keep her place.

'Are the audience numbers good?' Ella asked, careful to keep her voice from shaking.

'They certainly are. Kathleen is a big draw. She's only been performing for a week and already she's enchanted the audience. At this rate we'll have to put her higher up on the bill.'

'She'll be thrilled with that.' Ella forced the words from between stiff lips. This was getting her nowhere: she and Anthony might be complete strangers for all the contact they were making.

'Is your husband coming in tonight?' Anthony was the first to break the uncomfortable silence.

'Yes, Jolly will be here as soon as he can. I think he wants to go over the plans for next week's acts with you.'

Again there was silence and Ella rose to her feet, despairing of ever breaking through Anthony's impersonal manner.

'Anthony, I have to tell you what I feel.' The words rushed out of her mouth before she could think. 'If only you'd kept in touch with me – if only you had come to see me sooner – I would have been free – we could have . . .' Her voice died away as Anthony looked at her coldly.

'I wrote to you regularly, you never replied.' He shrugged. 'In any case, you are married now. Nothing can change that, can it?'

'But I don't love him! I care for him, of course I do, but not in the way I cared for you. Anthony, I never received any letters from you. I thought you were never coming back.'

'So you took the first man who came along.'

'It wasn't like that! My mother was ill and I needed help, and the only one offering it was Jolly. I owe him everything. He's been so good, taking care of my mother as well as me. I don't know what I would have done without him.'

Anthony's face softened. 'I know it must have been hard for you to manage, I do understand that, but if only you had waited for me I would have taken care of you.'

He made to rise from his chair but just then the door opened and Jolly came in. He was in his element at the Palace now, and it showed. He beamed at Anthony.

'Little Kathleen is capturing the attention of the audiences, Anthony. I suggest we give her a better deal so that we can keep her here on a permanent basis.'

Anthony sank back into his seat. 'I agree, but she won't stay long, you mark my words. Soon she'll be tempted by offers from bigger theatres than ours – there will be no containing our little songbird.'

'Ah, well, do your best to keep her as long as possible. That will please you, won't it, Helena?' He put his arm around her shoulders and hugged her. 'She's looking well, isn't she, this wife of mine? She carries her impending motherhood well. I think it's going to be a boy.'

Ella could see by Anthony's set expression that any softening in his attitude was wiped out by Jolly's mention of the baby.

'Ella looks very well,' he said stiffly. 'I'm very happy for you and I hope you have the son you long for.'

Jolly nodded, sensing the tension in the room. He took Ella's arm and led her to the door. 'Come along, my dear. I've invited Kathleen and Doris to join us for tea.'

As Ella allowed herself to be led out of the room, she met Anthony's eyes briefly and his cold gaze told her all she needed to know: he was no longer interested in hearing her excuses. She forced back the tears. She had made a choice when she married Jolly: she had promised to be a good and faithful wife, and in spite of her love for Anthony she would hold true to her vows, however much pain it cost her.

As Kathleen helped Doris into the hansom cab, excitement bubbled inside her. Of course she wanted to see Ella, to chat to her, but the real thrill was that she was being invited as a person in her own right, not just a cleaner but a real professional performer.

She was wearing her new outfit, a fine coat of pure wool and beneath it a dress that hung down over her slender waist, touching fashionably on her hips.

'Sure an' isn't this the life, Doris?' She sat carefully back in the leather seat, hoping that her dress would not crease too much on the journey. 'We're going to tea with the boss.'

Doris's smile was smug. 'I've done it all before,' she said. 'In the days when I was top of the bill I went to champagne parties in all the best houses.'

'And now it's happening to me.' Kathleen clasped her hands together in sheer delight. 'I know it's only Mr Mortimer's house we're visiting, but it's a good start, to be sure.'

'Don't get above yourself,' Doris warned. 'Mr Mortimer is an important man in the community. And he's got the power to recommend you to other theatre managers. Don't write him off as "only Mr Mortimer".'

'Oh, I'm not,' Kathleen said quickly. 'I know Mr Mortimer gave me a real start in the business and sure won't I always be grateful to him for that?'

'I should think so too.' Mollified, Doris sat back in her seat. Looking at her, Kathleen could see echoes of the performer Doris had once been. Her hair was neatly combed and her face rouged and powdered. She looked so different from the Doris who drifted about the theatre making a display of dusting the fittings that Kathleen smiled.

Doris looked at her suspiciously. 'What you grinning at?'

'I'm smiling because you look so smart. I can't help thinking of all those months we spent at the Palace as cleaners, scrubbing the floors for a living. Look at us now – we've come a long way, Doris.'

The cab jerked to a halt outside the imposing front door of Mr Mortimer's house, and feeling every inch a fine lady, Kathleen stepped down into the drive. She helped Doris to negotiate the steps and then rang the bell, her heart beating fast with excitement.

The maid opened the door and gazed in wonder at the two fine ladies standing before her. Kathleen let Doris explain that they were expected – Doris could assume a fine, cultured voice if she chose – and then they stepped into the elegantly decorated hallway.

Kathleen sighed wonderingly. Was she really here or was she dreaming?

The maid took their coats and led them towards the sitting room, where they were greeted by Ella. Her eyes were bright as she welcomed them. She had done the right thing marrying Jolly Mortimer, Kathleen thought. Ella looked well and prosperous, and so she should. She was mistress of a fine house and need never work again. Life had been kind to the three of them, Kathleen decided, but she had come off best of all.

CHAPTER TWENTY-ONE

Ella sat at the back of the theatre watching her dear friend sing her heart out on the brilliantly lit stage. Kathleen had gained in confidence over the past few months and now she was as good as any performer who had graced the boards of the Palace theatre.

Ella moved a little to accommodate her now full waistline. Her slim figure had given way to a roundness of her hips and breasts, and every day, even though she felt heavy and unattractive, Jolly seemed to love her more and more.

But Anthony had distanced himself from her and she couldn't even claim him as a friend now. He avoided her whenever possible and it hurt her deeply. She still felt a tug at her heartstrings as she remembered the hurt look in his eyes when he knew she had married Jolly. She could bear that, but what she couldn't take was his indifference to her.

Rising as quietly as possible, she made her way

out of the auditorium and into the network of passages that threaded through the large building; she wanted to be waiting in the wings to congratulate Kathleen when her performance was over.

It seemed a lifetime ago that she and Kathleen used to scrub these very passages. Their lives had changed so much since then. Now Kathleen was realizing her ambition to be a performer. And she? Well, she was a married woman, expecting her first child.

Ella reached the back stairs leading on to the stage and moved quietly to the cover of the wings, from where she could see Kathleen, her face flushed with happiness, trilling out the last notes of her song.

When the curtains swished across the stage, cutting off the audience from the performer, she intended to greet her friend. But before she could move, she felt rather than saw a figure slip past her. And then, in the full glare of the electric lights, she saw Anthony take Kathleen's hands and bend towards her as if he would kiss her.

Ella silently retraced her steps, her heart heavy. It had not taken Anthony long to turn his affections elsewhere. And yet, hadn't he believed the same of her when he had returned to Swansea to find her married?

She made her way to the theatre door and asked the doorman to call her a cab. She waited until she heard the rumble of wheels and the clip-clop of hooves outside before letting herself out into the evening chill.

When she arrived home all was quiet. Her mother would be asleep, resting under the influence of the medication the nurse regularly gave her, and the girls would be in their rooms. Ella stood for a moment, breathing in the silence, trying to forget the sight of Anthony and Kathleen standing so close together on the stage, unaware that anyone was watching their intimate moment.

She found Jolly in his study, leafing through details of new and experienced performers he wanted to hire. He rose at once when he saw her and kissed her soundly. 'I wish you wouldn't go out and about on your own, my dearest. Not in your delicate condition.'

'I'm perfectly healthy, Jolly, and I took a cab, so there's no need to worry about me.'

'But I do worry.' He rested a gentle hand on the swell of her stomach. 'You have a precious load in there, our baby, and I don't want anything to upset or distress you.'

Ella smiled. She was more likely to be distressed by events in her own home than in the theatre. Leticia was still hostile towards her and rejected all Ella's attempts to win her over. Fortunately the younger girls were not influenced by Leticia's attitude, and Mary, the youngest, was showing real happiness at the prospect of having a newborn baby in the house.

And then there was the constant worry about her mother. Selma was usually subdued by her medication, but now and again she became awkward and refused to swallow the pills the nurse gave her. At such times Ella felt overwhelmed with gratitude to Jolly for taking on the burden of her family.

She took his hand now from her stomach and kissed it. 'You are such a good man, Jolly. I owe you so much.' She only wished she could love him as he deserved to be loved, not as a father figure but as a husband. Perhaps love would grow from affection and respect.

'Come along, my dearest, we'll go into the drawing room and I'll ask Jenny to bring us a bite of supper.' He put his arm around her shoulder. 'I must look after you, my precious Helena.'

As she went with her husband into the elegant drawing room, Ella was struck yet again by the change in her circumstances. Only last year she had been a humble cleaner, and now here she was, living in the lap of luxury with a ready-made family all around her. She should be grateful and she was. Why then did this little voice keep whispering in her ear that if only she'd waited a while she might now be married to the man she really loved? And yet she knew that Anthony wouldn't have had the means to keep her and her mother in the comfort they now enjoyed. But was life all about comfort and compromise? It seemed so to her now.

Letty was seated near the window and Ella noticed her look of disapproval as she saw her father enter the room with his arm around his wife.

'I don't know how you can be so besotted, Father,' she said. 'You don't know how ridiculous you look. How can you make such a fool of yourself?' She was clearly in a bad mood, and warmed to her theme. 'Everybody is talking about you, don't you realize that? They say you were a fool to take on a cleaning woman for your wife, and to burden yourself with her mad mother into the bargain.'

'Please, Leticia, I'm not in the mood for an argument. You know perfectly well that I married Helena because I love her, and I'm honoured to have her for my wife.'

'But it's so unsuitable!' Leticia's face was twisted with spite. 'She doesn't even know the correct cutlery to use at the table. She treats the servants as though they were friends, she has no—'

'That's enough.' Jolly stood before his daughter and pointed to the door. 'Go to your room, my girl, and don't come out again until you have a civil tongue in your head.'

Ella sat down abruptly. How could she blame

the girl for her feelings when she shared them herself?

'Don't take any notice, my dear.' Jolly sat beside her and took her hand. 'She's a silly young girl and she doesn't know what really matters in life.'

Ella looked up at him. 'Do I embarrass you, Jolly? I mean when we have guests and I pick up the wrong fork, are you ashamed of me?'

He smiled. 'I'm the proudest man on earth to have you by my side, Helena. But if it bothers you, just watch what cutlery I use and follow me.' He touched her hand. 'It's not really important, my dear. The guests we have here are mostly artistic folk – actors, performers and the like. They are used to eating in lodging houses and don't give a fig for what cutlery they use.'

He touched her cheek. 'That reminds me: Anthony is calling over later for a nightcap with us and I do believe he's bringing your friend Kathleen. That will be nice for you, won't it?'

'Of course it will.' Ella forced a smile. 'I can tell Kathleen how wonderful she was on stage tonight.'

'She really has come on, that girl,' Jolly said. 'I don't think we'll be able to keep her to ourselves for much longer, though. Other theatre managers have got to hear of her and they all want to hire her.' He reached in his pocket and took out a letter. 'Here's one request for her from a manager in Bristol. I'm going to tell her about it tonight and let her make her own decision. I think that's the right thing to do.'

'Well, I'm glad for Kathleen,' Ella said. 'It's what she's always wanted and we can't think of holding her back.'

As she relaxed against the cushions, her feelings were mixed. Was Anthony's closeness to Kathleen that of a manager or was it more personal? Whatever it was, it had nothing to do with her, and yet the thought of Anthony holding Kathleen, kissing her, telling her he loved her was almost too much to bear. She sighed heavily and Jolly put his finger under her chin.

'Are you all right, my darling?'

'I'm feeling disgustingly healthy, Jolly.' She saw the relief in his face and, on an impulse, kissed his cheek. He lit up like a candle flaming in the breeze, and Ella clung to his hand as if she was drowning in a raging sea and Jolly was her only means of survival.

Kathleen was breathless as she took yet another bow before the appreciative audience. One curl of her red-gold hair had come loose from its pins and trailed becomingly over her forehead. She had no idea how lovely she looked; all she knew was that she had pleased her audience so much that they were calling for another song.

Kathleen glanced into the wings and saw

Anthony gesturing for her to give an encore. So she put her hands on her waist, thrust her leg through the gap in her skirt and gave a bawdy rendition of her special song about waiting for her lover in the park.

When at last she left the stage, Anthony put his arms around her and lifted her off her feet. 'You're wonderful, Kathleen! You're the best thing that's happened to the theatre in a very long time.'

She hugged him and planted a playful kiss on his cheek, and as she did so he turned his head and their lips met. She felt her heart miss a beat. This was no longer a game: Anthony was actually kissing her. Not the kiss of a friend, but the kiss of a lover.

At last he put her down and they looked at each other for a long moment.

'Come on, then, Kathleen. Let's go to my office and have a cup of Doris's tea, shall we?' Anthony said finally.

He was speaking in such a matter-of-fact way that Kathleen wondered whether she had imagined the warmth of his lips on hers. She followed him to the office and sank into a chair. Doris came in a few minutes later, followed by a stagehand carrying a laden tray.

'Thanks for your help, darling boy,' Doris said breathlessly. 'And please, darling, close the door behind you.'

As Doris sat down, Kathleen saw lines of weariness on her face. 'I swear that stove in the kitchen gets moodier by the day,' Doris declared. 'It took so long to boil the kettle I thought we'd never have a cup of tea.' Her eagle eyes rested on Kathleen. 'What are you looking so flushed about, Madam? Not letting the applause go to your head, are you?'

'Sure and why would I?' Kathleen said quickly. 'I'm that used to it by now I take it all in my stride.' She didn't say that her colour had more to do with Anthony lifting her off her feet and kissing her soundly than the reception she'd received from the audience.

'Oh, I forget to mention it.' Anthony sank into his leather chair and draped one leg over the arm. He looked so handsome, so in charge of everything, that Kathleen felt love for him beat in every pore. When had this happened? When had he changed from a friend into a man she could spend her life worshipping?

'Forgot to mention what?' She hoped her voice sounded normal.

'Mr Mortimer has asked us to call in for a nightcap before we go home. Do you feel up to it, Kathleen?'

Kathleen felt a thrill run through her. The prospect of going anywhere with Anthony pleased her more than she could say. 'Sounds lovely,' she said. 'Sure I find it hard to sleep after a performance, and maybe a little drink will settle me down.'

'I don't suppose I'm invited?' Doris asked sadly.

Anthony smiled at her. 'I'm sure you can come along, Jolly won't mind. What do you think, Kathleen?'

Kathleen struggled to hide her disappointment. She'd been looking forward to being alone with Anthony in the intimacy of the cab, of travelling home with him at the end of the evening. 'No, Mr Mortimer is such a nice man, he would have asked you too if he'd thought of it, Doris.' She put down her cup. 'I'd better go and get changed,' she said, rubbing her fingers on her cheeks. 'And to be sure I can't go out wearing all this greasepaint.'

'I'll come and help you.' Doris's eyes were bright. 'The sooner we get you ready, the sooner we can go to see Ella.'

Kathleen glanced back as she reached the door. Anthony lifted his hand and touched it to his brow as if saluting her, and suddenly Kathleen felt as if she was surrounded by a rainbow.

Kathleen would never get used to the luxury of Mr Mortimer's grand house. As the maid took the fur cape she'd borrowed from the costumes room she looked round at the deep carpets and the rich polished furniture, and vowed that one day she'd have a house just like this.

Mr Mortimer greeted them like old friends and Kathleen made sure she was seated next to Anthony on the large comfortable sofa. Sitting quietly in the corner was Leticia Mortimer, Jolly's eldest daughter. She was staring at Anthony with wide eyes and it didn't take Kathleen long to realize the girl imagined herself attracted to him.

The maid poured the drinks and then left the room, and Kathleen saw Mr Mortimer produce a letter from his pocket. She sensed that something momentous was about to happen.

'Kathleen, my dear,' he said, 'I've got a request here from the manager of the Bristol Music Hall. He wants you to be top of the bill in his theatre for a run of six weeks. It goes without saying that we'd all miss you, but the decision must be yours.'

He handed her the letter and she sat staring at the bold writing, her heart beating swiftly with excitement. 'Jesus, Mary and Joseph, this is such a great chance! Oh, Mr Mortimer,' she said, 'I don't know what to say.'

She turned to Ella. 'What would you do? Tell me as a friend.'

'It's a great opportunity,' Ella said. 'You will be making a name for yourself in Bristol and, who knows, it might lead to a London appearance. I don't think you can turn it down.'

'But I'd have to leave you all,' Kathleen said. 'I'd be with strangers in Bristol. And yet, as you say, it's a great opportunity.' She handed Anthony the letter and he read it quickly.

'You must accept this offer,' he said at once. 'I can find someone to fill in for you for six weeks and then, hopefully, you'll be back with us.'

'Ah, but we must recognize that once Kathleen appears in Bristol, other managers from other towns are going to want her,' Jolly said. 'I don't think we can keep you to ourselves indefinitely, Kathleen. But we'll be glad if you grace us with your performance when you can.'

Kathleen had wanted Anthony to beg her to stay, but he was too honourable for that. He would put her career first, whatever it cost him.

Leticia spoke for the first time. 'I think you would have a wonderful time in Bristol,' she said. 'Meeting new people, working with big names. I don't know how you can hesitate.'

Kathleen saw through the girl's words at once. She liked Anthony and she wanted Kathleen out of the way so she could claim his attention for herself. For such a young girl she was remarkably clever and cunning. But still, Leticia was just that – a young girl, and in all probability Anthony saw her as a precocious child.

'Let me think about it, at least for tonight,' Kathleen said at last. 'Sure I'm flattered at the request but I don't know if I'm brave enough to launch out on my own just yet.'

'You've got to be brave,' Doris said, leaning forward eagerly. 'I know it can be lonely being on the road but it's the only way to further your career. In any case, you'll be found good lodgings, doubtless with a theatrical family, and you'll soon make friends with the other performers.'

'I know.' Kathleen swallowed hard and handed the letter back to Jolly. 'I'll give you my decision in the morning, if that's all right.'

As she leaned back on the sofa, Anthony put his hand over hers in a gesture of warmth. Kathleen smiled at him gratefully, her feelings so mixed she couldn't think straight. All she knew was that this was one of the most important nights of her life and she must relish it.

CHAPTER TWENTY-TWO

Selma stared around the room with a feeling of unease. She felt she was in prison. In her lucid moments she knew that she was losing control of her mind and that the lock on the door was for her own protection, but sometimes she had the urge to kick the door and scream to be let out.

She sat on the bed, picking at the fringe on the edge of the quilt, and then looked up hopefully as the key was turned in the door. Ella came into the room and Selma rushed forward and flung herself into her daughter's arms.

'It's all right, Mother,' Ella said. 'Nurse Carmel has only left you for a few minutes to bring your tea. I've come to keep you company.'

Selma looked at her daughter. She was so different from the old Helena who had come home from scrubbing floors at the theatre in an old sacking apron and with her hands all chapped and sore. Now her hands were soft and white and she was dressed in fine clothes. And she was so

266

big. Helena was expecting a baby, that was it. Why didn't her daughter tell her the good news?

'Sit down, Ma,' Ella said gently.

Selma looked at her sharply. 'Don't call me that. You know your father doesn't like it.'

A look of distress came over Ella's face and Selma wondered what she had said wrong. 'What is it, Helena? Why are you so upset?'

'Father is dead. Everything's changed.'

'I know.' Selma looked around the room. It was comfortably furnished with a bed and table and chair, but where was she? Not in the house where she'd lived with her husband and child. A bout of panic seized her and she clung to her daughter, holding on to her dress in sheer desperation.

'Where are we, Helena? I don't know this place.'

'It's all right, Ma,' Helena said. 'I'm married now to Jolly Mortimer, remember? We're living with Jolly in his house.'

'Where's Arthur?' Selma was worried. Her husband would be expecting his food to be on the table when he came home from the tin-plate works.

'Father passed away – he had an accident. Try to remember.'

Selma put her hands over her ears; the reality was so painful she didn't think she could bear it. She sank down on the bed and looked up appealingly at her daughter. 'I'm quite mad, aren't I?'

'No, Mother.' Helena spoke quickly, too quickly. 'You're not well, that's all. You'll be better when you've had time to rest and recuperate.'

Weary now, Selma lay back against the pillows. She realized there were times when she slipped into a confused world populated by shadowy figures. And yet now, in this moment of clear-headedness, she wished to be back there in that shadowy world where it didn't hurt so much.

'Your poor father was scalded to death, wasn't he? They brought him home to me and when I looked at him I didn't recognize him. And money – we didn't have any – we had to leave our home and that's when I started to go mad.'

Helena sat beside her and took her hand. 'It's all right, Mother, I'm looking after you. You're safe here with me and Jolly.'

The door opened and Nurse Carmel came into the room, her starched apron rustling as she moved.

'Mother seems a little better,' Helena said to the nurse. 'Could she be coming back to us?'

The nurse shook her head. 'It's temporary, my dear. She'll never come back to us, not as she was.' She held out some pills. 'Take these, Mrs Burton. You'll soon be feeling fine again.'

Selma took the pills but kept them in the corner of her mouth. She knew the nurse was

268

fooling her: she wouldn't feel better, she would feel sleepy and would drift away into a world of nightmares and ghosts. She closed her eyes and pretended to sleep, and dimly she heard the silvery whisper of the nurse's voice as she spoke to Helena.

They left the room together and Selma spat the pills into her hand. She was never going to be right, that's what the nurse said, wasn't it? Well, she wouldn't live out the rest of her life as a burden to her daughter. Helena was settled now with a good man to look after her. Selma had done her job, and now it was time to go to her husband in whatever heaven he believed in.

'I'll have to go to Bristol, sure I know that.' Kathleen looked at Anthony as though expecting him to argue with her. 'It's too good a chance to miss out on, don't you think?'

Anthony smiled at her from his comfortable seat in front of Doris's cheerful fire. 'It's your decision, Kath. No one can tell you what to do, isn't that right, Doris?'

'Aye, it's right enough,' Doris agreed. 'Look, Kathleen, no one says it's easy to go to a strange place where you don't know a single soul, but that's the business you're in now, girl.'

'Will you come to see me, both of you?' Kathleen's voice was wistful. 'It wouldn't be so bad if I could see a familiar face in the audience.'

'Of course we'll come and see you,' Anthony said. 'Look, I'll even take you over to Bristol myself if it will make you feel better.'

Kathleen's heart warmed. Anthony really believed that she would be a success and that meant the world to her. She took his hand. 'Thank you for everything,' she said. 'I wouldn't have had the courage to go on the stage at all if it hadn't been for you believing in me. You too, Doris.'

'We'd better let Jolly know your decision as soon as possible,' Anthony said. 'He'll be sorry to lose you, even for a few weeks.'

'Well, I'll be back, don't worry about that. The Palace is my home, it's where I started to make my name.'

'You'll go far and wide,' Doris said dreamily. 'You'll be known all over London before too long.'

'Sure an' isn't that my dream, Doris,' Kathleen replied. 'I'm so excited, I can't wait to talk to Ella about it. Let's call over there again tonight. I'm sure Mr Mortimer won't mind.'

'All right,' Anthony said. 'We'll pop over for a drink after dinner.'

Kathleen clasped her hands together. She could hardly believe what was happening to her. She'd had a good run at the Palace, and now other theatre managers were sitting up and taking notice. 'It's a dream come true,' she said softly.

Doris touched her arm. 'Now don't start getting above yourself,' she said sternly. 'There's more to being a performer than pleasing the audiences. It means getting up early to practise, it means late nights, and there will be times when you have to go on stage feeling sick as a dog and not let the audience know it. Your feet will ache, and on the nights when you don't perform so well your heart will ache, and that's much worse.'

'I know,' Kathleen said. She watched as Anthony got to his feet and stood before the fire. 'You're not going, are you?' she asked.

Anthony shook his head. 'I'm just stretching my legs. I was even thinking of offering to make you a cup of tea.'

'Forget the tea,' Doris said. 'This is a special occasion. Now that Kathleen's made up her mind to go to Bristol I'm going to open a bottle of brandy. How's that suit you?'

Anthony sat down again and stretched out his long legs. 'That's a damn fine idea, Doris,' he declared. 'A drop of brandy will go down very well.' He smiled and reached over to take Kathleen's hand. 'We'll toast your future,' he said. 'I hope it brings all the luck and success you deserve.'

She allowed her fingers to linger in his and a bubble of happiness brought tears to her eyes. Right at this moment, she felt as though she had the world at her feet and she was going to enjoy every moment of it.

'What is it? You seem upset, my dear.' Jolly looked anxiously at his wife. She was even more beautiful now, with her pregnancy well advanced. Her dark hair was glossy and her cheeks were rosy, but her eyes, those beautiful eyes, were full of sadness.

'It's Mother,' she said. 'Some days she's almost back to normal and I worry about her being shut in that room looking at the same four walls all the time. Couldn't we bring her down to dinner tonight? There'll only be you and me and the girls.'

'What does the nurse say about it?' Jolly wasn't too sure about exposing his daughters to the strangeness of Helena's mother. Leticia was already frightened of her.

'I haven't talked it over with her,' Ella said. 'But Mother seemed more herself today and perhaps a bit of company will do her good.'

Jolly could refuse his beautiful wife nothing. 'Very well, my dear, we'll give it a try. But we'll have Nurse Carmel eat dinner with us as well. Then she can keep an eye on things.'

'I'll go and tell Mother right away.' Ella was as excited as a girl and Jolly touched her hand tenderly.

'Well, don't wear yourself out running up and

down the stairs. You have to look after yourself, my dearest.'

'I feel wonderful, Jolly. I've never been healthier, don't you worry about me. And as for Mother, she's been so good today, she's quite like her old self, whatever Nurse Carmel says.'

As Jolly watched her leave the room the smile left his face. He knew that Selma's mind was too far gone into confusion and sickness for her to make any real recovery. Her good times would be transient, both the nurse and the doctor had explained it all to him, and yet he hadn't the heart to throw cold water on Helena's feelings of hope.

Later, though, when they were sitting down to dinner, he could see for himself that Selma was better than she'd been in a long while. She sat quietly beside her nurse and seemed to be paying attention to the conversation, even making a comment occasionally, and Jolly hoped that the evening would pass without incident.

Just as they finished the last course, the maid came into the room and bobbed a curtsey. ''Scuse me, Sir. There's folk from the theatre come to see you.'

Jolly put down his napkin. 'Show them into the drawing room and tell them I'll be there in just a moment.' He turned to Ella. 'You go and join our guests in the drawing room, my dearest. Take Letty with you. And perhaps your mother would like to retire for the night.'

'Please let me stay up just a bit longer,' Selma said quickly.

Jolly shrugged, helpless in the face of such an entreaty.

'Go and see to your visitors,' Selma said. 'I want to dab some rouge on my cheeks.' Her eyes were clear and she seemed completely lucid. Jolly nodded to her. He left her in the hall – there seemed nothing else he could do.

Jolly greeted Anthony in the drawing room and smiled to see Helena and Kathleen hugging each other warmly, while Doris stood by dabbing her eyes with a scrap of lace. 'Good evening,' he said, smiling. 'This is an unexpected pleasure. I do hope you're not bringing me bad news.'

It was Anthony who spoke. 'Kathleen's decided to accept the offer from Bristol. It's such a good chance for her, as you yourself pointed out.'

Jolly gestured for Anthony to sit down and smiled at Kathleen. 'I suppose I'll have to let you go, then.'

Kathleen's red hair clung becomingly round her face, but she was looking at him anxiously. 'Are you sure it's all right?'

'Of course you must go – but only on condition that you come straight back to the Palace once you're finished in Bristol.'

'Sure you won't be able to keep me away.' Kathleen's eyes were suddenly bright with excitement. 'I look on the Palace as my home, so I do.'

'I think this calls for a toast.' Jolly smiled. 'Though by the look of Kathleen's shining eyes you three have begun celebrating already.'

Jolly was just about to ring for the maid when he heard Nurse Carmel calling from the hallway. 'Excuse me a moment,' he said.

Ella was on her feet and out of the door before he could stop her. Jolly could see at once that something was badly wrong: his daughters were huddled in a silent group on the stairs, as if afraid to speak. He went to Ella's side at once. 'What on earth's the matter?'

'Mother's gone. She's just vanished into the darkness all alone.'

'I just slipped upstairs to fetch Mrs Burton's pills,' Nurse Carmel said defensively. 'I wasn't gone for more than a few minutes.'

'It's all right, no one is blaming you,' Ella said. 'It's all my fault for having Mother downstairs for the evening.'

'Now be calm, my dearest,' Jolly said. 'I'll search the gardens. She can't have gone far – not in just a few minutes. You go back to the drawing room and try not to worry.'

Ella returned reluctantly to the drawing room and Jolly sighed. The evening had promised to be a pleasant one and now everything had gone wrong. Kathleen was leaving them, if only for a few weeks, and if that wasn't bad enough, now Selma had upset Helena. He must organize a search party at once.

It was misty in the garden; a haze drifted through the trees like ghosts rising from the grave. Selma heard Arthur calling to her. 'See?' she said. 'He's not dead, he just had to go away for a little while.' Unaware of the dew soaking into her indoor shoes, she made her way to where he was waiting for her.

There before her was the lily pond, but she didn't see it. All she could see was Arthur's hand waving imperiously, telling her to hurry up. She didn't feel the cold of the water, not even when it closed over her head. She was taking Arthur's hand and as she sank into the swaying reeds she felt she was finding peace at last.

CHAPTER TWENTY-THREE

Ella sat up in bed and brushed her hair away from her face. It was early morning and Jolly was still asleep at her side. It was two months now since her mother had gone out into the night and drowned herself in the lily pond, and although everyone told her it was a happy release for Selma, Ella couldn't help blaming herself. If she hadn't insisted on her mother coming downstairs to dinner that night, Selma would still be alive.

Jolly stirred and smiled his sweet morning smile at her. Ella felt a pang of affection for him. He sat up and ran his hand through his tangled hair. 'Good morning, dearest. How are you feeling today?'

'I'm well,' Ella said reassuringly. And she was well. Her pregnancy was proceeding smoothly, according to the doctor. 'I'm not made of china, I'm a healthy young woman, so don't worry about me. All you need worry about is the theatre.'

'Talking about the theatre, I must confess I'm

glad to have Kathleen back,' Jolly said. 'She's singing for us for the first time tonight since she went away. She's such a draw, the crowds absolutely adore her. I think Anthony's been secretly pining for her too – it looks as though those two are going to make a match of it.'

Ella's heart plummeted as she thought of Anthony, with his dashing looks and his charming smile. Yet her love for him went deeper than mere appearances: she loved the essence of him, the way he used to look at her when he walked her home from the theatre, the feel of his hand holding hers. But she must put such disloyal thoughts out of her mind. Anthony must make something of his own life without her.

At breakfast, Ella looked round the table at Jolly's daughters. They had all been subdued since the night Selma had died; even Letty was kinder to her now. Jolly was reading his paper as usual, ignoring the plate of hot food the maid put before him.

'Jolly,' Ella chided, 'eat your breakfast before it gets cold.'

'Yes, I will, my dearest, in just a minute.' He folded the paper and picked up his knife and fork. 'I was just reading the reviews of the show in the *Bristol Post*. It seems our Kathleen made quite an impression – they want her to return as soon as possible.' He smiled. 'We have a little gem there – I'm glad we found her first.'

'I think it was she who found us.' Ella smiled back. 'Kathleen was always singing, even when we were scrubbing the floors of the Palace.'

She saw Letty frown. The girl hated any reference to Ella's former life; she still felt her father had married beneath him and in a way she was right. Tactfully, Ella changed the subject. 'How are you doing at your lessons, girls?'

Mary frowned. 'I've got sums today. I hate sums. I can't never get the answers right.'

'You have to know your arithmetic,' Letty said sternly. 'And your English too. Those subjects are so important.'

'Well, I don't think so,' Mary retorted. 'I mean to marry a rich man who'll keep me so that I don't have to work at any silly old lessons.' She beamed at Ella. 'That's what you did, isn't it?'

Suddenly the room was wrapped in a thick silence. Ella flushed. Mary had spoken the truth, as children do. She had married Jolly for his money.

She was glad when breakfast was over and the children had gone to their lessons. She looked at Jolly and after a moment's hesitation took his hand. 'You know I have the highest regard for you, Jolly. I care for you deeply and I'm grateful that you are such a good husband.'

'But you can't say the word "love", can you, Helena?'

'Love can grow,' she said quickly. 'It's mutual

279

respect and friendship that form the basis of a good marriage – and we do have a good marriage, Jolly.' She smoothed her dress over her swollen stomach. 'This is the proof, wouldn't you say?'

He smiled and the lines on his face relaxed. 'Yes, of course it is, my dearest. Will you be all right if I go to the theatre for a few hours or shall I stay here with you?'

'You go,' Ella said. 'I told you, I'm feeling fine.'

'Are you sure? I know you are putting a brave face on things, but in your heart you are grieving for your mother and still blaming yourself for her death. Speak to Nurse Carmel about it – she'll tell you how Selma was beyond help. Her life was over long before she died.'

Ella wished Jolly would get rid of the nurse. He'd kept her on to look after her in her pregnancy, but she was a painful reminder of that awful night when Selma had walked out to her death.

'Just go, Jolly, you've got work to do.' She paused. 'Perhaps I'll come over to the theatre later and see Kathleen and Doris.' And hopefully catch a glimpse of Anthony.

Jolly looked concerned. 'Is that wise, dearest? After all, you're very near your time now.'

She kissed his cheek. 'Stop fussing over me, I'm all right. Now go to work before I get cross with you.'

When Jolly had left the house, Ella felt the silence wrap around her. She was not cut out to sit at home and do nothing. She wanted to work, to be at the theatre looking over the bookings, arranging new artistes with Jolly and Anthony. Anthony, her darling. No, not her darling any more, but Kathleen's by the look of it. Suddenly her life felt empty and hollow.

'Cheer up,' she said aloud. She must look to the future. Perhaps when the baby came things would be different. She would be busy then, fulfilled. But would she? Somehow she doubted it.

'It was wonderful of you to show me the reviews from Bristol, Jolly,' Kathleen said. They were sitting in the plush foyer of the Palace, a cup of coffee on the table before them. She smiled broadly. 'I didn't tell you, did I, that on my last night there I got a standing ovation.'

'And well deserved.' Anthony came up behind her and rested his hands on her shoulders. 'You were the tops, Kath.'

She blushed as her eyes met Anthony's. She was falling more deeply in love with him every day, and much as she loved her career, she knew she loved Anthony even more. Sometimes she could almost believe he loved her too, and yet deep down she knew he still cared for Ella – she could see it in his eyes when he looked at her. But Ella was far out of his reach now, married, expecting a child, settled comfortably in the plush life Jolly Mortimer had provided for her.

Could she stand to be second best in Anthony's life? Kathleen knew the answer: she could. She would take any scraps of affection that Anthony could offer her, and gladly.

'We've got a full house tonight,' Anthony said. 'Doris has just sold the last few tickets so you'd better be in fine fettle, my girl, we're all counting on you.'

Kathleen felt a sudden pang of nerves. 'I'll perform as I've never performed before,' she said with more confidence than she felt.

Jolly leaned over and touched her hand. 'Of course you will, Kathleen, you're a real professional. You're so good sometimes I forget how new you are to this whole experience.'

Kathleen blushed with pride, and yet the nerves were still there. What if she didn't do well on her first night back at the Palace? What if she let everyone down? It would be unthinkable.

Doris came into the foyer and sank into a chair alongside Kathleen. She looked well and happy and very elegant. It was clear she was pleased to be part of the team running the Palace, even though her role was a small one. 'Sell-out, then,' she said, leaning back happily against the cushion. 'What do you think of that, Kathleen?'

She rushed on without waiting for a reply. 'Even the gods will be full, you mark my words.'

Kathleen rubbed her hands together, feeling a sudden chill. Her head was aching and she wondered if she was coming down with a fever. She pushed the thought away – she would perform tonight, however sick she felt. She needed to recapture the attention of her audience after so many weeks away.

'I think I'll go to my dressing room and have a rest,' she said.

She was aware of Anthony's swift look of concern. 'What about your rehearsal? Are you all right, Kath?'

She flashed him a smile. 'Of course I'm all right – just a bit tired, that's all. I'll only rest for a little while and then I'll go and rehearse.'

She made her way along the familiar grey passageways to her dressing room, sank into a chair and put her hands over her face. She couldn't be ill, she mustn't be ill, she had work to do. She leaned back, closed her eyes, and in a moment she was asleep.

She woke abruptly to the sound of someone banging on the door. 'Kathleen!' It was Anthony. He pushed the door open and looked in at her. 'It's time to rehearse. We're all waiting for you and the pianist is moaning that he has a home to go to, even if we haven't.'

'Just give me a few minutes to tidy up.'

Kathleen's voice was thick with sleep and her legs wobbled when she stood up, but she smiled at Anthony, determined not to show how ill she felt.

A little while later, she made her way to the stage. It was in shadow – the footlights were not switched on – and a group of artistes stood talking together in the wings. The girls of the high-wire troupe in their tights and skimpy vests were dusting chalk from their hands. It was all so normal and yet she was afraid to go on the stage.

She made her way to where the pianist was tapping his fingers on his knees, impatient to begin.

'Sorry, Joe,' she said. 'I dozed off.'

He nodded and flexed his fingers before striking the keys with more force than was necessary. As soon as Kathleen began to sing, she knew she was not at her best. She missed a note and glanced apologetically at Joe. 'Can we begin again?'

Joe nodded wearily and Kathleen took a deep breath, forcing the air into her lungs. The second attempt was a little better, but her voice did not ring out across the stalls as it should have done. At last, she waved a hand at Joe, calling the rehearsal to a halt. 'You go home. I'll see you later,' she said as she turned to hurry back to her dressing room. It was a disaster – she was going to make a fool of herself tonight. She sat in front of her mirror and stared at her face as if seeing it for the first time. She was pale and there were shadows beneath her eyes: she would need an awful lot of make-up to look presentable.

The door opened and Doris came into the room. 'Not feeling too good? I've got just the pick-me-up for you, my girl.' She held a glass towards her. 'Don't look so doubtful, it will do you good.'

'What is it?'

'It's a remedy I've used for years: a little bit of honey, a drop of brandy and a splash of hot water. Take this, get some rest, then have another one before you go on stage and I guarantee you'll be as good as Marie Lloyd herself, you mark my words.'

Later, as Doris helped her to dress for the performance, Kathleen took the second drink and felt it run through her veins like fire. The heat of the brandy seemed to loosen her vocal chords and she prayed the effect would last until she'd completed her performance.

As she stood in the wings, she watched the dancers whirl on the now brightly lit stage and shivered. Any moment now, she would be out there alone with no one to depend on but herself.

The dancers twirled off the stage and drifted past her, whispering noisily. The curtains swished across the stage and Anthony stepped through them to address the audience.

'Our next act is one we've been waiting to

welcome back to the Palace,' he began. 'She sings like a bird and her charm is such that all who see her fall in love with her. Friends, I give you our very own Miss Kathleen and her now-famous rendition of "Parks Were Made For Lovers".'

And then she was alone on stage, feeling naked as the lights picked her out. She hesitated for a long moment and the audience looked at her expectantly. The brandy burned like fire in her stomach and, taking courage, Kathleen began to sing.

Her voice came out pure and strong, ringing around the auditorium and filling every corner, soaring to the gods with no effort at all. She performed her repertoire of bawdy songs, working the whole of the stage, gazing up at the rich folk in the boxes, then lifting her arms to the people in the circle and lastly to the gods.

Her final song was a sentimental one about a mother's love for her lost child. She'd sung it every night in Bristol, but never with such pathos. When the last notes died away there was silence, and then the clapping and stamping of feet began, and at last the audience rose from their seats, calling for more.

Kathleen stumbled her way off the stage and as Anthony reached out to hug her she collapsed into his arms and into oblivion.

CHAPTER TWENTY-FOUR

Kathleen opened her eyes to see the sun streaming in through the windows. She thought for a moment that she was in her digs in Bristol, but on looking round the room and seeing familiar objects realized she was in Doris's house. She tried to sit up, but she felt weak and faint and fell back against the pillows, wondering what was happening to her.

She lay quietly for a time, drifting in and out of sleep, and then she heard footsteps on the landing outside the bedroom. The door opened and Doris came in, carrying a tray.

'Oh, so you've come back to us at last!' Doris smiled and put the tray on the bedside table. 'You almost woke up when I looked in on you an hour ago so I took a chance and brought you some beef broth. I do hope you'll try to take some.'

Kathleen tried to speak, but only a croak came out. Doris waved her hand in disapproval. 'Don't try to talk. You've had a terrible fever and the doctor tells us it will take you a little while to get over it.'

Kathleen made an effort to speak again and a thin reedy sound came from her dry lips. 'What about the Palace? I should be there rehearsing, so I should.'

'Don't talk soft, girl. You're far too sick to think of performing. Don't worry about the Palace, it'll still be there when we're dead and gone.'

'But who's taken my place?'

'A very nice baritone called Tommy Dobson. Not the draw that you are, but he works well enough.'

'How long have I been sick?' Kathleen was finding it more difficult to talk now; her voice was little more than a whisper.

'Only about a week, girl. Take your time and give yourself a chance to get better. Pining over the theatre won't get you anywhere.'

Doris picked up the bowl of broth and sat beside the bed. 'Try to have some of this, Kathleen. It'll put the strength back into you.'

Kathleen dutifully supped a little of the broth, but she was so tired that just lifting her head was an effort and after a few minutes she waved the bowl away. Doris clucked her tongue in disapproval. She sighed and looked at the clock on the mantelpiece. 'I'd better be going,' she said.

'I've got to be at the theatre in case we have any last-minute ticket sales.'

Kathleen felt a pang of fear. She didn't like the idea of being left on her own.

Doris seemed to read her mind. 'Don't worry, Ella has been sending her nurse over to take care of you while I'm at work. Oh, and Anthony calls in between houses, so you won't be all alone.'

Kathleen's heart lifted. So Anthony had been keeping an eye on her – surely that meant he cared about her, if only a little?

After Doris left, Kathleen dozed again, only to be woken by the sound of voices coming from the landing. The nurse bustled in and looked approvingly at her. 'I can see you're on the mend,' she said, 'and you've got your visitor Mr Anthony here to see you, but first I'm going to give you a nice wash and then comb that unruly hair of yours.'

Kathleen put up with the nurse's ministrations impatiently, anxious for her to finish so that Anthony could come in. At last Nurse Carmel tucked the brush into her pocket and picked up the bowl.

'It's all right, Mr Anthony, you can come in now.'

He smiled when he saw that Kathleen was conscious and crossed the room quickly, taking her hands in his. 'Thank God you're on the mend, Kath, I've been so worried about you.'

She made an effort to smile, very aware that he was close to her. He looked so concerned, as if he really cared about her. 'How's the show going?' she croaked. 'Are you missing me?'

'We're all missing you,' Anthony said. 'We sold out after the first night when you made such an impression, but then once people knew you were not performing the sales fell off a bit.' He smiled. 'Never mind that, how are you feeling?'

She nodded her head. 'Better.' In truth she felt weak and ill, but she wouldn't admit it to Anthony – he looked worried enough as it was. She felt warmed by his concern and happy that he was holding her hand, but the precious moment was over all too soon: before long he was getting up from his chair and buttoning up his jacket, flinging a bright scarf around his neck, trapping some of his thick hair close to his face. He looked so handsome, so lovable, that Kathleen longed to reach up and kiss him.

'I'll call in tomorrow to check on you,' he said. 'But you are being so well looked after, and now you're over the worst of the fever I feel much happier about you.'

After he had left, Kathleen closed her eyes, examining Anthony's words. Did they mean he cared as a friend or was it more than that? At last she fell into an exhausted sleep, only to dream that Anthony was leading her up the aisle of a church that suddenly turned into the aisle between the seats in the theatre. When she awoke it was almost dark, the room only lit by the gas flame from the lamp near her bed. The house was silent – Doris must be asleep in her bed. Kathleen prayed for sleep to claim her again; she was impatient for tomorrow to come because then she would see Anthony again.

Ella moved slowly towards the window and stared out at the garden, but all she could see was a heavy darkness that seemed to close in on her, weighing down her spirits.

As she turned back into the warmth of the room her stomach felt heavy and burdensome and her back ached with a niggling pain. A wave of grief swept over her – suddenly she wanted her mother beside her. Selma could have reassured her, told her about childbirth, supported her in a way that only a mother could do. But Selma was gone now and Ella felt very alone.

Impatient with her thoughts, she moved restlessly to the desk and sat down, reaching for a piece of writing paper. Nurse Carmel had told her that Kathleen was improving, that she was fully conscious now and taking a little food. Ella wished she could visit her friend, but Jolly told her it was out of the question while Kathleen was so ill. Ella knew he was talking sense – she had her unborn baby to think of. Still, she could put her good wishes on paper and tomorrow the nurse could deliver her letter to Kathleen.

From upstairs she could hear the sound of the girls laughing as they got ready for bed. She wished she got on better with Jolly's daughters. It would have been good to laugh with them, to share their high spirits, but Letty's sharp tongue always spoilt the moment for her.

Ella looked at the clock: the second house at the Palace would have started by now. Jolly might stay to the end of the night, or if everything was running smoothly he would come home and she would be very happy to see him. Sometimes she felt like a bird in a golden cage, imprisoned by Jolly's love, and yet as her pregnancy advanced she was glad of his reassuring presence and unfailing good humour, and grateful for his ever-present wish to make her happy.

The writing paper was still blank and Ella took a deep breath and began to write. She told Kathleen that she was missing her and she would soon come to visit her. But the words seemed banal and empty and she scrunched the paper into a little ball and threw it on to the fire.

Ella sank into her chair and closed her eyes, wishing she could sleep. The hours seemed to drag by, but at last she heard the front door open and close. She sat up, expecting to see her husband, but it was Nurse Carmel who came into the room.

'A message for you, Mrs Mortimer. Kathleen hopes you'll visit her soon. She says she's lonely, but how can the girl be lonely when she's just woken out of her fever and in any case has company all the time?'

'Company?' Ella asked.

'Aye. Well, that old lady Doris is with her in the daytime, then there's me with her in the evenings, and Mr Anthony calls in between shows at the Palace. If you ask me, she's very lucky to get such attention. But then she thinks of herself as a star these days, I suppose.'

What was it about Nurse Carmel that got on Ella's nerves? Was it her bluntness, her close alliance with the girls, or was it just that she imagined the nurse thought her an unfit wife for such a well-to-do man as Jolly Mortimer?

'I'll go up to the girls,' Nurse Carmel said. 'I expect they've made a right mess of their bedrooms if that noise is anything to go by.'

There it was again – an implied criticism of Ella, but she ignored it. 'That would be a very good idea,' she said. 'Shall I ask Cook to bring your supper up to your room?'

The nurse nodded. 'I know my place, Mrs Mortimer.' Her tone indicated she knew it was not in the plush dining room with the master of the house.

Ella sighed as Nurse Carmel left the room; she seemed determined to be offended by every overture Ella made. It was daunting to think that this cold woman would be with her at her confinement and after the birth of the baby.

And then Ella was alone again. She looked at the clock: Jolly should be home by now. Suddenly she realized how much she would miss him if he was never to come home again. They had forged a bond between them: his great love for her was expressed constantly, and for her part she had vowed to be a good wife always.

'I'm happy to see you much improved.' Jolly sat beside Kathleen's bed and smiled at her. She still looked far from well: the flush of fever had gone and now she was pale, her eyes shadowed and her cheekbones prominent due to the weight she'd lost.

'She's looking much recovered, isn't she, Anthony?' he said brightly and the young man nodded, his hand reaching out to hold Kathleen's.

'She's got to take things easy for a while,' Anthony said. 'But we'll soon have her back on stage, enchanting the crowds the way she always did.'

'Don't talk about me as if I'm not here.' Kathleen's voice was little more than a hoarse whisper.

'Throat still sore?' Jolly asked and Kathleen nodded.

'Doris is going to bring me her special gargle – cures all but a broken leg, according to her.'

When she smiled she looked more like her old self, Jolly thought. Soon she would get the sparkle back in her eyes, her cheeks would fill out and she would be the vivacious Kathleen she'd always been.

'Well, it's about time I was getting back to my wife.' He patted Kathleen's arm. 'She'll be wondering where I am.'

He caught a glimpse of Anthony's naked misery before the young man forced a smile, and Jolly realized that the young man was still deeply in love with Ella.

'Is Ella keeping well?' Anthony's tone was polite, but he didn't meet Jolly's eyes. 'The baby is due quite soon, I understand?'

'Any day now,' Jolly said. 'And yes, Helena is fine and in good spirits. I expect she'll visit you soon, Kathleen, baby permitting.'

Kathleen nodded but didn't attempt to speak, lifting her hand in a gesture of farewell.

Jolly took his leave, hurried down the stairs and stepped out into the darkness. The moon slid from behind the clouds, sending a shaft of light across the pavement. As he walked briskly towards his home he was impatient to reassure himself that everything was all right with his wife and family.

After a few moments, he heard the soft scuffing noise of someone following close behind him. He lengthened his stride, but the sound of footfalls still pursued him. And then, before he could turn around, rough hands were grasping him, wrestling him to the ground. He felt fetid breath against his face and then a voice grated harshly in his ear.

'I want your takings from the theatre.'

Jolly struggled to see the face of his assailant, but the man had a scarf around his mouth. The words were followed by a punch in the stomach and Jolly gasped for air, trying to breathe through the pain. He was dragged to his feet and shaken like a rat. The man pushed him against the wall. 'You're coming with me,' he said harshly, half dragging Jolly along the empty streets.

The theatre was in darkness, the stage empty, the curtains closed. Jolly was being pushed towards the stairs. He hesitated and was rewarded with a blow to his kidneys.

'You know the way to your safe, don't you?' He was being pushed towards the stairs and as he stumbled the man dragged him upright. 'Don't fool with me, you bastard. I know you got money and I want it.'

In the office Jolly stood with his hands hanging

down at his sides. 'If you think I'm giving you any money, you can forget it,' he said. Another blow brought him to his knees.

'Look, let's do this the easy way,' the man said. 'Open the safe, otherwise I might have to drag that pretty wife of yours out of bed, or even those little girls of yours.'

Jolly knew then that he was beaten. He couldn't risk anything happening to his wife and family. He knelt on the floor and took the keys of the safe from his pocket. In the safe were several weeks' takings: money he needed to pay the artistes as well as his bills. He watched with hopelessness as the thief took the money and stuffed it into his pockets. Then a punch was delivered to the back of his head and Jolly slumped forward, his face against the floor. He heard footsteps running down the stairs, but it was a while before he could drag himself to his feet and out of the theatre into the dark.

He practically ran all the way home. This was the last time he would be alone, he vowed to himself. He'd hire a watchman, some burly chap who would fend off any ruffian. He wasn't going to take any more chances – the man who had struck tonight might well attack again.

The warmth of the house greeted him as Jolly stepped through the front door. The hall was well lit, the strategically placed lamps shedding a glow over the well-polished furniture. Helena was waiting up for him. She looked a little pale, but her smile was warm as she greeted him. She placed her hands on his shoulders and kissed both his cheeks. 'I'm so glad you're home, I was getting a little bit worried about you. Are you all right, Jolly? You've got a bruise on your forehead.' Her smile vanished. 'Was I right to be worried? Has something happened?'

'I had a fight with the scenery and the scenery won,' he said. He drew her close to him, very aware of her large belly pressing against him. He felt filled with pride – he had a lovely wife and a baby on the way; these were the important things in life, after all. But he'd needed the money the thief had taken from him. He'd spent much more on the opening of the theatre and on the performers than he'd ever anticipated. He'd borrowed from the bank, sure that he would repay the debt after a few months, but somehow it hadn't worked out that way. Perhaps he wasn't cut out to be a businessman, he thought worriedly; it might have been wiser to remain a well-paid manager at the tin-plate works.

'Are you sure nothing's wrong?' Ella asked. 'You're very late.'

'I went to see Kathleen.' He held Ella for a long moment before releasing her. 'She seems very much better now. Just a bit of a sore throat, that's all.' He had to protect Ella from the truth; if he told her that he'd been attacked she might be shocked and go into sudden labour.

He led her to a chair. 'You sit there for a minute. I'm going to say goodnight to the girls.'

Leticia and Charlotte shared a fair-sized bedroom at the front of the house overlooking the garden, while the twins and Mary shared a larger room at the back of the house. All of them except Letty were asleep.

Letty's face brightened when she saw him. She put down the book she was reading and scrambled out of bed. 'Papa, why are you so late?' She hugged him and pressed her head against his chest. He felt his heart fill with happiness and gratitude that he was home safely with the people he loved. No harm must come to them, however much it cost.

'Goodnight, my little chick.' He kissed Letty's head. 'Now back to bed, it's time you were asleep.'

As he retraced his footsteps back down the stairs, he tried to work out what he could do about the loss of the takings. He might have to borrow more from the bank; he would explain the situation to his staff and the cast – he was sure they would understand the delay in receiving their money.

Once Kathleen was back on stage they would

have a full house again and he would soon recoup his losses, but he must take care never to be in such a vulnerable position again. It was too bad when an honest man couldn't walk the streets in safety, but he'd learned his lesson. Now he must put on a smile so that his beloved wife would rest easy.

CHAPTER TWENTY-FIVE

Ella settled comfortably into the chair and smiled at Kathleen, happy to see her looking much better. 'Thank goodness you're up and about again, Kathleen. But you're still a little pale – how are you feeling?'

'I'm still a bit hoarse,' Kathleen said, 'but I'll live. Doris is looking after me well, her special gargle is working wonders. I'll soon be singing like a bird again.'

Doris came in with a tray on her arm and caught the last part of the conversation. 'It'll take a little while yet,' she warned. 'But the gargle will work. It is an old recipe that does a body more good than any of the modern muck they're peddling now.'

'I can't wait to get back on stage,' Kathleen said. 'I know I'm letting Jolly down, though the dear man never speaks a word of complaint.'

Ella could well believe it. Jolly never had a bad

word to say about anyone. She felt a rush of real affection for him.

The doorbell chimed and Doris smiled. 'I think I know who that is. We can't keep the man away these days, can we, Kath?'

Doris went to answer the door and Ella's heart missed a beat as she heard Anthony's melodious voice ring through the little hallway. He came into the room and his eyes met Ella's. It was he who looked away first.

Ella looked down at her hands, trying not to see the way Anthony kissed Kathleen's cheek as he greeted her warmly. It cut Ella to the quick to hear the tender note in his voice. 'You're looking so much better, Kath,' he said. 'We'll have you back on the stage in no time.'

'I hope so.' Kathleen held tightly on to Anthony's hand. With her gorgeous red hair clinging in little curls around her face, she looked very beautiful as she smiled up at him. 'I need to be out there in front of an audience again. I need it as much as I need the breath in my body.'

'Well, we've got a good list of artistes this week,' Anthony said. 'Though none of them can touch you for talent, Kath.'

Kathleen waved his compliment away. 'Who have you got?' she asked eagerly.

'We've got the Villions – you know, the acrobatic cyclists. We've had them before and they're a great draw.'

'Who else?' Kathleen's hands were clasped together now, the knuckles gleaming white. Ella could see that the Palace had become the whole world to Kathleen. Her eyes were alight and her cheeks were flushed pink as she waited for Anthony's reply.

'Let me think. There's Harry Raymond – he's a good comedian and he can dance the feet off anyone else. Oh, and for the finale we've got Rose Govetti, the dancer. There, what do you think of that?'

'It's all right,' Kathleen said, sinking back into her chair. 'They're all very good performers, but there are no big names this week, no real attraction.'

'You were going to be that.' Anthony leaned towards her and touched her cheek, and Ella steeled herself not to flinch as she watched them. Anthony and Kathleen were very close and she fought the pain of jealousy as she tried to be happy for them.

She felt a niggle of pain in the lower part of her back and became conscious of the largeness of her body. How could any man look at her with love? Except for Jolly; he loved her unconditionally.

'What about you, Ella?' Doris seemed to pick up on her feelings. 'Not long now before the little one comes. Are you excited? I bet Jolly can't wait.'

Ella wasn't sure how she felt. She wanted the baby, of course, but for the first time she wondered if she could deal with the responsibility of motherhood. She wasn't doing too well with Jolly's daughters: Letty still treated her as though she was an interloper and Ella didn't know how to deal with her hostility.

She became aware that the others were looking at her, waiting for her reply. 'I'm excited, but also apprehensive,' she said at last. 'I don't know how I'll cope once the baby comes.'

Doris's shrug was theatrical. 'Well, no good looking at us, girl. Kathleen and I don't know anything about having children.' Ella felt a pang of isolation; she seemed barred from being at one with her friends.

It was Anthony who saved the moment. 'You'll be a wonderful mother, Ella. I'm sure there's enough love in you for dozens of children, and in any case you'll have Jolly there to help you. He's a seasoned parent, he'll know what to do, so don't worry.'

He didn't realize that his every word was building a higher barrier between them. He was treating her as the wife of his employer, nothing more or less.

'I'm sure you're right,' she mumbled, relieved when the talk returned to theatre matters.

It was not long before the doorbell rang, announcing the arrival of Jolly. He would have come in the horse and trap; these days he seemed nervous of her being alone on the streets. She knew she should be grateful for his care, but somehow she felt stifled by it.

When he came into the room, he looked downcast and Ella looked up at him anxiously. 'Jolly, is everything all right? The girls . . . ?'

'The girls are well and happy, Helena, but I do have some bad news. Anthony, you've noticed nothing wrong in the office, have you?'

Anthony looked puzzled. 'What do you mean?'

Jolly shook his head. 'I tried to hide it from you. I wanted to put everything right myself, but the bank is refusing to lend any more money.'

'Why do we need more money?' Anthony asked. 'I know we operate on a shoestring, but the week's takings usually tide us over for the next week.'

'That's the trouble.' Jolly's shoulders sagged. 'I'm sorry I kept it from you, but I've been robbed and now I'm being blackmailed.'

'What are you saying, Jolly?' Ella said anxiously.

Jolly took her hand and squeezed it. 'I don't want to upset you unduly, my dearest, but these things are best out in the open. It's time to tell you all what's been going on.' He explained about the robbery, adding, 'The thief threatened to hurt you and the girls if I didn't give him the money, so I handed it over. I didn't know what else to do.'

305

'That's why you've taken on a nightwatch-man?' Anthony said.

Jolly took a deep breath. 'Yes, but it doesn't seem to have helped. Now I'm receiving threats in the post.'

'Look, Jolly, we have to go to the police,' Anthony said. 'This man must be brought to justice. I wish you'd told me earlier. We could have done something about it. I've got some money put aside, I'll put that into the theatre, we'll be all right.'

'You'd do that for me?' Jolly asked. Ella heard the catch in his throat and tightened her hand round his. He hung his head. 'But I couldn't accept a loan, I might not be able to repay it.' He paused. 'The bank people think I've mishandled the money. We'll have a hard job convincing them otherwise.'

'Leave it to me,' Anthony said quickly, 'and don't worry about the money. It's to help all of us – what would we do if the theatre closed?'

'It's so good of you, but I don't see how I can accept your generous offer.'

'You must,' Anthony insisted. 'And don't worry about paying it back. I'll manage.'

'Well, what about a partnership then, Anthony?' Jolly said. 'It would be a relief for me to hand over some of the responsibility for the maintenance and running of the Palace.'

The two men shook hands and Ella felt a

lump in her throat. Doris smiled and said, 'This calls for a glass of wine rather than a cup of tea.'

Suddenly Ella felt weary. All she wanted to do was to go home, lie on her bed and let sleep take away all her worries. She tried to enter into the spirit of celebration but somehow she didn't feel part of it all; she was just an onlooker at the theatre now, there was no role there for her. She was glad when Jolly noticed her silence and decided it was time to go home.

It was in the small hours of the night when the first pains came. Ella sat up in bed and clutched her abdomen, feeling suddenly afraid. She listened to Jolly's even breathing until another pain struck and then she shook his shoulder.

'Jolly,' she said, 'wake up! My time has come.'

He was awake at once. He scrambled out of bed and pulled on his dressing gown. 'I'll get the nurse,' he said, trying to hide his panic. 'Everything will be all right, don't worry.'

Nurse Carmel bustled into the room a few minutes later and took charge, and for once Ella was happy to see her. She had an air of professionalism about her that was reassuring.

'Let's just have a look to see how far things have progressed.' The nurse examined her and nodded in satisfaction. 'I think you'll be one of the lucky ones, you'll give birth easily. By morning there will be another addition to the Mortimer family.'

As the pains intensified and came more regularly, Ella didn't feel very lucky. If this was an easy birth, God save her from a difficult one. She wished her mother was there. Selma would have held her hand and murmured words of encouragement. She felt tears prick her eyes and Nurse Carmel gave her a brisk look.

'No need to cry,' she said. 'You're doing well, there will be no complications.'

The hours passed, and as the contractions intensified, to Ella's surprise, Nurse Carmel took her hand and spoke soothingly to her. 'There's a good little mother, then. Don't worry, you're doing just fine. The baby will be here before much longer. Just try to relax between the pains.'

Relaxation was the furthest thing from Ella's mind as her body struggled to give birth to her child. And then the pains changed, they became an urge to bear down. 'I think the baby is coming,' she gasped.

'Good, I can see the head crowning,' said Nurse Carmel. 'It won't be long now, my girl, so you just listen to me and do what I tell you.'

Ella wished Jolly was there with her, but husbands were always kept out of the way until everything was over and mother and baby were clean and neat, with no sign of the struggle that took place during childbirth.

'Right. Now, this is going to need a big push.' Nurse Carmel's voice was soft and steady. 'Just do your bit and it will all be over before you know it.'

Ella's body took charge. She felt the urgent need to push her child into the world, and nothing else mattered except that last effort to give birth. And abruptly, it was over. For a moment there was silence in the bedroom. Then the plaintive cry of her child shattered the silence, filling Ella's heart with happiness.

'You've got a fine healthy boy,' the nurse said in satisfaction, as though she had arranged the whole thing. 'Mr Mortimer will be so pleased.'

'Can he come and see me now?' Ella pleaded, but Nurse Carmel shook her head.

'We've a little work to do here first.' Efficiently she saw to the rest of the business of childbirth and then she carefully washed first Ella and then the baby. 'Out of bed and into the chair with you. Carefully now, this won't take a minute.'

She left the room to fetch some fresh bedding and returned with a smile on her face. 'Mr Mortimer is delighted to have a healthy son,' she said as she bustled around the bed.

'You didn't tell him?' Ella was swamped with disappointment. 'I wanted to tell him myself.'

'Doesn't matter who tells him, does it? Now back into that nice clean bed and thank your lucky stars that you've birthed your first child in comfort and safety.'

When Jolly came into the room he cupped her face in his hands. 'Are you well, my dearest?'

'Of course she's well,' Nurse Carmel broke in, in a tone that suggested she would accept nothing less than a healthy patient. 'She's young and strong enough to have lots of children.'

'He's a boy, Jolly.' Ella tried to ignore the nurse's comments. 'A boy – just as you wanted.'

Nurse Carmel shattered the intimacy of the moment. 'Here, Mr Mortimer, I'm sure you'd like to hold your son.'

Ella wished the nurse would leave them alone, but she bit her tongue and watched as Jolly cradled his son tenderly in his big arms.

'This is the happiest moment of my life,' he said. 'Thank you, Helena, for giving me a fine boy to add to my wonderful family.'

'Let me hold him,' Ella said, and Jolly carefully put the baby in her arms. As she looked down into the crumpled little face of her son, her heart melted. He was perfect, from his little shell-like nails to the dimples in his cheeks.

'He has his father's looks,' Nurse Carmel said, determined to get in on the picture. 'See, he has your eyes.'

Jolly shook his head. 'He's like Helena,' he

310

said. 'He has a fine strong jaw and a cloud of dark hair.' He touched his own receding hairline ruefully. 'He's the most perfect boy in all the world.'

The door was pushed wide and Letty came into the room. 'I heard that, Father,' she said. 'I don't suppose you'll care for us girls now you've got a son.'

Jolly immediately took her in his arms. 'My dear girl, you are very precious to me and of course I'll care for you always.'

After a moment, Letty disentangled herself from her father's arms. 'I'd better have a look at him, then.' She peered into Ella's arms and her face softened. 'Can I hold him?' she asked meekly.

Ella let her take the baby and Letty cradled him gently against her, touching his soft skin with the tip of her finger. 'He's lovely,' she said in awe. 'So perfect.'

Ella felt a pang of hope. Perhaps with the birth of the baby Letty's attitude towards her would soften. They might even become friends. But Letty's next words dispelled her hope at once.

'Don't think this makes any difference to us,' she said. 'You're not my mother and never will be.' She gave the baby to Ella and turned and left the room, and Ella felt tears spring to her eyes.

Jolly patted her arm. 'Don't worry, she'll come round in time.'

Ella let the nurse take the baby from her and lay back wearily against the pillows. 'I hope so, Jolly,' Ella said. But somehow Letty had managed to spoil the most sublime moment of her life.

CHAPTER TWENTY-SIX

As Anthony supervised the change of scenery ready for Kathleen's first performance since her illness, he felt both excited and apprehensive. In rehearsal Kathleen's voice had not been as clear and pure as it should have been, but perhaps tonight, with an expectant audience to encourage her, she would sing like the true professional she'd become.

'We'll have the park scenery up.' Anthony's voice echoed in the silent auditorium. 'Tom, fetch in the trees, there's a good lad.'

Tom clattered about the stage with the wooden trees. They were painted in garish greens and yellows, but they looked real under the lights. Tom was a new boy, fresh-faced and eager to learn. Anthony had taken him on a few days ago, impressed by the youngster's enthusiasm for the theatre.

'Anthony, I've got some good news for you.' Jolly Mortimer came on to the stage, his round face beaming with good humour. 'Sorry I'm a bit late, but I have the best excuse ever. Last night Helena gave birth to a fine boy, isn't that wonderful?'

Anthony forced a smile, but his heart was sinking. Ella was truly lost to him; the birth of her child brought it home to him anew that he had no place in her life. He took Jolly's hand and shook it warmly. 'Congratulations!'

'Thank you, Anthony, I knew you'd be pleased for us.' Jolly looked round approvingly at the stage set for Kathleen's performance.

'So Kathleen will open the proceedings tonight, then?' he asked.

Anthony nodded. 'She'll start the show and end it – she's top of the bill and the audience want to see as much of her as they can.'

'Quite right.' Jolly was beaming. 'Tell Kathleen about the baby, and Doris, of course. I know they'll both be so pleased.'

'Aren't you staying?' Anthony asked.

Jolly shook his head. 'The best thing about having a partner is leaving him to do all the work.' He paused. 'I'll get the solicitor to draw up the papers to make the partnership official as soon as I can arrange it. Is that all right?'

'Of course. Are the police making any progress? Do they have any clues as to who the robber is?'

'All they'll say is that they'll keep me informed. I suppose we'll just have to be patient.'

'It will all sort itself out in time,' Anthony said.

He swallowed hard. 'Oh and, Jolly, give Ella my congratulations. Tell her I'm delighted for you both.'

Anthony turned as Tom brought a few more fake trees and arranged them around the bench. The boy seemed to have the knack of knowing just what was required.

'New boy?' Jolly asked.

Anthony nodded. 'We needed someone young and strong to haul the scenery about and Tom was eager for work. He doesn't mind waiting a week or two for his pay. I hope you approve.'

'Aye, we lost a lot of good employees when the theatre was closed,' Jolly said. 'I suppose we need fresh blood around the place. Anyway,' he smiled, 'I can see you're coping perfectly well without me, so I'll get off home.'

'I'll be doing the books later,' Anthony said. 'If you want to come and check them you'd be more than welcome.'

'You know I'm leaving all that to you now, and glad of it,' Jolly said.

Anthony watched as Jolly left the stage and disappeared into the darkness of the wings. Although Jolly was on the plump side and was some years his senior, Ella loved him and had given him a son. He was very fortunate. Anthony sighed; there was work to do and he'd better get on with it and stop feeling envious of a good and generous man.

He brought his mind back to the matter in hand. 'That's right, Tom. Put that tree by the bench. We'll soon have this set looking fit for the return of our star performer.'

He took off his coat and helped the young boy manoeuvre the tree into place, and when he was satisfied he stood back and folded his arms. He'd done all he could to make tonight's show successful; now it was down to Kathleen. He only hoped she was up to the challenge.

Ella watched from her chair near the bedroom window as Jolly's daughters filed into the room, shepherded by Nurse Carmel. 'You can't stay too long now, we don't want to tire your stepmother out so soon after the birth, do we?'

Letty looked first at Ella and then at the nurse. 'Can I hold him again? I'll be very careful.'

It was Ella who answered. 'Be gentle with him. He's just had his feed and I don't want him to be sick all over you. It might be better if you sit down with him. He's quite heavy, despite being so small.' She watched as Letty carefully lifted the baby and stared down into his tiny face.

'What are you going to call him?' Mary was leaning over her sister, trying to touch the baby's face.

Ella smiled at her. 'I thought we might think of a name for him together. Perhaps we can write a list and give it to your father when he comes in.'

316

'I'd like to call him Richard after Papa,' Letty said firmly. 'No one uses my father's proper name. I don't think many people even know what it is.'

'I'm as guilty as everyone else,' Ella said, 'and you're right, Letty, the baby should have his father's name. What do the rest of you think of it?'

There was a chorus of agreement from the girls as they knelt on the floor around the baby and touched his hands and his face wonderingly.

Nurse Carmel took the baby unceremoniously from Letty and wrapped him up so tightly that his little arms were pinioned against his body. 'This child should be swaddled,' she said.

Letty held out her arms. 'Give him back to me, if you please.' Her voice held a tone of command and the nurse responded to it immediately, replacing the baby carefully in Letty's arms. Ella looked on in wonder. If only she could command the respect that Jolly's daughter did, how much more settled she would feel.

'If your father agrees with us then we'll call the baby Richard,' Ella said.

'I like it,' Charlotte broke in. 'It's a lovely name and he's a lovely baby, Helena.' This was a great compliment coming from Charlotte, who rarely voiced her opinions.

'What if we leave it to Letty to tell your father the baby's new name?' Ella asked.

317

'Can we all tell him? Please, Helena, we all want to tell him.' Mary looked at her pleadingly.

Ella looked at Letty. 'What do you think?'

'We can all be there,' Letty decided, 'but I'll be the one to tell Papa what name we'd like for the baby.'

Mary turned to Ella. 'Is the baby my brother, Helena?'

'Of course he is.' Ella smoothed back Mary's hair. 'The baby is your father's son so he's your brother.'

'Half-brother, to be exact.' Letty stared challengingly at Ella over the baby's head. 'Same father, different mother.'

'Well, I want him to be my proper brother,' Mary said, 'so that's what he'll be.'

Ella smiled at her.

'Now,' Nurse Carmel said firmly, 'it's time for the baby's nap.' She took him from Letty and put him in the crib, tucking the blankets firmly around his small body. 'A new infant needs all the sleep he can get, so come on with you, girls, get out into the garden and breathe some fresh air into those lungs of yours. I don't want your father thinking I'm shirking my duties.'

When the girls had gone, Ella leaned back in her chair and looked longingly at the bed. She was so tired, she just wanted to sleep. Nurse Carmel was still fussing round the baby and

318

Ella plucked up the courage to interrupt her ministrations.

'I think a little nap might do me good,' she said.

Nurse Carmel looked at her haughtily. 'I don't agree with lying in bed all day long. A new mother needs to sit in a nursing chair to feed her infant so that he doesn't get colic, and a spell out of bed with your feet on the ground is good for you.' She squared her shoulders. 'Don't you agree, Mrs Mortimer?'

'Yes,' Ella said wearily, 'I'm sure you know best, Nurse.' She wished Jolly was home. He'd only intended to pay a fleeting visit to the Palace, and when he returned he was planning to sit with her for a while. Then they could talk about the theatre, about the artistes they'd engaged and the finances – anything that took her fancy. She closed her eyes and tried to relax, but some part of her wanted to be up and about, involved in the real life outside the four walls of the house. She feared she wasn't destined to be satisfied with the domestic life.

By the time Jolly came home, Nurse Carmel had decided it was time for Ella to return to her bed. Jolly sat at her side and took her hand. 'How are you feeling, my dearest?'

'I'm a little tired, that's all. But, Jolly, don't talk about me, tell me about the Palace. Can we afford to go on hiring top performers?'

Jolly laughed. 'My dear little Helena, you must not worry your head about such things. Not now you're a mother.' He kissed her cheek. 'You'll have your work cut out bringing up our son, without bothering about the theatre.'

'But I want to bother about the theatre,' Ella protested. 'I love it all – the smell of it, all the excitement when the curtains open, the costumes, the scenery. Oh, Jolly, I can't just be a housewife and mother. I'd feel stifled.'

'There, there.' He patted her hand. 'I know you feel restless, cooped up in your room like this, but once you are up and about you'll be able to take the children for walks in the park, visit friends – your life will be full of other things and you won't be interested in the theatre any more.'

Ella sighed. The life Jolly was describing was not to her taste at all. 'But I have no friends,' she said, 'except for Doris and Kathleen.'

'You'll make new friends,' Jolly said easily. 'Others who have family concerns, just as you have.'

'But, Jolly . . .' she began.

He held up his hand. 'No arguments, my dearest. You need looking after and I mean to take great care of you. You know how precious you are to me.' He took her in his arms and she rested her head wearily against his shoulder. She would have to talk to him when she felt stronger. She couldn't live her life cooped up in the house or visiting women she didn't know, making polite conversation. But she was too tired to argue with him now.

There was a knock on the door and Mary pushed it open, peering at her father with questioning eyes. 'Can we come in, Papa? We've got something to tell you.' She yelped as Letty pushed past her and strode into the room, promptly followed by the other girls.

'I'll do it,' Letty said. 'We've been talking about a name for the baby,' she went on, slipping her arm around her father's shoulders. 'I hope you'll be pleased with it.'

Jolly hugged her. 'Well, let's hear what you've got in mind, then. I won't know if I like it until you tell me what it is, will I?'

Letty smiled at him. 'We want the baby named after you, so we've all decided to call him Richard. There! What do you think?'

Jolly looked at Ella. 'Is this what you want too, my dearest?'

Ella nodded. She watched, smiling, as Mary climbed on to her father's knee. 'It's what we all want.'

'Well, in that case I'd better do as I'm told, then.' Jolly smiled. 'What do you think, Charlotte?'

Charlotte pondered on the matter for a long time, a sober look on her face. 'I think Richard is too old for our baby, but we can always call him Rich for short.'

Nurse Carmel bustled into the room. 'Now, girls, out you go, it's time the baby was fed. You too, Mr Mortimer.'

Jolly rose obediently from his chair and kissed Ella on the cheek. 'See you later, my dearest. Take good care of our boy.'

Ella wanted to tell the nurse not to be so bossy, but she remained silent. She took the baby and held him to her breast, wincing a little as his mouth clamped on to her nipple. And then the baby began to suck and it was as if the boy's tiny mouth was drinking in all the love she felt for him.

'I'm really nervous tonight.' Kathleen looked past Anthony at the stage, set all ready and waiting for her behind the closed curtains. 'My voice isn't as good as it should be. I could hardly get a note out in rehearsal.'

'It's only natural you feel nervous, you've been away for a while and you've been ill. You're bound to feel a bit shaky the first couple of times you perform. Once you're out there on the stage you'll be your usual wonderful self, you'll see.'

Kathleen looked down at the dress she wore for her first number. It hung around her in folds and she realized how much weight she'd lost. When she jutted her knee through the split in the skirt the result was anything but bawdy. 'It's hopeless,' she said. 'Sure, I look like a scarecrow, not an entertainer.'

'Nonsense!' Anthony squeezed her shoulder. 'You look as beautiful as ever, Kath, and I mean that from the bottom of my heart.'

Kathleen's spirits rose. Anthony was being so kind to her – was that love she saw in his eyes? She took his hand. 'Are you sure, Anthony?'

'Of course I'm sure.' He bent forward and kissed her gently. 'No more fears now. You are the greatest draw this theatre has had the luck to put in front of the footlights.'

The musicians began to tune up their instruments and Kathleen's heart turned over. 'Not long now,' she said, clasping her hands together to stop them trembling.

'I'd better go and check on things,' Anthony said.

Kathleen looked up at him pleadingly. 'Oh, Anthony, stay with me, please. I'd feel better knowing you were watching me from the wings.'

'All right,' he said at once. 'If you need me, of course I'll be here for you.'

The band struck up the music for the opening number and Kathleen cast a panicky look at Anthony.

'Go on,' he encouraged. 'Your fans are waiting for you.'

And then Kathleen was on the stage, waiting for the curtains to sweep back and reveal her to the audience. The band played her cue and the audience began to clap. Kathleen walked to the front of the stage and struck a pose. The clapping grew louder. She opened her mouth to sing, but nothing came out. As she opened and closed her mouth like a goldfish, the crowd began to get restless. There was the rustle of people whispering. Kathleen tried again, but her voice had deserted her. She stood there, her hands hanging limply at her sides, panic rising in her.

The band played her cue notes again, but Kathleen was frozen. It was a disaster. She tried desperately to sing, but her throat closed up until she felt she was choking. A few moments dragged by and the musicians struck up the opening chords yet again, waiting for Kathleen to begin. She stood looking helplessly at the blur of faces, and her heart beat heavily in her breast as the clapping became slow and the catcalls and whistles began.

And then, as the tears began to pour down her cheeks, Kathleen turned away from the audience, who were stamping their feet now in anger rather than admiration. Almost fainting, she ran from the stage just as the curtains swept together, shutting her off from the baying crowd.

CHAPTER TWENTY-SEVEN

Ella looked into Kathleen's tearful eyes and crumpled face and a wave of pity swept through her. It was several days since the debacle at the Palace, but Kathleen was still sorely grieved by it.

'I'm sure you'll be all right, just give it time,' Ella said gently.

Kathleen looked at her with anguished eyes. 'But, Ella, I couldn't sing. I opened my mouth and no sound came out, and I just stood there looking a real fool. Sure I'll never be able to face an audience again.'

'Of course you will,' Ella said reassuringly. 'Didn't Anthony go out and explain to everyone you'd been ill?'

'So he did, the darling, but all those people who'd paid good money to hear me sing were badly let down. I don't think I'll ever get over the shame of it.'

'It's no shame to fall sick,' Ella insisted. 'The

crowds love you, they'll be waiting for you to get better.'

'An' in the meantime the Palace is losing money because the audiences are not coming any more.' Kathleen sighed. 'I looked in last night and the place was half empty.' She rubbed her already reddened eyes. 'And it's all my fault.'

'Things will pick up again,' Ella said. 'Don't worry about the money. The police have caught the man who robbed Jolly, and we'll be all right, I'm sure.' But she wasn't sure at all. Jolly still went about with a worried expression on his face all the time, and even with Anthony's injection of cash it was clear the theatre wasn't making a profit. It wasn't all down to Kathleen, of course. Poor Jolly insisted the decline was due to his own mismanagement of the theatre. Whatever the reason, the end result was the same: there wasn't enough money to pay for top performers, and the other theatres in the town were cashing in on the Palace's bad luck. But Ella wasn't going to tell Kathleen all that; she was upset enough as it was.

Kathleen picked up her bag and gloves and stared woefully at Ella. 'I'd better be getting back home. Doris will be wondering what's happened to me and I know you're busy now with the baby an' all, so I won't keep you.'

'I'm glad of the company,' Ella said firmly.

'Richard is asleep upstairs and the girls are all occupied with their lessons, so why don't you wait till Jolly gets back? He'll take you home in the horse and buggy.'

A smile warmed Kathleen's face. 'Sure an' aren't I used to walking about on my own? I'm from a poor Irish family, remember? And we both walked home in the dead of night when we were cleaners at the Palace – have you forgotten what it's like to be poor?'

Ella smiled. 'No, and neither have you, even though you're a star now. But you're not going home alone – there are some bad people out there.'

As she finished speaking, Ella heard the sound of the front door opening. 'Ah, here's Jolly now.'

Her husband came into the room and smiled broadly when he saw that Ella had company. 'Kathleen, how are you feeling now? Is your throat any better?'

Kathleen nodded. 'It's not so sore, but I'm still afraid to sing.'

'Well, don't worry about it,' Jolly said warmly. 'Once you're better you can come back and top the bill at the Palace. You'll soon be pulling in the audiences as you did before, you'll see.'

He dropped a kiss on Ella's head and she looked up at him, grateful for his kindness to Kathleen. 'How was the show tonight?' She prayed he'd put a gloss on the poor number of tickets they'd sold since Kathleen's disastrous appearance.

'Pretty fair, my dearest. But never mind that. How's that son of mine behaving?'

'He's such a good baby,' Ella said proudly. 'He takes his milk like the strong boy he is and he seems to be growing by the minute.'

Kathleen smiled, her tears forgotten. 'Let's go and see the little mite. I've been too wrapped up in my own misery to cuddle the baby yet.'

'We'll go and see him, but I doubt the nurse will let you hold him. Once he goes down for the night that's it as far as she's concerned.'

'The dragon! I don't know how you put up with her – she scares the life out of me.'

'She's a bit on the strict side, but she does her job well enough.'

'What's for supper?' Jolly asked. 'I'm starving and my little wife doesn't think of me at all these days.' He smiled and winked at Kathleen. 'Did you ever see a man so badly treated?'

Kathleen shook her head at him. 'You don't look like a man who's ill treated!' She burst out laughing. 'Sure you're a picture of health if ever I saw one. You must be looking after him well, Ella.'

'He's a spoilt boy.' Ella looked fondly at her husband. He was smiling at her, his eyes sparkling with happiness at being home with his family. 'But

328

then I'm spoilt too, so I can't grumble. Come on, let's face the dragon and see my darling Richard, shall we?'

As she led the way up the stairs to the nursery, Ella pondered on the twists and turns her life had taken. Here she was, mistress of a fine house filled with a ready-made family to care for. But was she happy? Most of the time she was, but at times like this, when she was with Kathleen who lived and breathed the theatre, Ella felt that somehow she was missing out on life.

The Palace was silent now, the crowds long since vanished, though the smell of perfume and cigarettes still lingered in the air. Anthony breathed it all in as he stood in the auditorium enjoying the atmosphere and the quiet.

And then he heard a noise, very slight, almost like the rustling of leaves. He tensed, and lifted his head to hear more clearly. It came again, the unmistakable sound of footfalls in the passageway.

He paused behind the door that led into the body of the theatre, pressing himself against the wall. The footsteps came nearer and on an impulse Anthony wrenched the door open.

Two men stood frozen in shock. Each wore a scarf around the lower half of his face and a dark hat jammed well down over his brow.

'What are you doing here?' Anthony demanded.

'If it's money you're after, you're out of luck. There's nothing here.'

Before he could say another word a fist struck him full in the face. Anthony was a big man, but the blow rocked him back on his heels.

'You'll get upstairs where the safe is kept,' a harsh voice growled at him. 'We know you keep the takings till Thursday night, so don't try to play the fool or it will be the worse for you.'

'We don't keep any money here,' Anthony protested. 'Not since one of your fellow crooks cleaned us out.'

He was grabbed by both men and dragged unceremoniously up the stairs to the office, where he was thrown violently to the ground. His head cracked against the floor and for a moment he was dazed.

'The keys!' One of the men bent over him and searched his pockets. Anthony heard the jangle of keys and the robber's grunt of satisfaction. But the safe needed a tap as well as keys to open it, and Anthony was rolled over on to his back. A face was held close to his own and fierce eyes stared manically at him from above the none-too-clean scarf. 'Where's the tap?'

'I've told you,' Anthony said, 'there's no money here.'

'Well, it won't hurt for us to look in the safe then, will it?' The man smacked Anthony in the mouth and he felt blood begin to flow as his pockets were emptied. The safe was quickly opened and to his relief Anthony saw there was no money inside it. Jolly must have taken it home with him.

He heard a curse and then a boot slammed into his side.

'Where is it?' The man who was asking all the questions leaned over him. 'Tell me or it will be the worse for you.'

'It's in the bank. Where do you think it is?' Anthony challenged, and was kicked again for his pains.

'You must think I'm a fool.' The man caught him by the throat and banged his head hard against the floor. 'I know you keep the money here. You need it to fund next week's show.'

Through the haze in his mind Anthony registered the fact that the robber knew the workings of the theatre a little too well.

'Well, this week it's different.' Anthony struggled to get up, but was pressed back by a boot stamping on his chest.

'What d'yer reckon, Tom? Is the bastard telling the truth?' The man spoke quickly, his voice jumpy with nerves.

Tom? Anthony tried to peer at the men standing above him. One of them was slight, just a boy in fact. Suddenly it all clicked into place. It was Tom, the new boy he'd taken on a few weeks ago, the scene-shifter. He must have told his friends about the way the theatre operated.

'I reckon Mr Mortimer's taken the bloody money home with him.' The voice was definitely familiar. 'He does that sometimes when he finishes late here.'

'I wish your father was here.' The man looming over Anthony seemed undecided as to what to do next. 'If he wasn't shut up in Swansea jail he'd tell us what was what.'

'If my father was here the job wouldn't have been botched.' Tom's voice was harsh, bitter. 'Look, we could go over to Mr Mortimer's house,' he added.

'No!' Anthony said. 'He wouldn't take the money home with him – he must have banked it earlier today.'

'Shut up!'

Anthony felt a boot make contact with his head and suddenly the world went black.

'Where can Anthony be?' Doris fretted, wringing her hands together as if she was taking part in a melodrama. 'He said he'd come for supper. He should have been here an hour ago.'

Kathleen shook her head at her. 'Sure an' won't he be drinking in the public bar somewhere. Don't worry, Doris, he'll turn up. He never fails.' Secretly Kathleen was worried too, but she told herself not to be foolish. Everything would be all right – Anthony was a little late, that was all.

'But I've got a bad feeling in the pit of my stomach,' Doris said. 'I know something's wrong.'

Kathleen felt her fears crowd in on her. 'I'll go over to the Palace and look for him. You just keep yourself calm, Doris. Don't go fainting on me. I couldn't cope with hysterics right now.'

She went out into the hall and pulled on her coat. Doris followed her, clutching at her arm. 'Is it safe to go out at this time of night, do you think?'

'Look, Doris, you and me and Ella walked home much later than this after clearing up the Palace.'

'I suppose you're right.'

'I won't be long, so don't fret.'

Kathleen opened the door and peered outside. There was a fog hanging over the house tops and the stink of the tin works was thick in the night air. 'I won't be long.' She closed the door behind her, shutting out the sight of Doris's worried face. 'We're making a fuss about nothing,' she said aloud, trying to give herself courage.

The streets were empty; even the public houses had closed their doors for the night. Somewhere a dog howled and Kathleen shuddered. 'Sure that's a bad omen if ever there was one,' she murmured.

The fog seemed to grow thicker, swirling around like smoke in the pools of light from the gas lamps. She was glad when the solid brick building came into sight, but there were no lights on in the place. It looked dead, deserted, as if it had never been filled with singing and laughter and music.

The side door was open, sure proof that Anthony was still inside. Kathleen moved cautiously across the dark foyer, the hair prickling at the back of her neck. As she climbed the stairs towards the office she heard voices, men's voices, muffled but speaking with evident aggression.

'You might have killed him!' The voice was familiar but she couldn't place it. And then the words trickled through her like iced water. Killed? Who might they have killed? Not Anthony, please God.

She crept closer to the open door of the office and peered into the room. Anthony was lying in a crumpled heap on the floor and two men with scarves covering their faces stood over him.

Kathleen clasped her hand to her mouth. What should she do? Where could she get help at this time of night? The streets outside were deserted.

'I say we get over to Mr Mortimer's house.' One of the voices spoke up, deep and strong, breaking the silence.

'And what will you do there?' The younger, familiar voice was challenging. 'Beat the life out of Mr Mortimer for a few pounds? I'm sorry I came in on this scam. I didn't know there was going to be rough stuff or I'd never have agreed to the plan.'

'Oh, grow up, Tom! Did you think kind words would get us anywhere? If so you're a bloody fool. Your father didn't stop at kicking five bells out of Mr Mortimer, did he? And why do you think he told you to do this stupid job? So that you could work for us, that's why.'

Tom? It must have been his father who attacked Jolly Mortimer. Kathleen felt sick to her stomach. She looked round the landing, lit only dimly from the lamp in the office, searching for a weapon – but there was nothing.

She stood quite still, wanting to stay near Anthony and yet knowing she should warn Jolly that these men were planning to attack him in his home. Well, she wasn't doing anyone any good just standing on the landing. She turned to retrace her steps and stumbled in the dark, almost pitching headlong down the stairs.

'Bloody hell, there's someone out there!'

Kathleen tried to run, but the man coming behind her was too quick. He caught her by her hair and swung her round to face him. 'Well, well, if it isn't Little Miss Songbird.' He dragged her back into the office. 'Look, Tom, see what I've found.'

'Let her go, Dai,' Tom said. 'Don't hurt her.'

'Oh, I won't hurt her,' the man said. 'She's far too valuable for that. No, let's take her with us. We'll get a fine ransom for her, you see if we don't.'

'But Mr Mortimer hasn't got much money. We was only expecting to get the week's takings, that's all.'

'He can go to the bank, like all these toffs do.'

'I don't like it. I wasn't in mind for a kid-napping or beating folk up.'

Kathleen strained to see if Anthony was alive or dead. He had a deep cut on his forehead and blood was coming from his nose and his mouth, but at least he was breathing. Incensed, she kicked out at the man behind her. Her boot connected with his shin and he let out an oath. He swung her round to face him and his eyes glittered above the scarf covering the rest of his face.

'You'll behave if you know what's good for you,' he said. 'I could have a good bit of fun with you if I had a mind to.' His hand strayed to her waist and Kathleen froze.

'None of that!' Tom said quickly. 'No one will pay good money for her if you hurt her, will they?'

'Aye, you could be right. Now where are we going to put her till we're ready to make a bargain for her?'

'Don't ask me,' Tom said. 'My mam's at home

in my house and she's not going to have anything to do with all this.'

'Right, there's that empty house in the woods – we'll take her there.'

'But the place is haunted,' Tom said.

'Don't talk rubbish, there's no such thing as ghosts. Now come on, follow me if you don't want to end up with your father in a prison cell.'

Kathleen's heart twisted in fear as she heard Anthony groan. Then she was being dragged down the stairs and out into the night. Perhaps she could watch which way they were taking her so that she could find her way back when she made her escape – because escape she would. These villains wouldn't hold her for more than five minutes.

Suddenly she felt a scarf being tied around her eyes and another around her wrists, binding her hands behind her back. Then she was being pushed forward and all she could feel was the dank night air swirling like a malign spirit around her body.

CHAPTER TWENTY-EIGHT

Awoken suddenly from sleep, Ella sat up in bed, her every nerve alert. There had been an unfamiliar sound from downstairs and she waited in silence, straining to listen. Jolly was asleep at her side, and as she glanced at him her gaze softened. He looked like a cherubic baby with his eyes closed and his whole body relaxed.

She lay back down; she must have been dreaming, for all was silent now. She was just slipping back into sleep when she heard the sound of a door being closed.

Ella climbed out of bed and pulled on her dressing gown. Cautiously she opened the bedroom door and heard a loud scuffling in the hall. 'Help! Someone help me!'

Ella peered over the bannister and through the gloom she saw two men and a woman, struggling together.

'Help me! Murder!' It was Nurse Carmel crying out in the hallway.

Ella crept back into the bedroom. 'Jolly! Wake up! There's someone in the house.'

Jolly was awake at once. 'Stay here, Helena, I'll go and see what's going on.'

Ella looked round her, panicking. The men who had robbed Jolly before had come back for more money and somehow Nurse Carmel had become caught up in it all. Ella stood on the landing, wondering if she should follow Jolly downstairs or go to the girls and lock them all in the nursery with the baby. But before she could make up her mind, Letty came along the landing, her hair hanging in two plaits down her back.

'What on earth is all the noise about?' Letty's voice was thick with sleep and Ella tried to hush her.

'We're being robbed,' she said. 'Go and get one of the servants to run for help.'

Letty stared at Ella in disbelief. 'Robbed?' she whispered. But before she could move there was a cry of pain from Jolly. Ella heard Letty gasp with fear. Unable to contain herself, Ella ran down the stairs and picked up a bronze figure from the hall table. One of the robbers had Jolly in a stranglehold. His back was turned towards Ella and he seemed unaware of her presence.

'Talk, you bastard,' the man barked, his voice heavy with menace. 'Tell me where the money is.'

'What money?' Jolly said. 'We don't keep any money in the house.'

'Don't fool with me, otherwise it will be worse for you. We've got your little songbird tucked away where no one will find her and she might just come to harm if you can't bail her out.' As he was speaking, the thug punched Jolly's head and Ella heard her husband gasp with pain. As the man raised his fist again, Ella darted forward, holding the bronze figure aloft, and brought it crashing down on his head.

He slumped to the floor, pulling Jolly with him. Ella stood protectively over Jolly and stared at the other man, who was holding Nurse Carmel in an arm lock. He seemed young and uncertain and Ella decided to try to reason with him.

'Let Nurse Carmel go,' she said firmly. 'The servants have gone for help.'

Jolly staggered to his feet and stood beside her. His head was bleeding and Ella caught his arm, restraining him as he moved forward. 'No, Jolly. There's no need for any more violence. Help is on the way.' She suddenly snatched the scarf from round the younger man's face, catching him unawares.

'Tom!' Jolly's voice was hoarse and tinged with shock. 'Why would you want to rob us? Don't you make a good living working at the Palace?'

'It was him – Dai,' Tom said, shamefaced. 'And my father too – he told me to make a living for our family while he served his time in jail. I'm sorry, Mr Mortimer, I didn't want to do it, not any of it.'

Nurse Carmel pulled away from Tom, huffing in outrage as she pulled her dressing gown around her.

'Look, Tom, you'd better tell us everything,' Ella said gently. 'Come on, you're not a thug really, are you?'

'It's true he's taken Kathleen.' Tom's shoulders slumped. 'The idea was to hold her until you gave us money and then set her free. I promise nothing bad would have happened to her.' He pointed to the man slumped on the floor. 'I stopped him hurting her, mind, but Anthony – well, he got a beating. I'm sorry.'

Ella felt her heart contract with fear. 'Oh, Jolly, what shall we do?'

'First we'll have to tie this villain up to make sure he does no more damage. Then I'll go for the police.'

'No need, Papa.' Letty rushed into the hall. 'Constable Timmins is on his way.' Her face was animated. 'Look, I'll fetch some rope from the stables.' Before Jolly could object she ran out again.

Ella looked at Nurse Carmel. 'Will you check on the baby?' she asked in a flat voice.

Nurse Carmel nodded and plodded upstairs, her feet bare, her hair in disarray. She was very pale and it seemed all her pomp and pride had gone; she was just a frightened woman stripped of all her authority.

Ella was relieved when Letty returned with a length of rope, her eyes glittering with excitement. They both watched as Jolly secured the robber's hands and feet. Jolly straightened up and as he looked at Tom he shook his head. 'I'm sorry, Tom, but you'll have to take your medicine for being involved in this sorry affair.'

Ella felt for Tom as he hung his head. 'I know, Mr Mortimer. I don't mean you any harm. I never wanted anyone hurt, and even if you did let me off he – ' he pointed to the man on the floor, ' – he would have shopped me anyway once the police got their hands on him.'

'Helena, what's happening?' Charlotte was standing on the landing and behind her were Lizzie and Vicky and little Mary. Behind them cowered Cook, her nightcap awry.

'Papa, are you all right?' Charlotte was hanging over the bannister, her hair swinging loose.

'I'm not hurt at all. Don't worry.'

'What are you girls doing out of your rooms?' The danger over, Nurse Carmel attempted to assume her usual commanding tone of voice.

Letty looked at her scathingly. 'The noise you made would have woken the dead,' she said. 'Did you really expect us to stay in our rooms not knowing what was happening down here?'

'Well, I don't know, all I wanted was a nice

342

cold drink of milk and I was attacked by those villains. Do you wonder I was screaming?'

'I notice you didn't do anything to help,' Letty said witheringly. 'Helena was the heroine. She tackled that man while you just stood by and watched. You were brave, Helena,' she said humbly. 'You probably saved my father's life.'

'And you were brave enough to get a message to the police.' Ella found she had tears stinging her eyes.

Jolly put his arm around Ella and smiled at Letty. 'You showed great presence of mind. Now, once the police arrive we'll get to the bottom of all this. Tom, where is Kathleen being held?'

'In the woods, Mr Mortimer, in the haunted house.'

'You can take the police there when they come,' Jolly said.

'What about Anthony?' Ella asked. 'From the sound of it, we'd better get a doctor for him.'

'The police can see to Anthony, so don't you worry, Ella. Why don't you bring some tea, Cook? We could all do with cheering up.'

Very quickly, it seemed to Ella, the hallway was filled with men in uniform. Jolly was a respected figure in the town and the police had turned out willingly to help him, even though it was the middle of the night.

'Sorry about all the bother, Constable Timmins,' Jolly said, 'but I don't want these villains in my house a moment longer than I have to. And, Timmins, we have friends out there needing your help. Young Tom here will tell you all about it.'

The constable looked sorrowfully at Tom. 'I thought you would turn out to be a good un', lad,' he said. 'Instead you're following in the footsteps of that father of yours. You're a fool.'

Ella noticed that Letty was standing beside Tom, looking him over with unconcealed interest. Letty caught her looking and the colour rushed to her face. 'Constable,' she said, 'from what I heard, Tom was forced into this. I don't think he wanted anything to do with it.'

'Well, he should have kept well away then, Miss Mortimer.' The constable stood looking at her for a long moment and then turned to his colleagues. 'Let's take these no-good fools away, lads.' He touched his helmet in deference to Jolly and followed the men out of the house.

When the door had closed behind the police, Ella sank into a chair and rubbed her hand over her eyes. 'What a dreadful night,' she said. 'I do hope the police get a doctor to Anthony as soon as possible.'

'Now,' Jolly took charge, 'did Cook bring us tea? Right then, take your drinks to your rooms, girls. There's nothing any of you can do now but go to bed.'

'What about you, Jolly?' Ella asked anxiously.

'I'll get over to the Palace and see what's happening there.'

Ella wished she could go with him, but she could hardly leave the house and the children at this time of night. 'Don't be long, Jolly. You're looking tired and that's a nasty graze you've got over your eye.'

Jolly smiled his sweet smile. 'I'm all right, my dearest, quite all right.'

When Jolly had gone, Ella looked at the girls gathered around her. 'Who wants to sit in the kitchen to drink their tea?' she asked. The girls chorused their assent and Ella led the way down the short flight of stairs, the girls trailing behind her.

'I'll make another pot, Mrs Mortimer.' Cook filled the kettle and put it on the stove, then fetched clean cups and saucers from the cupboard.

'Yes, make more for all of us, Cook, including yourself,' Ella said. 'This has been an unusual night and I think we all need plenty of tea to calm our nerves.'

'It don't feel right, Mrs Mortimer, me sitting down to drink tea with the master's wife.'

'I insist,' Ella said. 'We don't need to stand on ceremony on this night of all nights.' She sounded strong and confident and hid her fears well, but inside she was trembling. What if Anthony was seriously hurt? And Jolly was getting too old to put up with such rough treatment at the hands of some greedy villain.

Still, she must put her worries aside and keep up the children's spirits. Mary, she noticed, had tears in her eyes. She touched the girl's cheek. 'It's going to be all right,' she said. 'Your father will sort out everything at the theatre and then he'll come straight home. We're safe and sound now.'

Ella was surprised when Letty held out her hand. 'Friends, Helena?' she said, her tone reminding Ella that she was still only a child.

'Friends,' Ella agreed, trying not to cry.

Nurse Carmel came into the room looking sheepish. 'The baby is fast asleep. He never heard a sound.' She paused and smiled nervously at Ella. 'Can I be a friend too?'

Ella handed her a cup of steaming tea. 'That would be very nice, Nurse Carmel,' she said softly.

The nurse met her eyes. 'And please, will you all just call me Margaret? It's much more friendly.'

Ella looked round the large table surrounded by family and servants, and for once they all seemed in accord. She felt warm and included, as she'd never been before. Her only worry now was that Kathleen was found safe and well and that Anthony, her dear Anthony, had not been badly hurt.

The doors of the theatre were wide open and as Jolly walked through the foyer he heard Kathleen's voice coming from the direction of the office. He felt a wave of relief. The police must have found her straight away.

As he climbed the stairs, he felt a tremor of pain in his chest. That man must have hit him harder than he realized. He dismissed the pain as he made his way to the office.

Constable Timmins stood at the open door and Jolly could see Anthony still on the floor being attended by Doctor Frazer. 'How is he?' Jolly asked, bending over to see more closely. Anthony's face was swollen and bruised and already the skin around his eyes was turning black.

'Pretty bad,' Doctor Frazer said. 'The blow to his head is the worst injury. He'll be lucky if he hasn't got a cracked skull.' He stood up. 'But don't worry, we'll be taking him to hospital. He'll be well looked after.'

'Oh my darling, open your eyes and speak to me!' Kathleen voice was hoarse, her red hair standing up around her white face like a halo. She was kneeling on the floor beside Anthony and looked pleadingly at the doctor. 'He will be all right, won't he?'

'As I said, he'll be well looked after.'

'Can I go to the hospital with him?' Kathleen's

voice wavered. 'I don't want him to be alone when he wakes up.'

'I'm sure that will be in order.' Doctor Frazer was looking closely at Jolly. 'Are you all right, Mr Mortimer? I understand the villains went to your home. Did they attack you?'

Jolly waved the doctor away. 'I'm a bit shaken, that's all. What with my wife and children in the house it was all a bit worrying.'

'That's an understatement, Mr Mortimer. Anyway, come to see me tomorrow and I'll check you over.'

'I'll do that,' Jolly said. 'But I'll be all right when all this chaos is sorted out and I'm back home with my family.'

'You go home, Jolly,' Kathleen said. 'I'll wait with Anthony and go to the hospital with him.'

'I think I will, dear.' Jolly did his best to hide how groggy he was feeling.

'I'll walk with you,' the doctor said affably. 'You look a little shaken up.'

Jolly nodded; he was feeling too sick to argue. 'That's very kind of you.'

They left the theatre together and Jolly was glad of the cool night air on his face. He stared up at the blue-grey sky, watching the dawn bring the trees at the roadside into sharp relief. The moon was a pale orb; soon it would fade away as the dawn blush spread across the town.

When the doctor paused at his door, he looked

348

at Jolly with raised eyebrows. 'Sure you wouldn't like me to give you a sedative?'

'No, thank you, Doctor, I'm all right, I assure you.'

As the doctor's footsteps faded into the distance, Jolly felt the pain hit him like a blow to his chest. With a monumental effort, he knocked on the door, struggling for every breath. He saw the maid's face and behind her stood his dear Helena, and then, with darkness rushing into his mind, he fell into the hallway.

CHAPTER TWENTY-NINE

Ella sat at the bedside looking down fearfully at the decent kind man who was her husband. Jolly had changed overnight from a person full of life and vigour to a sickly old man who found even breathing difficult. He hadn't recovered consciousness since last night when he had collapsed in the hallway.

Margaret had taken charge of the situation; she had had the presence of mind to send the maid rushing out after the doctor. Doctor Frazer had done his best but at last he'd shaken his head and given Ella the dreadful news that Jolly's heart was failing and he might never recover from the strain.

There was a knock on the door and the maid came slowly into the room. She glanced fearfully towards the bed and then looked away quickly. 'Miss Kathleen is here, Mrs Mortimer,' she said. 'Do you want me to show her in?'

Ella nodded. 'Yes please, Jenny, bring her up

to the bedroom. She'll be anxious to know how Mr Mortimer is.'

Kathleen crept into the bedroom a few moments later and pushed back her red curls in a nervous gesture. 'How is he?' she asked in a frightened whisper.

'There's no change. Dr Frazer is coming back later to check on him. Bring a chair over, Kathleen, and sit with me. I'm so frightened and I can't let the girls see how I feel.'

Kathleen sat beside her and squeezed her hand. 'I'm glad you sent the maid to tell me and Doris what's happened. Sure haven't I prayed on my knees, asking the Blessed Virgin Mary to be merciful to us.'

Ella took a deep breath. 'How's Anthony?' She felt disloyal even saying his name but she had to know.

'He's going to be all right.' Kathleen's words brought a rush of relief and Ella's spirits lightened a little. 'Doris is at the hospital with him now, but it looks as if he will come home soon.' Kathleen paused. 'Those men have got a lot to answer for. Especially that Dai Johnson. He's older than young Tom and he's led the lad astray. If I could get hold of him I'd kill him with my bare hands.'

'The law will deal with him,' Ella said. She glanced at Kathleen and smiled ruefully. 'I think I gave him quite a headache, hitting him with that bronze figure. I didn't know I had it in me to be violent.'

'He got what he deserved,' Kathleen said. 'And you were protecting your own – sure that's an instinct that's in all our hearts.'

Ella sighed and took Jolly's hand in hers. 'It didn't do us much good in the end, did it? Anthony is still in hospital and Jolly – well, you only have to look at him to know he's a very sick man.'

'He's strong, he'll recover,' Kathleen said. 'Just give it time. Now why don't you go and have a bite to eat? I can sit with Jolly for a while.'

Ella shook her head. 'I'm afraid to leave him, even for a moment.' Her voice broke. 'Oh, Kathleen, what's happening to us all? Our lives have changed so much. I sometimes feel we were happier when we were just cleaners at the Palace.'

Kathleen put her arm around her. 'Don't say that. You've got a fine husband who loves you dearly, a ready-made family and a darling little baby of your own.' She grimaced. 'And sure wasn't cleaning them corridors and stairs the worst job in the world?'

Ella tried to smile, but she was swallowing her tears. 'You don't want to hear me moaning, you've been through the mill yourself and you must be so worried about Anthony.'

It was the first time Ella had admitted, even to herself, that Kathleen had a claim on Anthony's

352

affections. She knew she should wish them well – they were meant for each other, sharing such a great love of the theatre – but she couldn't help feeling a pang of regret for what she'd lost. Immediately she felt guilty.

Ella looked down at her husband. He was so dear to her: he'd married her, taken care of her, and now here he was brought to this, a sick man lying unconscious in his bed. She owed him all the love and loyalty she could muster.

Letty came into the room, breaking the silence with her softly spoken words. 'Has Papa improved at all, Ella?' She came to stand beside the bed and Kathleen moved out of the way to accommodate her.

'The doctor will be here later,' Ella prevaricated. 'He'll tell us then if there's been any change.'

Letty was near to tears but she held her head high as she fought for control. Ella saw again that Letty was little more than a frightened child. How she'd misunderstood the girl for so long she didn't know. All Letty's hostility was based on fear, fear of losing her place in her father's affections. Ella scolded herself for not realizing sooner that Letty was just a vulnerable young girl who didn't know how to handle her anxiety.

Kathleen rested her hand on Ella's shoulder. 'I'd better go,' she said quietly. 'I may be fetching Anthony home from the hospital this afternoon. He's going to stay with us at Doris's house.'

'Send Anthony my best wishes.' Ella got up. 'I'll come to the door with you.'

'There's no need,' Kathleen said, waving her away. 'I know you want to stay with Jolly and sure I'm big enough to see myself out, aren't I?'

Ella subsided thankfully into her chair. At the door Kathleen paused. 'I'm going to tell that maid of yours to bring you something to eat. A little bowl of soup, perhaps?'

Ella was too tired to argue and in any case she knew she had to keep her strength up to feed the baby. 'All right, Kathleen,' she nodded. 'That would be lovely, thanks.'

Kathleen closed the door quietly behind her and Ella took Jolly's hand again. Letty touched her arm. 'You should rest, Ella, you're looking so pale and tired. You've been through a lot lately and I haven't done much to help. Look, I'll sit with Papa and I'll call you if there's any change.'

After a moment, Ella nodded. She longed to see her baby, to reassure herself that her son was well. She missed holding him in her arms, kissing his downy head. 'All right, Letty,' she said. 'But please call me if there's even the slightest change.'

Letty looked at her with clear blue eyes. 'I know I've been a trial to you, Ella. I've been spiteful and vindictive, but I promise all that will change. I saw how you saved my father from that man and I know you must really care for him.'

Ella noted the girl's choice of words: she didn't

mention the word 'love', but then Letty was perceptive and knew that the marriage had been an unsuitable one – she had declared it often enough. Yet now she seemed willing to give Ella all her support.

It was strange to be out of the sickroom, seeing the sun shining in through the large landing window. Ella took a deep breath and eased her cramped shoulders. She felt released, if only for a short time, from the burden of watching Jolly struggle for every breath. Immediately she felt guilty: it wasn't much to ask of a wife that she sit by her sick husband's bedside.

She resisted the urge to run back to the bedroom and made her way along the landing to the nursery, where her darling baby was waiting for her. The prospect of holding Jolly's son brought her a modicum of comfort.

'Careful now, Anthony.' Kathleen helped Anthony down from the trap Doris had hired for them. 'You're still very weak, so you are. Now come on into the house. Doris will have the kettle on.'

Anthony stumbled a little and put his arm around Kathleen's shoulder for support, and she revelled in his nearness.

'Oh, my lovely boy!' Doris rushed to the door to greet them. 'Come in and make yourself comfortable. It's so good to see you out of hospital.'

Kathleen helped Anthony into the parlour and waited while he settled into a chair. He looked up at her and smiled. 'Don't look so worried, Kath, I'm getting better by the day.'

Kathleen touched his face gently. 'But look at your bruises. Your poor eye is still swollen.'

'I'm all right. But what about Jolly?'

'The poor man is still unconscious. The doctor thinks it's his heart.'

'Ella must be out of her mind with worry,' Anthony said and Kathleen felt a tug of jealousy. Anthony was always thinking of Ella, always talking about her. She pushed the bad thoughts away: Ella was her friend, and she was honourable and kind and would be true to her marriage vows.

She sat beside Anthony and took his hand in hers, and when he didn't draw away she took comfort from that. 'What are we going to do about the theatre, Anthony?' she asked. 'Will you take Jolly's place until he's better?'

'I'll do my best to fill Jolly's shoes for a while,' Anthony said. 'But let's hope he recovers soon.'

'But you could do all Jolly's work, to be sure you could,' Kathleen protested.

Anthony smiled at her and then winced. 'Damn these bruises! If I could get my hands on that Johnson man I'd give him a few bruises to go on with.' He pushed a stray lock of blond hair from his brow and Kathleen's heart melted with love for him. Even with his bruised face and uncombed hair he was still the most handsome man in all the world.

Kathleen sighed. 'I haven't helped things at the theatre by losing my voice. And now we've lost Jolly too.'

Doris tutted in disapproval. 'Jolly is going to be all right. He had a nasty shock, that's all. He's a fine-built man – he can survive all this upset, you'll see.'

'Jolly's not a fine-built man, as you put it,' Kathleen said. 'He carries too much weight and he's much older than us.'

'Older than you, perhaps,' Doris said. 'But he's a lot younger than me, remember. Jolly is in his prime.'

'I'll go to see him for myself this evening,' Anthony said.

'Oh, don't do that!' Kathleen protested. 'You're not strong enough yet to go out and about. Rest easy for tonight and go over there in the morning.'

Anthony shook his head. 'I'll be all right, Kath, don't you worry about me, I'm stronger than I look.'

'But you've taken a bad beating. You've been in the hospital, for heaven's sake.'

Anthony released his hand from hers. 'I'm not having any arguments. I'm going to see Jolly tonight – I've got to know how things stand.'

He wanted to see Ella. The thought ran through

Kathleen's mind but she swallowed her pain and tried to smile.

'Then I'm coming with you,' she said. 'Now how about us all having a cup of tea?'

The baby had been fed and was now fast asleep. As Ella looked at him, tucked up securely in his crib, she felt her heart ache with love for him.

'Helena,' Letty's voice drifted up the stairs, 'dinner is ready. Come and try to eat something, please.'

Reluctantly, Ella left the nursery and made her way downstairs to the dining room. She knew why Letty was insisting she ate regularly. If her stepmother should fall sick Letty would have no one to turn to for support.

The girls sat around the dining table waiting for her and Ella gestured to the maid to serve the dinner. Jenny was a good girl; although nominally the parlour maid, in reality she was maid of all work. She cleaned the house and lit the fires; she even kept the stove in the kitchen alight. And then she served the meals with a good heart. The household really needed a second maid but Jolly couldn't afford it now, especially not since he had taken over the ownership of the Palace; the theatre seemed to have drained away all his savings.

Ella did her best to eat the tender lamb's liver casserole Cook had prepared, but her throat seemed to close up every time she lifted the food to her mouth. The custard tart was easier to swallow, but as soon as she'd finished Ella pushed back her chair. 'I'm going to sit with your father, girls. I'll send Margaret down to get her food,' she said. 'You must all come and say goodnight to your father before you go to bed.'

Jolly lay as she had left him. His breathing was still laboured and his face twisted every now and again as though he were in pain. Ella felt tears come to her eyes as she sat beside her husband and watched his struggle to breathe. She brushed them aside impatiently. There was no point in crying, and anyway she didn't want the girls to see her with reddened eyes. She had to keep their spirits up.

Suddenly she felt Jolly's hand move in hers. She looked down at him and saw that his eyes were open.

'Jolly, my darling, you've come back to us.' She bent over him and kissed his cheek.

'I'm sorry, my dearest.' Jolly's voice was little more than a whisper. 'I'm so sorry to leave you. I love you very much – don't ever forget that.'

'Jolly, what do you mean? You're not going to leave me. You'll be here with me for always.'

'I'm dying, Helena,' he said simply, 'and there's nothing any of us can do about it.' He stopped for breath and Ella saw how white he was and how deep were the lines etched around his mouth.

359

He gasped with pain and held his hand to his chest. 'Call the children. I must say goodbye to them.' His voice trailed away and Ella watched in alarm as he closed his eyes wearily.

'Jolly, my darling Jolly, don't go and leave me!' She ran to the door and cried out for the nurse to come at once. The girls, hearing her desperate cries, hurried out of the dining room and ran up the stairs, their dresses flapping like a flock of restless birds.

'Helena, what is it?' Letty grasped her arm.

'It's your father. Oh, Letty, what are we going to do?'

Letty straightened her back and walked towards the bedroom. She hesitated for a moment at the door and then went to bend over her father. Charlotte, Mary and the twins ran straight into the bedroom after their sister. Mary took Ella's hand and looked up at her trustingly. 'Papa is going to get better, isn't he, Helena?'

'I don't know, sweetheart,' Ella said brokenly.

In the bedroom, Jolly was trying to talk to his daughters. His eyes met Ella's as she moved towards him. 'Fetch my son,' he said.

Ella looked at Letty. 'Will you go and get your brother?'

Letty nodded and left the room at once. Young as she was, she realized her father had little time left on this earth. She quickly returned with the baby and Nurse Carmel came behind her,

her starched apron crackling as she walked. She took Jolly's pulse and then her eyes met Ella's. 'There's nothing I can do, nothing anyone can do.'

'Bring the baby to me,' Jolly gasped, and Letty held the boy as close to her father as she dared, her hand under Richard's tiny head. Jolly kissed his son and looked steadily at his eldest daughter. 'Helena is going to need all the help she can get,' he said. 'I want to know you'll support her in all she tries to do.'

'We will, Papa.' Letty started to cry and her sisters, seeing her distress, cried with her.

'Helena, hold my hand. I must confess I'm a little frightened now that my time has come.'

Ella took Jolly's hand between her own and began to rub his fingers as if she could keep the life from draining away from him by her own strength of will. He half smiled, breathed softly for a moment, and then his eyes closed. Ella knew he'd gone from her and the tears spilled over, running saltily down her cheeks.

Margaret took a deep breath and then made to draw the sheet over his face.

'No, don't do that.' It was Letty who spoke. As Ella looked at her she saw not a child but a woman in the making. She would need to grow up fast now.

'Let's leave him in peace,' Ella said. 'Go on downstairs, girls, and ask Jenny to make some

361

tea. You too, Margaret.' There was a new note of command in her voice and for once her instructions were obeyed without question.

And then Ella was alone with her husband. She looked down at him through her tears. 'Goodbye, my darling Jolly,' she said brokenly. 'Rest easy now and don't worry about the family, I'll take care of them all.'

She kissed his cheek for the last time and then the tears came faster, flowing freely down her cheeks. 'Oh, Jolly,' she said, 'how am I going to manage without you?'

She slumped on to the bed and sobs racked her body. She was all alone now, and had only herself to depend on. But she would work her fingers to the bone to protect and care for Jolly's family. 'God help me,' she whispered.

CHAPTER THIRTY

Ella looked at the bank manager in consternation, unable to take in what he was saying. 'Please,' she said, 'will you go over that again?'

He sighed. 'I regret to inform you that there is a considerable debt outstanding on your husband's account and the house was given in surety. Naturally the bank will require you to reduce the balance at regular intervals.' He hesitated. 'Let's say once a month.' He looked at her keenly. 'Otherwise the house will be repossessed.' He fiddled with a paper knife on his desk. 'I knew Mr Mortimer well and had a great deal of respect for him, so I'm prepared to be lenient – up to a point.'

Ella sat back in her chair, fear running through her veins like ice at the thought of losing the house. Where would she go with no money and six children to look after?

'Give me three months, Mr Singleton,' she said desperately. 'I'm sure I can get the theatre in shape and start making a healthy profit by then.'

The bank manager looked at her doubtfully. 'I understand things are not looking so good at the Palace.' He fiddled with the paper knife again. 'With the talented Miss Kathleen unable to perform, you've lost the biggest attraction the Palace has ever had.'

'She's making a good recovery,' Ella said quickly. 'She will be completely better in a few weeks' time – her voice is improving every day. If only you could hear her rehearsing, Mr Singleton, you'd be as confident as I am.'

None of it was true but Ella had no choice but to play for time. She'd known that money was tight, even though Jolly hadn't wanted to burden her with business matters, but she hadn't realized that Jolly had put the house up as guarantee of repayment.

Mr Singleton looked at her for a long moment and then, to her relief, he nodded. 'I can keep the hounds off my back for three months,' he said with a wry smile. 'I wish you all the luck in the world, Mrs Mortimer.' He held out his hand and Ella took it, smiling gratefully.

'Thank you, Mr Singleton. You won't regret your decision.'

He saw her to the door and held it open for her, and then Ella was out in the street, listening to the rumble of the traffic along the busy High Street. A dray horse clopped past her, drawing a high cart filled with beer barrels that wobbled precariously as the cart ran over the cobbled road.

Ella stood still, taking deep breaths and trying to control the trembling that had suddenly come over her. In the bank she'd been bold, making rash promises, but how she was going to fulfil them she just didn't know.

She became aware that passers-by were looking at her strangely, and galvanized into movement she began to walk home. Changes would have to be made, and at once: there was no money to spend on anything that wasn't strictly necessary.

The nurse would have to go and so would the servants. It would be hard telling them the bad news, but it would have to be done. And from now on the family would have to live on plain fare: no more good cuts of meat or rich puddings. She was used to eating plain food, but Jolly's daughters were not.

And then there was the Palace to be sorted out. How she would pay for artistes to perform there she didn't know, but somehow she would make it work. She would have to.

It was good to walk into the warmth and brightness of the home Jolly had been so proud of. Ella felt tears choke her throat as she stood in the hall and let Jenny take her coat. She couldn't lose the house – she would be letting Jolly and his children down if she did. Somehow she must make the theatre the thriving enterprise it was before, employing big-name artistes to draw in the crowds again.

She could hear the girls arguing upstairs and her heart sank. They were trying their best to come to terms with Jolly's death, and now there were more difficulties for them to face.

Ella decided to deal with Margaret first – she was the person she dreaded telling most. Margaret Carmel had been a pillar of strength since Jolly's death. She'd been more like a friend than an employee lately, and telling her there was no longer a job for her in the Mortimer household was going to be upsetting for both of them.

Ella rang for the maid and Jenny came at once, her round face beaming as if she was glad to see her mistress back from her trip to town.

'Bring me a pot of tea, Jenny, and two cups if you please, and then fetch Nurse Carmel for me.'

Jenny nodded and left the room, but soon returned with a tray of tea and a plate of scones. 'They're fresh, Mrs Mortimer.' She pointed to the plate. 'Cook made them this morning. They're Miss Letty's favourite.'

'Thank you, Jenny. Just put the tray down there.'

Ella waited anxiously for the nurse to make an appearance, fortifying herself with the hot tea. In spite of her anticipation of the coming ordeal she was startled when there was a knock on the door.

Margaret came into the room with a rustle of starched linen.

'Would you like a cup of tea, Margaret?' Ella asked. The nurse nodded, seeming to sense Ella's distress. Ella coughed to hide her nervousness. 'I have to be honest with you, Margaret. My dear Jolly, through no fault of his own, has left me with considerable debts.'

The nurse looked down at her brightly polished shoes without saying a word. Ella took a deep breath. 'It means that I'll have no money to pay you or the servants – I'm afraid I can no longer afford to employ you.'

'I want to stay,' Margaret said. 'You're family to me now.'

'But don't you understand?' Ella said desperately. 'I have no money, I can't afford to pay your salary.'

'You'll need me more than ever now, Mrs Mortimer. I can see to the children while you are earning a living for us all. I'm happy to work for bed and board if that's acceptable to you.'

Ella sank back into her chair. This was the last thing she had expected. Margaret Carmel was a well-trained nurse; she could make a good living for herself if she took a post with one of the well-to-do families in the area. 'That would be wonderful, Margaret. But are you sure you want to stay on with us? Of course, I'd pay you once I have my financial affairs sorted out.'

'I've known Mr Mortimer off and on since Leticia was born and I won't let him or you down in your hour of need.'

'Thank you, Margaret.' Ella was near to tears. 'Thank you from the bottom of my heart. You don't know what a relief it is to me to have your support.'

The nurse sniffed back a tear too and busied herself smoothing down her pristine apron. She squared her shoulders and lifted her chin. 'I'd like to feel that you all considered me part of the family. Now, if that's all I'll get about my duties.'

When she'd gone, Ella closed her eyes wearily, moved that even in death Jolly commanded so much love and respect.

Ella saw Cook and Jenny together, and stood near the fireplace to deliver the bad news. 'I'm sorry, but I have to let you go,' she said. 'The plain fact is that I have no money to spare to pay your wages.'

Her words were greeted with silence and then Jenny began to cry. Cook put a comforting arm around the girl, shushing her gently. 'We understand, Mrs Mortimer,' she said, 'and I'm sure you'll give us the best references.'

'I don't want to go.' Jenny's voice was thick with tears. 'I love working here, Mrs Mortimer, and I'm sure I could take less wages or even no wages at all if I could stay.'

Ella shook her head. 'I've got enough depend-ants to worry about, Jenny. I'm sorry I can't accept your generous offer, but I'll speak to some people. I'm sure I can find you a place in a good house, so please don't cry.'

Cook nodded to Jenny. 'Come along, girl, I'll help you to pack your things.'

'There's no need to do that at once!' Ella said quickly. 'I can at least give you time to think things over. I won't throw you out into the street, don't worry.'

When Cook and Jenny had gone, Ella sank into a chair and put her hand over her eyes. She was frightened by the enormity of the task that lay ahead of her. She needed to make enough money to pay off the debt to the bank, and even if she could manage that, she now had five young girls to bring up as well as her son.

Children needed educating; they needed to be fed and clothed. Could she do all that on her own? She picked up her cup and held it to her lips, only to find the tea was cold. It was the last straw. Ella put down the cup and leaned back in her chair, feeling the salty tears run down her cheeks. She was lost, hopelessly lost.

'Pull yourself together, Ella Mortimer!' she said sternly. 'Otherwise it's the workhouse for all the family.'

★   ★   ★

Ella arrived at the theatre just as the first house was about to begin. The musicians were tuning their instruments and the atmosphere of the Palace seemed unchanged. The same pall of cigarette smoke drifted and danced behind the electric lights and the same odour of expensive perfume lingered in the air. What was different was the rows of empty seats that seemed to leer up at her, taunting her with the knowledge that the theatre's popularity was on the decline.

She sat in the back row and watched the show, and even as a non-performer she could tell it was poorly done. She needed big names to attract the audiences, but how could she pay for them?

Kathleen would have worked for nothing. She would have drawn in the crowds every night, bringing in more than enough money to attract big names to the theatre, and soon the Palace would have been a thriving business again.

Ella thought back to how Kathleen's career had begun. Suddenly, like a bolt from the blue, the idea came into her head: she would hold a competition at the theatre like the one that had given Kathleen her first taste of success, but this time it would be between professional artistes, performing for prestige rather than payment. Ella sat up straighter in her seat. She would invite editors of national newspapers to attend the event, offering them the best seats in the house. She would have to offer overnight accommodation as well: how was she going to pay for that? Perhaps good guesthouses and hotels would waive the cost of the accommodation in exchange for some good publicity? It was certainly worth finding out.

When the curtain fell on the last act, there was a sporadic burst of clapping and then the thump of seats as people took their leave. Ella felt more optimistic than she had done since Jolly's death. If there was even a chance of winning the battle against debt and eviction from her home, then she had to take it.

'I think it's a brilliant idea.' Anthony looked at Ella seated in the big chair in Doris's sitting room and was touched to the quick by her drawn face and shadowed eyes. He longed to take her in his arms and comfort her. If only he had made his fortune he would have handed it to her on a plate. But at least he could help with the practicalities of organizing a competition.

'I'm glad you came to talk things over with me,' he said. 'I know some newspaper editors personally. I'll go and see them. I'm sure I can persuade them to take part in the competition.'

'What about the performers?' Ella asked. 'I don't know how to approach them.'

'I'll do that too.' Anthony was confident he could gain the interest of the artistes he'd had dealings with previously, when the Palace was a thriving concern. 'I think I'll be able to gain support for the competition without much trouble.'

Ella smiled at him and he felt his stomach turn over with love. Sweet, dear Ella – how he longed to kiss her rosy lips and make her smile again.

'How are you feeling now, Anthony?' she asked. 'The bruises have faded and you look your usual handsome self.'

'Thank you for your kind words.' He made a mock bow and took her hand, holding it to his lips.

Just then the door opened and Kathleen looked into the room. 'I'm not going to be in the way, am I?'

Anthony shook his head, not noticing the droop of her mouth or the frown that creased her forehead. 'I'm just pledging my allegiance to the future most successful proprietor that the Palace theatre has ever known. And of course you're not going to be in the way, you silly girl. As it happens, you've arrived at just the right time to give us your views.'

'What nonsense is it you're talking now, Anthony? Why would you want my views on anything at all, if I'm such a silly girl?'

'Ella's had this wonderful idea.' Anthony reluctantly released Ella's hand. 'She's – well, we are going to organize a competition like we did before, but this time it's going to be for professionals only. Now what do you think of that?'

He watched the changing expressions on her face and thought how beautiful she looked in the soft lamplight. She would make some man a perfect wife one day.

'I think it sounds good,' Kathleen spoke hesitantly.

'But?' Anthony asked.

'Sure it all comes down to money again, and we haven't got any, have we?'

'Ah, that's the clever bit.' Anthony smiled. 'We don't pay them a penny, but we promise them good publicity in exchange for their efforts.'

'Is that enough, do you think?' Kathleen sounded doubtful.

'Well, how would you like to pit yourself against the likes of Minnie Palmerston and beat her? Wouldn't that raise a stir in the theatre world? You'd have more work than you could handle.'

Kathleen's face fell. 'I couldn't pit myself against a raw beginner now, but I can see what you mean.'

Anthony cursed himself for being so tactless. 'I'm sorry, Kath,' he said gently. 'But you'll sing again, I'm sure of it.'

'I wish I had your optimism, Anthony,' Kathleen replied. 'But I'm babbling. I've been sent in by Doris to ask if anyone wants a cup of tea.'

'I do, for a start,' Anthony said. 'How about you, Ella?'

Ella got to her feet. 'Thanks, but I'd better get back to the children.'

'You're not running away like that.' Doris appeared in the door with a tray on her arm. 'You shall have some refreshment with us and then tell me what all the excitement is about.'

'Have you been listening at the door, Doris?' Anthony took the tray and put it on the table.

'No, I have not!' Doris retorted. 'Now, is somebody going to tell me what's going on?'

Anthony watched Doris's reaction carefully as he explained what Ella had in mind. He saw her frown turn to a smile and a sense of excitement gripped him; Doris was a wily old bird and had been involved with the theatre almost from the time she could walk.

'You know what?' Doris said, looking as though she'd found the Holy Grail. 'I think this daft idea might just possibly work. Now let's all calm down, shall we? Nothing was ever gained by being hysterical.'

Anthony saw beyond Doris's rebuke: he'd caught a glimpse of tears in her heavily made-up eyes. A great feeling of hope gripped him. If they all pulled together, Ella's scheme might well be the saving of the Palace theatre.

CHAPTER THIRTY-ONE

Ella decided to take the girls to the big market in Swansea and show them the most economical way to buy food. There would be no more top-side of beef; they would have to make do with the cheaper cuts. And they would buy enough dry ingredients such as flour, oatmeal and salt to last a month or two, thus saving precious shillings from their small budget.

As they left the house, Charlotte protested at having to walk all the way to town. 'But, Helena, can't we go in the pony and trap as we always do?'

The twins linked arms and stared up at Ella. 'We don't want to walk either,' said Vicky, speaking for both of them as she often did.

Ella shook her head. 'I'm sorry, girls, but I've arranged to sell them. Have you forgotten I said we must cut our expenditure? We must just get used to walking and have done with it.'

'But it doesn't cost anything to run a pony and

trap,' Charlotte said indignantly. 'We can't walk to town – everyone will think we're paupers.'

Ella tried to be patient. 'A pony needs fodder and grooming and that involves stable hands. As for the trap, one of the wheels was coming loose and needed replacing,' she sighed, 'and we just don't have the money.'

'We always put the pony out to graze.' Mary's innocent eyes met Ella's as she reached out and caught Ella's hand. 'It didn't cost anything for the grass, did it?'

'We paid the farmer to let the pony graze in his field, Mary,' Ella explained. 'And how would we manage in the winter? The poor animal needs warmth and shelter from the cold and rain and you know the roof of the stable is leaking badly. You see, girls, it takes a good deal of money to keep animals.'

Charlotte opened her mouth to speak again but Letty nudged her. 'For goodness' sake, stop whining, Charlotte. The walk to town will do us good.'

'Well, Papa would never have treated us like this, that's all I'm saying,' Charlotte murmured.

Ella felt a lump rise in her throat. Charlotte was right. Jolly would turn in his grave if he knew the measures she had taken.

'You'll enjoy the market.' Ella tried to lighten the moment. 'You'll see women selling cockles and mussels. They use a big oyster shell to measure out the shellfish.'

'I don't want to go to the market.' Charlotte was determined to be difficult. 'It will be full of smelly people all pushing and jostling us. Cook and Jenny used to do the shopping and they knew what sort of food we liked.'

'And I know what sort of food we can afford,' Ella said sharply. 'Get it into your head, Charlotte, and the rest of you girls, we have very little money to spend.'

Vicky and Lizzie spoke together. 'We do understand, Helena.' Ella looked gratefully at the twins. Sometimes they were wise beyond their years.

By the time they reached the market Ella had managed to raise the girls' spirits. Even Charlotte was intrigued as she passed the cockle women seated at the entrance to the market, baskets full of shellfish set on the ground in front of them.

'Good day to you, Miss Mortimer.' One of the cockle women looked up at Letty. 'I heard the sad news about your father. He was a good man, one of the best.' The woman held out a large oyster shell with a few cockles in it. 'Try my shellfish, no charge,' she said.

Ella was amused to see Letty hesitate and then lean forward and pick gingerly at a cockle and pop it into her mouth.

'Fresh this morning they was caught.' The

woman held out a pristine white cloth. 'Here, wipe the vinegar off your fingers.'

Charlotte's face brightened. 'Can we have some shellfish for our supper, Helena?' She took one of the cockles. 'Mmm, they're delicious.'

Ella smiled, watching as the girls surrounded the cockle women and stared, entranced, at the array of shellfish on display. She opened her purse. It would do no harm to humour the girls: shellfish was a cheap meal and with a slice of bacon was tasty as well as economical. Still, the money she had found in Jolly's petty cash tin would not go very far and it was all she had.

She bought a jugful of cockles and then led the girls to the meat stall, where she haggled for offcuts of bacon, aware that the children were hanging back, ashamed to be involved in bargaining for food. She then bought some cheese and a freshly baked loaf, and looked longingly at the butter placed in neat pats on a tray. Her mouth watered as she saw the beads of liquid brought to the surface of the butter by the salt in it, but she couldn't afford to spend any more money and that was that.

Vicky and Lizzie had wandered away and Ella glanced over her shoulder to see the twins happily engaged searching through a basket of brightly coloured ribbons. She felt tears prick her eyes, knowing the girls would be disappointed if she told them she couldn't afford to buy any fripperies. When they came to her side, each clutching a ribbon of scarlet and gold, she opened her purse to check the change inside.

'We don't want to buy them, Helena – we just want to show them to you,' Vicky said quickly. 'We've got plenty of ribbons at home.'

Ella swallowed her tears. 'Perhaps we'll buy ribbons next time we come to the market.'

On the walk home, the girls went on ahead, chattering animatedly. Ella realized they'd never even seen the market before. Jolly's girls had been used to the best of everything, but now they would have to learn to economize.

When she turned into their gate she saw a horse and buggy near the door and her heart leaped as she realized she had a visitor. It could only be Anthony – she hoped he had good news for her.

Anthony was sitting on a chair in the hallway. 'The door was unlocked so I came in. I hope you don't mind – Nurse Carmel assured me it would be all right.'

'Of course it's all right.' She avoided Anthony's gaze, afraid her feelings for him would show. She was relieved when Letty ushered the girls in the direction of the kitchen.

'We'll cook the lunch,' Letty said. 'Come along, Charlotte, and no whining, understand?'

Anthony looked at Ella for a long moment without speaking.

'It's bad news, isn't it?' Ella led the way into the drawing room and sank into a chair, unconsciously twisting her hands together in her lap. 'Tell me quickly, Anthony.'

'It's the concert,' he said heavily. 'Only two of the performers we contacted have agreed to take part. The bigger names have pulled out – it seems they got word the theatre is in a bad way.'

'Could we put on a show with the ones you have lined up?'

'It wouldn't be worth us hiring an orchestra, even a small one, for such an event. It could hardly be called a competition with only two artistes.'

Ella sighed heavily. 'I had such high hopes, Anthony. Now I don't know what to do.'

'In the last resort we could sell the Palace,' Anthony suggested.

'We must try everything to keep it,' Ella said. 'When you work it out, we'd have very little money from selling it because Jolly owed the bank so much.' She looked around her hopelessly. 'The same goes for the house. No, we'll have to try and make the theatre pay, for your sake as well as mine. I know you've made sacrifices to keep the theatre going – I'm very grateful, you know.'

Anthony smiled. 'No need for thanks. I want the Palace to flourish again as much as you do.'

Ella drew a sharp breath. He was so dear to her that she could hardly bear to look at him.

'If only Kathleen could sing like she used to,' Anthony said. 'She could run a show practically single-handed. We could put in a few acrobats or jugglers to fill in the gaps in her performance and we'd know her name alone would bring in the crowds.'

Ella looked down at her hands. Jolly's wedding ring gleamed brightly against her fingers. Perhaps she could pawn it – at least then she'd have some money to tide her over the next few weeks.

'Look,' Anthony's voice broke into her thoughts, 'don't worry, I'll go and see some of the artistes personally. Perhaps I can persuade a few of them to take part in the competition.'

Ella smiled. 'I think you could soften the hardest of hearts if you tried, Anthony.' He met her gaze and held it, and it was Ella who looked away first. She knew she was blushing and cursed herself for being such a fool. Jolly was not long in his grave and here she was longing for another man's touch.

'I'd better go,' Anthony said. 'Try not to worry, Ella, I'll put on this show if it's the last thing I do.'

She saw him to the door and watched the horse and buggy recede into the distance. She stood for a moment on the doorstep and stared at the busy street beyond the gates. Her mind was turning round and round, searching for a solution to her problems, but none would come.

Anthony seemed to think she had enough money to last for the weeks or months it would take to organize the competition, but she had only a few shillings in her purse. Suddenly she was afraid.

Margaret came downstairs with the baby in her arms. 'Mr Anthony gone, is he? I hope I did right letting him in.'

'Of course you did, Margaret.' Ella realized the nurse was another mouth to feed, but she needed her if she was to earn a living for them all.

'I think our little boy wants his milk,' the nurse said. 'I've pacified him with a little boiled water and sugar, but it's not good enough for his lordship.' She spoke with genuine affection and Ella smiled at her.

'Thank you, Margaret.'

'What on earth are you thanking me for?'

'Everything.'

Margaret rubbed her eyes as she left the room; Ella knew now that the nurse's briskness hid a heart that was as good as gold.

She enjoyed the short time of peace as she held her son to her breast; she pushed her worries out of her mind because she'd heard it said that a mother's milk curdled if there was any anguish in her soul.

But her peaceful interlude didn't last long. Charlotte came barging into the room, her face flushed. She stared mutinously at Ella. 'Letty's burned the cockles,' she said. 'There's an awful stink in the kitchen – it's really put me off my food so I won't want to eat anyway.'

Ella put the baby into his crib and buttoned her bodice. 'Don't worry, we've got lovely fresh bread and some fine cheese so we won't starve. And I'm sure Letty was doing her best, so try not to upset her.'

'Too late,' Charlotte said. 'I gave her a real telling-off. I was looking forward to some bacon and cockles.'

'Never mind,' Ella said. 'We'll have the bacon with our bread and cheese.' She watched with a sinking heart as Charlotte shook her head.

'No, we won't – she's burned that as well.'

Ella fought the tears that threatened to spill down her cheeks. 'Well, everyone has to learn, don't they? I'm sure Letty will get used to the cooking and you must all help her, do you understand? Now go and set the table for lunch. We'll eat in the kitchen – it's pointless carrying food to and from the dining room.'

Margaret popped her head round the door. 'Perhaps we can rustle up more than just bread and cheese. I'm sure there's a sack of potatoes in the corner of the kitchen. I'll see what else I can find.'

Left alone, Ella twisted her ring on her finger. How much would she get for it? Surely a gold ring would be worth a few shillings. She sank back and closed her eyes, seeking a few minutes' respite from her worries, but she felt a heavy despair creep over her. She couldn't cope with it all – losing Jolly so suddenly and then learning that he owed money on the house as well as the Palace. It was all too much for her.

'Pull yourself together, for heaven's sake!' She spoke her thoughts aloud, her voice echoing in the silence of the room. She had to manage: there was no one else to do it for her.

A short time later, Mary came to fetch her. 'The lunch is ready, Helena,' she said. 'You should see what Margaret has cooked for us. There's potatoes and onions and a whole heap of cabbage. It smells lovely, just as it did when Cook and Jenny were here to see to us.'

Ella took the baby out of the crib and carried him down to the kitchen. The girls were seated round the scrubbed table, waiting as Margaret shared the food between them.

Margaret nodded to Ella. 'Come and eat, make some good milk for that baby of yours.' The nurse's hair was tied back from her face, which was shiny from the heat of the stove. Ella wondered how she could ever have thought of her as intimidating.

'Thank you, Margaret,' Ella said. 'It's very good of you to go to this much trouble. It's much appreciated.'

Margaret looked at her steadily. 'This is the first time I have ever felt part of a family, and it's I who should be grateful to you.'

Ella felt tears come to her eyes and she brushed them away impatiently. One thing about being poor – you certainly knew who your real friends were.

The next morning, Ella searched Jolly's drawers, looking for any money he might have left lying around. But her search proved fruitless. What she did find was a small case of jewellery that must have belonged to Jolly's first wife. There was a fine pearl necklace and a few rings set with precious stones, but the pick of the bunch was a gold watch on a very long chain.

She would probably make quite a bit of money on the jewellery. But after a moment's hesitation, Ella put the things back where she had found them. These trinkets belonged to the girls – they were probably all that was left to show for their mother's life.

Ella left the house with her wedding ring in a small box. It was all she possessed, the only thing that was hers to sell. She made her way along the rain-darkened streets and wanted to cry out her despair to anyone who would listen. But for once the High Street was silent; it seemed she was the only person out and about.

When she stepped into the dark interior of the pawnbroker's shop her mouth was suddenly dry. The man behind the counter stared at her from over the rim of his spectacles. He took the ring without a word and appraised it for a moment. 'Haven't you anything with jewels in, Madam?' he asked dispassionately. 'Gold is only bought on weight value and there's not much gold in a wedding ring.'

He offered her such a paltry sum that Ella was tempted to take back her ring, but then she thought of the empty larder and summoned all her courage. 'I want double what you're offering,' she said boldly.

'I'll meet you halfway and give you three shillings and sixpence.' He didn't wait for her assent, just took some money from a drawer and pressed it into her hand. Ella sighed with relief: they would eat now for the rest of the week.

As she emerged from the dark interior of the shop she blinked in the bright daylight, and stared at the money in her hand. This would not do. She needed to get a job, any job, and the sooner she did so the better.

CHAPTER THIRTY-TWO

Doris walked through the large empty auditorium of the Palace and stared round her with a heart that was near to breaking. She'd spent her life in the theatre and she loved it. How could she bear it if the theatre was sold off to some uncaring buyer?

Kathleen was on the stage, looking round her as if she wanted to imprint the memory of the place on her mind. Behind her was the backdrop for her favourite song, 'Parks Were Made For Lovers'. Doris felt tears spring to her eyes, blurring the image of cardboard trees around a park bench that was made of cheap wood but painted to look solid and weighty, like ornately wrought iron. It was all an illusion. The role of the theatre was to provide, if only for a time, an escape into a beautiful world where there was no pain, no suffering, no poverty.

She sat in one of the plush seats and thought about poor Ella, widowed and left with a large family and with no means of supporting them all. She and Kathleen were all right, there was a little money coming in from the lodgers who rented rooms in her house. They could survive on that, just. And Anthony was young and talented, he could find a job as theatre manager anywhere, perhaps even here in Swansea. But Ella – what did she have? Somehow they had to all pull together to make the theatre flourish again.

Kathleen came down from the stage and sat beside Doris. 'The Palace feels so empty, so sad,' she said. 'I wish there was something I could do to help Ella make a success of it again.'

Doris peered at Kathleen in the dim lighting, trying to see her expression. 'You could go and see a doctor about that throat of yours,' she said tartly.

'It would do no good,' Kathleen said. 'The last quack I saw told me it was all in my head, that I could sing if I really wanted to.' She sighed heavily. 'Sure an' don't I want to sing so bad that it hurts me even to think about it.'

Doris lapsed into silence, searching her mind for anything that might help Ella. 'Perhaps I could borrow money if I put the house up as collateral,' she said finally.

'She wouldn't let you do that,' Kathleen retorted.

'You don't know that for a fact.' Doris spoke with no conviction in her voice.

'Come on, Doris, where's your precious second sight now? It seems to fail you when we really need it.'

Before Doris could reply, the door swung open behind them and the tall figure of Anthony shut out the light from the foyer. 'I wondered why the door was open,' he said. 'I thought perhaps it was robbers again, looking for more money.' He gave a short harsh laugh. 'Not that they'd find any.'

'So you're back from your travels,' Doris said. 'Did you get any more big names to enter the competition for our gala night?'

'One or two,' he said. 'Look, if I'm honest my trip was a disaster, but then we're not offering much incentive, are we? A silver cup and a month's run at a failing theatre is not much of an inducement to anyone, especially artistes who can command a high price wherever they perform.'

'What are we going to do, then?' Doris asked. 'Do we ditch the whole idea of a competition?'

'I don't know,' Anthony said. 'I've been thinking of getting a job in one of the other theatres here in Swansea. At least then I could help Ella out a bit.'

'You don't know her very well, do you?' Doris shook her head. 'Ella is too proud to take anything from us.'

Kathleen shook her red-gold curls. 'There's no point in any of us running up debts, because Ella wouldn't have it, you know that.'

'What is the answer, then?' Doris put her hands up to her face, as if by blotting the theatre out of her sight she could blot out the problems they all faced. She stood up abruptly and waved Kathleen out of her way. 'Let's set off home,' she said. 'There's nothing to be done here.'

As she followed Anthony into the foyer, she looked at the dusty board showing a full bill of performers. If Kathleen's name was at the top of the list she would fill the theatre single-handed. Doris sighed. If wishes were shillings all their troubles would be over. As she closed the outer door behind her, Doris felt a tear slip down her cheek. She wiped it away angrily: if her life in the theatre had taught her nothing else, it had taught her that nothing ever came of tears except red eyes and a runny nose.

Since Margaret had taken over the duties of cook as well as nursemaid, Ella had found the running of the house much easier. It helped that the girls were cooperating; they had taken to shopping in the market as if they'd been doing it all their lives. She felt that her growing friendship with Letty was the one rewarding thing to come out of the whole business of losing Jolly and taking on his huge debts.

She was sitting in the drawing room trying to relax after putting the baby down to sleep for the night when she heard the doorbell ring. She knew it must be Anthony – he had said he'd be calling over. Her heart flipped uncomfortably as she got to her feet to welcome him.

When he entered the room he brought with him the chill of the evening. His face was red with the cold, but it was the stoop of his shoulders that told her his trip had been unsuccessful.

'Sit down, Anthony, please,' she said as he hovered in the doorway. 'I can see it's bad news so just tell me straight out what's gone wrong.'

'It's not all bad news,' he said. 'I've managed to get some performers to enter the competition.'

'But not the big names?' Ella sank back in her chair.

'I'm sorry, Ella, I had hoped for better news. But at least we can put on some sort of a show that might bring in the theatregoers.'

'I've been thinking.' Ella avoided looking into Anthony's eyes, afraid she would let him see how worried she really was. 'What if we extend the list of artistes by inviting members of the public to join in the competition – you know, like we did last year? But this time the amateurs will be up against professionals.'

'I don't know.' Anthony rubbed his chin. 'It might work, especially if we find someone with Kath's talent.'

Ella's heart did a flip. He was always thinking of Kathleen – he must be very much in love with her.

'Will you contact the newspapers then, Anthony?'

'We'd need money for any advertising we did, Ella. Have you thought of that?'

She hadn't. 'Leave it with me.' She tried to sound calm and self-assured, but she had difficulty controlling the trembling of her lips. 'Would you like a cup of tea before you go?' She got to her feet. 'Come to the kitchen, I expect the kettle is on the hob.'

She was very aware of him following her down the steps and she longed to turn and throw herself into his arms. She straightened her shoulders, putting such thoughts out of her mind. She had more serious things to think about than silly dreaming about a man she couldn't have.

They sat at the kitchen table and sipped their tea, neither of them talking, and the thought popped into her head that they could be an old married couple sharing a harmonious silence. Her eyes lingered on Anthony's features: he was so handsome with his hair falling over his brow and a bright cravat at his throat.

He looked up and met her eyes and she looked away quickly.

'I'd better be off, then.' He put down his cup. 'I expect Kath will be waiting up for me.'

She rose quickly. Of course he wanted to be with Kathleen. 'She'll be getting anxious, I expect,' she said. 'I'm sorry if I kept you.'

He held up his hand. 'No, you haven't kept me at all. I'm only sorry I couldn't bring you better news.'

She saw him out and watched him walk away from her, down the drive where frost silvered the grass and out into the dark street. He became just a shadow as she watched and reluctantly she closed the door.

The house was silent; everyone had gone to bed and she was alone with her problems, knowing only she could solve them. She returned to the kitchen and poured more tea. She had to think of a way through this morass of troubles. She had to be strong, but she had never felt so weak and alone in her life.

Kathleen had been watching through the palour window, looking out for Anthony's return. She saw his unmistakable figure loom up out of the darkness and her heart began to beat more quickly. She put her hand to her chest, trying to be calm. Anthony seemed to be turning more and more towards her, but she must be patient and not frighten him off.

Doris came into the room and clucked her tongue in disapproval. 'You're pining after that boy and it's no use. He's in love with Ella – see sense, won't you?'

Kathleen concealed her pain and anger. 'Sure an' isn't it natural to be worried about him? You know that those thieves' associates might still be out there waiting for him, wanting their revenge.'

'I know more than you give me credit for, Kathleen. Hear what I have to say, will you? Anthony is not for you.'

'You don't know everything, Doris,' Kathleen was stung to reply. 'If you did you'd get us out of the hole we're in and save the theatre.'

'I'm talking to you now as a friend, Kathleen, not a clairvoyant. Anyone with half an eye can see Anthony wants only one woman and that is Ella.'

'How can you say such things?' Kathleen burst out. 'Her husband is only a few months in his grave and you're trying to match Ella up with Anthony.'

'The two of them were meant for each other,' Doris replied. 'I saw it in the past and I see it now. It's only respect for Jolly's memory that keeps the two of them apart.'

Anthony came into the room and went straight to the fire burning in the grate, holding his hands out to the blaze. 'It's freezing out there,' he said.

'How was Ella?' Kathleen found herself saying and she held her breath as Anthony seemed to be turning thoughts over in his mind. He wanted to hide his true feelings from her. In her heart she knew Doris was right: Anthony was in love with Ella.

'She's a bit subdued,' he said at last. 'I didn't have very good news to give her, after all.' He sat in one of the easy chairs that Doris was so fond of. 'I only wish I could have told her that all the performers I approached were willing and anxious to come to the Palace.'

He rubbed his eyes tiredly and Kathleen resisted the urge to lean forward and kiss him. 'I'm sure you did your best, Anthony,' she said. 'Look, I'll go and make you a nice cup of tea, shall I?'

He shook his head and a lock of bright hair fell over his brow. 'No, thank you, Kathleen. I had enough tea with Ella to sink a boatload of sailors.'

It hurt her to think of Anthony and Ella sitting down together all cosy and close, drinking tea together. She wished Doris would go to bed. She couldn't probe Anthony's feelings with Doris watching her every move.

To her dismay, Doris sank back in her chair and steepled her fingers together, looking over them at Anthony. 'How was Ella in herself? I mean, did she seem downhearted?'

Anthony shook his head. 'She made a pretence of being cheerful, but Jolly mortgaged the house up to the hilt as well as the theatre. If he'd lived perhaps he would have sorted out his financial problems and got the Palace up and running successfully again. As it is . . .' His words trailed away, but Kathleen knew how much he cared for the theatre, longed for it to be successful again. How much of that desire was to see Ella safe and happy and how much was a genuine love for the theatre was more difficult to work out.

Kathleen looked at Doris. 'Why don't you go up to bed? You're looking very tired,' she suggested. She was hardly able to keep the irritation out of her voice. Couldn't Doris see she wanted to talk to Anthony on her own?

Doris returned her gaze, knowing full well that Kathleen wanted her out of the way but obviously determined to stay where she was. Kathleen pushed back a red-gold curl impatiently and tried to ignore Doris.

Anthony seemed to be in a trance, staring into the fire, his shoulders slumped.

'Are we really in danger of losing the theatre?' Kathleen asked.

Anthony met her gaze. 'It all looks pretty bleak to me,' he said hopelessly. 'There's no money to stage a new show and I've tried to find a job but no one needs a manager, not in Swansea. I'd have to go away.' He rubbed his eyes tiredly. 'I don't know how we're going to get any more money, but the fact is if we don't think of something soon, the Palace will sink without trace and every one of us with it.'

CHAPTER THIRTY-THREE

Ella alighted from the train and stood looking round her at the huge crowd that surged along the platform, everyone intent on their own business. She found the hustle and bustle frightening, but she had come to London fully prepared and knew where Ida Marlowe lived.

In the past Ida had been one of the finest singers in the land, though it was rumoured that her powers and therefore her reputation were diminishing. But no one in Swansea would be aware of that fact.

Ella had read about Ida Marlowe in an old newspaper she had found in Jolly's study, and in desperation she'd taken the liberty of writing to her, asking for a meeting. She had been surprised at the swiftness of the performer's reply. It was clear she was at least interested in the prospect of working in the provinces.

Ella rehearsed in her mind what she would say to Ida Marowe: she would make it clear that the singer would top the bill, but she hadn't yet explained about the competition. Soon it would be Christmas and Ella planned to make the competition the highlight of the festivities. Once Ida Marlowe's name appeared in the press and on the billboards, the show would most certainly attract other big names and equally big audiences. It wouldn't solve all of her problems, but at least the takings would be enough to fend off the bank for a little while.

When she reached the singer's home, a maid led her to a large drawing room. Pride of place in the well-lit room was given to a grand piano; the white keys, shining like teeth, seemed to smile at her.

She was reluctant to take a seat so she stood near the door, admiring the heavy drapes at the windows and the good, plump furniture. After ten minutes of waiting, Ella's nervousness had mounted. What if Madame Marlowe didn't want to leave London at Christmas? Perhaps she had bookings already for such a busy time of year. If that was the case, Ella feared that the Palace would be lost and she and the children would be faced with eviction from the comfortable home Jolly had provided for them.

Ida Marlowe came into the room with a flourish, her brightly coloured skirts swirling, the fur cape at her shoulders drifting with the breeze as though the creature it came from was still alive.

'Please be seated, Mrs Morton.' Ida sat down, spreading her skirts around her dainty feet. Everything about her spelled success, from the gleaming pearls at her neck to the soft satin of her shoes.

'It's Mortimer, my name is Mrs Mortimer,' Ella said.

Ida waved the mistake away with a flip of her long fingers. 'I've asked the maid to bring us tea. You must be in need of refreshment after your long journey.'

The deep timbre of her voice and the way she held her head revealed her imposing theatrical presence. It was no wonder she had commanded such fine audiences.

Ella's tongue seemed glued to the roof of her mouth. She didn't know how to frame her request; now she was here in the great woman's presence she was filled with doubts about the wisdom of her journey. She was grateful when the tea arrived and she was able to moisten her lips.

'You said you had a proposition for me.' Ida Marlowe's eyes were suddenly sharp. 'I understand you want me to come to Swansea to perform at the beginning of the Christmas season, but you must realize it would need a very large purse indeed to coax me away from London at such a time.'

Ella swallowed her nervousness as Ida Marlowe

continued talking. She could see she would have to play her trump card at once. 'I would like you to come to the Palace theatre for a month. You would be given top billing, that goes without saying, and you would be supported by a wonderful cast. I would also be happy to make you part-owner of the Palace if you choose to take up my offer.'

Ida Marlowe stared at her without speaking. After a long and tense silence, she was ready to reply. 'Part share of a theatre that to all intents and purposes is going out of business – that's not much of an inducement, is it? In any case, a month is a long time to be away from the London stage, you must realize that.'

'I've planned a competition,' Ella said, determined not to show her nervousness. 'It would be the professional artiste against the talented amateur.'

Ida Marlowe sighed. She clearly wasn't convinced that it was in her interest to throw in her lot with the Palace.

'Your name would be enough to raise the profile of the Palace, Madame Marlowe, and even if my venture failed and the Palace had to be sold off, your part-share of the building itself and the plot of land it's on would more than compensate you for your loss of earnings over the Christmas season.'

Ida Marlowe sat back in her chair, digesting

Ella's words. Ella watched her carefully: not by one twitch of her lips or flutter of her eyelashes did Ida reveal what she was thinking.

'I believe you are not yet booked up for Christmas?' Ella said at last, breaking the long silence. 'Though of course the offers will come flooding in soon, I'm sure.'

'Of course they will.' Madame Ida pursed her lips and stared at Ella thoughtfully. 'I have tentative offers from theatres in Bristol and Cardiff, so I might be able to tie everything in with an appearance at Swansea. On reflection, I am willing to consider your offer favourably. That's if no other offers come through in the next week or two.'

'That's not good enough,' Ella said boldly. 'I need an answer now if I'm to do the advertising required to pull in the audiences. You must see that.'

'I don't know if this offer of part-ownership of the theatre is enough to convince me. Who knows whether the enterprise will be a success?'

'It will be.' Ella's voice rang with a confidence she didn't feel. 'I mean to turn one of the many rooms below the theatre into a coffee shop and I have several businessmen who are very keen to obtain the lease.' She didn't add that she'd only just thought of the idea. She was all too aware that any such offers would only be made if the Palace showed a profit again.

'I'll sleep on it,' Madame Ida declared theatrically, 'and I'll write to you tomorrow to let you know my decision.' She rose to her feet and Ella realized the interview was over. 'It's been a pleasure meeting you, Mrs Morton.'

'Mortimer.'

Ella had to wait a long time for a train to take her back to Swansea. It was cold on the platform and she shivered, wondering if the money she'd borrowed from Doris for the journey had been wasted.

Still, while talking to Ida Marlowe she'd had the idea to offer out space for a café within the theatre. The costumes room would be ideal – it was large, with ample space for tables and chairs. Or better still, she could utilize the empty rooms alongside the office, which had the benefit of lovely views over the sea.

She felt suddenly cheered. There was so much potential in the huge building – it could accommodate a sweetshop, a tobacconist, even a taproom where men could drink beer while their good ladies treated themselves to a glass of cordial. Ella was surprised that she hadn't thought of this before, and as she watched the train belching smoke as it reached the platform, she felt cheerful for the first time since she had lost Jolly.

Once she'd boarded the train, she closed

her eyes and leaned back in her seat, sighing contentedly. She was more hopeful now, with new ideas for the use of the theatre spinning through her mind. And on reflection, she felt sure Ida Marlowe would agree to perform at the Palace. At least she hadn't turned the offer down flat, she was willing to think about it. Ida Marlowe had mentioned other offers in Cardiff and Bristol. Both had good solid theatres – would that be enough to tempt her to leave London?

Ella felt the long journey home would never end, but when at last she stepped down from the train she felt she had done all she could to give the Palace a new lease of life. Her heart leaped as she saw Anthony's familiar figure waiting for her. She hurried towards him, eager to tell him all about her meeting with Ida Marlowe, knowing that he was as keen as she was to save the Palace from closure.

He took her hands in his as she reached him and Ella fought the impulse to stand on tiptoe and kiss him. He smiled at her and she thought again how handsome and dear to her he was.

She could not reveal her feelings for him, not with Jolly so recently gone to his rest. In any case, Anthony's future seemed to be bound up with Kathleen's; any show of love or even affection would only embarrass him. She drew her hands away and squared her shoulders. 'I've lots to tell you, Anthony, but let's get home as soon as possible. I'm in need of a drink, and I don't mean a cup of tea.'

Anthony smiled down at her. 'I've got a pony and trap waiting outside, borrowed, of course, and a bit on the rickety side, but it'll see us back to your house.'

As he took her arm and led her from the station, for a moment Ella was able to pretend that they were lovers and not just good friends.

'Sure I don't know if I'll ever sing again, Ella.' Kathleen stared gloomily into the fire. 'My dearest wish would be to impress such an important lady as Ida Marlowe with my voice. Anyway, forget all my problems. Come on, Ella, tell us all about your visit. What did she say to you?'

Doris slapped Kathleen's hand. 'Let the girl draw breath, won't you? Ella didn't expect us to be sitting in her house waiting to hear all her news.' She smiled at Ella. 'I know you must be tired. London is hard on the heart and on the feet, believe me. I performed there many times when I was younger.'

'She's going to let me have her decision tomorrow,' Ella said. 'I think she'll agree to come, but I haven't told you what inducement I offered her.'

Kathleen sat up in her chair. 'What have you offered her? Sure don't keep us in suspense.'

'I offered her a part-share in the Palace.'

Kathleen saw Anthony's forehead crease with worry. 'Was that necessary?' he asked, his voice gentle, his eyes drawn as always to Ella's face.

'It's a gamble, I'll admit,' Ella said. 'But just offering her top of the bill wasn't going to influence her at all, and she seemed interested in sharing the business, even though she knew the Palace wasn't doing so well financially.'

'I see,' Anthony said worriedly. 'But if she's so well informed about our troubles, why should she be interested in owning a share of the Palace?'

'Well, she was. I expect she checked up on us the minute she got my letter.'

Kathleen saw the beginnings of a smile soften Ella's face.

'I told her a pack of lies, but by heaven and all the angels, I came up with some very good ideas while I was at it.'

'What ideas?' Kathleen was full of curiosity at the thought of Ella lying. 'Come on, tell us everything.'

As Ella outlined her plans, Kathleen saw a bit of the old Ella return, a spark of the light and enthusiasm that had been absent since Jolly's death.

'First of all, I thought we could offer a lease to the right person for the setting up of a café on the premises. That way we'd take no risks but we'd bring some much-needed money in. And we needn't stop there: we could sell toffee and cordial and all sorts of things.' She sighed. 'There's so much we could do with the unused parts of the building.'

Anthony leaned towards Ella, his eyes alight with hope. 'That's a wonderful idea,' he said. 'And if we get Ida Marlowe on the bill we'll get other artistes to compete.' He took her hands in his – neither he nor Ella realized what he'd done. 'If we charge the public a small sum to enter the competition we'll be certain to make a profit. Well done, Ella.'

Kathleen slumped back in her chair. Anthony was making it quite clear that he had feelings for Ella. Why hadn't she admitted it to herself? After all, Doris had kept trying to make her face the truth. She wanted to curl up into a ball and disappear from sight. The pain inside her was tearing her apart; she loved Anthony with every fibre of her being, but she could see clearly now that he thought of her only as a friend. It was a bitter pill to swallow and she caught Doris giving her a sympathetic smile. She'd harboured silly dreams but now they were gone, wiped out by the look in Anthony's eyes as he held Ella's small hands in his own.

CHAPTER THIRTY-FOUR

As soon as it was announced in the press that Ida Marlowe was to appear at the Palace for the Christmas season, applications began to flood in for the competition. It seemed that anyone with ambitions to work in the theatre relished the notion of being on the same stage as Ida Marlowe.

Ella was sifting through the forms and at her side Anthony was counting the entry fees. After a while he opened the cash box and shovelled the coppers and shillings into it. 'Even if we squeeze in applicants every night of the week, we're not going to make much money from this competition,' he said.

Ella looked at him and their eyes locked. Ella felt her heart begin to thump, but she made a determined effort to speak normally. 'The entry fee is just a part of it,' she said. 'Think of all the relatives and friends of the people applying to be in the show – I think you'll find that the theatre will be booked solid.'

Anthony touched her hand and Ella felt a blush rise to her face. She drew away quickly. 'And we have Ida Marlowe appearing on our stage. That's even impressed the hard-faced bank manager.'

Anthony closed the cash box. 'You have a fine mind, Ella. I'm dazzled by your courage and commitment to the Palace.'

'It's my only means of making a living and well, keeping going.'

Anthony sat back in his chair. 'I know you have a difficult time ahead of you,' he said, 'and if there is any way I can help, please just ask me.'

His formal tone reminded Ella that she had a family – it seemed to have formed a barrier between them. She couldn't blame him; Anthony was a single man and he had feelings for Kathleen. He was just being kind.

'Anthony,' she said firmly, 'I don't expect you to give up all your free time helping me. I know you have your own life to lead.'

He sighed. 'I want to help, Ella,' he said. 'The Palace is partly mine too, remember?'

'I know you love working here and that you still feel loyalty to Jolly, but promise me that if this venture fails you'll leave Swansea and find work wherever you can. You have too much talent to waste it on a failing project.'

'You want me to go away?' He looked so

downhearted that Ella wanted to take him in her arms and comfort him.

'If my latest plans fail I think it would be for the best, don't you?'

She glanced at the clock on the office wall. 'I'd better get back home. I have to feed my baby and the girls will be needing me.'

She drew on her thick coat and tucked her hair into her hat. 'Anthony – ' She hesitated, and he looked up at her hopefully. 'I am grateful to you, I really am.'

'Are you sure you don't want me to walk you home?'

Ella shook her head. 'Since those robbers who attacked us were put in prison I feel quite safe on the streets. Thank you, all the same.'

As she hurried down the stairs and into the belly of the theatre she noticed that the corridors and, more importantly, the stairs the public would use were in need of a good scouring. She smiled ruefully. It looked as if she would have to do a bit of cleaning herself, and hopefully Kathleen would tuck her skirts up into her bloomers and give her a helping hand.

It was cold out in the street and Ella turned up her collar against the bitter wind. She could feel the milk fill her breasts and she hurried past the railway station and down the High Street, anxious to be home with her children. That's how she thought of the girls nowadays: her children.

Her responsibility but also her joy. She had a great deal to be thankful for. She just hoped that her gamble would pay off and she would have enough money to make the Palace the thriving theatre it once was.

'I don't want to go to an ordinary school.' Vicky pouted.

'Neither do I.' Lizzie's rejoinder was predictable; she always agreed with her twin.

Letty looked at them sternly. 'The days of private tutors have gone,' she said firmly. 'We're poor now that Papa has passed over – ' she couldn't bring herself to say the word 'dead', 'and we all have to make the best of it.'

'Can't Helena bring us money from the theatre, like Papa did?' Vicky persisted. 'She's always over there, never here with us. The only person we see is Margaret, and she's either with the baby or busy in the kitchen.'

'It'll do you good to get to school, then,' Letty retorted. 'You'll be meeting enough people to satisfy even you. Now come on, get your coat, it's cold outside.'

'But the children who go to school in town are poor,' Vicky murmured. 'I've seen them: they're raggedly dressed and most of them haven't even got shoes.'

'Well, then, thank your lucky stars that you have decent clothes to wear and perfectly good shoes.' Letty was losing her patience. 'Now come on. Mary's ready, look, and she's the youngest. Good girl, Mary.'

'Why isn't Charlie coming with us?' Lizzie began to grizzle. 'I don't want to go without Charlie.'

'Charlotte has a bad cold, as well you know.' Letty opened the door and a blast of icy air made her shiver. 'She's got to stay in bed until she's better.'

'But you don't have to go to school. It's only Vicky and me and Mary going, it's not fair.'

'Letty's too old to go to school now, you dunce!' Vicky said pompously. 'Don't you know anything?'

'Shut up, clever sticks!' Lizzie shouted and made a lunge at her sister's hair.

Letty stamped her foot in frustration. The twins didn't often fall out, but when they did it usually ended up with one or both of them crying. 'I'll be glad to have you lot off my hands,' she said feelingly. 'Now out, before we freeze the whole house out with the cold.'

It took twenty minutes' hard walking to reach Robertson's school, and even Letty's footsteps faltered as she approached the tall, gloomy building. It had cruel-looking iron fencing all around the perimeter, and looked more like a prison than a school. Resolutely, she marched the girls across the yard and into the building. It was only a little warmer inside the school than it had been outside and Letty felt her heart dip with fear. How would her sisters fare in this unfamiliar atmosphere?

A man came bustling along the corridor and to Letty's relief he was tidily dressed, with a high white collar showing beneath his dark coat. In his hand was a thin stick and he thrashed the air with it with apparent enjoyment.

'The Mortimer family, I take it?' He looked down at them from a great height and Mary crept closer to Letty, hiding her face in the folds of her sister's coat.

Letty swallowed hard. 'Yes, Sir. These are my twin sisters, Victoria and Elizabeth, and this is Mary. I'm Leticia, the eldest in the family.' She wanted to ask if the girls would be well looked after, but something about the man's officious manner stopped her.

'I'm Mr Wallis, headmaster of this establishment.' His tone was cold.

'How do you do?' Letty held out a hand, which he ignored. 'What time shall I come to fetch them home?' she asked timidly.

A door opened along the corridor and Mr Wallis waved Letty and her sisters aside to allow the crocodile of subdued children to pass. None of them were without shoes, Letty noticed, though one boy seemed to be wearing a pair that might have been his mother's. They were

412

scuffed with a hole in one of the toes and seemed much too big for him. He caught her staring and glared defiantly back at her. She looked away quickly.

'Well, off you go, Miss Mortimer. I will see the children are allocated the most suitable place in the school.'

Letty jumped as Mr Wallis's doom-filled voice blared out his dismissal of her.

Mary wouldn't let go of Letty's skirt and Lizzie began to grizzle again. Mr Wallis frowned his disapproval. 'Enough of that. Stop crying this instant.' He thrashed the air with his stick frighteningly close to Lizzie's rear and Letty looked at him in alarm. Mary began to wail, a high-pitched cry that outdid Lizzie's miserable snuffling. Mr Wallis caught her arm and dragged her away from Letty. 'Stop it at once, child!' He raised the stick and brought it down with a swishing sound on Mary's back. Mary yelped with pain and Letty rounded on Mr Wallis, her cheeks flaming.

'How dare you!' she demanded. 'My father never struck any one of us and you are not going to lay a hand on them, do you hear?'

'That explains the lack of discipline here,' Mr Wallis snapped. 'Spare the rod and spoil the child. I'll have you know we don't tolerate dis-obedience here, not in my school.'

Mary howled and, through streaming eyes

and nose, pleaded with Letty to take her home.

Mr Wallis looked on in disgust. 'The child is wetting herself. Are these well-brought-up girls, I ask myself. But I'll soon tame them.'

Letty's chin jutted forward. 'Oh no you won't. I'm not leaving my sisters here to be abused by the likes of you.'

Mr Wallis grew red. 'You will do as I say. Now go home and try to act like a grown-up and let me do my job.'

Letty gathered the girls to her and led them to the door. 'You can keep your school, Mr Wallis,' she said. 'But this is not the last you'll hear from me, I'm warning you.'

She hurried the girls out of the door and into the cold winter air. Mary was still sobbing and clinging to Letty's coat and, subdued, the twins walked silently behind her.

Helena wasn't in; she was probably at the theatre, working as hard as ever. Letty ordered the girls to take off their outdoor clothes and go into the sitting room.

'What are we going to do, Letty?' Vicky said. 'Who'll teach us now?'

'Charlotte is the bright one,' Letty said. 'She can teach you, and I'll help her all I can and so will Margaret. We'll get by. In the meantime just read your books, I've got a letter to write.'

She sat at the desk near the window, the

pale sunlight slanting through on to the sheet of headed notepaper she drew towards her. Mr Wallis wouldn't like it one bit when he saw her indictment of him revealed in the pages of the *Weekly Recorder* for all to see.

CHAPTER THIRTY-FIVE

There was an air of excitement in the theatre as the musicians, performing free for old time's sake, tuned their instruments, smoking and coughing, stirring restlessly as they always did before a show.

Ella stood in the wings, her heart pounding with anticipation as she peeped through the curtains at the packed auditorium. A haze of cigarette smoke rose up towards the footlights and the heavy scent of perfume hung in the air. It was like old times, the good old days when all she did was scrub the floors and enjoy the occasional performance, with no responsibilities.

'Please, Mrs Mortimer,' a young stagehand appeared at her elbow, 'Madame Ida wants you in the dressing room.'

Ella left the stage at once, alarmed. Ida Marlowe should be ready to go on stage now: as well as topping the bill, she was making an appearance at the start of the competition.

Ida was seated before the mirror in her dressing

room. Her face was pale and she flapped her hands in front of her, making the feathers on the shoulder of her gown dance and wave as if they had a life of their own. 'I can't go on,' she said. 'I've just received a message from London. I'm wanted at the Pavilion – their main act has let them down and I'm to be the replacement. I need to travel to London at once. Please send someone to help me change my clothes.'

'You can't do that!' Ella said. 'We need you here. The audience is waiting to see you.'

Ida got to her feet and towered over Ella. 'But you don't understand,' she insisted. 'This is my big chance to make a comeback on the London stage. I can't possibly turn it down.'

'But what are we going to do without you?' Ella said desperately. 'The audience is here to see you. You can't disappoint them.'

Ida began to pull off her dress. 'I have to take this chance, you must see that. I simply cannot turn down an offer like this. The manager of the Pavilion has sent a motor car for me. Don't you realize what a very important person I am?'

Ella felt like crying, but she knew nothing would move Ida Marlowe. She meant to go to London and nothing would change her mind. She watched Ida change out of her stage clothes, carelessly throwing them over the back of her chair.

'My fur coat, where is it?' she demanded.

Ella pointed wordlessly to the worn-out screen that had once been boldly coloured and upright and now sagged drunkenly on uneven legs. She followed as Ida picked up her belongings and made for the stage door. Outside stood a gleaming car, the first one Ella had ever seen. Gathered around it was a crowd of curious onlookers. A small boy touched the paintwork, staring in awe at the gleaming vehicle.

'Now you can understand how much they want me in London.' Ida waited for the driver to open the door for her. 'This car is owned by the boss of the Pavilion and he's sent it all the way to Swansea just for me.' She preened as she slid inside, pulling her fur coat around her shoulders. 'Goodbye, my dear, and best of luck for your little competition.' She waved a gloved hand as the car drew away from the kerb and Ella watched hopelessly as the car disappeared along the High Street, heading away into the night.

As Ella stood in the doorway, panicking at the thought of telling the eager audience that Madame Marlowe wouldn't be performing after all, Kathleen came up behind her, breathless from running along the corridors of the Palace.

'Is it true that Ida Marlowe is not taking part in the competition after all?' She clutched Ella's hand. 'One of the stagehands told me there was a grand new motor car waiting to take her to London. It's not true, is it?'

'It's true,' Ella said softly. She wanted to stand there and scream, to rail against Fate, which seemed to defeat her whatever she tried to do. Instead, she linked her arm with Kathleen's and forced a cheerful note into her voice. 'Come on, let's just make the best of it, shall we?'

Letty chivvied Mary along, exasperated as her sister played with her mittens instead of putting on her outdoor clothes. 'If you don't hurry, we won't be able to see the show,' she said.

Lizzie and Vicky stood patiently waiting by the door and at the last minute Charlotte came downstairs, her cheeks still pale but with a determined look in her eyes.

'If you're all going to the theatre to see this marvellous singer then I'm not going to be left out.'

Letty looked at her in concern. 'Are you sure you're well enough, Charlie?'

'If I'm well enough to teach these little monsters their lessons then I'm well enough to go to the theatre.'

'Wrap up warm, then.' Letty took the scarf from her own neck and wrapped it around Charlotte. 'You do realize we won't be able to have seats in the audience, the show is a sell-out. We'll have to stand at the back of the theatre. Mary, you can stand in the aisle so you can see what's going on.'

'I'll put up with that, I just want to see the

show,' Charlotte persisted. 'I'm curious about this wonderful Madame Marlowe, and anyway I'm sick of staying indoors.'

Letty shrugged. 'Come on then, all of you, let's go.'

'Wait!' Margaret came running up the steps from the kitchen. 'The supper's all done for when we come home and I've made up my mind, I'm coming to the theatre with you. Wait while I fetch the baby and I'll walk along with you.'

Letty opened the door and led the girls out to the road. Margaret followed at the rear, a thick Welsh shawl wrapped around her with the baby tucked up inside its warm folds. Letty flashed her a grateful smile and then dug her hands deep into her pockets to keep them warm.

Her fingers encountered the stiff letter that she'd carried with her for days. It was from Mr Summers, editor of the *Weekly Recorder*. He wasn't accepting her piece about Mr Wallis, it was what he called 'too hot to handle', but he liked her style and wanted to meet her with a view to her writing a regular women's page for the paper.

She wasn't stupid – she knew that at first she would not be paid very much, if anything at all. But one day she'd be a professional reporter and her heart filled with excitement at the thought. She'd always liked to scribble poems, but had never imagined she'd one day be a real writer. She was looking forward to telling Helena the news. It was about time something good happened to the family.

Letty blinked in surprise at her own thoughts. She actually felt warmth towards Helena these days, thought of her as one of the family. Over the months she'd seen how hard her stepmother was working to keep the family together and she could only admire her for having the courage and love to take them all on.

The bright lights of the theatre spilled out on to the road as Letty ushered her sisters into the warmth of the foyer. A strange man stood near the door, wearing a smart uniform. He held up his hands to prevent Letty from going any further. 'Full house,' he said, looking down at her. 'And this isn't a nursery school. Why have you brought all these children here?'

Letty lifted her chin. 'I expect you're a temporary doorman,' she said icily, 'otherwise you'd know we are Jolly Mortimer's children.'

He rubbed his chin. 'I don't know if I should let you in. Perhaps I should go for Mrs Mortimer, she'd soon tell me if you were spinning me a story.'

Letty's haughty manner didn't change. 'Go and fetch her if you dare, but I don't think my stepmother would approve of you dragging her away from other more important matters, do you?'

'Are you with this lot?' He directed his question to Margaret.

'I'm their nurse,' she said, 'and I guarantee they will be right as sixpence once you let them in.'

'All right, then,' he said grudgingly. 'But if there's any noise or trouble you'll be out on your ear, do you understand?'

On their best behaviour, the girls filed into the theatre, looking in awe at the heavy red curtains that hid the stage from view and the brilliant lights that gleamed like the sun, dispelling the darkness.

Letty spotted one empty seat at the end of the back row and gestured for Margaret to sit there. 'Take Mary on your lap if you can manage with the baby as well,' she whispered. 'She might fall asleep if she's comfortable.'

Letty felt, for the first time, the excitement of the theatre, sensed the anticipation that ran through the audience as the band struck up a rousing march. Soon the big red curtains would sweep back and they would see the wonderful Madame Ida Marlowe, who was the talk of the town.

Helena had told her in detail how the evening would progress. Madame Marlowe would introduce the show and bring on the contestants, and then, at the end of the evening when the best act was announced, she would perform her repertoire and everyone would fall silent, privileged to hear a singer from the London stage.

She thrust her hand in her pocket, reassuring herself that the letter was still there, and an idea suddenly struck her. Perhaps she could weave the Palace and its performers into her column – that would help to advertise the shows, especially now when funds were low.

She leaned against the door, wrapped up in her own thoughts, determined to make mental notes on the show and translate them into writing once she got home. One day, she would repay Helena's kindness in taking on the Mortimer children, but for now she was happy just knowing that some day she would be able to contribute to the up-keep of the family.

Ella stood behind the curtains. She was dreading having to tell the audience that Ida Marlowe was indisposed and wouldn't be appearing after all. Her eye was caught by a movement in the wings and to her surprise she saw Kathleen dressed in her stage outfit, the velvet skirt tucked up to reveal a shapely leg. Kathleen tiptoed towards her, her finger pressed against her lips.

'What are you doing?' Ella whispered. 'Why are you dressed like that?'

'I'm going on,' Kathleen whispered back. 'Even if I can't sing, I can talk, break the news to them gently that there is a change to the programme.'

Ella shook her head. 'I can't ask it of you, Kathleen. It's my duty to break the bad news.'

'Go on away and take that long face with you before it makes me cry.'

Anthony came on to the stage and drew Ella away. 'Let her do it,' he said. 'I think she's eager to be in front of an audience again.'

He stood with his arm still draped around her shoulder and Ella leaned against him, glad of his support. Doris came to stand close by and she took Ella's hand, rubbing it as though to comfort her.

Taking a deep breath, Ella gestured to the stagehand to raise the curtain, and she watched in breathless anticipation as Kathleen struck a pose with her hands on her hips and her head on one side.

'I've got something to tell you.' Her lilting voice carried clearly to the back of the auditorium. 'There's been a change to the advertised show.' She moved from one side of the stage to the other, staring at the audience as though challenging them to protest. 'Ida Marlowe is indisposed, but you'll enjoy the performance, so you will, 'cause we've got fine artistes waiting to entertain you.'

There was a stir and exclamations of disappointment, and then one man got to his feet and shouted to her, 'Why don't you sing to us then, Kathleen? We all love you and we've missed you.' Someone pulled his coat-tails and he sat down.

The band struck up the music to 'Parks Were Made For Lovers' and Ella froze as she saw Kathleen hesitate.

'Oh, Anthony, what's going to happen? They'll lynch her if she doesn't sing.'

He hugged her close, but she could see he was dismayed at the turn the evening had taken.

The music dwindled and finally stopped, and it was as though the whole theatre was holding its breath. And then Kathleen began to sing. Her voice was loud and clear, echoing across the theatre as true and strong as it had ever been. The band struck up again as Kathleen paraded across the stage, showing a shapely leg and pulling the top of her dress aside to reveal just a little of her full breasts. Her voice soared through the auditorium as she gained confidence. She tossed back her red hair and flipped her hand towards the box nearest her, as though inviting the occupants to join her in song.

When the last triumphant note faded away, there was a moment's silence and then the clapping began. It filled the theatre as Kathleen made curtsey after curtsey. At last she held up her hands for silence.

'Now we come to the important part of the show.' Now full of confidence, she announced, 'The competition will begin.' She swept off the stage to enthusiastic whistles from some of the men in the audience. Breathless, she threw herself into Ella's arms and clung to her. The compère for the night took the stage to introduce the first contestant, and the rustle of the audience settling down to enjoy the show was music to Ella's ears.

'It's back! Sure by all the saints, my voice is back.'

'And better than ever,' Anthony said warmly. 'Perhaps you should follow Ida Marlowe's lead and go up to London.'

'I'm determined on it,' Kathleen said. 'But I'll see the Palace on its feet before I go.'

Ella drew Kathleen to one side. 'What about Anthony? Will you take him with you?'

Kathleen shook her head. 'I would take him like a shot, but it's not me he wants.'

'What do you mean?' Ella frowned.

'He's in love with you, you soft ha'peth.'

'Don't be silly,' Ella protested. 'Why would he want a woman like me with so many problems?'

'Go and ask him, with my blessing.' Kathleen pushed her away. 'Anthony, take this girl away and give her a stiff drink. I think she needs it.'

Anthony took her arm but Ella shook her head. 'I don't want a drink, Anthony, really I don't. I'm fine standing here watching the competition.'

426

The first half of the show went well and an excited buzz from the audience filled the auditorium as the interval started. Ella's heart lifted. The night was going to be an even greater success than she'd dreamed of. She heard a rustling behind her and turned to see Letty lead the other children up the steps and into the wings. With them was Margaret, rocking the baby in her arms.

'It's going really well, Helena.' Letty seemed to be in charge of the situation. 'You should hear the comments made by the people around us. They are loving the show and some of them are praising Kathleen to the skies. It's a great success, and it's all down to you.'

'Quite right, young lady,' Anthony said warmly.

Ella brushed away her tears as love for her family ran through her veins like wine.

Letty came to her side and, after a moment of hesitation, kissed her cheek. 'You are a real mother to us, Helena,' she said. 'Papa would be proud of you.'

Ella couldn't hold back the tears then. They ran down her cheeks unchecked as she hugged and kissed each of the girls in turn, and then took her own precious son and kissed him on his downy little head.

Anthony leaned towards her, wiping away her tears with his fingertips. 'I know it's far too soon to tell you this, but I'm a patient man and willing to wait for as long as it takes. I do love you, I've always loved you and I'll wait for you for ever if need be.'

'Go on, Helena,' Margaret said. 'Tell the man it's worth his while waiting for you.'

The children crowded around her and Letty nodded her head silently.

A warm feeling tingled in Ella's heart. The Palace was on its way to being a success again, and though it would take a lot of time and effort for her to pay off all the debts, she was sure now, with the support of her dear family and friends, that she would do it.

Ella smiled up at Anthony. One day she would feel free to give her love to him, and as they stood side by side without even touching Ella knew that they couldn't be closer. One day, all her dreams would come true, and as she looked up into the gods she felt as if Jolly was giving her his blessing.

THE END

BARGAIN BRIDE
by Iris Gower

Young Charlotte Mortimer loves her new job as
the teacher in the local school. She wants to
help the poor of the neighbourhood. She loves
Luke, a fellow teacher, but has to take lodgings
with Justin Weatherby, a wealthy businessman
with two children whose wife has died.
Charlotte resents his position of wealth and
influence as a Governor of the school. Justin,
however, needs to marry again, in order to
inherit the fortune which his uncle has left to
him. His eye falls upon Charlotte, and she
has little option but to agree . . .

9780593056028

NOW AVAILABLE FROM BANTAM PRESS

BANTAM PRESS

THE ROWAN TREE
by Iris Gower

Manon Jenkins' cherished childhood in the sleepy village of Five Saints in the heart of Wales ends abruptly when her beloved father dies. She is left homeless and alone. The handsome blacksmith, Morgan Lewis, cares deeply for her, but she won't marry a man she doesn't love. She longs for Caradoc Jones, son of a famous Welsh cattle drover and, in desperation, she accepts a job as chaperone to Caradoc's spoilt sister Georgina on the jouney to Smithfield market in London. She plans to seek her fortune as a herbalist, preparing medicines for sale to both the rich and the poor.

Life on the trail is hard, and Manon struggles to be accepted by the other women as they walk long miles over rugged terrain. One heady, star-filled night Caradoc finally becomes her lover, but she is devastated when he refuses to marry her. She is determined to survive without him in London, but when she realizes she is pregnant, she finds that it's not easy to escape the clutches of the Jones family . . .

The first in her magnificent new series about the cattle drovers of Wales

9780552150347

CORGI BOOKS

FIREBIRD
by Iris Gower

Llinos Savage found herself in charge of the family
pottery while still a young girl. As she attempted to
keep the business afloat, there were many problems
to overcome, including her mother's untimely
death and the plotting of Philip Morton Edwards,
the powerful and rich owner of the rival
pottery in Swansea.

Her world was further complicated by the two young
men in her life: Eynon Morton Edwards, Philip's
son, a gentle and sympathetic figure who became
her best friend but who was despised by his father;
and Joe, an exotic outsider, born of an unlikely
union between a cultured English businessman
and a Native American squaw.

How Llinos grew up and coped with running the
pottery, while suffering from the hatred of the
Morton Edwards family and her efforts to suppress
her own feelings for the man who seemed her most
unlikely suitor, unfolds into a compelling story
of tragedy, riches, poverty and love.

The first book in Iris Gower's exciting new series.

9780552144476

CORGI BOOKS

THE SHOEMAKER'S DAUGHTER
by Iris Gower

When Hari Morgan's father died, he left her nothing but an ailing mother and the tools of his shoemaking business. But what he also passed on to his daughter was a rare and unusual gift – that of designing and making shoes that were stylish and different. One of the first to realize this was Emily Grenfell, spoilt, pettish daughter of Thomas Grenfell, one of the richest men in Swansea. Emily, who resented the beauty and courage of Hari Morgan, nonetheless was delighted with the dancing slippers she made for her début at the Race Ball, one of the grandest events of the year. It was to be the beginning of a lifetime of friendship, hatred and rivalry between the two girls for, as Hari's business and fame began to grow, so Emily's fortune began to decline.

And between the two girls lay an even deeper tension, for Emily was about to be betrothed to her cousin, Craig Grenfell, a man whom Hari could not help loving and wanting for herself, a man who finally betrayed her. From then on, Hari was determined that nothing and no-one would prevent her rise to a triumphant success.

The Shoemaker's Daughter is the first book in Iris Gower's enthralling series, *The Cordwainers*.

9780552136860

CORGI BOOKS